DEATHLESS & DIVIDED

The Chicago War, Book One

BETHANY-KRIS

Published by Bethany-Kris

www.bethanykris.com

eISBN: 0-9947909-6-5
eISBN 13: 978-0-9947909-6-5
Print ISBN: 0-9947909-7-2
Print ISBN 13: 978-0-9947909-7-2

Cover Art © Jay Aheer
Editor: Dominique S.

DEDICATION

For Eli … because you're perfectly awesome. And you should know it.

CONTENTS

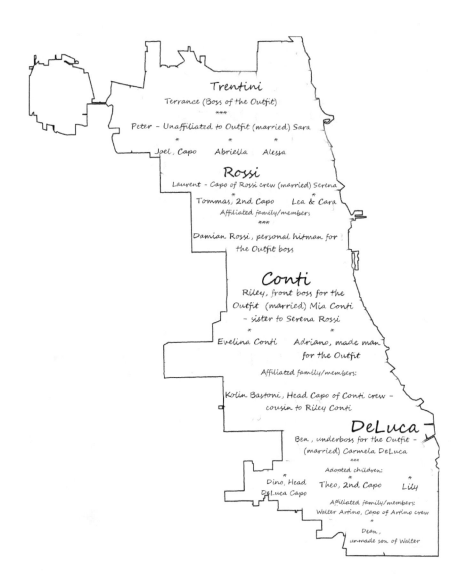

Trentini

Terrance (Boss of the Outfit)
***

Peter - Unaffiliated to Outfit (married) Sara
*

Joel, Capo   Abriella   Alessa

Rossi

Laurent - Capo of Rossi crew (married) Serena
*

Tommas, 2nd Capo   Lea & Cara

Affiliated family/members
***

Damian Rossi, personal hitman for
the Outfit boss

Conti

Riley, front boss for the
Outfit (married) Mia Conti
- sister to Serena Rossi
*   *

Evelina Conti   Adriano, made man
for the Outfit

Affiliated family/members:

Kolin Bastoni, Head Capo of Conti crew -
cousin to Riley Conti

DeLuca

Ben, underboss for the Outfit -
(married) Carmela DeLuca
***

Adopted children:
*   *

Dino, Head   Theo, 2nd Capo   Lily
DeLuca Capo

Affiliated family/members:
Walter Artino, Capo of Artino crew
*

Dean,
unmade son of Walter

PROLOGUE

Lily DeLuca felt like stone as she stared at the two-storey yellow home from where she sat across the road on the sidewalk. Immovable and cold. Someone must have resided in the house—new people—because it used to be a pale blue. A sidewalk of colorful stones now led up to the walkway of the front entrance as well.

Time changed everything.

Everything but Lily.

Well, she knew she was different, of course. Older. A woman now and not a child anymore. She knew homes didn't keep dreams and love protected and safe within their four walls, but instead, only gave the semblance of those things. She was no longer naive and stupid to the things and people around her.

No one was deathless in their world.

Even the innocents couldn't be saved.

Blowing out a puff of air, Lily tilted her head up again and blinked at the home. She swore she could still hear her older brothers' encouragement and hollering as she finally learned to ride her bike without training wheels. At four-years-old, they got her stuck in a tree in the backyard the first time they taught her how to climb it. She kicked her oldest brother Dino in the balls just after her fifth birthday in the front driveway when he let her spider out of its jar.

Dino and Theo DeLuca always let her tag along back then. They never acted like she was some annoying little sister out to ruin their fun.

Lily glanced down the quiet street, wondering if anyone recognized her. Melrose Park had long been home to a large American Italian community as well as the Chicago Outfit. A lot of people in the area probably knew who she was, but if they didn't, they would surely recognize her name.

Maybe she shouldn't have come here at all.

"Miss," the cab driver called, chomping loudly on his wad of gum. "You almost done or what?"

"Is the meter still running?" Lily asked back, not even bothering to look at the man parked beside where she sat.

"Yeah."

"Is my credit card still good?"

"Yeah."

Lily shrugged. "Then no, I'm not done."

"Whatever, kid," the guy muttered.

The cell phone in Lily's pocket rang for the fifth time since she left Dino's place a couple of hours earlier. Dino had gave the damn thing to her and took the one she had away, saying something about burner phones.

Lily figured that was just one more way for Dino to keep an eye on her.

She ignored the call.

The two-storey house, however, couldn't be ignored at all.

An ache stabbed in Lily's chest, spreading outward. It only continued to grow in intensity. The longer she stared and thought about the day her so-called family took away what that house was supposed to mean and murdered the dreams it held, the more she hurt.

Oh, she hurt all over.

"Time to stop running, Lily."

The words Dino spoke to Lily when he ordered her to leave Europe and travel back to the States plagued her mind.

He was right.

She ran.

Lily still wanted to. Coming back to Chicago felt like a death sentence.

What did this place want from her?

God knew she didn't have much left to give.

She could finally start college, maybe, but she didn't even know what she wanted to study. Her brothers owned a dozen and one different businesses around Chicago to keep her busy working, but how long would that keep her interested?

She couldn't be *just* Lily DeLuca in Chicago, Illinois. She couldn't be just anyone here. Not a tourist or a traveler, not a pretty face in a crowd of people. No, she was Lily fucking DeLuca; the daughter of a turncoat, dead father and mother; a sister to rival Capos in the Chicago Mob. And while she didn't want to think about it, her age made her a prime target for the Outfit to look at her for other reasons, too.

Christ, she should have fought Dino harder.

How long would it take before the Outfit took something else away from Lily that she loved?

"What is this place, anyway?" the cab driver called out the driver's window. "S'not anything special to look at, girl."

To him, it wouldn't be.

To Lily ...

It didn't even matter.

She pushed up from the sidewalk, brushing off the legs of her skinny jeans.

"Nothing," Lily said. "It's nothing."

CHAPTER ONE

The weight of a debt could crush a man. It was one of those things a person knew always followed close behind. It never really left, even if it seemed like it was gone.

Damian Rossi lived for a decade waiting to finally pay for the debt he owed. Dino DeLuca never once mentioned when Damian would be required to step up and answer for the dues he owed, but it still hung there ... waiting like the anvil ready to fall.

"Come on over. It's time to talk about paying up, Damian."

Eleven words had never felt quite as heavy as those did.

For Damian, life was dominated by the mafia. Or rather, The Chicago Outfit. Being only twenty-seven-years-old meant Damian answered to everyone else before he ever got to give himself what he wanted. It didn't matter that he had finally received his button—his in to the family—a little over a year ago. Nobody cared that Damian was just as made as they were in the Outfit. No, because he was still a fucking young gun to them.

If an older Capo needed an extra pair of hands and called on him, Damian had to go. If the boss wanted something from him, regardless of how seemingly unimportant it was, Damian needed to find it. It didn't matter if he was running on four hours of sleep in three days, Damian didn't get to make his own choices when it came to the Outfit.

The Outfit made those goddamn choices for him.

Always.

Most times, Damian didn't mind. He chose the life, and he was good at it. But he also didn't know anything different. After his mother and father died in an automobile accident when he was five, the only thing he had left was the Outfit and the people inside who raised him when his drunk aunt and uncle couldn't.

"You owe me, D."

Debts never went away in the mafia. They could disappear for a short time but someone always came back to collect, eventually. Damian supposed it was just his time to pay up. He didn't exactly like that Dino hadn't given him much of a reason why now was the time or how he could pay it back, but it just was.

That was how it worked.

Dino DeLuca's home rested on a large estate of thirty well-protected acres outside of the city limits. After he'd been let in through the gate and parked his car, Damian pulled out a cigarette and lit up. He still had twenty-minutes before he needed to meet the Capo, after all.

"It's windy for such a nice day."

The voice came from the line of trees to Damian's left. He turned on his heel in just enough time to see Dino emerge. The man swung a set of keys around his index finger and held a manila file with his other.

"Shit, make some noise, Dino."

Dino chuckled. The sound surprised Damian considering Dino was serious in all things—business, family, and life. Lightheartedness and nonsense wasn't in his game. Damian supposed he could understand that. He'd never been one for whims and fantasy, either.

"Aren't you supposed to be the ghost?" Dino asked, his teeth flashing as he grinned.

"Wish they'd forget that name."

"You earned it, D."

Damian shrugged. "Whatever. That doesn't mean I like it."

Growing up without his parents meant Damian spent a lot of time under the feet of others. He'd been a small, scrawny kid. Instantly forgettable. The only thing that made living in his aunt and uncle's house bearable was his cousins; Tommas, Lea, and Cara. Not that they had it any better. Laurent and Serena Rossi hadn't been made to have kids. The four kids spent more time moving from family to family than they spent actually living with their guardians.

Yeah, easily overlooked.

A little ghost.

Damian ended up being raised by several people instead of the ones delegated to the task. When he should have been focusing on school, he'd been shoved knee-deep into the mafia and that lifestyle. Looking back on it all, he knew the reality was simple. He'd been groomed for the life. Numbed to violence and business. Accepting of the expectations and rules of their family and ways. He liked it, though.

Damian supposed that worked out well for him. Being forgettable as a kid ended up carrying over to his adulthood and his career in the Outfit. Not every man was cut out to be a killer. No one ever saw him coming. They didn't get the chance to see him leave. Rarely was he suspected when a body showed up. He simply took the call, did the job, and moved on. No questions ever got asked.

"Figured you would be inside filling your face with food," Damian said.

Dino eyed his large home. "Enjoying the outside while I can."

"Trial is coming up, right?"

"A little over two months," Dino said under his breath.

Getting in some kind of trouble was unavoidable when it came to the mafia. Dino refused to take a deal on the racketeering, laundering, and fraud charges that had been plaguing him for a couple of years. He wouldn't plead guilty, either. The man had a damn good lawyer though, but everybody knew what he was looking at.

Twenty years max when totaled up.

Damian knew the bastards wanted the maximum and were going for it, too.

"Do you ever wonder why I liked you so damned much way back when you were a kid?" Dino asked.

Damian laughed. "No."

"Life hasn't treated either one of us very fairly, I suppose. I probably saw a lot of me in you when you were just a punk-ass kid following us around."

"You're not that much older than me."

"Five years."

"What is your point, Dino?"

"You never sat around waiting for your pity party, D. When your parents died, you got shuffled around from place to place. When my parents died, we had to pretend like they didn't even exist. You just accepted the hand dealt to you; we were forced to. So, I guess I liked that about you and the fact we had a common loss helped, too. Made me sympathetic, if anything. Rarely does someone get that from me. Hell, even Theo doesn't get a goddamn Christmas card from me anymore. You got an invite to the dinner table."

Damian hid his surprise with a cough. Dino rarely spoke of his siblings. Even when Dino and his younger brother Theo needed to spend time in the same room together, the rival Capos acted like strangers instead of brothers. A five-year age gap separated the two men. Dino's sister, on the other hand, had been MIA from the DeLuca family for a few years.

If Damian thought about it hard enough, he was pretty sure he could remember a blonde-haired, brown-eyed girl following Dino and Theo around way back when. Apparently, the majority of the girl's teen years were spent at a private boarding school. Dino didn't talk much about her. An even bigger age gap separated them, as far as Damian understood.

"Lily is your sister's name, right?" Damian asked.

Dino cocked a brow. "Why?"

"Curious."

"It is. She's twenty-one, almost twenty-two. Her birthday is coming right up. She spent the last three years after she graduated gallivanting across Europe. Backpacking, mostly."

"Kept out of trouble?"

"Yes, which I appreciate. Well, as far as I know. Lily isn't ... fond of me. She checked in once a month. It was my only demand."

Damian was beginning to feel like this conversation might turn into some kind of therapy session. Nobody wanted that shit.

"What did you need me for today, anyway?"

Dino smirked, but it faded fast. "I wasn't the only one who took a liking to you, was I?"

Damian didn't know what the hell his friend was getting at. "Pardon?"

"Terrance."

The Outfit's boss.

"I do okay with him, if that's what you're dancing around," Damian replied.

"Just okay. Right, Damian."

"What?"

"You don't even realize it, do you?"

Obviously not.

Damian was too tired to play word games. "I do what the boss wants, Dino."

"Christ, Damian. If you spent the same amount of time paying attention to your surroundings as you do working to blend in, you would have it made."

"It's not killed me yet," Damian said, grinning.

"Good thing." Dino shoved his hands in his pockets. "Joel's never gonna make it as boss, not under Terrance's watch."

"He's his grandson. It would make sense for Joel to take over when it's time."

"So? Like I said, Terrance knows better. A good boss is partly made, but mostly born, Damian. Joel doesn't have it. Terrance knows it. Hell, the Outfit knows it. What nobody really knows, is who will take it." Dino barked out a laugh, adding, "Well, I think I know who Terrance is looking at for it."

"Oh?"

"Yeah, I'm looking at him."

Damian turned to ice in the June air. "You're fuckin' kidding me."

"Hey—"

"That's not even funny, Dino. I've never wanted that or even suggested that I did."

"I'm aware," his friend murmured.

"So what the hell?"

"I didn't say you did want it, Damian. That knack of yours, being invisible, wouldn't work very well if you're the boss."

"Exactly," Damian said. "And I like being able to come and go as I please."

"But you don't, not really."

Damian didn't challenge Dino on that because he knew it was true.

"Terrance has never mentioned anything of the sort to me," Damian said, wanting to get Dino's mind away from that.

Whatever plans the Capo was scheming up, Damian didn't want to be a part of them. If someone got wind of that shit, he'd be six-feet under in a makeshift grave before he even got the chance to apologize for anything.

Damian liked being alive.

"He wouldn't. You're still young to him, but he's looking at you. He's watching you, D. Because to him, you've got it. You fucking *listen* instead of running off at the goddamn mouth. You follow the rules, take his calls, and do what he asks. Haven't you wondered why you don't have a crew of your own, yet?"

Damian avoided Dino's heady gaze. "Sometimes."

"Because you're too busy with him. Why would he give you more than you've already got with everybody else and the boss put together? That would mean you would have less time for his bullshit. And he likes having you close. How many times do the guys call you for the boss, anyway?"

"A few."

... *times a day*, Damian held back from adding.

"You know what I heard Ben say to Riley when he called for the boss the other day?" Dino asked.

Ben DeLuca was Dino's older uncle and the right-hand man to Terrance. Damian didn't particularly like the guy, but he gave him the respect he was owed.

"What did Ben say?" Damian asked.

Dino nodded at Damian. "Said the guy might as well call you on whatever it was first."

Damian shifted on his feet, uncomfortable. "So?"

"So, Ben is Terrance's main guy—always has been. The underboss, that's important. Like how Riley is important as the front boss on the streets and to the feds. Terrance takes Ben and Riley to the Commission meetings, runs shit past them for a second and third voice, and all that other good nonsense."

"Why do I hear a *but* in there?"

"But ... he kind of does that with you, too, huh?"

"I haven't noticed," Damian said quietly.

"I think you have. You went along with them to the last Commission, didn't you?"

"Yeah."

"How was that?" Dino asked.

Interesting and enlightening.

Damian had done passing business with the major families in New

York, including the biggest and dominating Marcello clan, but that was his first time seeing them all together. He supposed he now understood why the families talked about the Marcellos like they were untouchable. They kind of were. Damian held a great deal of respect for the Marcello family. After all, it was better to know who your biggest rival was and admire their ability to be a challenge at all.

"Figured out Terrance isn't fond of the Marcellos," Damian said.

Dino shrugged like that didn't make a difference. "We're big time in Chicago. They're big time in New York. Keeping the peace is better than starting a war with another family. Terrance knows that. Nonetheless, he invited you along. You're the first person he's done that for aside from Ben and Riley, of course."

"It would make sense for Ben and Riley to go, Dino. Underboss and front boss, man."

"But not you."

"There were other lower associates at the meeting for the bosses."

"Capos, likely," Dino said. "Probably men who had a stake with one of the other families. Something to gain for their bosses. You, on the other hand, went there to learn. Terrance just didn't tell you."

Damian swallowed hard, feeling an invisible weight bearing down on his shoulders like never before. "I don't want to be a boss."

That was not one of his life goals. Being a boss meant constantly being watched. From officials, from your own men, and from the public. It never fucking ended. It also meant being one huge target for anyone that had eyes for your position. Damian liked being invisible when he wanted.

He liked being *him*, for fuck's sake.

"Not even ten, fifteen years from now?" Dino asked.

"No."

"Funny, Ben thinks you're up to taking on the role, Damian. I wonder what gave him that impression."

"Not me."

"He doesn't like it at all," Dino added like it was an afterthought.

Well, that really caught Damian's attention.

"Ben?" Damian asked.

Dino nodded once. "That's what I said. Seems my uncle thinks you're too independent for the job—you've got your own mind, you know."

"A man with his own mind is a problem for him?"

"It is when he can't manipulate the boss," Dino said, chuckling. "God knows he's tried for years to manipulate Terrance to his bidding and sometimes, he has succeeded. Most times, Terrance already has his decisions cemented before Ben DeLuca even gets thought about. Ben could be a boss if given the chance, but he prefers to sit on the sidelines and have others do the work, not actually be front and center doing it himself. That's a problem."

"Good bosses do their own work."

"Ben just likes to manipulate," Dino said, sighing. "Getting it, yet?"

Damian wished he wasn't, but reality was starting to sink in, and fast. When a man was headed to somewhere another man didn't want him to be in the mafia hierarchy, the best way to fix that situation was by ending the problem.

"Ben is going to come after me," Damian said.

Dino's quiet, cold stare didn't waver as he replied, "It's a good possibility. He only needs a reason to explain the hit away to Terrance. Something that would justify it in Terrance's mind. Ben did it to my parents; you're not even family to him."

Damian wasn't hearing Dino, not really.

"Because Terrance likes me."

"Shitty world we live in when being liked gets you killed, huh?" Dino asked, humor coloring his tone.

Damian found nothing about this funny. Mostly, it bothered the fuck out of him. He wasn't frightened of Ben, as far as that went, but it was something he'd have to deal with in one way or another. That wouldn't be particularly easy considering Terrance held a fondness for old DeLuca.

There was also the little matter of Dino. The guy was Ben's nephew, but he was giving Damian a major heads-up about his uncle's possible plans. Dino had no reason to be doing that unless he was looking for something, or rather, wanting something from Damian.

Somebody always fucking wanted something.

"But what Ben wants with you isn't important. He's not on that path quite yet." Dino sucked in a deep breath, glancing up at the cloudy sky. "I've had enough fresh air for the day. Let's go inside and get some coffee."

"We're done talking about it? Just like that?"

"Oh, no. There's a lot more left to discuss yet, Damian."

Yeah, Damian figured that.

"Drink," Dino ordered.

Damian tossed back the remainder of his coffee, still as silent and stoic as he'd been an hour ago when he entered Dino's home. Dino sat across from Damian behind his large desk, drinking his own coffee. By the smell wafting from the drink, Dino had doused it with a good shot or two of whiskey.

"Why tell me?" Damian asked.

"About my uncle?"

What else was there?

"Yes."

Dino shrugged. "I've got to get things in order around here before I can't anymore."

"Twenty years isn't that long, Dino."

"In a cell with bars for windows, cement walls for art, and God knows who for a bunkmate? It's Hell."

True enough.

"And I'm not planning on making it that far," Dino said lower.

Damian passed a look Dino's way. "I beg your pardon?"

Dino waved it off. "Nothing."

"You still didn't answer my question about why, man."

"No, I suppose I didn't." Dino placed his cup to the desk before tapping one finger on the manila file he had with him earlier when Damian first arrived. "Family is important to me. Despite what the Outfit tries to project about *la famiglia* and all that bullshit, it means little to me. Because that's all it is—bullshit. Every man in the Outfit is in it for him and he always has been. We're greedy, we're excessive, and we know it. Everybody is jealous of somebody else, Damian. You're lucky you don't give a damn enough to notice."

Dino smirked, shaking his head as he added, "It wouldn't take much at all for the Outfit to crumble in around itself, not with the way its run and all. My father, back when he was still alive, used to say the Outfit was better when they ran it with the old school rules."

"Cosa Nostra rules, you mean."

"Sure. Men didn't steal from one another. Honor was held to a higher standard. Making money wasn't the only important thing."

Dino had a point. Even Damian had to admit the Outfit's main focus was money, making it, and who had the most of it. But wasn't that the mafia way?

"You can't call something a family if we're all enemies making nice at a dinner table," Dino said.

Damian laughed. "Sounds exactly like my family."

"Mine, too, as awful as that is. We put on a good show, of course, but we barely manage that." Dino slid the file closer to Damian before he rested back in his chair and picked the cup again for another long swig. "Open it."

Plucking the file off the desk, Damian flipped over the top and came face-to-face with the picture of a beautiful young blonde with brown eyes ·and a teasing smile. Underneath the picture rested papers filled with information on the smiling, carefree girl. Damian felt like he was intruding on the life of a woman he didn't know, so instead of going through the rest of the documents, his attention was taken back to the picture on the top of the pile. The small photograph had been printed on what looked to be a postcard. Flipping it over, Damian read the words written in a messy scrawl on the back.

Wales, England.
The beer could be better. I'm loving the accents, though.
Checking in a different way this time.
Miss you, D.
Love,
Lily.

Damian took note of the full date written in the left hand corner under Lily's name.

"Pretty, isn't she?" Dino asked.

The question seemed innocent enough.

It rarely ever was where Dino was concerned.

"Sure," Damian admitted.

Lily was beautiful. Wide, clear brown eyes with flecks of green and gold in her irises. Pretty pink lips curved high with her genuine happiness. Her blonde hair, waved and long, framed her features.

Damian looked away from the picture.

"She looks like our mother. Especially in that one there. Like nothing in the world could ever hurt her as long as she smiled back. I always remember that first about my mother. I'm glad Lily was able to carry it on even if she doesn't talk much to me anymore."

"Was this when she first started backpacking?" Damian asked.

"A couple of months into it," Dino answered. "That is the only full-frontal picture I have of her that could be considered even remotely recent. She sent a few more after that one, but someone else was always in the picture and you couldn't see all of her features. I wanted you to see who she was. She doesn't look all that different, really, but I didn't think asking her if I could take a picture after I forced her home would do me much good. She's pissed off enough as it is."

Wait, what?

"You asked Lily to come home?"

"Demanded, actually," Dino replied. "Then, when she refused, I threatened to send someone after her. She chose not to challenge me, thankfully. I wanted her to make the choice."

Damian snorted. "Doesn't sound like much of a choice, Dino."

"Lily's twenty-one. I've let her have her fun. She's gone and done all the exploring and learning she felt she needed to do before life came around to kick her in the ass and settle her down. I didn't hold her back. At first, she'd call me once a week and send me a postcard whenever she hit a new place. I figured her doing the traveling thing, learning how to live off what she made by working small jobs and the goodness of other people was a good life lesson. Something to better her."

Damian didn't see anything wrong with Dino's reasoning. "I get that."

Hell, he would have killed to do something like that. Instead, he'd only left the state of Illinois a handful of times and always for business.

"It was more than Theo and I ever got," Dino said, a hint of bitterness twisting his words dark. "Ben made sure my brother and I knew exactly what we were headed for. The Outfit was our destiny—in our blood, don't you know?"

Damian wasn't sure how to respond to that, so he stayed quiet.

Dino didn't seem to mind. "My father wanted out. Did you know that?"

"No. I thought he was forced into working with the officials, not that he wanted to."

"Yeah, he wanted out and he tried. Worked with the officials on the low for a while, recorded some things for them with a wire, and got caught in the process. Ben found out my father was working with the FBI and took both my parents out. Anyway," Dino muttered, rapping his fingers to the desk. "I never could figure out why Ben killed my mother, but the older I got, the more sense it made. She would have taken us kids and ran, I bet. Ben couldn't have that."

"He doesn't have any of his own, yeah?"

"None. Good thing, because he'd probably sell off every daughter his wife gave him and manipulate his sons right into a grave." Dino made a dismissive sound under his breath, but it felt laced with something Damian couldn't understand. "Look at how well he's separated my brother and me. We let him do it, too, not even realizing it."

Damian was learning a lot of things he hadn't known before. "It might not be too late to fix that, Dino."

"Trust me, those bridges are good and burned. Nonetheless, I was old enough to be the one who looked out for my sister. Ben always tried stepping in at times. He wanted her in schools he picked; I let her choose her own. He wanted her back in Chicago the moment she graduated; I let her go on to do whatever the hell she wanted."

That didn't sound like a bad thing, necessarily.

"I had to keep my distance, though," Dino continued, rubbing at his forehead. "Ben's a nasty fucker when he wants to be. I let him believe my choices with Lily were about controlling my family how I saw fit. That, when I was ready, I would bring my sister home and do what he deemed appropriate for a girl of her status and name."

"Which is what?"

"Marry her off to get her and us higher," Dino said.

Damian wished he could be surprised. It wouldn't be the first time the daughter of a made man was forced into a marriage she didn't want because of her family's ambitions.

"If Ben thought for one second I was letting her live the life she wanted because he took away everything else she had, my sister would have buried me, too," Dino said. "When it comes to us DeLuca siblings, Theo's the only smart one because he did everything Ben wanted and didn't question it. I did, too, but I always had some underlying goal."

It wasn't like Dino to be open about his personal shit, but Damian was getting it from the man in the tenfold tonight.

"So?" Damian asked.

"Lily was the only one of us three with her head stuck in the clouds. I just yanked her back down to earth recently. Keep that in mind when you meet her."

"Meet her?"

Dino grinned a wicked sight. "You owe me."

Damian froze in the chair. For the majority of a decade, the non-monetary debt Damian owed Dino DeLuca hung over his head, ready to fall at any moment. As a younger man, Damian had been rash and reckless. He'd made more than one bad decision. A particularly stupid one where he took the life of a made man in the Outfit could have cost Damian his life.

Dino stepped in, gave an excuse to the boss, took the blame for the death, and then proceeded to make Damian an understudy of sorts. Mistakes like Damian had made were enough to put a man six feet under. It had, essentially, been Damian's first real *in* to the Trentini crime family. Being close to Dino put Damian straight in Terrance Trentini's path and got him noticed.

It also meant Damian was indebted to Dino for saving his life, even if that meant years of waiting to finally give his dues.

"You owe me," Dino repeated as if he knew exactly what Damian was thinking.

"What do you expect me to do?"

Dino pointed at the folder. "Lily."

"Lily," Damian echoed, more uncertain than ever.

"I liked something about you back then, Damian. Time to pay up."

"How?"

Dino smiled a cold sight. "I have to protect what is important to me, Damian. My sister and my brother, they're important. Theo will do okay, no matter what. He's fucking resilient like that—as long as he keeps his heart out of the game. Lily though, she's not the same. She's too stubborn for her own good and I don't want to think about somebody taking that from her. When I'm not here, somebody else needs to be watching over her. And it can't be Ben DeLuca."

Christ. Dino made prison sound like a death sentence.

Maybe it was to the man. Damian didn't know.

"And I come into this how?" Damian asked.

"You're going to marry my sister."

Damian's thought process dropped off the radar.

Surely he was too tired and hadn't heard Dino correctly.

Right?

Damian's jaw fell slack. "What?"

"A life for a life, D. That's how it works in this life. Besides, this'll work out to your favor, too. We both know you're a happy little fucker in your spot doing what you do, Damian. There's nothing wrong with that."

"I don't understand," Damian muttered.

Well, he got the marriage deal.

Yeah, he fucking got that shit.

Dino just smiled. "Like I said, you're going to marry my sister. Sounds pretty simple to me."

CHAPTER TWO

"Lily, get a move on! We're late as it is!"

"Go to hell, Dino."

Lily refused to move the blanket covering her head. It was far too early on a Sunday morning for Dino to be going on like he was.

"I'm serious, Lily. Get up."

"No."

"Lily."

"Dino," she mocked, knowing damn well she sounded contrite and childish.

Lily couldn't even bring herself to care.

Lily DeLuca liked to be on the move. She was the kind of girl who didn't like to stop. Maybe that was why traveling appealed to her more than settling down into a stable life did. Now that her oldest brother forced her back from Europe, the only thing Lily seemed to want to do was nothing. Drag her feet, sleep in until noon, and ignore the world she would rather be seeing.

Chicago was pain to Lily.

She was nearly six when her parents were killed but she still remembered them. In her mind, their memories were vivid. The dreams she had of them were even more so. She despised how everyone else around them, including her brothers, acted as if the people who gave them life didn't exist; as if the people they called family didn't take them away.

She spent more time than she wanted to admit running from life and reality just so she didn't have to feel pain. Chicago had been the last thing on Lily's mind. If she could've helped it, she wouldn't have ever came back.

Dino didn't give her a choice.

"All right, this is fucking ridiculous," Dino grumbled.

Lily felt the blanket yanked from her body before a good cupful of cold water rained down on her face. It might as well have been ice. She spluttered and screeched, throwing her arms up to dodge the attack. It was pointless.

Dino just laughed above her. "Get up, I said."

"I hate you," Lily spat, soaking wet and sad in her heart.

"Time to make face at church, little one."

Lily scowled. "Don't call me that."

For a brief second, Dino's face darkened. "What happened to us, huh? We used to be close, Lily."

She didn't even have to think about it.

"You're just like everybody else. You didn't care, Dino."

Sighing, Lily sat straighter and stared forward at the priest of the parish as he took his place, dressed in his robes, and began the rite of Mass. Lily couldn't say church was particularly her favorite way to spend a Sunday, but she didn't know anything different.

Even when she backpacked across Europe, she always managed to find a Catholic church to say her grace, pray if needed, and do her penance. Lily wasn't an angel, but she believed in God. If she didn't believe in something, then she was supposed to accept those who passed on were forever gone.

She couldn't do that.

"Are you paying attention?" Dino asked at her side.

"Yes," Lily replied. "Stop hovering, Dino. I am fine."

"I'm just checking, Lily."

"I am fine."

Fine was a relative term that didn't apply to Lily. Dino pissed her off by forcing her home when she was doing so well out on her own without the Trentini, DeLuca, Conti, and Rossi families surrounding her. Her oldest brother put her through private school, let her spend most months out of the year away from home, and then signed over a quarter of her inheritance for Lily to use as she saw fit after graduating.

What changed?

Why did he force her back to a place where he should know she didn't want to be?

"Will you talk to me, now?" her brother asked. "You've ignored me for the last two weeks."

For good reason.

If Lily didn't ignore Dino, she'd try to rip his throat out with her fingernails.

"I was staying out of trouble, Dino," Lily said, trying to keep the heat out of her tone. "I checked in like you wanted me to."

"We had an agreement, Lily. And really, I let you go over that by two years."

Lily frowned, knowing his statement was true. After she graduated, Dino agreed Lily could backpack across Europe for a year before starting college. Preferably, a college in the states. But she loved traveling, meeting new people, and learning about the world around her. One year turned into two, and then to three. He never once asked her home.

Lily was appreciative her brother let her do what she wanted for as long as he did. He was essentially her guardian until she became an adult. Dino seemed to think he still made all the calls for her. The distance between them had grown over the years. Sure, the eleven-year age difference probably didn't help, but the more immersed Dino became in the mafia, the less Lily cared. Instead of being angry with the people who hurt them when they were just kids, Dino surrounded himself with them.

"You're angry with me," Dino murmured, keeping his gaze locked on the man standing at the altar.

"Very."

"You needed to come home," her brother said, completely unaffected. "It was time. You're a grown woman, Lily. It's time to accept what that means to *la famiglia*."

Lily barely held back from scoffing.

The priest surely wouldn't appreciate that.

"*La famiglia*, Dino? What has the family ever done for me?"

"Raised you."

"Raised me?"

The question came out as a sharp whisper. Dino winced in response. Lily took a little bit of satisfaction in that.

"Us," Dino corrected quickly.

"No, *la famiglia* turned us into orphans. And since when is my life of any importance to the Outfit, Dino?"

"It just is, little one."

Lily's teeth grinded at his casual use of that pet name.

Again.

"It doesn't matter," Dino said softly. "Whatever you think I'm doing is unimportant. What I am doing is for your best benefit, Lily. Trust me."

"I don't know anything about what you're doing, Dino."

"Well, you're probably not going to like it either way. Nonetheless, I'm trying to save you a lot of trouble and heartache if you would just give me the chance to do so."

Nothing her brother said made sense.

Lily was over the runaround.

"I'm a grown—"

"You're a mafia child," Dino interjected swiftly. "You're a born and bred DeLuca. You're a woman, sure, but you also know what that means.

You don't get to make the choices here, Lily. Follow the rules and everything will be fine."

Rules.

She shuddered in the pew, disgusted at the thought of what her brother's vague words could possibly mean.

"I've let you run away long enough," Dino said, his mouth tugging down into a frown. "It's time for you to come back to the family and do what we need you to do, now."

Lily's heart stopped as she looked her stoic brother over. "What does that even mean?"

"I've let you run away long enough," he repeated simply.

Lily didn't want to be immersed in their world. As a child, she hadn't been given a choice. As an adult, it should be only hers. She was not some pretty Mafioso *principessa* for her brothers to show off and dangle in front of others' eyes.

She was *her.*

It was her life.

"Dino—"

Lily's words were drowned out by the sound of the congregation standing.

"Please," Lily heard Father Garner say from the altar as she also stood, "… join me in a Mea Culpa to cleanse our souls and minds for the beginning of this Mass."

Dino smirked. "Funny how that works. It's automatically assumed we've sinned—that we're all sinners in need of repenting. We're not even given the option to be saints."

"We are sinners," Lily muttered.

Their whole family was full of them.

Dino shrugged. "We are."

"Confíteor Deo omnipoténti, et vobis, fratres, quia peccávi nimis …"

"I confess to almighty God, and to you, my brothers and sisters, that I have greatly sinned …" The words echoed through the church from two-hundred or more voices. It was almost melodic in effect, healing to some, she knew. A way of asking for forgiveness alongside everyone else so you didn't have to do it alone.

For some, it was the confession they would never give otherwise.

"Cogitatióne, verbo, ópere et omissióne," Dino murmured in perfect Latin.

"In my thoughts and in my words, in what I have done and in what I have failed to do," Lily said along with the congregation to follow the priest's words in English.

Something in the corner of her eye caught Lily's attention. Subtly, so it still seemed as if she were staring at the front, Lily turned her head and glanced to the side. Across the aisle stood a man she hadn't noticed earlier.

With his head slightly bowed and his lips moving along with the prayer, it looked as though he was fully engrossed in the confession.

Except he was staring at her, too.

"*Mea culpa*," rang out from the crowd of worshippers.

The next would come louder, Lily knew.

She was still stuck staring at the man. His eyes were a steel-blue. Dark hair fell over his gaze as he blinked and tilted his chin upward in Lily's direction. The action surprised her though she didn't know why. With chiseled features, a jaw wrought tight, an expression born from indifference, and a stance that spoke of an uncaring confidence, he reminded her of stone. Hard and cold. Beautiful ice, maybe.

There was something else about him, too. Something familiar. Like she maybe knew this man. It wouldn't be such a shock, considering the people who gathered at this church had been going for years. As did her family.

Who was he?

"*Mea culpa*."

The man flashed a quick smile and Lily turned away.

"*Mea máxima culpa*," she whispered.

It was only when the prayer turned to English for the verse did she realize that she could distinguish the man's voice in the people around her. She focused on the deep tenor in the pew across from hers just three feet away.

She shot him another look, not even caring if her brother noticed her staring or sudden distraction. The man was still watching her, too.

"Through my fault, through my fault, through my most grievous fault," he said.

Who are you, Lily wondered.

"*My bad*," the man mouthed.

Mea Culpa.

"Lily DeLuca, look at you," Terrance Trentini said with a smile that was far too wide for Lily's liking. She stayed still as he hugged her, held her cheeks in both his palms, and kissed her forehead. "You've grown up into a beautiful young woman, *mia bella*."

"Thank you," Lily said quietly.

She didn't like this man.

In fact, she didn't like any of the men or most of the women gathering in the foyer to welcome Lily and Dino into the large Trentini mansion. She knew better than to think that way—Lily didn't know most of them enough to say whether or not she liked them. What she did know about them, some of them, bothered her.

Lily wished Dino would have warned her about the lunch after church.

"You should be proud of this girl, DeLuca," Terrance said to a silent Dino.

Dino only smiled in response, but it didn't feel true.

"Oh, we're proud," came a voice from behind Terrance.

Lily couldn't help but grin at Theo as he came to stand beside Terrance. She hadn't seen him since arriving back to Chicago. Theo and Dino didn't get along well. Despite her misgivings about her brothers at times, Lily did miss them.

Especially Theo. At twenty-seven-years-old, he was closer to Lily's age than Dino.

"Welcome home," Theo said.

"Thanks," Lily replied.

"Don't let the crowd bother you," Terrance said. "It's larger than normal; Ben wanted to properly welcome his niece back."

Lily beat back the scowl threatening to form at her uncle's name. Terrance hadn't lied. Guessing by the number of voices coming from the connecting room, there were a lot of people. She knew some of the faces from spending her summers and holidays in Chicago during her years at private school. They weren't strangers to her, but she didn't feel entirely comfortable around them, either.

She quickly glanced over some of the faces, taking them in so she knew who was there. Joel Trentini's sisters, Abriella and Alessa, stood off in the corner, talking quietly to one another. Their parents, Sara and Peter, weren't very far away. The DeLuca siblings grew up calling them their aunt and uncle, although there was no real relation.

Lily also recognized the face of Tommas Rossi as he tossed a wink in Abriella Trentini's direction before acting like it hadn't even happened. She suspected if Tommas was there, the rest of his family was somewhere in the home, too.

One of the faces Lily knew and found instantly was Evelina Conti. The girl had gone to the same private schools Lily attended. As teens, they were mostly inseparable. But where Lily had been allowed to go on and do her own thing, the Conti family didn't let Evelina or the girl's younger brother, Adriano, do anything that wasn't to the Outfit's benefit.

"Lily!"

Evelina pushed past the men blocking her way, including Theo. Lily almost missed the way Theo tried to avoid staring at Evelina.

Almost.

She figured it wasn't important at that moment.

Lily accepted the embrace from her friend, hiding her grin in Evelina's hair. "God, I missed you."

"We just talked a couple of days before you came home," Evelina said, laughing.

"So?"

"Yeah, I know. I missed you, too." Evelina pulled back from Lily just enough to showcase that knowing smile of hers before whispering, "I know you're pissed, but I'm glad to have you back. It's fucking terrible here without you. You make it fun."

Lily made a face. "Later?"

"Later," her friend agreed.

"How was Europe?" Joel Trentini asked as he took Lily's cardigan and Dino's suit jacket.

"Beautiful," Lily said honestly. "I would have preferred to stay another year."

"Ah, but you have business here, my dear," Terrance said with another one of his wide smiles.

Dino gave Lily a look that silenced her before she could even say a thing. "She does. We're getting to that."

Ben DeLuca emerged from the entryway that led into the common room and dining area. "Is everyone here?"

"Not yet," Terrance replied.

"Who's missing?" Ben asked.

"Damian."

Who?

"He's on his way," Dino assured. "He was right beside us in church. Quiet, as usual."

Oh.

Steel-blue eyes. Dark hair. Sly smile.

Lily's pulse picked up.

"They'll make a good pair," Terrance said to Dino. "And he needs a wife. She's a good match."

Wait, what?

Lily felt like she was part of some cosmic joke that nobody had let her in on until now. And it was a really shitty time for her to be finally figuring it out.

When Terrance turned to speak with his grandson Joel, Lily spun on her heel to face Dino. She was sure her older brother could see the rage swimming in her gaze. Disbelief, heartache, and sickness rolled like one giant ball of hateful poison in her gut, flooding into her veins.

"Dino—"

"Not now." Dino jerked his head to the side and with a quick apology to the family and friends, he led Lily down the hall and away from the eyes of others. When they were alone, Dino let out a loud sigh, loaded with tension. "Take a second to think about it all before you say anything, Lily."

Take a second?

Her brother was about to sell her off like fucking cattle at the meat market. He wanted her to take a second and consider it? Like what, it might be a good thing?

Lily barely held back her scream of frustration. "You fu—"

Dino grabbed Lily's hand she raised to strike him. She wasn't the hitting kind of girl. She didn't like violence all that much. Funny, considering her entire life had been drowned in some kind of violence. All the mafia knew was violence.

"Stop," her brother hissed.

Lily tried to yank her arm back, but Dino held firm. "You bastard."

"You don't know a thing, so stop it right now." Dino squeezed Lily's hand just enough to make it hurt and to quiet her. "This is not the time or the place for any kind of bullshit, Lily. And you know damn well you're not the first to have something like this happen to them. Really, you're lucky you lasted as long as you did. If it were up to Ben, he would have married you off the day after you turned eighteen. Stop acting like a brat."

Lily's heart hurt and her lungs ached.

She couldn't breathe.

"What I need you to do is go back in there, greet Damian when he gets here, smile for those people, and make nice during dinner. It will be two hours—tops. Play your part like the good little DeLuca you are, like I know you can be."

"Why would you do this to me?" Lily asked.

Betrayal stung the back of her tongue as bile spilled into her throat.

Dino *tricked* her. He said nothing about marriage or anything of the sort when he told her it was time to go home.

Of course, he didn't, her mind taunted. *You would have run.*

She still could.

Dino seemed to pick up on her inner dilemma. "Your accounts have been frozen. You will not receive another penny of your shares or inheritance until you are married to Damian Rossi."

"A Rossi."

"He's a good man," Dino said. "And if I didn't pick you a husband, Lily, Ben was going to. I'm on a one-way train to prison for the unforeseeable future very soon. Theo will have little to no control at his age, especially where you are concerned. That would mean your welfare and choices are left to Ben. Is that what you want? Because if you think for one minute he would consider anything that you wanted, you are sorely fucking mistaken. Ben wouldn't care—he'd use you for his gain and nothing more. Even if that meant marrying you off to an abusive prick or a man twice your age."

"I'm a human being. I am a free woman, Dino," Lily snapped back. "I can make my own decisions about my life without anyone's input. I will marry who I want, not who you deem appropriate for me."

"You know that's not true. You might have liked pretending for the better part of your life like you're not involved in *la famiglia*, Lily, but we both know better. Please understand why I did this."

She couldn't.

"Lily—"

"Go to hell."

Dino barked out a bitter laugh. "I've already got one foot in the door, Lily. I'm just biding my fucking time while I wait."

Lily spun fast on her heel and pushed past Dino, needing to get away from him. She only took two steps before coming to an abrupt stop against the form of a familiar but still strange man.

Lily's hands splayed across the man's chest as she squeaked in surprise, not even realizing he had intruded on her moment with her brother. She felt her cheeks heat up because not only had he heard a very private conversation, but she was touching him, too.

He didn't seem to mind.

The same steel-blue gaze that had regarded her earlier at the church looked Lily over once again. She swallowed hard, feeling the bands of his muscles roping across his pectorals under her fingertips jump. His lips pulled into a smirk that looked entirely too wicked for Lily's liking.

Getting a close up look at this man was bad for Lily's insides. He was fit with a body built like a boxer's. The black suit he wore hugged his over six-foot frame perfectly and it only seemed to add to the confident, cool air he sported. A strange disinterest colored his features, but in his eyes, it seemed like he was looking straight through her.

She glanced down between their bodies, noting he stood relaxed and seemingly unbothered by the situation they were in. Even his hands were tossed into his pockets as if he were waiting for something and not like Lily was touching him.

His nonchalant attitude only added to his dark, mysterious demeanor.

Lily still didn't know how he managed to slip down the hallway without her or Dino noticing or why he was as quiet and still as he was now. What game was he playing?

Who in the hell was this man?

Lily's heart beat a little harder in her chest, remembering the name Dino uttered earlier.

Damian Rossi.

"Hello."

Lily blinked.

His voice was a dark tenor dripping with richness. The one word slipped from his mouth without his lips even needing to move. She had the pleasure of hearing many accents in her travels, but his was something else entirely.

"Damian," Dino said, bringing Lily out of her stupor. "Good to see you finally arrived."

"Ran over a nail in the church parking lot and came out to a flat tire."

"Ah, I see."

Lily stepped back from Damian. His gaze didn't move from her for a second, not even when he talked to her older brother like they were old friends.

Were they?

"Hello," Damian said again. "Lily."

Lily snapped out of whatever daze she was in. "Hello."

"It's Damian," he murmured.

"I know who you are."

Damian lifted a single, dark brow high. "Oh?"

"Yes."

"You don't seem pleased," he said quietly.

"That I'm forced to marry a man I don't know and don't want to know?" Lily asked bitterly. "I'm sorry to disappoint you, Damian."

Damian's smirk grew into a grin. "You know me."

"I—"

"You do," he interrupted before she could argue the point further. "Just not that well."

Lily blew out her frustration in a breath of air, gritting her teeth. Resolve steeled her spine straighter and she reminded herself of what her brother asked her to do. Turning, Lily faced a stone-faced, unbothered Dino.

"I will make nice and play good at this dinner," she said.

"Thank you," Dino replied.

"But I'm not marrying that man."

Dino's expression didn't waver. "It's not your choice."

"I am not marrying him, Dino!"

"Yes, you are," Damian said.

The words rolled over Lily's skin like liquid gold. She could feel the heat of his breath on the back of her neck.

This would be a great deal easier if she didn't find him attractive.

And why the hell was he agreeing to this, anyway?

"In two months, whether you agree or not, you will be my wife, Lily

DeLuca."

Lily couldn't help it; she shivered.

CHAPTER THREE

Damian sipped on a glass of cognac, letting the flavors of vanilla, spices, and flowers wash over his palate as he stayed immobile in the corner. He liked the shadows. It was the best place to watch people, after all.

While the guests mingled, drunkenly laughed, and went about their merry day, Damian observed. Mostly Lily, though. She was not a happy girl. And not just because of the forced engagement, he suspected.

"Almost didn't notice you over here," Tommas said as he slipped in beside a quiet Damian.

That was the point.

Damian gave his cousin a silent nod of acknowledgment but kept his eyes on the blonde ten feet away chatting with Evelina Conti and the Trentini sisters.

"You're really going to do this, huh?" Tommas asked, following his cousin's stare.

"Yep," Damian answered.

"Didn't think you were the marrying type, D."

Damian chuckled dryly. "I'm not."

"Then—"

"Dino," Damian interjected simply.

Damian knew he didn't have to say more and Tommas wouldn't question him further on the statement. Tommas was aware that Damian had been indebted to Dino for a long time though the two men didn't discuss it.

"Well, she's pretty," Tommas said.

Damian sighed. "Yeah."

If being pretty was the only thing a girl needed to make her something special, then Damian had seen more than enough of those kinds of females in his life. He wasn't interested in having another one. Lily was beautiful, though. Damian couldn't deny that.

Her brown eyes sparkled, especially when she was animated about something. He noticed while watching her during the dinner and party that Lily didn't smile a lot, for whatever reason. But when she did, her plump lips curved in the sexiest way. With high cheekbones, small features, and standing a good six inches shorter than him in her heels, she wasn't exactly what he would call a common beauty.

No, she had classic beauty. Like an old black and white movie actress.

She was not the kind of girl he'd go for. He didn't like the combative, stubborn type. He intended for his agreement with Dino about the marriage to be solely business. Damian owed Dino, this was what his friend demanded from him to pay it back, and Damian planned on following it through to the end. Every last bit of it.

Lily wasn't the least bit afraid to show her emotions. In a world where everybody wore a mask, Damian liked genuine things.

"I think she might be feisty," Damian said.

Tommas laughed lowly. "Trouble, you mean."

"No, she's not trouble."

Lily, no matter how much time she spent away from the Outfit and its suffocating rules for the women in the family, knew how to behave. Damian kind of liked that, too. He wondered what it would take to get her to let loose.

"What does Theo think of this?" Tommas asked. "I know he's fond of her. At least he always talks about her like she's still a kid instead of a twenty-one-year-old woman."

Damian shrugged. "What does Joel think about you fucking his little sister?"

Tommas choked on air. "What the hell, man?"

"Just saying, Tommy. I imagine Theo feels the same way about Lily being made to marry a man six years older than her, one she barely knows for the sake of business, as Joel feels regarding you and Abriella."

"Joel doesn't know about me and … yeah, he uh … nobody does, shit, I thought you didn't."

Damian scoffed under his breath. "Yeah, I know."

"How?"

"You smell like that fucking shit she wears—perfume or whatever— when you come into the club first thing in the morning looking like you didn't sleep all night. And I saw your car parked down the street from her parents' one night when Terrance called about something and I had to head over there."

Tommas cursed. "Have you told—"

"No," Damian said quickly. "I won't, either."

"Should I say thanks or what?"

"No, but she's eight years younger than you, Tommas, with a mob boss for a grandfather and a fucking idiot for an older brother. They're looking at men for her and you're not one of them. You should clean house of that nonsense before it becomes a habit you can't break and she gets you killed."

Guessing by the look on Tommas' face, it was already a damned habit.

Perfect.

Damian decided to let it go. He had enough of his own problems as it was.

Like Lily and what Dino wanted him to do for her.

Damian's gaze found Terrance Trentini in the middle of the room engaged in conversation with his grandson Joel, Ben DeLuca, and a Capo for the Outfit. Business never ended when it came to the family.

Dino wanted Lily to be safe and he earned Damian's loyalty a long time ago—Damian needed to pay up. Men like them were nothing without their word and too many men in the Outfit seemed to forget about that. Damian followed through on his word every single time. Lily DeLuca would be no exception, even if that meant she hated him for it.

Lily and Damian didn't have to like one another to be married, apparently. People around them proved that fact all the time.

"What do you think of the Outfit?" Damian asked. "Inside, I mean. Not business, but what does it make you think of?"

Tommas hummed. "It's family, man."

"Really, that's all you've got to give me? Family?"

"The only family we know."

True.

"Sometimes family hurts," Damian said.

Tommas nodded. "Ours certainly does."

"Someone's been watching you for the last half hour, Lily."

Damian hid his smile with his glass of cognac as Lily shot him a piercing look over her shoulder. Oh yeah, the girl was still pissed. He pretended not to notice she had caught him watching her and instead, surveyed the room while keeping her in his peripherals.

Lily was three sheets to the wind if her fifth glass of red wine was any indication. She hid her buzz well. Damian gave her credit for that.

"Yes, I'm aware," Lily grumbled under her breath.

Evelina laughed lightly as Lily's gaze left Damian as quickly as it found him. "He's very handsome and since he's my cousin, that's all I'm willing to give on the topic."

"Shut up, Eve."

"He is, Lily." Evelina shrugged. "Hey, at least Dino picked someone for you that looks decent, can take care of you, and likes your brothers."

"Yeah, because that's everything that matters right there."

"Just saying. You could be me."

"What is that supposed to mean?" Lily asked.

Evelina scoffed. "It means, I'm just waiting for the highest bid to come in, Lily. That's what happens when your father is the front boss for the Outfit and you're his only daughter. Think about it, he needs to compete with Ben and whoever the hell else Terrance likes. Men like my father only want to go up and that's all they give a damn about. If they can't get up there by their own hand, they'll use somebody else's to get there. My hand happens to be the one he's going to use, maybe even for another family."

"Which one?"

"Who knows? New York, Boston, maybe the fucking Vegas crew. He might as well slap a few stamps on my forehead and send me through the mail."

Lily's head turned just enough to give Damian a glimpse of her profile. Her frown and crumpled brow spoke of worry and disgust.

Why did she care so much about what happened to someone else?

"That sucks," Lily said.

"Yeah, it does," Evelina agreed. "And I was kind of liking on somebody, too. Daddy would have a righteous fit if he found out."

"Oh, who?"

Evelina shrugged. "Nobody."

"Eve," Lily pressed.

"Nobody, Lily, seriously. Better for us both that you don't know."

Damian was learning all kinds of new things tonight.

"What about Adriano?" Lily asked. "Is your father going to do the same thing to your brother?"

"I don't know," Evelina admitted. "We're not ... like we were way back when. And he's just like our father sometimes. Plus, he's got a dick between his legs, right? So, boys get to be in with it all. Completely different thing, I guess. Whatever. Anyway, enough of this sad shit. We're supposed to be the fun ones. Talking about this isn't fun and I was trying to point out that Dino did consider you for this."

Evelina's voice lowered, but Damian still heard her as he acted like the dancing, laughing people had all of his attention. "Damian's a nice guy. And I'm not just saying that because he's family, either. You've not been around for a long time. You don't know him well enough to pass judgement."

"You're not the one being married off to him like a cow on the market, Eve," Lily said sharply.

"I'd rather see you go to Damian Rossi than another man in the Outfit."

36

Lily spat out a laugh. "You're just saying that because it's not you. Had your father or brother tricked you like Dino did to me, you would be pissed off like nothing else. All that rebellion you did on the down low would suddenly get a hell of lot louder. Deny it, Eve."

Evelina didn't bother trying to. "I'm already pissed at my father so that's pointless. Listen, Damian is kind of quiet like you are and doesn't like the spotlight. He used to hang out with your brothers when Theo was twelve or something. They're the same age. Don't you remember him at all?"

Lily's face darkened as she passed another glance toward Damian. "Did he?"

"You really don't remember?"

"No," Lily said.

Damian surveyed Lily from the corner of his eye, noting how she chewed on her bottom lip in her curiosity.

"He was kind of like you guys."

"How so?"

"You know, like being shuffled around from place to place, people to people. Just … you two might have something in common where that's concerned. They're not going to give you a choice, Lily, and obviously Damian agreed to the arrangement for whatever reason. It's settled—your opinion bears no importance to them. I know it's barbaric and ancient, but it's going to happen."

Damian's unofficial fiancée grew silent like she was considering Evelina's words and taking the warning for what it was. Unofficial for only a short while because soon word would pass about the murmurings of the agreement between the Rossi and DeLuca families. The Outfit loved gossip and the news would spread like wild fire. Since Dino wanted the wedding to happen before his trial, dinners like the boss had thrown today could be considered an engagement announcement and party.

"Maybe," Lily finally said quietly. "I don't have to like it, Eve."

"Yeah, I know. You want another glass of wine?"

"Hmm, yeah, I think—"

Damian decided to step in and shut that idea down before Lily could agree. Dino would have a shitfit if Lily got any drunker than she already was. "Thanks, Eve, but she's good for the evening."

Lily glared over her shoulder at Damian still unbothered and still in his corner. "Excuse me?"

"That's your fifth glass of wine, your eyes are drowsy, and your brother never was one for a drunk woman," Damian informed like they were breaking bread over a dinner table. "While drinking probably seems like a good way to deal with this shitty night—I don't blame you, honestly—I can bet you'll regret it in the morning if you act like a fool and embarrass yourself and your brothers. You're not that kind of woman, Lily."

Damian gave a wide-eyed Evelina a charming smile. "Again, thanks, but no more."

"All right," Evelina said faintly.

Lily spun around and pressed her fisted hand to her hip. "Who in the hell do you think—"

Damian's gaze cut to Lily and she quieted instantly. "I'm not saying it to be an asshole, Lily. Go on, drink yourself stupid if that's what you want to do. You're the one who'll have to face these people again when you're sober."

Lily handed the wine glass to a stunned Evelina without a word.

"Thank you," Damian said with a smile.

"I didn't do it for you," Lily retorted.

Damian laughed.

No, girls like Lily never did things they didn't want to do. He liked that, too. Too bad the whole engagement thing wouldn't work out that way for her.

"Sure," Damian said with a wink.

Lily's gaze narrowed a second before she stormed off into the crowd.

Damian made sure to take note of which direction she went just in case. Evelina sighed with a shake of her head.

"That's not going to help your case," Evelina said softly.

Damian answered that with a shrug.

"Do you even care if she likes you, D?"

"Does it matter?" he asked back. "She doesn't need to like me to have my last name."

Evelina pursed her lips. "Damn, you're proving me all kinds of wrong tonight."

"How so?"

"I didn't think you were that kind of guy, Damian."

He cleared his throat and avoided Evelina's gaze. Him and her, they were mafia kids. He had six years on Evelina and eight on her brother, but he spent time in the Conti homes as well growing up. All of their families intertwined in that way.

"Guess you don't know me all that well, huh?" Damian asked, reverting back to his usual self.

Evelina didn't look away as she said, "No, I just think you're awfully good at making others believe you're doing what they want."

She was right.

"How much have you drank?" Damian asked.

"Too much."

"Where's your father?"

"Hitting on someone's wife," Evelina replied. "Ma's probably watching from the corner—she likes that nonsense, you know. Gets off on it. I think the fight is like their foreplay. It's disgusting."

Damian laughed hard. "Yeah, you've drank too much. Hand it over, Eve."

Evelina walked over and passed him her wine glass and Lily's, but not before she emptied hers of the contents. "You always were a fucking spoil sport, D."

"What'd you find out about the shipping deal with New York?" Tommas asked his boss. "It would be great if we could start working through there again. It's cheaper and all to have it slide through their ports and then straight to ours since they've got the labor rackets and the bribes going on there."

Damian pretended to sip on his cognac and seem disinterested in the conversation going on in Terrance's personal office. He'd only followed the men when the boss asked them upstairs because he liked to know what was going on around him, not because he had to be there. Damian didn't worry about crews, tribute, and bullshit like the rest of Terrance's guys did. Damian's work for the Outfit didn't fall in line with that unless someone needed an extra pair of hands for something.

Usually Damian worked with Tommas on those things, anyway.

"Marcello isn't going to let us in on that again, not after that mess a few years ago," Terrance said before tossing back the remainder of his red wine.

"I don't know why you bother making nice with them," Joel muttered under his breath. "With the Calabrese and the Donati families working with us, we could easily cull the Marcellos down to nothing. We could set up a syndicate—"

"Oh, shut up with that fucking nonsense," Terrance barked.

The quiet chatter in the room silenced.

"If your men had done what they were supposed to do in the first goddamn place when working in New York, we wouldn't have this problem with the Marcellos, Joel," Terrance said, scowling. "Instead, they decided to trade bullets with the dominating family. I might not like the Marcellos all that much, but I'm not an idiot, either. They control New York for a reason. They hold power over the other families because they earned it. They're closely aligned with the Sorrentos in Vegas. So yes, let's go right on ahead, act like bulls in a China shop, and start a war we can't finish. Why don't we do that, huh?"

Joel looked like he had taken a bite of something sour. "Grandpapa—"

"Shut up, Joel. *Dio*, you're working my last nerve and I'm not even drunk."

"I was just saying that—"

"Shut up or get out, Joel."

Damian supposed he understood why Joel wouldn't ever make it as a boss. The man didn't know when to sit down and be quiet.

"We hold the power in Chicago," Terrance continued. "That's what matters here. We work here. We have our own dealings to manage here. The Outfit dominates and unlike New York, we don't have to worry about or work with other families because the Chicago Mob controls even them. Forget about New York, it isn't ours and I don't want it."

"Fine," Joel said through clenched teeth.

"So, that's a no then?" Tommas asked.

"Yeah," Terrance said gruffly. "That's a fucking no."

"Pay a little more to get it straight through to here, that's all," Damian's uncle Laurent said. "Keep doing what we're doing."

"Can we talk about giving someone their in to the Outfit?" Joel asked.

Damian perked at that, curious. Usually the boss would bring something like that up, not another made man.

"Who?" Terrance asked.

"James."

"Poletti?"

"Yeah."

"No," Terrance said.

"Why the hell not?"

"Because he's a fucking Poletti and half of his mother's family is involved with the Lazzari guys. I'm not going to let some kid of another family weed their way into mine, Joel. That's ridiculous. Just because you work with them on things doesn't mean they're Outfit material."

"You don't even know—"

"The answer is no," the boss interrupted coldly.

Damian watched a couple of men filter out of the office quickly and silently as Terrance and Joel had a stare down. More meetings than Damian cared to count went down in this way. Joel had some crazy kind of superiority complex because his grandfather was the boss. Terrance refused to give his grandson any legroom to move.

No fucking wonder.

Damian wasn't sure Joel understood what respect was. How Tommas was as good of friends with this man as he was, Damian didn't know. He suspected it was because Tommas and Joel were the same age and grew up together. They weren't anything alike, though.

"Out, Joel," Terrance said. "No arguing. And the rest of you, too. I need a break. Get out."

"We're going to talk about this again," Joel said.

Terrance pointed at his office door and said nothing.

Damian turned to leave with the remaining men but stopped when his boss said, "Not you, Ghost."

It wouldn't matter how many times someone called him that, Damian still didn't like it. The damn nickname just reminded him of how forgettable he'd been as a kid and not the shit it referred to now in the present time.

"Yeah, Boss?" Damian asked.

Terrance waited for his office door to be closed, glaring at the last man who left with a glower: Joel. "Christ, he's a problem waiting to happen that boy. I wish his father would have pulled his head out of his ass and joined the Outfit like I wanted him to. He would have made a good boss. Joel makes a damn good fool and nothing more."

Damian chose not to dignify that with a response. He figured Terrance wasn't looking for one, anyway.

"What did you need?" Damian asked.

Terrance rapped his fingers down to the desk in a fast beat. "That boy he mentioned … James. Do you know who he is?"

"Of him."

"Me, too. His father was a habitual gambler that got beat to death when he couldn't pay his bookie repeatedly. Made the kid's mother a young widow to four kids she barely managed to take care of. I don't want that family's mess anywhere near the Outfit."

Damian didn't blink at that omission. "Interesting, but what does that got to do with me, Boss?"

"Joel needs to understand he doesn't get to make calls like this, you see. And his little show like he did tonight has been happening far too often lately. I don't know what has gotten into him but I feel the need to remind him of just who is in charge and why. So, you're going to do that for me."

Damian wasn't sure he understood the job correctly. "You want me to teach Joel a lesson?"

He couldn't think of a single time in his career as a hitman for Terrance that he ever had to make a move on the boss's close family or friends.

"Of a sort," Terrance mused. "If Joel wants to behave like a child, then I will punish him like one by taking away something that he wants. Clearly, he wants this man in with the Outfit, so that can't happen. Make sure Joel understands that in a way that is permanent, Damian."

Yeah, Damian got it.

James Poletti would need to go.

"Joel won't like that, I imagine," Damian said.

Terrance made a dismissive sound that came off as cold as his demand when he said, "I've let his nonsense go on long enough. It's high time he begins to learn he is not the one man who runs this show, my boy. And it seems you now have a job to do, so why are you still standing there?"

Damian didn't know. "How do you want it done this time?"

"Oh, make it easy on the kid, I suppose. It isn't his fault, after all."

No, it certainly wasn't. Damian didn't feel much about the entire thing and he wasn't all too surprised about the demand, either. This was who he was and a part of living the life he chose. The killing didn't always have to be justified or even make a whole lot of sense, not when the boss made the call. Men like Damian didn't get the option to refuse, not if they liked being alive.

"You want a call when it's done?"

"No, I'll be watching the news."

"All right, then."

"Thirty-k for this one, Damian," Terrance said. "It will be transferred into the account when I first get word."

Thirty-k.

That was the price of the man's life.

Damian probably could have argued the number with his boss and tried for something higher, especially since the man's death was pointless and Damian didn't usually go for that nonsense, but he didn't. Obviously Terrance had his mind set on what he wanted and killing the Poletti man was it.

"What about his mother's family?" Damian asked.

Terrance didn't look like he gave much of a damn if his disinterested expression was any indication. "What about them?"

"They might retaliate."

"So be it."

Damian reached for the doorknob and pulled the door open.

"One more thing," Terrance added.

"What is that?"

"Congratulations on the DeLuca girl, Damian. Getting married puts you one step closer to where you need to be. It'll work out well for you, I'm sure. You're twenty-seven, so it's time to settle down anyway and have a couple of kids to keep you busy. She'll make a good and proper wife for a made man—her brothers have seen to that."

Terrance's words hammered home what Dino had said to Damian two weeks earlier about the man looking at him for the head of the family.

It only reinforced his resolve to do what needed to be done so he could keep his life the way he liked it.

As his.

Damian didn't give his boss a reply as he walked out of the office.

The guests were finally starting to disperse from the Trentini estate when Damian made his way back downstairs. He noted Joel and a few other men in the family that had been in the office to witness the boss and his grandson's disagreement had left also.

That was the thing about the Outfit—everybody had a side to pick.

Damian said his goodbyes to his cousins and ignored his uncle and aunt when he passed them by in the dining room. Instead of parking his car in the Trentini's large driveway and take the risk of getting blocked in if he wanted to leave early, Damian had parked his cobalt blue Porsche 911 GT3 in the back of the home. The car was his baby. He didn't live in an excess of luxury, considering his small two-bedroom loft was as modest as they came in Chicago's Wicker Park. The Porsche was his one show of wealth.

Damian wasn't in the Outfit for money. If that were the case, he probably would have dropped out of the business long ago. It took a man years before he was really able to start pulling in any kind of decent cash of his own where the Outfit was concerned. Most revenue went to the boss— seventy percent of everything.

Damian supposed that was another reason why he liked his choice in career. Working with the Rossi crew for Tommas from time to time earned him decent cash. But being Terrance's personal hitman when needed was Damian's real payday. While he never stopped working for the Outfit, and other people seemed to think he was their personal soldier to do with as they wanted, Damian knew he could step back from that.

So, why hadn't he?

Damian frowned as he made his way toward the back of the house, realizing then how Terrance had been grooming him in some ways. Christ, Damian hadn't even noticed it was happening and that sickened him. Terrance often shoved demands from his men onto Damian when it was something he didn't want to handle. Thinking back, Damian could remember more than once when Terrance openly asked Damian's opinion on certain things.

Damian thought it was innocent.

Fuck.

It wasn't just about what the boss had been trying to slowly and quietly teach Damian, either. It was about the men around them and the Outfit as a whole. The Outfit's men were getting glimpses of another person of importance, someone with a voice being heard and a hand in the game.

Except Damian didn't want his hand in that fucking game. Lots of men would make a good boss—Damian could be a good boss. But he didn't want to be.

In the back of the house, where the guests didn't go during parties and dinners, Damian found the hallways quiet and dark without windows. Large homes like the Trentini's had very few windows on the bottom floor but the ones that it had were higher than normal. No boss wanted to give someone an easy way in, after all.

The figure leaning against the shadowed wall by the backdoor stopped Damian in his tracks instantly. The bit of light coming in from the frosted glass window on the backdoor haloed around her shape and washed her in a stream of color.

For a brief second, she actually looked calm and happy.

Alone, but happy.

Lily DeLuca.

A memory flashed into his mind so quickly he almost missed it.

"Damn, Uncle Ben's gonna be pissed, Lily," Theo said, the twelve-year-old's voice cracking on his uncle's name.

Lily sniffed, moving away the tattered piece of her summer dress to look over the damage on her knee. It was scuffed up and bloody something awful. It probably hurt but other than her sniffling, Lily didn't cry.

"Ow," Lily muttered.

"Shouldn't have let her tag along, maybe," Damian said. "Dino's not going to like that, either."

Or maybe the boys shouldn't have decided to climb the fence.

"But I always come with Theo," Lily whispered.

Most of Damian's friends didn't let their kid sisters hang out with them, but since Theo and Lily didn't have parents and Dino was too busy with whatever he did, Lily was always around. She didn't have a lot of friends because she was too busy following her brother around. Damian didn't mind since she was quiet.

Damian liked quiet people.

"The fence is rusty, too," Damian said.

Theo groaned. "Great."

"What does that mean?" Lily asked.

"Means we have to tell Uncle Ben so he can take you to the hospital."

Lily's brown eyes widened and tears started to well. "But—"

"You're gonna need a needle, I think."

"No!"

Damian winced. Whenever a girl cried, his stomach went weird. Girls shouldn't cry. "It doesn't hurt, right, Theo?"

Damian lied.

Those needles hurt a lot.

"Uh, right. It doesn't hurt, little one."

Lily sniffled again. "All right."

Damian blinked out of the memory, surprised it had come back to him at all. A great deal of his childhood had somehow been lost to the recesses of his mind over the years. He didn't have a lot to remember that he wanted to, really.

Did Lily remember him tagging around sometimes back then, too?

Damian, knowing she probably hadn't heard his approach, cleared his throat quietly.

Lily didn't even blink. "I figured Dino would come find me. Or maybe Theo. Definitely not you, anyway."

"I wasn't looking for you," he said honestly. "My car is parked out back to avoid someone getting killed if they scratched my car."

"Fascinating."

"Really? Because you sound bored as hell."

She also seemed a lot calmer than earlier.

Damian wondered what had changed for Lily in the span of a couple hours. He brushed it off. It didn't matter. Damian had a job to do so that meant he had to go out and get the info needed to get it done as quickly as possible.

Resuming his walk down the hallway, Damian passed a quiet Lily by.

"Do they still call you little one?" he asked as he unlocked the backdoor and opened it.

Lily stilled but didn't answer.

It was enough for Damian to know her brothers did still call her that.

Damian turned to face her. The breeze from the outside wafted into the hallway and blew the scent of Lily's flowery perfume through the space. She watched him from under her thick, dark lashes and he wondered if she wanted to bolt as far away from him as she could.

There wasn't a whole lot of space in the hallway, so turning like he did put him directly in front of her. Lily had to look up and Damian could plainly see the anger still warring in her gaze. It made her all the more pretty with just a glimmer of defiance behind her brown gaze. The frustrated pout of her lips demanded attention.

She had a mouth made for kissing.

Shit.

Damian didn't need more added onto his plate than what he already had but he figured out in that moment that he liked angry girls.

"You know, you don't have to hate me, Lily DeLuca. It might make this whole thing a hell of a lot easier if you just accept what is going to happen and get it over with."

"Get it over with, right," Lily scoffed. "Being sold off like cattle, you mean. I should just accept that I don't get to choose my husband or future."

"I never bought you—that wasn't the deal put on the table."

Lily looked away. "Oh."

"Nope."

"Why are you agreeing to this?" she asked.

Damian didn't even crack a smile. "Because I have to."

"Don't you want to pick your own wife, not have one given to you?"

"Who said I wouldn't have picked you, Lily?"

CHAPTER FOUR

"Theo, tell him!" Lily waved helplessly at Dino. "Tell him this isn't fair!"

Theo sighed. "Dino—"

"Not your choice to make, Theo," Dino cut in firmly.

"Yeah, I got that," the younger of the two brothers replied. "You could have told me ahead of time, though."

"Wasn't important."

"Is this for the sentencing thing?" Theo asked vaguely.

"Essentially," Dino replied.

"Ben doesn't like it—he hid it well today, but he said so."

"Terrance approved."

Theo chuckled. "Wonder why."

"You know why," Dino said.

"I know D, too."

Dino smiled faintly. "We all do. He'll do what I need because he needs something, too. Helping hands don't exist in this world. They're all trying to grab something back for them. I figure he's starting to learn that."

"What about Lily?"

Dino dropped his fork and napkin to the table, rested his arms along the sides of his plate and stared his brother head-on. "Do you think Damian is a bad choice?"

"No, I think he's a fine choice," Theo replied. "For a man in the Outfit, anyway."

"For a man in general, you mean."

"Whatever, Dino."

"If I had discussed it with you, who would you have picked to get the job done?"

Was that all Lily was, a *job*?

Disgust rolled thick and strong in her gut, threatening to spill her casserole and salad all over the dinner table.

"Joel Trentini, maybe?" Dino continued, his voice dripping with sarcasm as a smirk twisted his mouth upward.

"Hey," Theo barked. "I'm a fucking DeLuca, too."

Dino nodded. "Then you know why I picked a Rossi."

"Well, I know why you picked Damian."

"Same thing."

Theo cocked a brow. "Could have picked Tommas—he's good for the job."

Again with that fucking title.

"I am not a job!" Lily snapped, finally meeting her wit's end.

Dino and Theo acted like she hadn't said a thing. Neither man looked away from one another.

"Tommas is good for the final job. Make sure you know the right side to be on when the time comes," Dino said. "Besides, I did think of Lily here, regardless of what she believes. A man like Tommas, already sniffing around a tree he shouldn't be, isn't going to do right by her in the end. Tommas will do right by his, to be sure, but Lily isn't his."

What?

Lily was so confused it wasn't even funny. Her brothers might as well have been talking in riddles for all she understood.

"She's not Ghost's, either," Theo said quietly. "Did you think of that, or are you only thinking of the past, Dino?"

Dino's expression barely flickered with emotion as he said, "We both know D, Theo. Give him time to catch the fuck up before you start running off at the mouth, huh?"

Theo blew out a steady stream of air, nodding. "Fine."

"I appreciate it."

Theo shot Lily a look that was anything but apologetic. "Sorry, little one. You're in this one for life."

Lily's jaw dropped.

How could he?

Not only had her brothers' entire conversation been spoken as if she wasn't even in the room, but they still managed to talk her in circles without including her. Lily glanced between her brothers who had both resumed eating without barely an acknowledgment to one another.

She still wasn't sure where she went wrong here.

Theo showed up earlier without a reason, said less than a few words to Dino when their older brother invited him in for supper, and now they were acting like strangers again. What in the hell had become of their lives?

"Theo!" Lily said, desperation pitching her voice high.

"Dino's doing right, Lily."

That was it. That was all her brother said.

Lily dropped her fork to the table with a clatter, gaining both her brothers' attention as she stood from the table and pushed her chair roughly away.

Dino eyed her plate of food. "We're not finished eating, Lily."

"I'm finished, or do you plan on telling me how many calories I have to consume in a day, too? Maybe you would like to give me a list of things I should and shouldn't be doing, like the miles I jog in the morning or the color of my lipstick. What should I wear, how should I speak and walk? Come on, Dino, what more can you do to me? Let me have it."

"Lily—"

"Why are you doing this to me?" she asked. "Why, Dino?"

"Because I have to."

Damian's words a few days before clanged around in the back of Lily's mind like a warning bell.

"I am not your way to the top!" she shouted.

Dino didn't blink. "I'm not aiming to get there."

Lily couldn't begin to understand her brother. And God knew she tried. "Dino, *please.*"

"Stop begging, Lily," Dino said, his words sharp like the edge of a blade. "You're a DeLuca whether you want to be or not. DeLucas don't beg, we never have, and you're sure as shit not going to start now. As far as what you can and can't do, you already know the answer to that, so don't start looking for direction from me. You know what is expected from you; what more do you want from me?"

"To let me live my life," Lily said.

"I'm trying."

Abriella Trentini dropped the stack of magazines on the coffee shop's small circular table and took a seat with a huff. The white lace, pearl buttons, and flowing silks on the covers of the magazines made Lily sick just by looking at them.

"Do you have a style you like?" Abriella asked. "That'd help to narrow it down a bit."

"She's going to make this extra difficult," Evelina informed before taking a drink of her chai latte.

Lily gave her best friend a dirty look. "Classic, A-line, lace."

"Someone was wrong," Abriella said in a sing-song manner, grinning.

Evelina shrugged. "Give it time."

"All white?" Abriella asked.

"Off-white," Evelina said.

Lily laughed under her breath. "She knows. Definitely off-white. The less whispering I have to listen to, the better. No need to give the mob bitches anymore reason to act like barking spiders than they already have."

"Hey," Evelina said, mocking offense with her hand pressed to her chest. "Is that how you think of us—mob bitches?"

"No, just bitches."

All three girls' laughter rang out in the quiet coffee shop, drawing the attention of several annoyed gazes. Lily didn't even care about them. Their life wasn't being upturned and decided on without their input or approval. They weren't being forced to plan a wedding they didn't want or being made to marry a man they didn't know.

"Seriously though," Abriella said, sobering. "How are you doing with all of this?"

Lily sighed and eyed the magazines. "I've spent the last week arguing and yelling at Dino."

"And?"

"And here I am looking at bridal magazines."

Lily thought that statement was self-explanatory without her needing to go into further detail.

"How in the hell did Dino get the church to agree to overlook the mandatory six-month couple's counselling?" Evelina asked.

Lily scoffed. "Paid the church off, probably."

"Ah, the smell of old money, bribery, and religion first thing in the morning," Abriella said in a long sigh. "Smells like home, girls."

Evelina laughed under her breath. "Just like home."

"And the mob," Lily added bitterly.

"Is that all it is for you?" her best friend asked.

Lily didn't know how to properly answer Evelina's question. "Partly, but it's about me, too. Why let me just begin my life away from all this and then drag me back into it?"

Evelina shrugged. "Maybe Dino and Theo never really let you go; you just thought they did."

"Dino picked the date," Lily added. "I couldn't even pick my own wedding date, he had to."

"Why?" Abriella asked.

"I don't know. It's a little less than a month before the start of his trial."

Evelina's gaze widened. "That's like … That puts the wedding almost two months from today."

"Yep," Lily mumbled.

"Shit."

"Yep."

"They're not wasting time, then," Abriella said softly.

"Nope," Lily replied, sadness twisting at her insides.

"Damian didn't want a little more time or something?" Evelina asked.

Lily shrugged. "How the hell should I know?"

"Pardon?"

"I haven't seen him since the dinner at the boss's. He's not been around, he's not asked for me, and we've not spoken otherwise. I have no idea what Damian wants but I can bet it isn't me."

"What if he did?" Abriella asked.

Lily snorted indelicately. "He doesn't."

"I didn't ask that. I asked about if he might, what would you do if that were the case?"

"Nothing," Lily said honestly. "I would do nothing."

Evelina watched Lily like she was a deer ready to bolt over the rim of her cup. "You're already doing nothing, babe."

"Talk to me when this is you, Eve. Let me know how you feel then."

"I will. It's bound to happen. And I expect you to let me bitch, moan, and cry my goddamn eyes out because I'm not marrying the man I want. Simple as that."

Lily felt thunderstruck at her friend's blatant statement. "I will."

"Good. Carry on with your bitching and moaning."

"I'm not crying," Lily pointed out.

"Yet," Abriella muttered.

"DeLucas don't cry," Evelina said before Lily could.

"We don't."

"Not to other people, anyway," Evelina added.

Grumbling, Lily flipped open one of the many magazines Abriella brought along for their lunch date. Abriella Trentini was a lot like Lily and Evelina in the way she had been brought up in and around the thick of Outfit business. She was a mafia child through and through, so she, like Lily and Evelina, likely knew there wasn't any way around the arrangement made.

"They're planning a huge party," Lily said. "Dino was working on the guest list this morning. It was ridiculous."

"How big?" Evelina asked.

"At least three-hundred guests. Probably more." Lily made a face. "I didn't even know most of the names on the list. How do you plan a wedding that big in less than two months?"

"Money," Evelina said like that explained it all.

Lily supposed it did.

"Big thing for two families to merge," Abriella said. "I'm not surprised Dino went for a Rossi."

Lily wasn't even sure she wanted to know but because she had been so out of the loop with the Outfit and the families involved for the last several years, she didn't have a choice but to ask. "Why is that?"

Abriella raised a single brow high. "Really?"

"Yeah, I asked, didn't I?"

"Terrance made the call, Lily," Abriella said quietly. "If Dino wanted to align you with another family, it makes sense for him to do it with one he trusts. The Rossi family had very little to do with what happened. Terrance and your uncle made all the calls on that mess, you know."

Lily still didn't understand. "No, I don't."

Evelina cleared her throat, shooting Abriella a look Lily couldn't decipher. "She's never been around a lot, Ella. Dino's kept her out of a lot of it, especially the Outfit. She doesn't even talk to me about that stuff, all right?"

"Can't blame him," Abriella muttered.

"I'm right here, okay," Lily said. "Talk like I am."

Abriella sighed. "Your parents. Terrance and Ben did all of that."

Lily's spine straightened in the chair. "I know."

"Then you know why Dino would choose a Rossi and not someone closer to your family or a Trentini to align you in marriage."

"So, what? Dino doesn't think someone in the Trentini family would marry me because our father was a rat? That's—"

"No, because Dino doesn't trust them," Evelina interrupted gently. "It's been a long time, sure, but wounds like those don't ever heal as well as people think they do."

Lily swallowed hard, trying to force the lump in her throat down. It didn't help. Her wounds certainly weren't healed. They had barely faded at all.

"Yeah, tell me about it," Lily whispered.

"Okay, enough of this," Abriella said, grabbing the magazine from Lily's hand.

"Hey!"

Evelina just laughed at Lily's wide eyes.

"Seriously, enough." Abriella gathered the magazines and tossed them into her messenger bag. "This day is ridiculous. This wedding is ridiculous. Pick a dress another day. Dino will have everything planned and going ahead regardless of us, so we might as well let him do it. We have better things to do."

Lily gaped. "Like what?"

Abriella shrugged. "How about a club?"

Evelina made a face. "Should we?"

"Who's going to tell? One of us?"

"What is the problem?" Lily asked, glancing between her two friends.

"Nothing," Abriella replied, giving Evelina a pointed look. "We do this all the time. Go out and have some fun, shake off the stress, and forget about the day. Nothing is wrong."

"As long as nobody sees us," Evelina said. "Daddy would be in a right fit and you know your grandfather would flip, Ella."

"Terrance will never know."

"But—"

"He hasn't found out about all the other times, Eve."

"True, but it still makes me nervous. I mean, Lily is getting married and they know we're all friends. Terrance probably has a half of a dozen enforcers trailing us on a daily basis just to make sure we're being good."

Being good?

Lily scoffed. What fucking world did they live in? They were adults, right? "And what if they did find out?"

"They don't, so it's not important," Abriella said. "Eve is just overthinking, like she always does."

"I am not!"

"Okay, you're not. Shut up about it. Tommas' place?" Abriella asked.

Evelina nodded. "He's the only one who won't run his mouth if he sees us out."

Abriella smiled. "He is. And I always know how to lose the enforcers trailing me. They're too embarrassed to call Granddaddy and tell him they lost me because they know how much shit they'd be in. How about we take my car, stop at the place Tommas' rents for me after I lose the—"

"Whoa, hold up," Lily said, leaning forward with interest. "What did you just say?"

For the first time, Abriella actually looked nervous. She wouldn't meet Lily's gaze. "It's nothing."

"A family Capo is renting you a private place and that's *nothing*?" Lily repeated dully.

"It's nothing to *you*," Abriella said firmly. "Better you don't know, Lily. Trust me."

"I don't know, either," Evelina said with a grin.

Oh, she clearly knew.

Abriella didn't take her eyes off Lily for a second. "Listen, what I do is what I do, Lily. And I'm going to make damn sure I have fun while I can before I can't anymore. I'm not looking for anyone's permission here. Are we good?"

Lily thought so. "We're good."

Tommas Rossi's club couldn't fit another soul inside. Lily was sure of it. How the club didn't have fire marshals knocking on the door to clear bodies out, she didn't know.

"What are you doing here?" Adriano asked his older sister.

Evelina didn't turn from the bar as she ordered.

"Hey, look at me," Adriano barked. "Don't act like I'm not talking to you, Eve."

"Shut up, Adriano," Evelina said with a huff. "You're not even legal. Who the hell let you in?"

"Tommas."

Abriella rolled her eyes. "Figures. Where is he?"

"In the back office dealing with some shit."

"Work, you mean," Abriella said. "Somebody's dealing in here for him. God, he's never going to learn."

"Something like that," Adriano replied with a shrug.

Lily took the bright green grasshopper drink Evelina offered and tipped it back to take a big sip. The alcohol flooded her mouth instantly right along with the intense flavor of the drink. Christ, it was good.

"Not so fast," Evelina said, laughing. "You'll be so hammered I might not be able to get you home without Dino knowing."

"Screw Dino," Lily replied before taking another drink.

Lily's attention went straight back to the brother and sister who were glaring at one another.

"You shouldn't be here," Adriano said.

"Tommas is here, right?" Evelina asked sweetly.

"I said that already, Eve."

"Exactly. Someone is here. He'll keep watch over us. What is the problem?"

Adriano's teeth gritted beneath his jaw. "You know what the damn problem is."

Evelina waved a hand flippantly at her brother before taking a drink of her Sourpuss and Seven-Up mix. "Not really, little brother."

"You're fucking impossible," Adriano muttered. "I'm trying to give you some warning here and you're ignoring me."

"Are you going to be a little rat and run to Daddy?" Evelina asked.

Adriano's gaze narrowed as he glanced between Lily and Abriella. "No, but you're not the one someone might flip over tonight, Eve."

"Turn cheek, Adriano. Isn't that what everybody keeps telling me?"

"You owe me."

"Whatever."

"I'll keep my mouth shut about you, but somebody else needs to know about her," Adriano said, nodding at Lily.

Who the hell would care if she was at the club?

Adriano disappeared back into the crowd without another word.

"That was easy," Lily said.

Evelina didn't look all too pleased at her brother's parting words.

"Fucking spoil sport."

"How long do you think we have?" Abriella asked.

"An hour, maybe."

Abriella pouted. "I'll go find Tommas and see what he can do."

Evelina scowled. "Nothing, probably."

"Give him a chance."

"What am I missing?" Lily asked, sipping on her grasshopper again.

She needed one of those for each hand. They were that damn good.

"It's nothing," Evelina assured. "Let's just have some fun and dance while we can."

That sounded perfect to Lily. The music practically pumped through the floors and vibrated the borrowed heels Lily stood in.

She had come to find out Abriella Trentini's rented apartment might as well be a second home with an entire wardrobe included. Lily chose not to ask questions when she noticed a man's suits hanging alongside Abriella's dresses earlier. Then again, she figured Tommas Rossi's name had been mentioned more than enough for it to be kind of obvious.

Someone wasn't going to like it when their secret was found out.

"Let's dance!" Evelina shouted, giggling as she tugged on Lily's hand.

Lily grinned. It had been too long since she was able to just have fun, especially with Eve.

"Let's dance."

Strobe lights flashed from all angles in rapid succession, making the crowd nothing but a blinking black and white blur to Lily. She turned with her arms thrown high, swallowed by the club goers, drunken laughter, sweaty, swaying bodies, and music.

She wasn't the partying kind of girl. Sure, Lily had her fun every once in a while, but she never really let loose. It felt so good to dance and be just another face in the crowd—someone unrecognizable and unknown.

Not a DeLuca.

Not a girl affiliated with the mob.

Not the daughter of a turncoat or the sister of made men.

No, just Lily.

It reminded her of traveling all over again and of being free.

Lily realized she had lost her friend somewhere in the crowd. She didn't really care. Evelina had probably gone back to the bar for another round of drinks. The buzz slipping through Lily's veins said she probably had enough of her own for the night.

Large hands found Lily's waist from behind before her body was drawn into the firm chest of someone. A man. He smelled like the club, liquor, and unfamiliar cologne. He wasn't the first person to randomly grab Lily and bring her in for a dance or two, so she didn't mind. Her hips moved in time with the man's and the music. Lily wanted to see who it was that decided to dance with her, so she turned in his embrace to find a good-looking stranger with a wide grin.

"What is your name, pretty girl?" he asked.

She didn't think giving her name would be an issue. It wasn't like she planned on taking this man home.

"Lily."

"Carter," the man replied.

"Hello, Carter."

"Hello, Lily. Beautiful dress."

"Thank you."

His grin melted into a sensual smirk. "Let's see if I can get it off you before the night is through."

Lily wasn't sure how to respond to that. She liked the sound of his voice, though. "You'll have to work awfully hard."

And he didn't have a chance.

"We'll see about that," Carter murmured.

Lily let Carter bring her closer as his hand skimmed up her exposed back. All the while, she swore she could feel someone watching her.

Someone who wasn't Carter.

CHAPTER FIVE

"Oh, come on, Tommas," Abriella said, her cheeks pinking. "You're such an asshole. How is Lily having a little fun any different than—"

"Stop it, Ella," Tommas snapped. "It's entirely different. I keep a damn eye on you when you're out."

"Because I come here," Abriella replied hotly. "And I do it for *you*. I brought her here so what is the fucking problem?"

"And you shouldn't have done that, either!" Tommas growled.

"You—"

"Enough, Ella."

Abriella glowered at her companion.

Damian acted like the two weren't glaring daggers at one another. In fact, he wished he didn't know anything about his cousin's relationship with Abriella Trentini. Tommas was going to get himself killed over that shit someday—Damian was sure of it.

"Adriano took Eve home, then?" Damian asked.

"A few minutes ago," Tommas confirmed.

"Is he going to keep his mouth shut about the girls being out at a club without supervision?"

Tommas nodded. "Of course, he will. The kid is golden, you know."

"Fun suckers, the lot of you," Abriella said with a huff.

"No, we're keeping you out of shit with your fathers and grandfathers," Tommas said with a frown.

Abriella sneered. "Right, that's what you're doing. Where am I going tonight, Tommy? With you or to Granddaddy's? How do you plan on explaining that when you drop me off, huh? Maybe you'll take me back to my apartment where the stupid enforcers are waiting for me like always. I've been drinking, right? I can't drive. God knows you don't trust a soul around me, so you'll have to take me home ... or maybe we'll go back to our place and—"

"Stop, Ella. You're drinking and I don't want to deal with this nonsense. Do you know the kind of position you put me in tonight?" Tommas asked.

"Like the kind you put me in?" Abriella asked back sweetly.

Tommas' jaw fell slack. "Ella!"

Ouch.

The girl had balls, anyway.

Maybe Damian could understand why Tommas was doing the crap he was with Abriella—whatever it was. Tommas always had liked his women a little rough around the edges and difficult. Abriella sure fit that bill.

Damian cleared his throat. "All right, enough of this. You two fight or fuck it out. I don't care. Where's Lily?"

"On the floor somewhere," Tommas said, not moving his piercing gaze from Abriella. "She was dancing the last I saw."

"Thanks," Damian said.

"No problem, man. It's only ten; Dino probably hasn't starting flipping his shit that Lily didn't show up home, yet."

Damian waved his cousin's statement off. No way in hell would Damian be able to take Lily home to her brother without Dino finding out what happened. Especially if Lily was drinking like Tommas said when he called earlier. Dino would not be happy about that bullshit. Better for Damian to get Lily to a safe place for the night and excuse it in the morning when he did get her back home.

"Didn't you have that job tonight?" Tommas asked. "Poletti and all?"

Damian shrugged. "Yeah, but you called, so …"

More important things.

Plus, the night wasn't exactly over. Damian could still get the hit in if the Poletti man stuck to his normal schedule. There was a certain art to being a hitman, after all. Watching your victims and planning before you struck was an important piece to the puzzle. The chance of leaving something behind or fucking up lessened.

Damian Rossi didn't know how to do messy.

"Terrance isn't going to like that, I suppose," Tommas said.

"I'll get it done."

Tommas snatched the tumbler full of red liquid from Abriella's hand just as she tried to take another drink. "Oh, I think you've had enough, *mia bella donna.*"

"Go to hell, Tommy."

"Goddamn, Ella, you know I lo—"

Damian turned on his heel and walked away before he had to hear something else he didn't want or need to know. He quickly slipped into the crowd of club goers, searching through the unfamiliar faces for the one he knew.

He was pretty damn sure Lily wouldn't appreciate him just showing up and ordering her out of the club, but she didn't give him much of a choice, really. It wasn't Lily's fault, as far as he was concerned. Abriella and Evelina knew better than to be kicking it in a club owned by a Mafioso. Their parents and the Outfit expected those girls to be above reproach at all times. There couldn't be a single reason for gossip to start spreading.

They weren't fucking angels. Damian didn't pretend they were, but he didn't want to see them getting in any kind of trouble because they wanted to have a little fun, either. Lily, especially. Since she was Damian's fiancée—technically—Tommas called him first instead of Lily's brothers. Damian was supposed to be looking out for Lily, it was one of Dino's requests, but his week had been swamped with getting his plan perfected to fulfill Terrance's order on the Poletti man.

Lily fell through the cracks.

Damian figured she would be okay for one damn week, but apparently not.

Damian, bothered when the people all but swallowed him whole, moved to the wall and walked alongside the less crowded space as his gaze scanned the floor. When he did finally find Lily, something unfamiliar burned hot and fast through his stomach. It pooled there and threatened to overwhelm him with the sensation.

Lily danced with a man like they were cozy. His hands were on her body, grabbing at her waist and hip before traveling higher over the tight, black dress Lily wore. The guy's hands might as well have been all over her, for fuck's sake. The damn dress was short as fuck. Too short, maybe. Damian might have liked seeing the bodycon-style dress on her any other time, actually.

In fact, he might have really liked seeing her dance any other time, too.

Damian had to admit, Lily was one hell of a sexy sight.

She moved in time to the music perfectly, the sway and swell of her ass drawing in his gaze and holding it as the tempo picked up. With her hair in loose waves, the blonde strands covered her back and shoulders as she danced. A sly, almost coy, smile curved her lips into the sweetest grin while her dark eyes twinkled with a wicked gleam.

Yeah.

Sexy as fuck.

Her black dress hugged every curve. She showcased a toned, young figure made to fit a man's hands. Not the ones holding her now, though.

Damian hadn't expected to feel jealousy. Women weren't property to be owned in his mind, even if the deal with Dino kind of put that situation on the table for him and Lily. Watching his fiancée dance with another man; seeing that man touch her ... Damian couldn't do that shit. Something in him burned like crazy, running straight out of control.

He decided in that moment, right then and fucking there, Lily DeLuca was his and she was damn well going to know it, too. Even if it took a bit of convincing to get her there.

When the man's hand drove down Lily's back, coming dangerously close to her ass as he pushed her smaller frame into his, Damian jolted forward. A harsh heat balled in his middle as his teeth and fists clenched.

"Whoa, too close," Lily said, trying to take a step back from the guy.

She hadn't even seen Damian coming.

Not yet, anyway.

"What the fuck do you mean, too close?" the guy asked. "We're just dancing."

"Your hands can stay off my ass," Lily replied.

"Goal is to get you out of this dress—"

"That's not going to happen. Back off a little, okay?"

He still wasn't letting her go. He didn't back off like she told him to, either.

Damian came up behind Lily, put a hand on her waist, and grabbed her tight. "Remove your hands from her body, or I will cut each of your fingers off and stuff them down your throat, asshole."

Lily spun around, her brown eyes wide but dimmed with drink. Guessing by the tightness in her lips and the way her hand pressed on his midsection as if to push him away, she wasn't pleased to see him show up. "Damian? What are you doing here?"

Damian didn't pay her any mind. He was too busy staring down the fucker who looked like he was going to reach for Lily again.

"Go on, do that," Damian goaded. "Touch her again, man. Let's make my night perfect by spilling blood all over the floor of my cousin's club. Here's a fucking history lesson you ought to know before you go around handling females that don't belong to you. Rossi. DeLuca. Trentini. Conti. Do those names ring any goddamn bells for you? This is Chicago— they're the first names you grow up learning to stay the hell away from when you play on the streets."

The man took a step back, his hands flying upward in a prone position. "Sorry, my bad."

Damian laughed. "Yeah, that's right. Get the hell out of here and don't make me ask again."

Lily's lips popped open as she turned to watch the man slip into the crowd of moving bodies. Nobody seemed to notice a thing out of place.

"Damian!" Her tiny fist smacked his chest hard. Pretty brown eyes glared up at him with a fierceness that said she was ready for a fight. "You … you …"

"What?" he asked.

"Oh, my God. Why would you do that?"

Damian lifted a single shoulder. "He shouldn't be touching you, Lily. You shouldn't be surprised."

"We were just dancing," she half-cried. "And you … you come in here like you own me or something."

"You're my fiancée. That means I—"

"Fuck you," Lily spat, sneering. Disgust colored her words thick. "No man owns me, Damian. Not you or anybody else."

"It's not about owning you, Lily. It's about the respect. And if you want to go out and drink, party, or do whatever, you need to make sure you've got the proper chaperone with you. Especially now that you're set to be married to me. Evelina and Abriella might run around behind everybody's backs doing whatever in the hell they want to do, but you know better, and frankly, so do they."

Lily's fists met her hips. "Says who?"

"Me. Dino. Any man in the Outfit."

"Screw the Outfit. I'm twenty-one-years-old. I stopped needing to check in for permission when I hit eighteen."

"Sorry, sweetheart, but it doesn't work that way. We're trying to keep you out of trouble here. Don't you get that?"

"No." Lily's laugh was full of scorn. "What I get is you thinking you've got some kind of say on the things I do or don't do. Reality check, Damian. You don't. At all."

Lily spun on her high stiletto heels. Damian didn't let her get too far. He caught a shrieking Lily around the waist, picked her up as she fought against his hold, and cradled her over his shoulder like she weighed nothing more than a bag of flowers.

"You're a bastard," Lily hissed, smacking the spot between his shoulder blades with her opened palm.

"Ouch, hit a little lower. I didn't know you liked it rough."

Lily stilled in his grasp before her wiggling started up again. "You're ... *impossible*."

"You'll grow to like it."

"I doubt it," Lily bit out.

Damian ignored the curious gazes watching them as he strolled through the swarm of people separating on the floor while he walked past.

"I look like a child, put me down right now," Lily ordered. "I can walk, you know."

"No, if you act like a child, you'll be treated like one."

"Damian!"

"How many drinks did you have?" he asked.

"A few."

"A few?"

Lily huffed, pressing the perky mounds of her tits into his shoulder. "You're not my goddamn babysitter, Damian. You can't tell me how much I can or can't drink. This is undignified. Put me down."

"Would you rather I call Dino to come get you?"

Lily froze. "No."

"Stop fighting and let me get you out of here, then."

"Fine," Lily said quietly, all the fight in her voice gone.

"Seriously, how many drinks?" Damian asked as a familiar bouncer waved him through the front entrance.

"Five, maybe."

"Maybe?"

"Definitely not seven," Lily muttered.

Damian chuckled and he felt Lily tense all over as the sound rocked her body against his. "Why the party tonight?"

"Abriella suggested it earlier. Trying to get my mind off things."

"The wedding?" Damian asked.

"Something like that," Lily replied under her breath. Damian felt Lily's elbow dig into his shoulder as she propped her hand into her palm. "Who called you?"

"Tommas."

"Little rat."

Damian didn't grace that with a response. The late June air outside of the club was cooler than inside, packed with all those drunk, dancing people. Lily sucked in a huge breath as Damian strolled across the parking lot with her still slung over his shoulder. At least she'd stopped fighting. He appreciated that.

"Did you tell Dino or Theo?" Lily asked.

"No."

"Why not?"

"Because you're my responsibility," Damian answered honestly.

"Since when?"

"Since we became engaged."

Lily made a disgruntled noise under her breath. "Great."

Damian had parked his car at the far end of the parking lot. He walked the dark space in silence, letting Lily's attitude and anger bounce off him. The girl could have her feelings—he didn't begrudge her right to them as far as that went. What he did hope was that she would eventually settle herself to the idea of their marriage.

It was for life, after all.

Neither of them got much of a choice in the matter.

Damian would like for his future wife to tolerate him, in the very least. He didn't want to live the next fifty or sixty years in a household like the ones he grew up in with the couples fighting all the fucking time and hating one another.

Frowning, Damian tried to shake those thoughts off. Whether he wanted to admit it or not, he liked Lily a great deal. He'd started to remember more and more flickers of memories from when they were younger and he used to chum around with Theo. Lily DeLuca was a sweet, honest piece of Damian's past he'd forgotten about.

Lily's fingers drumming on the back of Damian's neck brought him out of his inner turmoil.

"So, what difference would it make if you told my brothers I was out partying without a babysitter, anyway?"

"Well, for one, you were just having some innocent fun. I don't fault you for being young and wanting to go out with friends. Dino might not see it the same way, is all. Except that asshole you were dancing with. That's unacceptable, Lily. I won't stand for that."

Lily snorted. "We were dancing. It was nothing."

Damian's grip around her waist tightened like he didn't want to let her go. "He was touching you. His hands were on you. That can't happen again."

Her voice went lower when she said, "I told him to back off."

"And he didn't."

"And then you acted like a damned barbarian," Lily said.

Damian could practically feel her eyes rolling.

"Listen, if you want to go out, we'll do that. You just have to ask or tell me. Whatever. I don't care. But you can't be going out like that alone. It doesn't look good on your brothers or me for you to be kicking it free without someone—"

"Babysitting me," Lily interrupted, clearly annoyed.

"I'm trying here," Damian said softly. "The least you could do is try, too."

He had a feeling it wouldn't work out that way, though.

Lily mumbled something unintelligible under her breath.

"What was that?" Damian asked.

"Nothing."

Damian used his free hand to tickle up the side of Lily's calf. She couldn't have hid her breathless giggle even if she tried. "Do I have to ask you again?"

"Mr. I-don't-like-to-repeat-myself, huh?"

"Caught that, did you?"

"Yes," Lily said. "You didn't have to scare him off, you know. I was doing just fine by myself, Damian."

"Well, I didn't fucking like it, all right? Maybe you could have handled it, but I did, so let's move on."

Lily hummed under her breath, the sound coming off playful and teasing. Maybe that was the alcohol in her system making her do it, but Damian liked to hear it all the same. "Oh?"

"Yeah, don't think on it too hard."

"You know ..." Lily poked Damian in the back as he came up to the side of his Porsche. "... Abriella said something to me today."

Damian fought the urge to scoff. Abriella Trentini said a lot of things.

Nearly getting his girl in some kind of trouble put Abriella on the top of Damian's shit-list. Sure, Lily was an adult capable of making her own good or bad decisions, but Abriella damn well knew better.

"I don't care to hear much of what she has to say or what she thinks at the moment," Damian admitted. "That girl likes to find trouble wherever she can. One of these days it's going to catch up to her but you're not going to be one of the ones suffering from the backlash, Lily."

"Aw, are you pissed off because she took Eve and me out?"

Her sweetness act didn't convince Damian for a second.

"Yes."

Lily sighed. "I'm not. This was nice. I needed it."

"She knows better."

"So do I," Lily confessed softly. "Everybody likes to use the excuse that because Dino let me spend so much time away from home that I don't know what is expected, but I know, Damian. I do."

Damian set Lily to her feet. Her sexy black heels clicked on the pavement as she righted her dress and stared up at him. "You *knew*, huh?"

"Yeah."

"Why did you go, then?"

Lily shrugged like that was supposed to explain it all. "I told you, I needed it."

Damian waved at himself. "Am I some kind of fucking death sentence for you, or what?"

"Well ..."

"Well, what?" Damian demanded. "Does the thought of marrying me sicken you; does it make you want to run for the hills; is forever with a man who will care and provide for you that awful, Lily?"

Lily's brow furrowed before she pointed at her chest. "Nobody thought to ask *me*, Damian. It's my life and I was having fun doing what I wanted to do."

"No, you were running."

"Hey, you don't know—"

"Yes, I absolutely do know," Damian interjected sharply. He ignored Lily's wince. "I have had more than enough discussions with your brothers and time to myself when I was able to think it all over. Dino let you go because you couldn't handle the Outfit. You couldn't handle seeing your family pretending like your parents didn't exist and that they didn't love you with all they were. Because they did, right? Your dad loved you kids enough that he wanted what he thought would be better for you—a free life, a clean one. So, there you go. Dino let you run for as long as he could. You can't run anymore, Lily. Stop blaming him; it's not his fault."

Lily wouldn't meet his gaze. "He's marrying me off like a piece of meat."

"No, he's trying to save you from that. Christ, girl, think about it."

"But—"

"But nothing, Lily. You don't get to know everything, okay? You just don't. It's better for you and everyone involved if you know as little as possible in this life. Learn to trust people for once instead of depending on only yourself. You never know what might happen if you do."

Lily barked out a bitter laugh. "Trust, right. That's a joke. After everything the Outfit did to me when I was a kid, trusting them or anyone in it is fucking impossible."

Damian was over her pity party. He waved a hand in her direction dismissively, done with the charade. "Poor you, Lily. Here's a newsflash for you—you're not the only person in this parking lot holding a fucking membership card for a club no one wants to be a part of."

"Excuse me?"

"You're an orphan, right? That's how you feel. Guess what? You're not the only one standing here without parents. You're not the only one who grew up without them and you're certainly not the only one who was raised by the Outfit. Got it? Mine might not have been killed like yours were, but I still lost them all the same. It's time to move the hell on. Leave the past where it needs to stay. Behind."

Lily sucked in a hard breath, her bottom lip catching between her teeth. "I'm—"

"Don't apologize. That's not what I want or need to hear. I don't look for sympathy from others. It does nothing for me."

"Okay," Lily said quietly.

Damian crossed his arms and willed his irritation to leave. "I'm not sorry about earlier—that asshole deserved it and he's lucky I didn't break his face just for breathing. But, I am sorry about this past week."

Lily mimicked his pose, hugging her frame in the bodycon dress. "Oh?"

"You're my responsibility," Damian said, repeating his words from before. "I should have been around this week, maybe asked you out to eat or something just so we could talk. Tried, at least. Clearly you've got shit on your mind you need to get off. You're angry, I get that. You can be angry; you need to take it out on the right people, but you can't do that if you don't even really understand what you're angry about.

"Nonetheless, I didn't try this week," Damian continued, the corner of his mouth tugging down into a half-frown. "I was busy and something else came up I had to take care of. I figured you wouldn't want me anywhere near you for a while as it was. Maybe you still don't."

Lily shrugged. "I figured you didn't want to be around. This is just … a duty for you, right? You have to do it and you don't get a choice, either."

Partly.

It might have been a little bit more, too.

"Unless you try to get to know me a little bit, you don't have the first clue about this, us, or why I am doing it, Lily."

"True," Lily said. "But you're not like me, Damian. Everybody will turn their cheek to what you do after this is followed through. Nobody will care a bit who you're fucking or what you're doing even if you have a wife. Me? I'm stuck with you even if you don't have to be stuck with me."

"Back up a second," Damian said, cocking a brow. "Is that what you think my plans are? To marry you and keep you looking pretty on a shelf like a proper trophy wife while I have a dozen whores on the side?"

"Seems like that's the norm, doesn't it?"

Damian shook his head. "Not for me."

"So, what, I'll just be your warm body in the bed whenever you feel like using me?"

That was disgusting in more ways than Damian cared to explain.

"I'm not going to force you into my bed. I'm not into that nasty shit, but I kind of hope I don't have to force you, Lily. I want you to come all on your own because you want to."

She swallowed audibly, a pink tint coloring her cheeks. "I beg your pardon?"

"Just like I said. I'm not going to make it some kind of mission to seduce you, but I don't think I have to. You're young, beautiful—incredibly vibrant and sexy. I would be stupid and blind not to notice. So no, I won't force you into my bed now or ten years from now, but chances are, you'll make your way there all on your own. I want you to come to me willingly."

"Wow," Lily murmured. "I did not expect to hear that. You're either terribly arrogant or mighty cocky."

"Both, actually. I'm also honest," Damian added, chuckling. "Despite what my profession may say about me, I am upfront with my motives. So why don't I show you some of them right now, huh?"

"Like what?" she asked.

"We don't have to be strangers. You don't have to hate me and I really don't want you to. You're goddamn gorgeous—I wasn't looking for a wife but I think I'd like to have you as mine. We'll work out the details and while we do …"

"What?" she asked, her brown gaze meeting his, unashamed.

"You make all the calls. Just know the marriage will happen. It has to."

Lily's jaw clenched. "Yeah, I got that. Dino made that perfectly clear."

Damian figured Lily needed to be let in on a part of her brother's plan so she could finally—maybe—understand what Dino was trying to do for her. "Do you know what he asked me to do for you? What he wanted from me as the other half of this equation with the marriage?"

"What is that?"

"He asked me to take care of you and keep you safe when he couldn't. Think about it, Lily."

Lily shifted in her heels. "He's going to prison soon."

"Well, it sure seems like it."

"He won't be able to keep me safe from there."

"He let you run for as long as he could."

Lily blew out a shaky breath. "You still haven't told me why you're doing this."

"I did. Because I have to."

"That's a non-answer," Lily pointed out.

Maybe so, but it was the best he could give for now.

"You're looking at a pretty decent future if you would just quit fucking fighting it, Lily DeLuca."

Lily blinked, a soberness clearing her vision. "Actually, I'm looking at you, Damian."

"And I am not that bad of a choice, considering the men you could have been married off to."

"Maybe so," Lily agreed. "I still didn't get any say in the matter."

"There's no maybe about it, sweetheart. Give me a little bit of time, and I'll give you back everything you need."

"That's a pretty heavy promise," she said. "And this life does nothing but break them, Damian."

"Do I fucking look like a fairy godmother to you? I'm not handing out wishes, Lily."

"Well, I didn't exactly wish for this, did I?"

"Exactly," Damian replied. "So make the best of it."

Damian cut the lights to his Porsche and let the car roll down the quiet, dark street. Checking his phone, he could see none of the sensors inside his apartment had gone off, meaning Lily was still safe and sleeping in his bed where he left her hours earlier.

If all went well, he would be back at his place before she even woke up with her none the wiser that he left.

The east side Chicago neighborhood was quiet for it being early morning. Most of the homes in the middle-class suburb were still dark as the sun had yet to rise. No one liked to be up before dawn, after all. With the sun still below the horizon, the roads offered little light but for the street lamps up above.

Damian found a place to park his Porsche, cut the engine, and waited. Sometimes, his job was all about the wait.

Terrance had probably wondered why the hit hadn't already taken place, but the boss knew better than to question Damian's motives and choices when it came to carrying out business. Damian did it on his terms and his time so the job was done correctly and without fuss.

Damian didn't plan on spending his life behind bars.

No other man's life was worth that price.

He'd watched the Poletti man for a good week. The guy had a variance of routines between working some schemes, running between his favorite places, and making his way home every night. Damian had taken note of the fact the guy had no wife or girlfriend and probably no children. The guy hadn't visited any during the week, anyway.

Damian hoped this little lesson Terrance wanted taught to Joel did the job. Senseless deaths were just that—senseless and useless.

Regardless, Damian let his thoughts and feelings on the matter bleed away so he could do the hit, get the fuck home, and start the day out fresh. It was always better if he didn't let this kind of nonsense work its way into his conscience.

The mafia was what it was. Death came hand in hand with living the life.

Damian was no exception and neither was anyone else.

No one was deathless in this world.

As a light turned on down the street, illuminating a split-level home and the front yard, Damian leaned over in his seat and opened the glove compartment. He pulled out the glock he'd chosen for the job, checked the clip, slid it back in, and turned off the safety.

James Poletti pulled his hood over his head and did a few minutes of stretches on his small front porch. Damian rolled down the window on the passenger side of his Porsche, letting the late June air wash through his car. The breeze was just enough to keep the mugginess down to a bearable temperature with the AC in Damian's car turned off.

Before long, James Poletti started his usual morning jog down the dark street. Damian had wanted to do the job at another location, but this one worked just as well.

Damian didn't make much of a fuss about killing. He didn't make a show of it unless asked to, either.

Quick, Terrance had said.

When James was nearly at the passenger window, Damian turned the key and gunned the engine as he flicked on the car's lights. The man outside the car stumbled but caught himself easily enough. With a mumbled curse, James tossed a glance inside the open window, straight into the barrel of

Damian's gun.
Lights out.

CHAPTER SIX

Lily hugged the dress shirt tighter around her frame, well aware it did nothing to hide the expanse of her bare legs as she padded down the short hallway of an unfamiliar apartment. With sleep-tousled hair, weary eyes, and a sinking feeling in her stomach, she kept moving to find the sweet smell of coffee wafting.

She remembered the night before clearly. She hadn't tumbled into an unfamiliar bed out of drunken stupidity, but instead, climbed under Damian Rossi's sheets without so much as an argument. Then again, he took the guest bedroom.

Why he just didn't take his own bed and gave Lily the guest bed, she wasn't sure.

The tiny kitchenette gave a view of the large living room. Lily damn near tripped over her own two feet at the sight of Damian bare-chested with track shorts riding low on his hips. With every pull as he lifted his fit, muscled frame over the bar set between the doorjamb of a connecting room, his body barely reacted to the exercise. Like it was nothing at all, he did several sets of chin-ups while he watched a news program turned on low.

Lily's throat went dry.

The expanse of his muscled chest drove straight down over a railroad path of abs into the hard cut V of his groin. Damian's skin was clean of any ink and other than a small scar on his right pec, his body was unblemished. The slightest sheen of perspiration dampened his skin while his dark hair fell over his gaze glued on the flat-screen. Any female within the vicinity of this man looking like he was right then would probably throw themselves at him. He was the perfect vision of a male personified. Sex on fucking legs right there in flesh and blood.

Even Lily found herself shifting on the spot and rubbing her thighs together to soothe the sudden ache between her legs.

Jesus Christ.

What was wrong with her?

I want you to come to me willingly.

Lily sucked in a breath and forced the sudden desire pooling in her stomach away.

She couldn't help but wonder how this ridiculously attractive man seemed to go as unnoticed around people as he did. How could he slip into a crowd and disappear when he practically screamed for someone to look at him?

A vibrating sound stopped Damian's chin-ups. He dropped to the floor without making a sound, crossed the space to the couch in two fluid steps and swiped at something on the cushion. Damian wiped at his bottom lip with his thumb; Lily licked hers in response.

What did his kiss feel like?

She shook her head to rid that insane notion.

"Yeah, Boss. Morning."

"Ghost," came a familiar reply.

Terrance Trentini.

Lily had the distinct feeling she shouldn't be standing there listening.

"You watching this?" Damian asked, his gaze still surveying the silent television. His body blocked Lily's view of seeing what the screen showed. She didn't mind. The sight of his muscled back roped with chiseled lines was much better.

"Breaking news," Terrance replied. "Well done."

"Something like that," Damian muttered.

"I did happen to notice the mention of a blue vehicle. What was it they said?"

"A striking color," Damian said. "Nothing more."

"Still too close for comfort, my boy. That isn't like you."

"I wanted to hit him elsewhere. It worked like this, too."

"What happened?" Terrance asked.

"Plans changed. It doesn't matter, the witness couldn't give an adequate description of the car or license plate. The suburb isn't well-off enough to have cameras in that area. I did my fucking homework before I decided."

"Thirty-k has been transferred," Terrance said.

"I already checked."

"I thought you would have this done sooner. I'm happy to see it finished either way, but still, you took your time."

"I did my job," Damian said drily. "Is there anything else, Boss?"

Lily swore there was a smile in Terrance's voice as he replied, "Hmm, no. Time to deliver the terrible news to Joel, I suppose."

"Just keep my name out of it."

"I always do, Damian."

The call ended without another word.

Damian didn't turn around as he said, "Eavesdropping is a bad habit you should break before it gets you into trouble, Lily."

Lily bit her bottom lip. "Sorry?"

He shot her with a heated glance over his shoulder. The sight alone seemed to strike her in the chest with the intensity. "There are things you are better off not knowing."

"I didn't actually mean to eavesdrop."

Damian smirked. "No, you were spying on me."

Lily's arms tightened around her frame again. She suddenly became hyperaware of Damian's gaze raking over her figure with a slow intent. He didn't hide his staring at all and his smug grin only seemed to grow into a sight of satisfaction the longer he took her in.

She felt unnerved under his surveying.

"I look like hell," Lily said, unsure of why she even let the words out in the first damn place.

"You look incredible," Damian said quietly. "Like you spent the night rolling in someone's sheets, which I suppose you did."

Lily laughed. "Just not with someone, huh?"

"Not by my choice, sweetheart."

She shivered.

Goddammit.

Damian was clearly playing for keeps in whatever game he had decided on.

Lily wasn't sure she was ready for this.

Needing to get her mind away from the sexy, panty-soaking worthy place it had quickly gone to, Lily asked, "Is this usually what you do in the morning?"

"Talk on the phone?"

"No, work out."

Damian nodded once. "If I have time, I try. It's a good stress reliever."

"What else do you do besides track girls down at clubs, work out, and watch news broadcasts on silent?"

"Are you asking about my job?"

Lily pursed her lips, her stare flitting between him and the spot where he'd answered the phone. "Yeah, I suppose I am."

"I do what the boss wants me to do, Lily."

"Anything?" she asked.

"Yes."

The second shiver that crawled up her spine came for an entirely different reason than the first. It was a hell of a lot colder, too.

Anything was vague enough for Lily's imagination to run wild but pointed enough for her to understand without him directly saying it.

"So, you're not like my brothers, right?" she asked.

"And I'm not like Tommas, either," Damian said.

"Huh."

"That bothers you, doesn't it?"

"A little," she admitted.

"There's a reason why they call me Ghost, Lily."

"Oh?"

"Yeah, because they never see me coming and they don't hear me leave."

Lily thought about Dino and the vague reasons she had been given as to why Damian was his first pick for her. Maybe aligning her with one of the most dangerous men was Dino's way of keeping her safe. She wasn't sure how she felt about that.

"Because you're invisible," Lily said.

"In the most important ways."

"How?"

"The ways that keep me from getting caught," Damian answered.

Damian turned all the way around and crossed his arms over his broad chest. He nodded at her and said, "You look good in my shirt."

The statement was so random it took Lily off-guard. His voice had lowered an octave, turning it into that rich, dark tone. An instant heat bloomed in her sex and spread to her stomach.

"Do I?" Lily whispered.

"Yeah. It's a shame you have to take it off only to put that damn dress back on."

Good God.

"I don't know how to do this," she said softly.

Damian didn't move a muscle. "Do what?"

"Be okay with this."

"The marriage thing?"

"No," Lily said, her gaze flicking away from him. "I've been told more than enough times to know I don't get a choice in the matter."

"Then what?"

"I don't like what you do. I don't like the things you're a part of. I don't like that you agreed to this at all, regardless of your reasons."

"And?" Damian asked.

"And maybe I might like you."

"Yeah," Damian said, his laughter coming out like black molasses. Slow, thick, and covering every inch of her it could reach. "That's a bitch, right?"

Who was this man?

"You're late," Dino said, his words coming out as a sharp whisper.

Damian shrugged. "I called."

"At one in the goddamn morning," Dino growled.

Lily pretended to ignore the way her brother looked her over like he was searching for some sign of her defilement. She hated to be the one to break it to him, but that defilement happened years ago when she was sixteen on a summer vacation to Germany.

"Church steps," Lily said quietly, reminding her brother of where he was. "People are watching us."

Dino scowled. "Why didn't you call?"

Lily waved a hand in the air. "I forgot. Damian did instead. It was late, Dino. I was having fun."

Her brother didn't look like he believed her for a second.

"She was with me, so what is the damn problem?" Damian asked. "Didn't you call Tommas?"

"Yes," Dino said.

"And?"

"And I don't want her at that club again, supervised or not."

Lily faced her brother. "Why not?"

"Because Tommas does business in that place, Lily, and not the drinking kind."

"Fine, I'll take her elsewhere next time," Damian said.

Dino's glare turned on Damian. "Make sure it isn't owned by the Outfit."

"Will do."

"Fine," Dino muttered.

"Perfect."

Lily sighed, annoyed with the entire day already. "Church, then?"

Damian's hand found her lower back and Lily tried not to react to the touch. She seriously needed to get her head, heart, and body on the same page.

"Yes," Damian said. "Church."

"Okay, now that's something else," Evelina said.

"She looks like a well-priced hooker," Abriella replied, roaring with laughter.

"I didn't say it was nice. I said it was something else."

Lily didn't even bother to hide her own snickers as she took inventory of the slinky silk number in the mirror. It was held together by thin silk and two small straps and was weighted down with heavy jewels along the neckline. A slit at the side cut the ivory fabric all the way to the top of Lily's thigh.

The wedding dress was sexy, to be sure, but it was not Catholic material.

"Oh, God," Lily said, eyeing the piece. "Could you imagine Dino or Theo's face?"

"Can we take a picture just to send for a joke?" Abriella asked.

Lily posed and let her friend snap a quick picture. Abriella typed a message before dropping her phone back into her bag.

"Next," Abriella ordered.

"Not the style we're going for," Evelina said to the store manager. "Think classic, not classless."

The lady nodded tightly before ushering off to find another dress.

Despite loathing the very idea of spending hours in a dress shop searching for that perfect dress to wear, Lily's friends had convinced her to give it a try. It hadn't turned out to be such a bad thing, really.

Lily brushed her hands down the silk. "I do like the feel."

"You can do silk," Evelina said. "Just not like that."

"Or," Abriella drawled with a leer, "You can do silk for the wedding night."

Lily turned away from the girls, not wanting them to see the heat in her cheeks. She forgot about the goddamn mirrors she faced.

"Hey, what did we miss?" Evelina asked.

"Nothing," Lily said maybe a little too quickly.

"Oh, I'll tell you what we missed," Abriella replied, her reflection showing her knowing grin. "Sunday morning, Tommy got a phone call."

Lily spun on her heel. "Mind your business, Ella."

"You were with Tommas on Sunday morning?" Evelina asked.

"Early before I skipped back to mine and Alessa's apartment. I had to arrive at church alone, you know."

Of course, Lily thought.

Abriella was playing with fire and when that happened, somebody always ended up with burns.

"Anyway," Abriella said.

"Ella, please," Lily pleaded. "Just leave it alone. It was nothing."

"All right." Abriella tossed her hands up in defeat. "The bride is always right. We mustn't anger the DeLuca princess."

Lily's gaze narrowed. "You're one to talk, Trentini Queen."

Abriella snorted. "Cute."

Evelina didn't look as though she was about to let it go like Abriella had. "What aren't you telling me, Lily?"

"It was nothing," Lily assured. "I was drunk, Damian came to the club and didn't want to take me home to Dino like that—"

"So she ended up at his place," Abriella finished with a wide grin. "The entire night and then D got Tommy to lie for him when Dino called as a backup about the club."

Lily huffed. "You tell it like there's a lot more under the surface, Ella."

Abriella shrugged. "Don't blame me for having an imagination, babe."

"Well, there's nothing to imagine."

Evelina raised a single brow. "Nothing?"

"Is that so hard to believe?" Lily asked.

"No," Evelina replied. "But you look like there's something on your mind. Talk to me."

"Us," Abriella corrected.

Evelina hushed her friend. "Come on, Lily. What is up?"

Lily gestured at the wedding dress. "I don't want to do this."

"That's not news."

"But he is not what I expected," Lily added.

Evelina's expression turned stony. "Oh."

"Yeah."

"I like Damian," Abriella said quietly. "He's ... I don't know, genuine. That's hard to find in the people around us. With him, you get what you see. He's not out to purposely hide things."

"You know what really sucks about the entire thing?" Lily asked no one in particular.

Evelina smiled but it didn't ring true. "What?"

"I've only spent two meetings with the guy, one of which informed me he was my new fiancé, the second was when I acted like a fool and spent the night in his bed."

"So?" Abriella pressed.

"Two meetings," Lily repeated. "And I kind of like him. I don't know how to deal with that."

"I think that's a good thing," Evelina said.

"Maybe it would be. If I wasn't so confused and screwed up about my opinions and thoughts, it very well could be. It's like a fucking hurricane in here," Lily said, pointing at her temple. "I'm attracted to him because he's entirely different from what I thought he would be, at least he seems so. I'm bothered by the things he's involved in. I can't help but wonder what would happen if I just ... let it all go."

"But?" Evelina asked.

"Feels too easy," Lily said.

"You're making it too hard," Abriella replied with a smile. "Lily, not every arranged marriage works out in a way where the woman gets what she wants."

"I'm not getting what I want, though," Lily tried to explain.

"All right, let's look at it a different way," Abriella said.

"How?"

"What if you had spent those two meetings with Damian under similar circumstances but with the engagement non-existent? What then? Would you still be attracted to him?"

"Probably," Lily admitted.

"Would you still be bothered by the fact he's involved with the Outfit?" Abriella asked.

"You know I would."

"Would you see him again?"

Lily didn't know how to answer that or her stupid pride wouldn't let her.

Abriella wasn't looking for a response, apparently. "Yeah, I thought so."

"Give it a chance," Evelina said with a tiny grin beginning to form. "What will it hurt, Lily?"

Her heart.

Her beliefs.

Lily blurted out the first thing to come to her mind. "He said he wanted me to come to him willingly."

"What do you mean?" Evelina asked.

"His bed."

"Well, then …"

"Yeah," Lily said with a sigh. "I didn't expect that either. You know what that means, right?"

Abriella nodded. "Means he wants you, too."

She was so fucked.

Lily's gaze caught the store manager bringing back a beautiful slightly off-white, A-line dress with intricate beadwork along the sweetheart neckline. The gown, covered by delicate lace and trimmed with personal touches, instantly reminded Lily of the silver screen.

God, it was beautiful.

And she hadn't even tried it on.

"That's perfect," Lily said softly.

Evelina and Abriella admired the wedding dress as the lady hung it on the opened door of the stall.

"It's definitely classic," Evelina said. "And you. It feels like you."

Abriella glanced down at her vibrating phone. "Oh, got a response on the silk number."

Lily laughed, happy for the joking reprieve from the seriousness. "Yeah?"

"Yep, from Damian."

Lily's heart found her throat. "You sent it to Damian?"

"I sent it to Theo and Dino, too."

"Abriella!"

The girl just shrugged.

A troublemaker; that's what she was.

Lily couldn't help herself but ask, "God, what did he say?"

"That particular number is a definite no for the dress. Too showy for the church."

"But?" Lily asked.

She could hear the but in there somewhere.

Abriella smirked a wicked sight. "He's good with taking silk off you in the evening."

Jesus.

Evelina laughed, hiding it poorly with her hand. "Sounds just like a man."

Abriella glanced down when her phone buzzed again. "But he prefers black lace."

"You're awful," Lily told Abriella.

"You'll thank me eventually."

Lily bit the inside of her cheek, considering the choice in lingerie. It wasn't something she'd given much thought to before. "Black lace?"

"That's what he said."

"Huh."

Evelina grinned. "I know a shop just down the street, Lily. They've got some great stuff that would look perfect under that dress."

Lily made a face. "Don't encourage me, Eve."

Her friend didn't even blink. "You know I'm going to."

Yeah, she did.

"Lily, you have a guest."

Lily peeked over the top of the book in her hands as Dino's form darkened the sitting room. The window bench seat had become Lily's personal resting spot since she arrived home. The sunlight kept it warm and comforting. She also had a great view of the large backyard property. It gave her private, quiet time to think and read, or just do whatever.

Dino rarely interrupted Lily when she climbed into her spot.

"A guest?" Lily asked.

"Last minute thing, I guess. He's waiting in the foyer."

"He?"

"Damian," Dino explained. "You'll need to change into something more appropriate. A dress, preferably. It's for a dinner with the Trentini and Rossi families at one of Laurent's higher end places. Damian is wearing black on black."

Lily blinked. "Something more appropriate?"

"When did you turn into a parrot, Lily?"

She tossed Dino a dirty look before shoving her novel under the pillow on the window bench. Upstairs, Lily made quick work of finding a dress that would work for the dinner, silver heels to match and give a pop of color, and then she quickly dabbed a bit of rose tint on her cheeks and lips. Mascara helped to fan her eyelashes and black kohl darkened her gaze.

Lily made her way down to the foyer with a silver clutch in hand to meet Damian. Dino hadn't lied. Damian wore a fitted black suit topped off with a black vest, tie, and shirt underneath. Even his damn leather shoes were a shined black. He looked really good with his hands clasped together and his head tilted down.

Damian was the total vision of dark, mysterious, and sexy standing there in his suit looking like he was. Her waiting fiancé smiled as he appraised her outfit.

"Perfect," Damian said quietly. "You look beautiful."

Lily wasn't sure how to take his compliment. It seemed honest enough, but Lily didn't know if she wanted to play his games or not, yet. "Thank you. You look fit to be in the Secret Service."

Damian smirked. "I like black."

"I can tell. You could have given me a heads-up that you were coming today," Lily said.

"It was a last minute thing."

"So Dino said."

"You can't refuse an invitation with the boss, Lily, even if you have a million other things to do. He is the most important thing."

Lily shrugged. "In his mind."

Damian laughed under his breath, the sound coming out sexy and deep. "Well, we just don't tell him that. Are you ready?"

"As I'll ever be. What is the plan, anyway? Dino said something about a dinner at one of your uncle's restaurants."

"We have a show to go to first," Damian said. "It'll help pass the time before the dinner later. I figured we might as well take the chance to go out and actually do something together."

"Oh?"

"Yes. How do you feel about ballet?"

Lily met his heated blue gaze and searched it for any kind of ulterior motive. Could he possibly know somehow that ballet was one of Lily's favorite things? Damian didn't give off a single hint that he was playing at anything again.

"I like ballet a lot," Lily finally settled on saying.

"Have you seen *Giselle* preformed?" Damian asked.

"Once when I was a girl."

"And not since?"

"Nope," Lily replied with a smile. "But I remember enjoying it the first time."

Damian flashed a sensual grin. "Let me be the one to reintroduce you, then."

"Did you know the role of Giselle is considered one of the most sought after roles in a ballet dancer's career?" Lily asked, never removing her gaze from the stage.

Damian lowly hummed his no. "I didn't, actually. Why?"

"It's a classic. One of the most favorite and memorable ballets. It shows true emotion and is an honestly beautiful dance. Even the music is amazing." Lily caught the sight of Damian's smile out of the corner of her eye. "What?"

"Nothing. I'm just glad you're enjoying yourself, Lily."

"Where did you get the tickets, anyway?"

"Theo, actually. His date for the day flaked on him."

Lily's brow rose high. "My brother had a date today?"

Damian laughed. "Hey, don't come looking for answers from me. He didn't say who, just that they couldn't come. Theo's always been private about that sort of thing, and I'm not the kind of guy who asks questions."

Lily couldn't help her curiosity. "I wonder who she is."

"Someone, obviously."

"Obviously," Lily mocked, teasing.

"Like I said, I don't know who his date was, just that it didn't work out. Nonetheless, when I called to ask if he got a dinner invite to Laurent's place—he didn't, by the way—he asked if I'd be interested in taking you to a ballet. He didn't want the private balcony tickets to go to waste and apparently you've got a taste for these things."

So that was how he knew.

"I do," Lily admitted. "I was able to see a couple in Europe, too. They were amazing."

"I bet."

Lily sighed, sitting back in the plush chair and folding her hands on her lap. "Thank you for bringing me."

Damian mimicked her position, except his arm stretched over the back of her chair. "Don't ever thank me for that, sweetheart."

Silence covered the balcony, blanketing Lily in a sense of comfort and awkwardness all at the same time. She wasn't even sure how that was possible. From her peripherals, Damian's gaze caught hers and he held it. The man didn't blink and he didn't even look like he was breathing.

No, he just watched her.

Something warm bloomed in her chest under his heavy regard. It was as if he seemed to get some kind of pleasure from simply watching her. Lily realized then that Damian had no other reason to bring her to the ballet other than to spend time with her and to make her happy with something she enjoyed.

But why?

We don't have to be strangers.

We don't have to hate one another.

"What?" Lily asked softly.

"I like it better when you're smiling at me and not glaring," Damian said.

"I'm trying."

"I'm grateful." His murmur washed over her skin like a slow wave. It slipped over every inch of her exposed skin like her nerves were open for his attention. Lily didn't have the first clue why Damian had such an odd effect on her. "And you do look beautiful, Lily. Beautiful things should be admired. Let me admire in peace."

When he said things like that, she found it difficult to gage his intentions. What she did know, was that he clearly liked the influence he had on her. Damian's grin turned almost satisfactory in nature as his gaze darkened.

"I thought you said you weren't going to seduce me, Damian?"

Damian's expression didn't flicker as he said, "I'm not."

"Oh, really?"

Why else would a man shower a woman in compliments, take her out to do things she enjoyed, and watch her like she was a precious jewel that might be stolen away at any moment?

"No," Damian said with a shake of his head.

Those steel-blue eyes of his never wavered from Lily's direction.

"If not that, then what are you doing?" she asked.

Damian chuckled. "Keeping my promise, *dolcezza*."

Which one was that?

"Rossi table," Damian said. "Damian and guest. Party was undetermined last I knew."

The woman behind the podium nodded once and waved the couple back. Damian's hand found the small of Lily's back as they were led through the restaurant without a word, passing by several tables of well-dressed patrons. The woman veered to the right, taking them into a private section with wide wall-to-wall windows with a view of the quiet street at the side of the restaurant.

"Damian Rossi and his guest," the woman said with a wave at Lily and her companion. She turned on her high black heels and disappeared back into the common dining area without so much as a smile.

Lily quickly took note of the people sitting at a long table. Several tables must have been pushed together for the meal as it looked more like a board meeting than a private dinner. Lily's uncle Ben sat alongside Terrance Trentini. Laurent Rossi and his wife Serena sat across from the Outfit boss with Tommas at his father's side. Lily hadn't expected to see the Trentini sisters at the dinner, but both Abriella and Alessa sat in their respective chairs beside their mother and father on their grandfather's side of the table. Joel, Abriella and Alessa's brother, sipped from a glass of wine beside his father. Even the front boss for the Outfit was there, Riley Conti and his wife Mia as was Evelina and Adriano.

Considering the highest members of the Outfit had been invited to the dinner along with their family members, Lily had to wonder if this was more than just a regular meal. The table was empty of food, but everybody had a glass of something to drink.

"Smile, Lily," Damian said quietly as Terrance rose from his seat to greet the two newcomers.

"You're late," Tommas said, reaching over to grab a bread stick from the basket.

"Lily had a chance to meet the dancers after the ballet and I couldn't very well let her pass up that offer."

"Of course not," Terrance replied as he rounded the table. "Was the ballet good?"

"Very," Lily said, plastering a smile on her face for Damian's sake.

Her comment about the ballet wasn't a lie, but her smile for Terrance was. Lily still couldn't manage to feel comfortable around this man. He had ordered the hit on her parents all those years ago and her heart wouldn't let it go.

Terrance grabbed Lily's hand, squeezed gently, and then leaned in to press a kiss to her cheek. She suppressed the disgust and the immediate anger rolling hard in her stomach when Terrance finally released her and took a step back.

Damian's hand on her lower back pressed gently, reminding Lily he was there. For whatever reason, she was appreciative for his silent, knowing support.

"You look lovely, Lily," Terrance said.

"Thank you."

"I'm glad to see you were able to steal Lily away from Dino for the evening," Terrance said to Damian, smiling widely.

"He was headed to the south end for a pickup, so he didn't mind me stealing her away for the night," Damian said.

Lily's brow furrowed. She didn't remember Dino mentioning anything about work. In fact, she was pretty sure he had planned to stay in for the night and watch a rerun marathon of one of his favorite TV shows. Then again, Dino didn't tell Lily a lot about his job as a Capo for the Outfit. Probably for the better, really.

"Sit, sit," Terrance demanded with a wave at the table. "I'll have Laurent let the servers know we're ready for the food to be brought in."

"You already ordered?" Damian asked.

"A buffet spread. There'll be more than enough to choose from."

Terrance took his seat as Damian's uncle stood from his. Lily accepted the greetings from everyone else at the table while Damian pulled out her chair, tucked it into the table, and then took the open one beside hers.

Serena Rossi sat directly across from Lily and sipped on red wine like it was water. Actually, everyone at the table had a glass of wine, even Adriano Conti who wasn't old enough to be drinking.

Lily couldn't help but notice how Abriella and Tommas avoided looking at one another at all costs. While quiet chatter passed over the table as a large spread of food was brought in to be served, the two only spoke to each other if they had to. No one but Lily seemed to notice.

They played their parts well.

How long would that last?

"What ballet?" Evelina asked from down the table.

Lily smiled. "*Giselle.*"

"Oh. I love that one. How old were we the first time we all saw it together?"

"Eight, maybe," Lily said. "Didn't a group of us go? I can't remember."

"Yes, we all went," Evelina replied.

"All?"

Evelina nodded. "A bunch of us—you and Theo, me, Adriano, Abriella, and—"

"Me," Damian interjected in that dark tenor of his.

Lily stilled in her seat, catching Damian's stare with her own. Why didn't she remember that? It wasn't the first time someone said Damian had been around when Lily was younger, but she just couldn't find those memories. The truth was, Lily had spent so much time trying to wipe away those first few years after her parents' murder that apparently, it worked.

"Did you?" Lily asked Damian.

"Yes and I hated it."

Lily laughed. "Why?"

"I was a teenage boy with better things to do," Damian said, grinning.

"Did you hate it today, too?"

"No, I didn't."

Lily believed him. But if she were honest, Damian spent more time staring at her during the ballet than he did watching the show. At least, it sure seemed that way.

"Damian was staying with us then," Riley said offhandedly as he reached for a bottle of unopened wine chilling in a bucket. "For a couple of months around that time, I think. Wasn't he, Mia?"

Mia Conti nodded. "Yes, he was."

Damian stiffened, shooting his aunt and uncle a look across the table. Neither Laurent nor Serena seemed to notice the tension Riley's statement seemingly caused for Damian. Lily had.

"You were quiet as a boy," Riley added.

Terrance laughed loudly. "Ah, yes, Ghost preferred to be in the shadows even as a child, didn't you?"

Damian's tense back didn't relax as he said, "Something of that nature."

Joel scoffed down the way. "He's still fucking quiet."

"Joel," Abriella chided. "Come on, watch your mouth at the table at least."

"You're one to talk," Joel muttered. "Seriously though, Damian is still quiet now like he was when he was a kid. Makes a guy edgy sometimes; that's all I'm saying. How far can you trust a quiet man?"

Terrance cocked a brow. "You might learn something from Damian, Joel, if you took the time to pay more attention. Like the fact that listening instead of running his mouth gets him a hell of a lot further."

"To where, Grandpapa?" Joel tipped his chin in Damian's direction.

Lily felt second-hand offended just at the sight alone. "Where the hell has it gotten him, then?"

Damian reached for two over turned, cleaned wine glasses and handed one to Lily. "Well, I'm still alive, aren't I?"

"That's supposed to be a feat?" Joel asked snidely.

"I'd say so."

"Why is that?"

Damian took the opened wine bottle and poured a glass for him and Lily. His silence only seemed to irk Joel Trentini more.

"Damian, I asked a question," Joel said.

Lily caught Damian's smirk out of the corner of her eye before her fiancé said, "How many other men can say the same?"

CHAPTER SEVEN

Damian surveyed the guests at the dinner table as they ate, chatted, and discussed the upcoming events.

Like his wedding.

Thankfully, Lily took the discussions in stride and joined in when needed. He figured she was a lot like him in the way she didn't like being the center of attention, not to mention she wasn't entirely fond of everyone sitting at the table.

So yeah, he was grateful for her cooperation.

It wasn't like Damian wanted to be there, either. Terrance hadn't given him much of a choice when he called earlier about the dinner. It wasn't uncommon for the boss to gather his closest men and their families for a meal that didn't involve business, simply because Terrance liked to be in the loop on everything, but Damian had rarely been invited before.

As the guests ate, topics flowed from the studies Evelina, Alessa, and Abriella were focusing on in school to what Lily planned on doing regarding the same thing after the wedding. Tommas and Laurent vaguely discussed business the best they could with the Outfit's front boss, Riley, and with Ben while attempting to keep their words veiled for the women's benefit.

Damian stayed quiet in his seat beside Lily, carefully gaging his companion's mood throughout the meal. After all, breaking bread with these three families could be a hell of a taxing event. Someone always had to bring in drama. Damian avoided that shit like the plague. Others found it like flies and shit.

"We're going with peach and a powder blue, right?" Abriella asked.

Lily nodded and swiped her fork through Damian's fluffy pastry when she thought he wasn't looking. "Yes," she said before sticking the bite in her mouth.

Damian leaned over and whispered in Lily's ear, "I can order you one of those, you know."

"Yours is fine. I just wanted a bite."

Sure.

That was why she'd eaten half of it already.

Damian let her have the pastry.

"Is Damian going to be wearing the peach?" Serena asked.

Her words slurred together at the end of the sentence, reminding Damian his aunt had already tossed back a half of a bottle of wine since he and Lily arrived an hour before. He didn't know how much alcohol Serena had consumed before they got there.

Knowing her, probably a lot.

"No, the blue," Lily replied, keeping her attention on her pastry.

"Good, good," Serena muttered. "God knows we don't want him looking like a fool on his wedding day."

"Serena," Laurent snapped harshly.

Serena, like the drunk she was, didn't act like she heard a thing her husband said. Everyone else at the table had stilled and quieted, watching the scene unfold between the two women at the middle of the table.

"He's already done enough of that for himself with this whole thing as it is," Serena added. "He'll be lucky if even half of the Rossi family is able to show up without wearing something to hide their faces. The shame, my God."

"Serena!" Laurent said again, much louder the second time.

"That's quite enough," Damian said, refusing to feed into his drunken aunt's nonsense. "You've said what you wanted long before this, so I don't want to go through it again."

"Oh," Serena drawled, wagging a finger in the air. "But she hasn't, Damian. She should know we don't—"

"Laurent, control your wife and her liquor or neither of you will be invited back to dine with my family," Terrance said from the head of the table.

Serena scoffed loudly.

Damian's brow rose at that. Clearly his aunt had guzzled a lot more alcohol than he previously thought if she was even showing her nastiness to Terrance. Serena knew better than to pull that kind of crap with the boss.

Serena had her issues, to be sure. Especially where the marriage was concerned. Unfortunately for her, she didn't get to make any calls when it came to Damian and Lily. He also didn't give a flying fuck what his aunt thought. She hadn't cared much about him when she was supposed to, so what was the damned difference now?

Guessing by his aunt's behavior, Serena was about to have one of her meltdowns that usually came along when she drank too much. Damian wasn't interested in sitting through it, so he figured it was time to leave. Pulling out his cellphone, he texted a quick message off to let Dino know he would be bringing Lily home soon as the man asked him to do when he picked her up earlier.

"Serena—"

Laurent didn't even get the chance to say another thing.

"Oh, shut up, Laurent," Serena hissed, swiping her hand in her husband's direction without a care. "We all know, don't we? I mean, come on. Even she has to know."

Lily stared at Serena through her dark lashes. Damian swore he saw her eyes narrow. "Know what?"

Serena laughed a high, sharp sound. "Really? You're asking me?"

"You said it, didn't you?" Lily asked softly. "I'm only asking for you to spit it out instead of chew on it. Whatever it is."

Damian had to give his fiancée credit where it was due; Lily didn't blink a lash at Serena's behavior.

Serena attempted some odd cooing noise that came out entirely wrong. Instead of sickeningly sweet like he supposed she meant for it to sound, it rang like a garbled mess mixed heavily with her alcoholism. Most likely because she was three sheets to the wind and ready to topple over, Serena didn't even understand the consequences of her actions. She usually had a little more control than she was showing now. Damian had enough and he wasn't about to let Lily go through a round of his aunt's abuse just because the bitch couldn't hold her liquor.

Hell, she never had.

Damian still had a fucking scar on his pec to prove it.

Tommas had a few, too.

Standing from his chair, Damian offered Lily his hand. She took it without question, leaving her unfinished pastry on the plate and standing from her chair. "Sorry, Boss, but I think we'll have to call it a night."

Terrance frowned. "Yes, I—"

"You're *running*, now?" Serena grinned wickedly, the wine in her glass sloshing as she waved at Lily. "Since when do you run, Damian? Didn't we teach you better than that growing up? Don't you want me to explain to the poor girl how terrible she's making you look?"

"Serena, that's damn well enough!" Laurent exclaimed, his face turning red.

Lily stiffened at Damian's side and her hand tightened around his. "Me?"

The question had been posed with a dangerous edge, like Lily couldn't believe what she had heard.

"Lily, let's go," Damian said firmly. "She's not important and she's drunk."

"Which isn't anything new," Tommas muttered under his breath about his mother.

"Damian, I'm your *aunt*! And I expect you to treat me with respect!"

Damian snapped. Any and all control that he had managed to keep for the day was lost with three simple words. Turning on his heel to face the bitch across the table, Damian glared. Rarely did he show emotion in the presence of others and certainly not Mafioso. It was a dangerous game to play and while Damian was mighty good at his, he didn't ever like to give someone an opening to one of his weak spots.

Serena Rossi just hit the right one on the goddamn head with a sledgehammer.

"That's right," Damian said, sneering. "You're my aunt. My drunken, useless, bitch of an aunt. So fucking useless in fact, that you aren't even capable of keeping your husband home. But you were mighty fucking good at spreading your legs and making children you didn't want and couldn't care for. A woman who couldn't even be bothered to raise me and instead, handed me off to any and every person who would take me in. But not even me, no, your own kids, too. And when we were with you, shit ... Tommas and I spent the majority of our time dodging your abuse and taking the hits in-between so Cara and Lea wouldn't have to.

"Yeah, my aunt," Damian repeated, spitting the words through his clenched teeth. He waved at Mia Conti, Serena's sister. "You want to talk about how I'm embarrassing the family, huh? Why don't we go straight for the fucking jugular and talk about how even your own goddamn sister doesn't like to share a dinner table with you because you're too busy trying to fuck her husband half the time?"

A sharp gasp sliced through the quiet dining area. Damian didn't even know where or who it came from. He also didn't care.

"If you think I give a single fuck about what you think regarding me or the deal with the DeLuca family, you are sorely fucking mistaken, Serena. Toss back another glass of wine, your blood isn't sour enough, yet."

Damian wished he could be surprised that not one person had stepped in to stop him from verbally knocking his aunt down a peg or two, but he wasn't. Nothing he said to Serena was a lie. Shit, there was a hell of a lot more he left unsaid and probably for the better.

Even Lily's uncle at the end of the table beside Terrance sat silent and stoic with his gaze down on the wine swirling in his glass. That wasn't such a shock, either. Damian figured his tirade had been to Ben's benefit, anyway. It didn't exactly make Damian look good to be going off half-cocked in front of family and important men in the Outfit, not to mention the boss. Ben DeLuca played his part well, but chances were, he was scheming on Damian one way or another.

Fucking Christ, Damian didn't even care at that moment. He just wanted to leave.

Lily had practically turned to ice at his side as she stared up at him with sad, wary eyes.

"Can we go now?" Damian asked her.

Lily nodded but she didn't say a word.

Damian urged Lily ahead of him as he turned back to the table one more time. He owed one person at the table an apology and that was only for the sake of respect and little else. "Boss—"

Terrance held up a single hand. "Perfectly fine, Damian. I will see you tomorrow at tribute, yes?"

"Of course," Damian said.

Damian hadn't even turned away from the table completely before Serena let out a shriek. Her rage boiled over, pitching her voice high. Damian should have known better than to turn his back on his aunt when she was angry and drunk. Actually, he did know better but his concern about getting Lily out of his crazy aunt's presence had been more important than the life lessons he learned growing up with an abusive alcoholic for an aunt.

"You ... you little bastard!" Serena screamed.

Damian barely caught sight of the wine glass flying in his and Lily's direction in enough time to react. He stepped in front of Lily as the crystal caught the side of his jaw, shattering across his face and splashing red wine and sharp shatters of glass along his cheek. Pain bloomed as something wet and sticky dripped onto his shirt and suit jacket.

"Oh, my God," Lily whispered.

Damian blinked, stunned as Lily's soft hands ghosted over his face. He could hear the sounds of his uncle and the others at the table finally starting to react to Serena's very public display. While Laurent berated his wife's bad behavior, someone else was demanding an apology.

Lily kept patting at Damian's cheek with her fingertips. "Shit, you're bleeding."

Damian shrugged. "Just ... let's get out of here before—"

"Tell her, Damian!" his aunt goaded.

"Serena Rossi, you will shut your mouth or I will shut it for you," Laurent ordered.

That threat didn't stop Serena.

"Go to my car, Lily," Damian said. "Please."

Lily didn't move. She was too focused on dabbing at the stinging cut on Damian's cheek with the sleeve of her black dress.

"She's always going to be that fool's daughter, Damian," his aunt warned. "She might be a DeLuca, but she's still his daughter. A rat's child— a turncoat's seed. She's got traitor marked all over her. It might as well be tattooed on her forehead. It's in her blood and there's no bleeding that out. How long will it take before she spills on you, too, huh? Her own daddy couldn't keep true to the Outfit, what will she think of you when she finally gets a good look at who you are, Damian?"

Lily's breath caught as her stare met Damian's. Pain flooded her eyes as tears welled.

Don't cry, he wanted to tell her. *Don't ever let a woman like Serena Rossi see you cry.*

Lily DeLuca was far better than Serena Rossi could even dream of being, regardless of her father's past actions. Lily, Theo, and Dino weren't their father. Sure, their parents had made them, but their futures weren't dictated by past actions. Serena could spout her nonsense off all she wanted, but it wouldn't make a difference to what Damian thought.

The Outfit was supposed to be about family. Lily's father might have broken that rule a long time ago, but there were a lot of men—some closer than any of them knew—that worked goddamn hard to bring the Outfit back to what it was supposed to be.

La famiglia.

The family.

Serena didn't know the first thing about family. Not hers, the Outfit, or anyone else's. She certainly didn't know anything about Lily's or how goddamn much that girl's brothers cared and loved her.

Damian didn't have to tell Lily a thing. She squared her shoulders, gave a single look behind Damian at a pissed off, red-faced Serena, and dismissed the older woman with a tick of her chin and the bat of her lashes.

That was it.

Lily didn't say a word. Her indifferent, unfazed attitude was more than enough. Lily simply rejected Serena in a way that allowed her to keep her own dignity while stripping Damian's aunt of hers in front of an entire table of people. Unlike Serena's very vocal disdain, embarrassing and undignified, Lily's was silent and a great deal louder. A good woman, a smart and strong one, didn't need to make a scene to shame someone.

She clearly understood respect in a way Serena didn't.

Damian appreciated that.

Wiping at the slice on his cheek with his thumb, Damian glanced over his shoulder at his aunt. Serena stood at the table, glowering and huffing like a pissed off bull. She looked like a damn mess. Drunk, foolish, and looking for another fight. Damian wouldn't be the one to give her the battle she clearly wanted.

Everyone else at the table seemed to be having their own moment of shock, unable to speak or react. He didn't blame them. Sure, they'd all witnessed one of Serena's moments over the years, but never like this, in such a public place. It was only then he noticed the servers had rushed to the doorway of the private dining area as well.

"Let's go," Damian said to Lily.

Lily nodded. "Sure, okay. Let's find a bathroom first. I'll clean that mess off your face."

Damian's stance softened. She was genuinely worried about him and he wished she wouldn't be. It wasn't the first time something like this happened. Without another word to the people at the table, Damian guided Lily past the servers rushing into the room. Clearly their little scene hadn't gone unnoticed by the regular patrons if the way they were stared at was any indication.

The first bathroom they came to happened to be for women. Lily didn't seem to care as she pushed open the door and tugged Damian inside with her. A woman stood at the row of sinks washing her hands.

The woman squeaked and her cheeks reddened at the sight of a man inside the bathroom. It might have had something to do with the fact Damian was bleeding, had shards of glass on his shoulder, and his suit was wet with red wine.

Fuck. He smelled like a goddamn winery.

"Get out," Lily ordered.

"This is a—"

Lily's heel stomped to the tiled floor. "I said get out. *Now*."

The woman rushed out of the bathroom, making sure to keep a wide berth between her, Damian, and Lily as she went. He didn't fucking mind.

Lily crossed the bathroom to where clean, white facecloths were rolled into tiny folds and placed just so by the sinks. She waved a stoic Damian over and dabbed at his cheek with the dried, soft cloth to wipe off some of the blood dripping down his chin and neck. Once she wetted the cloth, Lily took her time dabbing at his wound, picking out pieces of glass from the slice, and brushing off the other bits on his shoulder.

"This suit is ruined," Lily muttered.

Damian shrugged, trying to ignore the way her warm hands felt roaming over his skin. "Oh, well."

"There's blood all over the collar and on your shoulder. It's not coming out."

"It's just a suit, little one."

Lily's eyes flicked away from his. "I'm not so little anymore, you know."

Damian grinned, unable to stop it. "I'm very aware."

"Did you call me that, too?"

"Once or twice. It fit, way back when. That age gap between you and your brothers sure made you quite a bit smaller than them in the grand scheme of things."

Lily smiled. It came off honest and true. Damian could count on one hand the amount of times this woman smiled in his presence and really meant it. He liked it; he wanted to see more of it.

"I was the oopsie baby."

Damian's brow furrowed. "The what?"

"The oopsie baby," Lily repeated, still dabbing at his cheek with tender swipes. "I remember Mom telling me once that after Theo, she didn't want another baby because she was scared she'd end up with three boys raising hell."

"And then you came along."

"Just like a little oopsie."

"Not a mistake, though," Damian said with a cocked brow.

Lily laughed. "No, she never said that. She got her girl, right?"

"Well, she got you."

"And I make up for everything," Lily said with a roll of her pretty brown eyes. "What a shame, I liked this suit."

Damian couldn't help but notice the slight tremor in Lily's hand as she tossed the bloody cloth to the sink. "Did you?"

"Yes."

"Lily—"

"God, that woman is vile. How did you grow up in her house?" Lily asked.

"I spent as little time with her as possible but mostly, we were raised by other people. Listen, don't pay her any mind."

"Easier said than done," Lily muttered.

"Hey." Damian caught Lily's cheek in his palm. He swept his thumb over the delicate line of her jaw and tilted her head up so she would look at him. The wetness gathering along her bottom lashes said Serena's words had affected Lily a lot more than she was letting on. "That right there," he said, still keeping a hold on her while pointing at the unshed tears with his free hand. "Don't you do that, Lily. She isn't worth a damn to what I or anyone else thinks when it comes to you. Serena thrives on her need to manipulate and create some kind of drama—don't be one of her victims."

Lily blinked the wetness away. "It's not her or what she said, not really."

"What is it, then?" She wouldn't answer him, but Damian had a pretty good indication of the problem. "Your father?"

"Partly."

"I thought it wasn't about what she said?"

Lily waved at the closed door with a fierceness and anger that came suddenly. "Those ... *people*. All of them."

"You're going to have to explain it more to me, sweetheart."

"They just label him as a rat. They don't even care that he was a man with children and a wife, like his life didn't matter in the end because he didn't follow their rules. He was more than the Outfit—he was my father. *My father*, okay. And it bothers me that he can't be my dad, he has to be the man who betrayed them. He's still my dad."

"I know," Damian murmured.

"He is, right?" Lily asked quietly. "Mine? Why do I have to pretend like he was worthless?"

"He's still yours, regardless of what anyone else says or thinks. And you'll never see him like they did because you're not like them, Lily. For the record, I don't believe that his actions determine your future, either. There's a huge difference between being blindly loyal and being faithful to your family."

"They're the family," Lily said. "Isn't that what we've always been told?"

"Your family is what you make it. The family is the people who protect and love you no matter what it costs them in the end. Family is who you keep coming back to even when all you want to do is run away."

"My brothers, you mean."

Damian shrugged, still sweeping his thumb over the line of her jaw. "Sure, but I'm hoping you'll put me in that category eventually, too."

Lily shivered in his hold. "How can I do that when I don't even know you?"

"You know enough," Damian replied truthfully.

All that she needed to know.

"I don't," Lily argued. "You still won't tell me why you agreed to this."

"Yes, I have. Twice."

"Because you have to."

"Exactly, Lily."

"That's still not an answer, Damian."

"Maybe you're not asking the right questions, sweetheart. If you spent half as much time looking at other people as you do stuck inside your own head, you might find the answers are right in front of your pretty face."

Lily bit her bottom lip and fidgeted on the spot. "I'm sorry."

Damian hadn't been expecting that. "For what?"

"Not remembering much about you. I meant to tell you before, but now seems like a good time."

"When you were younger, you mean?"

"Yeah."

Damian chuckled, caught her wrist with his other hand, and pulled Lily a step closer to him so that her nose grazed his when he looked down at her. Her eyes widened as her hand splayed out against his chest. She didn't push him away, though. Damian took that as a good sign.

"When I hung around with Theo, you were young and your parents had just died. I was moved around a lot, so there was only a brief time when Theo and I had been close as kids. For you, that particular time was traumatic. Your parents being killed, moving in with your uncle, and Dino leaving the home. You were so focused on Theo and being stuck at his side because everybody else around you had left."

Lily sniffed but the tears didn't come that time. "You remember a lot."

"Seems where your memories are a blank because of bad feelings, mine are coming back because of good ones. A lot of my childhood was spent listening to screaming, keeping out of everyone's way, and trying to be invisible."

"Oh?"

"Yes, so I don't care to remember it all that much. But you seem to be a sweet spot."

Lily's lips curved into a small smile. "Huh. Imagine that."

"Back then isn't all that important anyway, Lily."

"No?" she asked.

"No. Now is. Today. Tomorrow. Whatever you want to do or wherever you plan on going. Those are the important things; those are the things that matter to me. I told you we'll work out all the details as we go along. I wasn't lying."

"I want to trust you," she whispered.

"You will."

That kind of thing came with time. Damian certainly wasn't trying to get this girl to fall in love with him, but he wouldn't pretend like he didn't have some residual feelings for her; something inside that clenched around his lungs and heart with a vise-like grip to keep him steady and clear. He wanted her safe and happy, but it wasn't all because of her brother and his debt.

"Your dress is a mess," Damian noted, angry over the wine stains soaking the side of her black dress.

"The wine got me, too." Lily reached up and pressed the pads of her fingertips along his cut. "It's not so bad, really. I don't know why it bled so much."

"Flesh wound on the face."

"*Hmm.*"

"I should get you home and then you can maybe salvage this dress," Damian said.

Lily shrugged like it didn't make a difference. She had yet to take her gaze off his cheek and she continued touching him with a tenderness that said she was concerned. Damian caught her hand with his own, wanting to ward off whatever nonsense she had going on in her head.

"I'm fine, Lily."

"She really doesn't like me."

Damian laughed. "Do you care?"

"No."

"Good."

"Why is that good? Shouldn't I want your family to like me?"

"I don't give a damn if Serena approves of my choices or not. They're not hers to make. There's only three people with the Rossi surname I consider family and my aunt and uncle aren't them."

"But—"

"And soon enough, I'll be adding a fourth person to that list as well," Damian said, giving her a slow smile.

Lily froze, her stare flitting down to Damian's mouth before jumping back to his eyes. "You're too smooth for your own good, Damian."

"Yeah, well, I try."

With that, he bent down and caught her surprised gasp with his mouth. The moment her lips touched his, sweetness bloomed over his mouth. He could taste her flavor edging at the tip of his tongue, and Damian was lost. Lily's hand fisted into his suit jacket as he took another step closer to her until her body was pressed against his and her back was pushed into the counter top. He'd just wanted to distract her worries, but now that he could feel the way her lips felt moving with his, Damian wasn't about to stop. His hands slipped under her skirt, skimmed around to the back of her toned ass and grabbed tight. He lifted her onto the counter in one fluid motion, needing her higher so he didn't have to bend down to get that mouth of hers on his like he wanted.

Lily sucked in a ragged breath, her lips parting just enough to allow Damian to deepen the kiss. His tongue found the delicious heat of her mouth. As he kissed her harder, letting his teeth scrape over her bottom lip while she watched him under dark lashes, his hands roamed over the curve of her waist and up her sides until he was cupping her jaw again. His cock thickened under his dress pants and the way her body moved was just enough friction to get him harder than steel and ready to rip her fucking dress off. It was already ruined, right?

Damian forced Lily's head back, baring her neck and making her eyes widen. She was fucking beautiful. Her lips, red and pouting from his kiss, trembled. Her slick tongue darted out to wet her lip before it disappeared back inside that goddamn candy mouth of hers.

Yeah, candy mouth.

Because it was too sweet and far too addicting to stop at just one.

Lily's dress had ridden up, exposing the shape of her hips and a flash of black lace at the junction of her thighs. Her chest expanded and dropped fast with the harshness of her breaths.

"I was not expecting that," Lily said, a heat coloring her words.

Damian grinned. "The best moments come when you're not looking for them, Lily."

"I didn't say it was bad."

"I wasn't going for bad, sweetheart."

Lily's legs tightened around his waist. "Are you going to do that again?"

"Maybe."

Lily swallowed hard. "I don't—"

"Hush," Damian demanded.

"Damian—"

"Lily, be quiet."

His tone offered no room for argument. Damian wanted to enjoy the few moments he had with this defiant, interesting girl while she was giving them. He didn't want her worries or second thoughts running away with her.

"Hush," he repeated.

She nodded slowly. "Okay."

"Yes."

"What?" she asked.

"I lied. Yes, I'm going to do that again. I'm going to kiss you again because I like the taste of your mouth and I always take what I want. And I'm really looking forward to finding out if you fuck like you kiss because if so, I can't wait."

Lily's eyes blazed with lust. "What game are you playing, Damian Rossi?"

"No game."

"Are you sure?"

"Yes, but if I was, you should know I play for keeps."

"And you always take what you want," Lily said, throwing his words back at him.

"I absolutely do."

CHAPTER EIGHT

Damian's fingertips came in contact with Lily's lips and she jumped the moment he touched her. The simple action sent a lightning bolt of want and heat coursing through her entire body. The ache between her thighs increased as the tingling in her lips spread to her tongue.

Without a word, Damian leaned down and pressed a feather light kiss to Lily's mouth. He didn't claim her mouth with the furious, demanding strikes of his tongue like the first time. His teeth didn't tug and bite on her bottom lip like before, either.

No, he just ... kissed her.

Soft and sweet.

Gentle and quick.

When he pulled away, Lily's tongue darted out to draw the taste of him into her mouth again.

Damian's eyes darkened. "Every time you do that, lick your fucking lips, it makes me want to give you something to taste, Lily."

She knew better than to poke at a monster when he was showing himself, but Lily couldn't help it. "Does it?"

"*Mmm*, and I bet you would like that, too."

Lily shuddered. From the tips of her toes in her pumps all the way up to her goddamn shoulders, she felt the promise lacing his words crawl over her skin and body with damning intent.

Damian stepped back from Lily and offered her his hand. "Get down from there and I will get you home so you can change out of that dress. You've probably got wine stains all over your skin, now."

Her mind went to the dirtiest place possible. A place where his tongue, mouth, and lips cleaned all those wine stains off. Damian wasn't even trying and already Lily was second-guessing what she thought she wanted.

Would a marriage with this sexy, dangerous man be such a bad thing? If he wanted her and would treat her like she mattered to him, what more could she want? Lily hadn't been given much of a choice regarding who Dino picked for her to marry, but she was starting to think if he had, Damian might have made the top of her list.

Lily slid off the counter and fixed her dress just in time. The bathroom door swung open to expose a frowning Evelina.

"There you are," her friend said.

Evelina didn't act like the close proximity between Lily and Damian was anything unusual. She barely gave Lily's obviously mussed hair, wrinkled dress, and smeared lipstick a once-over as she stepped inside the bathroom and let the door close.

"I wanted to see if you would like some company tonight," Evelina said to Lily. "You know, bitch about your in-laws with someone or whatever."

Damian snorted. "Careful, Serena's ears burn when you talk about her."

Evelina shrugged. "I hope they fucking fall off. She was awful today."

"I don't care about that woman," Lily said.

She meant it, too.

"She was awful," Damian agreed. "I'm sure if Laurent doesn't put her in line, Terrance will. Serena knows her place, even if she didn't act like it today."

"Someone ought to take her damn wine away," Evelina muttered, shooting Lily an apologetic look.

"Hard to believe you're related to her," Lily said to her friend.

"Damian is, too."

"Imagine, Tommas, Lea, and Cara came from her," Damian added.

That had to be fucking impossible. Those three were nothing like their mother. Actually, they were nothing like their father, either. Well, what Lily knew of the Rossi twins. It wasn't a lot, but she doubted they were as awful as their mother. Especially if Damian talked about them with fondness.

"Anyway, when I noticed Damian's car was still in the parking lot, I came looking for you." Evelina smiled brightly. "I couldn't help but follow the blood drops this way. Found you in here ... together."

Yeah, there it was.

Lily had the distinct feeling her friend wouldn't leave her alone if she didn't invite Evelina over for the night.

"I cleaned his cut."

Evelina winked. "Sure. So, tonight?"

"Yeah, all right," Lily said. "Damian's going to take me home and then we can do whatever."

"Sounds like a pl—"

Evelina's words cut off as echoing pops followed the sound of shattering glass and screams. So many screams. Ice slipped through Lily's veins, freezing her on the spot. Suddenly, her heart felt like it was hammering out of her chest and her lungs wouldn't expand to bring in the air she needed to breathe.

Something was so wrong.

Lily's mind screamed it.

She knew that sound. That pop, pop, *pop*.

Gunshots. Repeated and fast.

More screams followed.

Evelina reached for the bathroom door to open it and the moment she did, the sound of squealing tires screeched in the background of volcanic noise and panic out on the restaurant floor. Lily tried to step forward but Damian's hand fisting into the back of her dress rooted her in place. Fear saturated her from the inside out.

"Don't move," she heard Damian order.

But ...

Lily wanted to argue. Her friend was already running out of the bathroom back in the direction of her family and friends. Lily understood why Damian wouldn't release his hold. Inside the bathroom, they were safe for now.

"Eve!" Lily yelled.

She finally snapped out of her shocked reverie. Jerking hard enough for Damian's grip on her dress to slip, Lily fled the bathroom on Evelina's heels. Damian's shout behind her was a distant warning she barely heard.

"Lily!"

People moved in all directions outside of the bathroom. Patrons, in their panicked state, rushed for the exits of the restaurant as fast as they could move. Servers shouted for calm while others demanded someone get on the phone for emergency services. A distinct Chicago breeze, one that was felt even in the summer throughout the city, blew through the building. It was too much for it to be coming from the doors opening for the fleeing patrons.

So wrong.

She could feel it in her heart.

Lily moved as if she'd been placed in a bubble—a daze. Evelina was maybe a few steps ahead of her, but she could practically feel the fear radiating off her friend in thick waves.

"Lily, wait," Damian said from somewhere behind her.

She didn't stop.

Lily rounded the partition that separated the main floor from the private one where they had dined earlier. The breeze from the outside was stronger the closer she came. Lily's gaze swept the carnage and confusion. People moved, people she recognized and knew, but she couldn't discern what was truly happening in front of her. The large wall-to-wall windows were broken, the shards of glass scattered all over the floor and long table. Gaudy, terrible, morbid red stained the white table cloths and splattered up the wall.

Someone was screaming again.

Someone else was gasping a gurgling, terrible sound. Like they couldn't breathe or speak. Like they were choking on something as words fought their way out.

Evelina was so close Lily could reach out and touch her.

"Jesus," Lily whispered.

"Call nine-one-one!" Tommas shouted.

"Who the fuck was it?"

"White car, I think."

"You fucking *think*?"

"Definitely white!"

"Dark windows. Too dark," Tommas spat. "Shit, it's not stopping. I can't get it to stop."

"Mia? Mia ... baby ..."

The gurgling continued, but it was becoming faint.

"No, breathe!"

Where was Tommas? He was talking but she couldn't see him. Lily tried to discern the voices and the people, but the haze just wouldn't clear no matter how many times she tried to blink it away.

"Lily ..."

She felt the arms of Damian wrap around her waist and pull her back. She fought against his hold, seeing Evelina crumple into a heap of limbs and tears on the floor. Lily needed to help her friend—she had to.

"Let me go!" Lily cried. "Let me go, please!"

Damian kept pulling her backward. Lily fought harder.

"Move, move, move!" Ben DeLuca shouted. "Out, Boss. *Now.*"

Lily watched as her uncle pushed a stunned looking Terrance from the space. They brushed past Lily and Damian without so much as a single glance backwards at the devastation and pain they were leaving behind.

Protect the boss.

Always.

Lily felt sick.

She wasn't the only one, apparently. Serena Rossi vomited in a corner while her husband backed against a wall, pawing at a bleeding wound on his shoulder.

"Through and through," she watched him mutter to himself.

Joel Trentini was the second to leave the space, following behind his grandfather and Ben quickly.

Shock was a terrible place to be.

It ate away at everything. It debilitated worse than even fear did. At least with fear a person had a chance to fight or flee. With shock, there was nothing ... just stillness, slowed reaction, and total uncertainty.

"We have to go," Damian said in Lily's ear.

She couldn't let him drag her out of there, no matter how much her instincts screamed for her to leave. Her friends were inside that restaurant. Evelina was still a crying mess on the floor begging through sobs that Lily couldn't understand.

"Please," Lily begged, jerking against Damian's hold. He was relentless in his intent to get her away. No matter how hard she struggled, he didn't let go. "Damian, *please!*"

Lily blinked again and the haze began to clear. Under the table on the other side, where one of the table cloths had been ripped down, lay a body prone and bleeding. The one side of the person's face was unrecognizable. Blood pooled in a dark puddle of red around the person's head, staining the beige carpeting.

Tommas palmed the person's face, tilting their head back as he shouted again for them to breathe. Riley Conti sat on the floor, his face in his hands and his shoulders shaking. Lily started to glance around at the faces, taking inventory, realizing who was still there, talking, crying … breathing and alive.

"Mia …"

"Mom," Adriano said hoarsely.

Adriano's voice came out croaking and aching. The young man's body shook as tears spilled. He fell alongside his mother's body, pushing Tommas aside and took over chest compressions.

"Lily, we have to go," Damian said.

Her throat was tight, choking her silent. At her sides, Lily's hands balled into fists until her fingernails cut into the palms of her hands and pain bit through her skin. She stopped fighting. Damian was warm, strong, and comforting. His arms felt safer and the further he took her from the screams and the blood, the better her chest felt. She let him drag her out and away from … that.

She didn't want this.

Lily had never wanted this.

No matter how hard she tried, Lily couldn't stop the shakes rocking her hands in her lap. Damian cut the engine on the car, blanketing the driveway to her brother's home in darkness again. He watched her warily from the driver's seat as she shook her hands and tried to get the dirty feeling off her skin.

"Do you want to talk about it?" Damian asked.

"No."

That, she was most sure of.

"You were a guest at the restaurant, specifically of Terrance's, so you should be aware—"

"I might be questioned," Lily interrupted.

"Yes."

She shrugged. What fucking difference did it make?

"I don't know anything."

"Stick to that," Damian said quietly.

"Eve …" Lily wet her lips, feeling the dryness in her mouth. "What about Eve?"

Damian sighed. "Let's go inside. You should lay down or something. It'll give you time to think."

Lily didn't have the strength or desire to argue. A part of her wanted to demand he take her to Evelina so her friend had some form of comfort. Another part of her screamed to find her bed, hide in the blankets, and sleep the rest of this horrible, unbelievable day away.

"Okay," Lily agreed quietly.

Damian got out of the car, walked around the front, and then helped Lily out like the gentleman he was. The man didn't act like anything had happened just less than an hour before. He didn't act like a woman was gunned down and had they stayed in that dining room, they might have been dead, too.

The front door was locked. Lily's hands trembled too much for her to unlock it. Damian took the keys and opened the door, exposing the silent home within. Not a light was turned on. Lily thought that was odd considering Dino's car was outside.

Hadn't Damian said Dino was working somewhere?

And …

"Hey, look at me," Damian said, his tone firm but gentle.

Lily glanced up at him cautiously, feeling unsettled and sick in her heart. "Yeah?"

"Do you want me to stay for a little while until you're settled?"

Did she?

Lily didn't know what she wanted except for this day to be over. "Who did it?"

Damian's expression didn't change as he said, "Someone with a goal, I guess."

"But Mia isn't … someone important, right?"

"Maybe they weren't aiming for Mia, Lily. Besides, killing anyone at that dinner would have caused a stir given who they were married to or children of."

"Oh," she mouthed silently.

Damian's hand found her wrist, his fingers locking around her hand tight before he squeezed just enough to make Lily feel like she had some form of solid ground to steady her.

"Stay," she said.

"Sure, sweetheart."

Lily walked through the quiet, dark foyer. She kicked off her heels, barely registering the ache in the soles of her feet as the coolness of the floor met her toes. The lingering daze still edging around her senses was a bitch to kill. It just wouldn't go away. Damian followed behind in his usual quiet state, but she didn't mind.

As she rounded the bottom of the stairs, Lily's walk came to an abrupt stop. A light flicked off to the right, drawing in her gaze. The downstairs bathroom door opened and Dino walked out with a towel wrapped around his waist and another in his hands. He didn't seem to notice his sister and Damian standing there as he ran the towel through his short hair with one hand while looking at the screen of his cell phone in his other. Then he hung the towel around his neck, padded further out of the bathroom, and kept looking at his phone.

"Dino," Lily said, still confused about the darkness of the house and her brother's presence.

Christ.

She wasn't sure about anything.

Dino should know, though.

"Dino," Lily said again, louder the second time.

Her brother finally looked up from his phone. "You're back early."

"Someone said you were working," Lily said.

"Got the job done early." Dino gave Damian a nod. "Thanks for the message."

Damian didn't say a thing.

Lily was confused. "What message?"

"I let him know I was bringing you home," Damian explained.

Oh.

"Something happened," Dino said, gracing his phone with all of his attention again. He didn't seemed surprised or bothered at all. Why wasn't he panicked? Why wasn't he demanding answers and wondering what happened? "My messages are going crazy, nothing makes a lot of sense."

"Mia was shot," Lily said, feeling distant all over again.

"Killed," Damian added lower.

Dino's left brow arched high as he regarded his sister again. "When did you get the call?"

Damian shook his head. "We didn't."

"Didn't?"

"We were there," Lily whispered.

A brief flicker of concern crossed Dino's features before it disappeared and the blankness returned. "Damian?"

The one word was laced with something Lily couldn't decipher. It sounded a hell of a lot like a threat tangled in with a million and one warnings. Why would Dino look to Damian for an answer on that? Her brother damn well knew they had been at the dinner.

"Serena had a spell," Damian said drily.

Dino still didn't look all too pleased. "Oh?"

"Got me in the face this time."

"I can see that. Shit, with what?"

"Wine glass," Damian muttered. "We were in the bathroom cleaning up the mess when the show went down."

"Lucky," Dino murmured.

"You could say that."

Lily's mind went back to Eve. As Damian and Dino discussed the shooting in vague, clipped sentences, Lily pulled her phone out of her clutch and tried to call Eve. She dialed her friend's number over and over but it went straight to voicemail each time.

"Who are you calling?" Dino asked.

"Eve," Lily replied, turning her back to her brother and trying again. "She won't pick up."

Lily didn't care. She needed Evelina to know someone was there to talk to when, or if, she was ready. Lily wished now she hadn't let Damian force her from the restaurant until her friend had been calmed or at least, given some sense of support.

"Lily, stop," Dino demanded. "She isn't going to pick up. She's probably at the hospital being questioned by police. This shit happens. Wait a couple of—"

Spinning fast on her heel, Lily faced her brother. "This shit happens?"

Dino shrugged, looking so blasé and unruffled it made Lily sick. "It's too bad Mia ended up being caught in the crossfire, but there's nothing that can be done. Obviously someone is out to prove a point with someone else in the Outfit, it's just a matter of time until their meaning is clear. This isn't the first time an innocent's been killed. Right now we have to focus on keeping what is important safe. I thought someone already understood that."

Damian scoffed. "She was safe, man."

Whatever little silent exchange passed between the two men only pissed Lily off more. Dino stood there entirely unaffected by the fact someone had lost their life because they were doing nothing except sitting at a table with connected men. Lily couldn't breathe. All over again, her shock, anger, and panic seemed to swallow her whole and drown her under the weight.

"Dino, someone died today. *Died.*"

"I realize that."

"My friend's mother!"

Dino sighed and gave his phone another glance. "I don't have time for this, Lily. You'll have to deal with this at your own speed because I don't have the patience to sit down and explain it all to you."

What in the fuck was there to explain?

"This is why, Dino!" Lily yelled.

"I beg your pardon?"

"This right here." Lily waved between them, so frustrated her voice pitched high. "This is why we're not close anymore. You keep asking and you want to know, well here it is. Because you're just like them, you don't give a damn about anything or anyone. You're so fucking cold it burns."

Dino laughed a hollow, dull chuckle. "That's really what you think?"

"No, I'm sure of it," she spat.

"Lily," Damian said, his tone darkening in warning. "Think about what you're saying right now. It's shameful and you know it."

Oh, well.

The truth hurt.

"No," Dino murmured with a shrug. "Let her think what she wants, Ghost. Someday, she might actually understand."

"I think I already do," Lily said with a flick of her wrist at her brother. She grabbed Damian's arm and tugged firmly on his coat. "I don't want to be here. I want to go somewhere else, anywhere but … here."

Damian passed Dino a questioning stare.

"Whatever," Dino said. "She's your responsibility. Keep her out of trouble and—"

"I do just fine on my own, thank you," Lily cut in fiercely. "And I am not his child to be tended."

"Again, I don't have the time," Dino replied, not even gracing Lily with his attention. "Damian, I will spill blood. You're aware without me needing to explain it all again."

Damian nodded. "Yeah, I got it."

Damian's apartment was quiet and dark as he closed the door behind Lily but it felt a heck of a lot safer and comforting than her brother's. Lily dialed Evelina's cell number and held the phone to her ear, willing her friend to pick up.

Instantly, the call went to voicemail.

"Hey, you've reached Eve. Leave me a mess—"

"Goddamn it, stop," Damian barked.

He grabbed at the phone in Lily's hand before it went flying across the room and straight into the wall. It snapped into three or four pieces on impact and left a sizeable dent in the paint and plaster.

"Damian!" Lily hissed.

"Stop right now." Damian leveled a glare on Lily that pinned her in place and took her breath away. "She is not answering because she can't, Lily."

"But—"

"Nothing. She can't."

Lily hid her trembling hands by tucking them together and folding her arms over her chest. "That was my phone."

Damian's stance softened. "I'm sorry. I'll buy you a new one tomorrow."

"That's not the point, Damian."

"I know." He sighed and raked his fingers through his hair. The strands fell over his eyes, hiding his feelings from Lily's scrutiny. "But you can't do this, okay. Calling her over and over does nothing but hurt you, trust me. When she can, she will see you called. That's enough for now."

"I should have stayed."

"I didn't give you a choice," Damian said quietly. "And better you didn't."

"But who was there for her?"

"Adriano, her father, and Abriella. Tommas and the rest of my family didn't leave. The Conti family will be there at the hospital or whatever. We have to stay away and hope the official side of things blows past us."

"That's not fair at all."

Damian's mouth drew thin. "That's how it has to go. I'm sorry."

Lily sighed shakily, wishing she could take the situation in better like Damian was. He didn't appear to be totally unaffected like Dino, but he was calm. That was more than Lily could say for how she felt inside. Her heart was a thunderstorm out of control and her mind was the hurricane ready to ravage through what was left.

"I should have stayed," she repeated.

"Hey, hey," Damian murmured, stepping closer. His hands found her jaw with the lightest touch as he tilted her head up to stare at her with worry creasing his brow. "First thing tomorrow morning I will take you wherever you want to go or to wherever Evelina is. I promise. You can be her shoulder to cry on and believe me, she will absolutely understand why you couldn't stay at the restaurant. She was probably too upset to know most of what was happening around her, anyway. She's going to need someone when she wakes up—be that someone when you're capable and ready."

Lily sniffled. "Okay."

"Come on, Lily. Don't do that."

"What?"

"Cry."

She made a face. "I'm not crying."

"You're thinking about it. Even your eyes are watery. Don't cry or I'll be forced to do whatever you need to make you stop. I don't like women crying. I don't do well with tears. Please don't put me through that nonsense."

Lily laughed bleakly. "I think that was the most selfishly sweet thing I've ever heard someone say. You'll do whatever I need to make me stop just so you can feel better."

Damian shrugged one shoulder. "Yeah, well, that's me. Just don't."

"I'm not a crier. It's just been a really shitty day, that's all. I'm still processing."

"Good. I don't think I'd manage with a woman who makes a scene at every little thing."

Lily wet her lips, forcing back the lingering emotions. "No, you seem to like the shadows, huh?"

"Very."

"Why?" she asked.

"Because my raising taught me it was better to be invisible and men like me don't work well out in the open."

"And what kind of man are you, Damian?"

"Not a particularly good one, sweetheart."

He'd been good to her so far, even when she had acted rude or nasty to him. Sure, there were still a lot of questions hanging in the air between them and the arrangement for the marriage, but Damian didn't once treat Lily like she was anything less than a woman who deserved his respect and care.

"And I like being this way," Damian added quieter. "On my own time, doing my thing. I get to choose where I'm going from here but at the moment, and probably for a long while, I'm going to stay just as I am because I'm good at it and I enjoy it."

Lily considered his words for a brief moment. She liked that he didn't have a desire to be front row and center like everyone else seemed to want. He was content in his place, even if Lily didn't like what his statements about his profession implied.

"Why did you join the Outfit?" she asked, honestly curious.

"I didn't know anything else and I didn't really want to. It was the only family I ever trusted enough to want to protect."

His frank, straightforward answer took her by surprise.

"Do you still protect it?"

Damian smiled. "The most important parts. The parts I think should be kept."

Lily didn't respond because she really didn't know how to. Damian tugged off his suit jacket and loosened his tie before kicking off his shoes. When Lily still didn't make an effort to remove her own heels, Damian bent down, lifted her right foot and slid off the stiletto. His fingers ghosted along the arch of her foot before he dropped it back to the floor and repeated the motions with her left side.

Instead of standing when he was done, Damian stayed down on his one knee as the warmth of his hands skimmed over her calves. His touch traveled higher until his palms rested along the back of her thighs and the tips of his fingers pressed into the hyperaware skin under her dress. Desire swept over her senses like a tidal wave, dragging her under the current quickly. She didn't think it was a devastating feeling but instead, heady and lovely.

"It's been a long day," Lily said.

"It has."

"I suppose I should thank you for taking care of me today."

Damian's lips curved into a sinful smirk and his blue eyes glimmered with wickedness. "I didn't mind."

"And that kiss was … nice," Lily said. "Before the whole killing thing, you know."

"So you said."

"I'd like to do that again. With you, soon."

"Now?" he asked. "Because here, I'm not liable to stop at kissing your mouth, Lily."

Lily laughed, feeling so off-kilter it wasn't even funny. "Aren't you supposed to protect my honor or something until the wedding?"

"That was not discussed and you're old enough to make that decision. Not that I think something physical would be bad between us—I told you I wanted that, anyway. What was discussed, was that the marriage would happen, regardless of how it came about so long as it did."

"You're not such a bad pick," Lily admitted.

"Besides, I don't think your brother is so stupid that he dumbly believes you are some kind of angel, Lily. And neither do I."

She laughed. "I'm certainly not one of those."

"We don't have to be strangers."

"So you said," she replied, throwing his words back at him.

"All you have to do is trust me," Damian said, a huskiness deepening his tone.

"Your motives are not clear."

"They don't have to be."

"But I'd like them to be," she replied with a sad smile.

"My intentions are thoroughly wrapped up in you as of now, tomorrow, and beyond. That's all you need to know, sweetheart."

Lily sighed as Damian's hands skimmed higher under her dress to find her backside. The pads of his fingers slipped under the lace of her panties and swept along the flesh of her ass where the curve of her backside melded into her thighs. She couldn't help but give into the feeling of his hands touching her. It took away the anxiety still lingering in her chest and the horrible visions playing on repeat in her mind.

She didn't want to think about those things, so she focused on the sensation coursing through her body instead.

"Black lace, *hmm*?" Damian asked while he wrapped his fingers into her panties and began to tug them down.

Lily played coy. "Someone said you had a fondness for that."

"I do. And your skin is just light enough to make it look damn fucking good."

She stepped out of her panties when he drew them down around her ankles. His fingers skipped back up her calf and straight under her dress before she'd blinked. Without warning he stroked her bare sex.

"Waxed," he noted.

"Completely," Lily agreed.

"Damn. Christ, you're soft like silk. I bet you're like wet satin inside, sweetheart." Damian's knuckles grazed the sensitive folds of her sex before two of his fingers swept them. He parted the lips of her pussy and stroked her soaked slit with one finger while his thumb edged around the hood of her clit just close enough to make her whine. "I'll always give you what you need as long as you use that mouth of yours, Lily. And right now, I want to hear all the sounds you make while you're being thoroughly fucked and worked. When you're screaming my name, make sure the neighbors hear it. I want to hear what I do to you."

Damian's words were practically growled against her thigh. They only served to get her wetter than ever. Her sex clenched every time his finger came in contact with her entrance.

"I especially want to hear you begging, demanding, and needing," Damian said, his tongue striking out to taste her skin. Something beautiful twisted in her stomach and shot straight down to her pussy. "Because as long as you're willing, I'll make sure you're good and fucking pleased come morning. You'll never want to leave my bed again. I might not own you yet, but you'll sure as hell want me to."

"Oh, my God." Lily swallowed the moan building in her chest. His light touches made every inch of her burn in the best way. His promises, filled with sex and sin, only added to her lust. "Stop teasing me."

"Wider," Damian demanded. "Let me see what you're hiding under this dress, Lily. Show me that pussy of yours and how wet it is. I want to see how pink and soaked you are for me. I should have told you this that night I saw you dancing in the club with that man, but now seems a good time, too."

Lily widened her stance as she asked, "What is that?"

"You're mine."

CHAPTER NINE

Damian's words were punctuated by two of his fingers finding heaven and home inside Lily's hot, tight pussy. He was right. She was drenched, slick with her arousal and it wet his fingers beautifully. Her body took his fingers in without a lick of tension. She opened for him, her sex flexing around his digits as he spread them wide on the withdrawal and then plunged them right back in again.

"Mine," he repeated strongly. "This is mine, how wet you are is all mine, and everything I do to you is mine, Lily. Only I get to do this, see you like this, and feel you like this. The next man who touches you in a way that is anything less than innocent will get the pleasure of feeling a bullet rip through his skull."

"Jesus," Lily breathed.

"Say it," Damian said, keeping the rhythm of his fingers fucking her at a tempo just fast enough to get her need to come rising. "Tell me what you know, what you know you want to say, and I'll give you everything you need."

"B-but ..." Lily trailed off, canting her hips into his palm with every thrust. Damian fucked Lily a little harder, curling his fingers to learn the inside of her pussy so he would know the right spot to get her raining all over his hand.

"There are no buts, Lily," Damian said lowly. "I intend for you to be my wife, that makes you mine, and every time I touch you like this, I expect you to know it, too. Tell me that you know, sweet girl. Every inch of your body is mine to taste, fuck, and have. None other but me."

"You," Lily echoed.

Damian grinned in satisfaction, watching Lily's eyes flutter closed as her sex began to shudder around his fingers. "My name in your mouth, Lily. That's what I want to hear every time you come tonight."

Lily whimpered. "Every single time?"

"Oh, I can guarantee there will be more than just the once."

"God, Damian."

"Yes, that's exactly what I want to hear." When her body released around his fingers, Damian kissed in the inside of Lily's thigh before he bit the same spot. The tartly sweet smell of her arousal soaked into his lungs as her come trickled down his palm. The second cry of his name came out louder, breathless. "Fuck yeah, Lily, just like that."

The tremors rocking her from top to toe satisfied Damian like nothing fucking else. He withdrew his hand from between her legs and stood, yanking her dress up with him in fistfuls until he could pull it over her head. Lily didn't shy away from the roughness in his actions as she worked at undoing the buttons of his dress shirt and loosening his tie. She pushed the silk shirt over his shoulders and down his arms. Damian only let go of her long enough to let the shirt hit the floor along with his tie.

"Christ, leave it," Damian ordered when Lily tugged at his belt.

Her wide eyes lit up with confusion. "But—"

"Not important," he said before his mouth crushed down on hers. Lily's plump lips parted to let his tongue strike into her mouth. She tasted of him and heat as his teeth scraped along her bottom lip and down her chin. Damian explored the expanse of her creamy, silky skin with his hands and mouth, licking a wet line down her throbbing pulse point and then nipping a path at her collarbones. "What do you sound like when you're being fucked, Lily? Are you wild and loud or soft and quiet?"

"I ..." Her words drifted off into a low, aching moan when Damian pushed her back against the door. He caught her wrists in his hands and lifted them high above her head, pinning them to the wood. Her chest and breasts, still stained with the red wine from earlier, arched against his body. "Depends on how you fuck me, Damian."

"Raw." He forced the word out through gritted teeth and caught her wild gaze with his own. "Raw, Lily."

"*Mmm*."

"I'm going to fuck you raw. Until every inch of you feels me everywhere. Until I know all the sounds you make and how all of you tastes. Fucking raw, sweetheart."

Lily's lip disappeared under her top teeth. "Yes, please."

Damian jerked her away from the door, spinning her fast so he could push her along the hallway with his hand at her back. Lily didn't stumble as he moved in closer, caught the ends of her hair in his fist, and tugged her back into his chest.

"You're not a goddamn china doll."

"No," she whimpered.

"I am not going to treat you like one, Lily."

"Good."

"Bedroom," he said.

Lily turned left at the end of the hallway and Damian let her go the moment she stepped into his bedroom. He flicked the light on, illuminating the space and her gorgeous figure to his eyes. She spun to face him as she walked backward until her legs hit the edge of his bed.

Lily DeLuca was a beautiful creature—wide, clear eyes, bitten red lips, mussed hair, and a body begging to be fucked by him. Her chest heaved with her ragged breaths and all he could think about was being buried nine inches inside her pussy and fucking her until he couldn't think.

Her arms fell to her sides and her palms turned up in his direction like she was inviting him in. It looked almost innocent in nature, submissive even in the way her gaze flitted downward so she could stare at him through her lashes. The girl had no idea the effect a simple look could have.

Damian was so hard his cock fucking hurt. The thick ridge of his erection strained against his slacks, the line of the zipper biting through his boxer-briefs into his dick. He reached down and unbuckled his belt before pulling it slowly from the loops. He didn't look away from her once as he unbuttoned the slacks, opened the zipper and pushed his pants down until he could step out of them.

She came to him willingly. Just like he wanted.

Damian had thought it might take a little more because Lily was so goddamn stubborn when she wanted to be, but he wasn't about to complain that it worked out this way.

She needed to be safe; to be taken care of; to be cared for. Dino wanted a certain type of man providing those things. That was Damian's promise—the deal. He planned on keeping it.

A life for a life.

His cock sprung free from the confines of his boxer-briefs as he slipped his thumbs around the waistband and tugged them down. Lily tried stepping backward again when he stepped forward, but she had already hit the bed. Instead, her ass hit his sheets and a blink later, Damian was on her.

Lily moved further onto the bed with Damian's urging. His lips touched down over and over to her fevered, pebbling skin. She tasted like woman, sex, and sin already. When his hands fisted into her hair, she tilted her head back with a loud groan, giving him perfect access to her throat. He took the chance to mark her there, wanting to see as much of him covering her body as he could.

Before the night was over, she'd be feeling him everywhere.

"Fuck me," Lily said, the words a soft whisper.

"I will. Soon."

He wanted to learn her first like he promised to. Gliding the tip of his tongue around the swell of her breast, he listened for the hitching of her breaths and the quiet mewls she released when he found her sensitive spots. Damian sucked and licked the red wine stains on her skin until all he could taste was her flesh and want in his mouth.

Lily's legs tightened around his waist and she grinded her hips into his dick. The slickness of her arousal glided along his shaft with every slide of her body. Damian traveled further down her body, kissing a path around her navel before roaming lower. Her thighs opened wider the moment he buried his face into her pussy and got the first real taste of this woman and her sin on his tongue. Her flavor was tart and heady, so fucking good. Her juices flooded his taste buds and Damian only wanted more.

She hadn't been expecting it if her loud shout was any indication. Lily jerked away from his tongue diving into her clenching core, but he pressed a hand flat to her stomach and pinned her to the bed. He fucked her harder with this tongue, thrusting it as deep as it would go until her sex was clamping down around him with every plunge.

"Holy shit," Lily stuttered out, her cries turning louder and more desperate.

"Amazing, sweetheart," Damian murmured before teasing her swollen clit with his tongue. "That's how you taste. Scream for me, Lily."

Damian drew her tiny clit in between his lips and sucked hard. Lily's air rushed out of her chest along with a broken cry of his name. He practically felt the orgasm tear through her nervous system as her arousal seeped from her sex. Damian took his sweet fucking time lapping at her come until she was clean, shaking, and begging him for more.

He kissed a quick path back up her toned stomach, feeling her legs tremble around him as her heels dug into his lower back.

"Tell me you're safe," Damian said, pressing his lips to hers gently. "Because I don't keep condoms here, sweetheart. Women haven't been invited into my home to fuck."

It was the truth. Damian kept this space to himself and he'd never had a reason to need protection in his apartment. In his car, sure. Brand new pack of condoms in the dashboard. But he wasn't interested in going down six flights of stairs to grab them.

Lily grinned a sexy sight. "I am. Four shots a year since I was sixteen. I've never fucked without a condom, either."

Damian kissed her again, more forcefully the second time. "Perfect. This will be a first for us both, then."

"Yeah?"

Something soft and unsure in the lilt of her tone caught his attention.

"Yeah," he confirmed honestly. "But what did I say earlier, huh?"

"Yours," she swore quietly.

"Mine, Lily."

"You better hurry the hell up and get a start on making that a fact, Damian."

His smirk matched hers. "Demanding girl."

"Shut up and fuck me."

That was what he wanted to hear.

Damian leaned up and flipped Lily over onto her stomach at the same time. Her hair blew out in waves around her face as he wrapped an arm around her stomach and lifted her to her knees so her beautiful, rounded ass was on display for him. He took the chance to admire her backside with his hand, grabbing the flesh to make it pink under his handling.

"Here, too," Damian said, dragging two fingers down the crack of her ass.

"*Hmm?*"

"I want you here, too. Everywhere I can have you, Lily."

She stilled.

"Not tonight," he added, using his other hand to grab the base of his cock. He rolled the tip of his dick along her wet slit, loving the silk feeling of her juices on his bare length. "But soon."

"Good God."

"No, Damian, I said."

Lily laughed. It faded into a sharp gasp the moment he entered her. Like earlier with his fingers, Lily's body opened so well for him. She took his cock in with three swift thrusts until he was balls deep and unable to breathe.

"Shit, you're tight," Damian ground out.

She was, crazily so. She was also a hot, blazing paradise, searing him straight down to his blood and bones.

Lily muttered something completely unintelligible. Her hands fisted the bedsheets as she tossed him a heated look over her shoulder. He wanted to hold her like that for a moment, feel her walls flex around him while her juices dribbled down to his balls, but he couldn't.

Damian grasped her hips firmly, pulled out to the tip, and yanked her body back into his groin. Lily sighed, the sound full of content and pleasure. He didn't give her a break between the second thrust and the third. The fourth and fifth came harder and faster. With each slap of skin and every shout of his name, something crawled over his skin and twisted in his stomach. It promised release and bliss. Damian's balls tightened, the sensation of fucking Lily bare as he rammed into her over and over driving him insane.

He wouldn't last long like this—not with her pussy holding him strong and contracting around him like she was already on the edge of her third orgasm.

"Christ, there … like that," Lily said, her teeth cutting into her lip.

"Get your hand down there and play," he demanded. "Feel how fucking wet you are for me, Lily."

Damian didn't need to tell her a second time. He felt the tips of her fingers graze his throbbing dick. Her wetness smeared as her fingers explored and teased. Her inner walls crushed around his cock so snug it nearly fucking blinded him. Ecstasy swept over his senses as he came hard, marking her in an entirely different way. When Lily's back arched inward and her muffled scream cut through the air, he was gone.

So gone.

"Yeah, I got it," Damian said, pressing the pads of his fingers into his temples. "Noon, Carmela's joint. I'll be there."

With a frustrated sigh, Damian hung up the phone call and tossed the cell onto the table. It was going to be a long fucking day if that call was any indication.

"Who's Carmela?" Lily asked from the kitchen entryway.

There wasn't a hint of jealousy in her voice, but her pretty brown eyes lit up with something unknown and a sassy grin split her lips.

"A place, not a person," Damian said.

He took his sweet time taking the sight of her in first thing in the morning after spending a proper night in his bed—one that included him being in there with her. Lily's hair was a tousled mess, but it looked damn good all the same. She wore one of his dress shirts with only two buttons done up in the middle and nothing else. Barefoot, wide-eyed, and smiling.

It was a much better sight than the night before.

"What kind of place?" Lily asked.

"Bar," Damian answered. "Partly."

Lily lifted a brow and without saying a thing, Damian caved.

"A strip joint."

"Oh," Lily muttered, her smile fading.

"A lot of business goes on there, meetings and whatnot."

She still didn't appear particularly pleased. Damian didn't want to be the one to explain that a great deal of business went down in places like those. They were the best ones to funnel illegal funds in from. Restaurants happened to be another one. Anything where cash could be hidden, the Outfit had a leg and an arm in.

"Are you jealous?" Damian asked.

Lily snorted. "Of strippers, Damian?"

Point taken.

"Good, you shouldn't be anyway," he said. "But I do have to head over there after we get something to chow down on."

"About the shooting yesterday?"

"Yeah."

Lily hummed, sadness dimming her pretty features. "Back to life, right?"

Damian nodded. "Back to life."

"I thought you were going to take me to Eve?" she asked.

"Still will. Her parents' place is on the way."

"Parent," Lily reminded him gently.

Damian flinched. "Yeah. That's where she is, anyway. I got that info before you woke up. She's not ... doing well."

Understatement. Evelina Conti was in the midst of a nervous breakdown, a lot like her father and brother. Questions were being asked. Answers were wanted. No one had any. This was going to be messy.

"She'll appreciate you coming, though," Damian said.

"What are we doing now?"

"What do you mean?"

"You and me," Lily said quietly. "What are we?"

"Whatever you want to be."

Lily laughed drily. "That's not entirely true, Damian. We're still getting married and I still didn't choose it."

"I don't know what you expect to hear from me, Lily, but my stance remains the same as it did before last night. Besides, what is the problem with being able to stand one another, huh? Isn't that a good thing?"

"Is that all it'll ever be?" she asked.

"I'm not asking for you to fall in love with me."

Lily didn't bat a lash. "Touché."

"The car was white, I don't give a fuck what anybody says," Tommas said sharply. "You weren't facing the window, Joel."

"How fast did that drive-by happen, huh?" Joel demanded. "Three seconds, maybe four if we were lucky. It was silver—grey, even."

"It was white!"

Damian leaned against the wall beside Dino, watching the scene unfold. Why the fuck the color of the car that had been involved with the shooting was important, Damian didn't know. He supposed they were trying to discern who had been driving, but since everyone who had seen the car agreed the windows were tinted dark, no one knew the shooter.

"What do you think?" Damian asked Dino.

"I think we're going to have a problem on our hands," Dino replied.

Damian chuckled. "Theirs, anyway."

"Something like that."

"Could have been the East Side gang," someone put in. "We've had a lot of issues with them."

"No," Dino said, jumping to the main conversation. "It wouldn't be them. They're the type of thugs that enjoy bragging about the shit they've done. We would have known already if they were the problem."

"Very true," Terrance said, his gaze on the tumbler glass of whiskey in his hand. The boss was another man in the place that seemed to be taking the entire scene in silence. He always had liked to observe more than participate. "We've cleared out a lot of those little problem gangs, anyway. I don't think that's where we should be looking."

"It was white," came a whisper from the far, shadowed corner.

Damian cringed at the pain in the man's voice. Riley Conti didn't even look away from the glass of rum in his hand as he spoke the words. He was still shaking and Damian had been counting. That was the man's fourth glass in an hour. Riley was shitfaced and thoroughly working on forgetting what had happened.

It was going to hurt a hell of a lot more when he was sober again.

It always fucking did.

"The car was white," Riley spat. "It's not a fucking gang. This is … personal, right? I mean, if they wanted to go after the boss, why not just damn well do that, huh? S'not about the boss, you goddamn idiots."

Terrance's brow rose but for once, the Outfit's leader didn't correct his front boss's ignorance and rudeness. Your wife getting killed was a pass on that shit, obviously.

"What, inside job, then?" Ben DeLuca asked.

Dino stiffened beside Damian.

"I didn't say that," Riley said, his words slurring at the end. "I said it's personal, meaning someone pissed someone else off and they're making a point."

The thirty or so men chatting quietly in the strip club silenced instantly with that suggestion. While they had all been discussing back and forth for a good hour about possibilities and what needed to be done, the very whisper of an inside job stopped them all. Immediately, men glanced between one another in a hushed state, tension climbing higher with every passing second. Damian could see the unspoken questions, accusations, and suspicion in their eyes.

Terrance leaned back in his chair. "That's a bold statement, Riley."

"Makes better sense than a fucking gang," the front boss replied in his drunken stupor. "Who'd you piss off, Terrance?"

The boss waved it off. "Laurent?"

"Yeah, Boss?" Laurent asked from where he sat at a booth with five other men. The bullet he took in his shoulder the day before didn't seem to be causing him any issues. Then again, Damian's uncle always did hide things well.

"I didn't get the chance to say something what with the bullets and blood, but make damn sure your wife understands we're not to have a repeat of yesterday."

"Got it," Damian's uncle said quickly.

"What was that all about, anyway?" Dino asked Damian too low for anyone else to hear.

"I told you, she had a fucking spell," Damian said, unaffected.

His cheek still hurt something awful, too. The nice row of scratches on his back that Lily had given him in the shower after their first round made up for that, though.

"About what?" Dino asked.

"Lily."

Dino scowled. "Our father?"

"Yeah."

"Fucking bitch. I suppose she forgets her father was the dirtiest cop that ever lived."

Damian laughed darkly. "I know."

"Doesn't apply to her, right?"

"He was dirty, maybe that's why she overlooks it," Damian suggested.

"Probably."

The conversation still happening drew in Damian's attention again.

"They drew blood first," Joel said. "I want to know who it was and soon."

"Patience comes in handy for times like these," Terrance replied. "You'll do well to remember that."

"He has a point, Terrance," Ben said. "Doing nothing feels like we're sitting ducks waiting for the next bullet to hit one of us. Perhaps Mia was just an accident, maybe whoever it was had been aiming for you."

Riley choked out a pained sound in the corner. No one paid him any mind.

Ben continued like he hadn't been interrupted. "Who's to say? What if the next mistake is one of your granddaughters, hmm? You've always got them around and close. The next stray bullet might just have their blood all over it, Terrance."

The boss barely reacted to the idea of Abriella or Alessa being caught in the crossfire of another shooting, but Damian knew better. Terrance's gaze narrowed and his lips twitched, fighting to pull into a sneer. Anyone else probably overlooked the small ticks, but not Damian.

Terrance was worried.

As he should be, Damian mused.

"What about the Poletti kid?" Theo asked as he took a seat across from Terrance.

Damian froze in place. How in the hell did Theo know about the Poletti hit? Theo asked his boss about it like he knew Terrance had been the one to make the call. But that was impossible. Damian hadn't said a word to his friend about the hit.

Dino knew …

Damian passed Dino a questioning stare.

Dino simply shrugged and lifted his beer to his lips without a word.

"What about the Poletti kid?" Terrance asked.

"Are we looking at a situation of retaliation here?" Theo asked back.

Joel's stare snapped to his grandfather. "What in the fuck is that supposed to mean?"

"Nothing," Terrance muttered with a wave of his hand to dismiss the concerns.

Theo didn't relent. "You put that hit out on him, didn't you, Boss?"

"What did you just say?" Joel asked, his tone taking on a threatening edge.

"Just what I fucking said," Theo said without any heat to his words. "You're not deaf or stupid so clean out your ears. Boss decided to cull that issue before you got a big head and invited the enemy in. Shit like that happens when you think you make all the calls and you don't, Joel. Welcome to the big boy world where you are not the most important person in the room. I imagine that must be hard for you, but grin and bear it, yeah? God knows we've done it enough for you."

Ouch.

"Damn," Dino whispered like he was fucking proud or something.

Damian figured it out then. Terrance had told Joel of the hit on James Poletti, but he obviously hadn't explained to his grandson that he was the one who made the call for it.

Terrance opened his mouth to speak. "I—"

"Did you kill James?" Joel demanded, cutting in on the boss.

Terrance heaved a sigh. "Joel, you are one more word away from getting my boot in your teeth."

Riley stumbled out from the corner, waving his glass wildly as he pointed at the boss. "You did this?"

"I beg your pardon?"

"You … you did this!" Riley shouted. "My Mia—she died because of you?"

"Somebody needs to stop him before he does something he regrets," Dino said.

"I think you've had quite enough," Terrance said calmly to his front boss. He gestured at one of the enforcers leaning against a chair behind him. "Ruck, take him home or—"

"I will not go home!" Riley took another stumbling step forward before his glass fell from his trembling hand. It shattered across the floor, the rum slipping along the lines in the tiles. Everyone else in the room seemed too frozen to speak or move. "Did you do this, Terrance? Tell me."

"I wasn't the one holding the gun, Riley."

"You didn't have to be," Riley said. "Isn't that what you always said, *Boss?* The man who orders the gun is just as bloody as the one who pulls the trigger."

"Take him home," Terrance repeated to the enforcer, still unruffled by the threatening tone Riley had taken on. "Sober him up and get him thinking clearly."

Riley cackled with a drunken laugh as the enforcer stepped forward to shuffle him out of the strip joint. The rest of the men who had gathered for the meeting stayed quiet until the front boss for the Outfit was out of the building and it was safe to speak again.

"He'll be fine once he cleans up," Ben said to Terrance.

The boss didn't look like he believed a word of it.

"It could be retaliation," Terrance said instead. He subtly passed a glance in Damian's direction before going back to the conversation at hand. "The hit wasn't entirely clean when it was followed through. There might have been someone who saw something, figured out the hit came from the Outfit, and didn't come forward to the police."

No one turned to Damian for answers.

This was exactly why he liked being on the boss's payroll and not anyone else's. The only person he needed to answer to for his fuck up was Terrance. Even so, he didn't think the boss was blaming him for it.

"You fucking bastard," Joel hissed. "And for what, to teach me a goddamn lesson?"

Terrance shrugged his thick shoulders like it didn't make a difference either way. "You will learn my lessons one way or another, Joel."

Joel gawked with his jaw wide open and hatred brimming. "Who did the hit, then?"

"I want enforcers on all the women," Terrance said instead of answering his grandson.

Another lesson Joel needed to learn was to never expect answers from a boss. Terrance wasn't required to explain his decisions.

Terrance ticked his chin in Chris's direction, an enforcer that tended to work a lot with the Conti crew. "Chris, stick close to Adriano and Evelina. I'm sure Riley will agree with me once he's clear-headed."

Laurent spoke up, too. "I have a couple of men from my crew keeping an eye on my wife."

"Already." Terrance didn't even pose the word as a question. It felt loaded with something Damian couldn't place. "Why is that, Laurent? You had no reason to believe this was a situation of retaliation on anyone's part."

"Being safe, Boss."

Even Damian had to wonder about that.

"Sure, sure," the boss drawled before giving his right-hand his attention. "Ben, I'm sure you'll figure something out for the DeLuca side."

"Of course," Ben replied.

"And Damian," Terrance added.

Damian perked, but barely. "Yeah?"

"I know your time is well-spent with the Rossi crew lately, but you'll be drawing back on that until this mess has blown over."

"Oh?"

"Lily seems to like spending time with my granddaughter. I'm sure over the next little while they'll be together a lot, given Abriella is in the wedding. I'll have an extra guard on Abriella. But otherwise, I expect you to be their shadow at every point when they are together."

Joel scoffed, obviously still pissed and reeling over the information he learned today. "And he's so fucking good at being in those, right?"

Damian acted like Joel didn't say a thing. "Will do, Boss."

"Good," Terrance said.

Tribute went forward as it always did every month. The men paid their seventy-percent due to the boss without question. No one was short. No one ever was. All the while, Damian couldn't help but notice how the mood had changed between the men. Where some would chat away in comfortable groups usually, most were off by themselves.

The paranoia had set in already.

All it took was a suggestion of something that nobody had even confirmed: inside job.

CHAPTER TEN

Lily blindly waved her hand over her nightstand while her face was still shoved into a pillow. She didn't know what that god awful ringing was, but it needed to go away. Finally, she found the cell phone ringing and pressed the home key, knowing it would ignore the call.

She eyed the alarm clock on her stand, noting the early morning time. Whoever was calling at six in the damn morning could make their way straight to hell where a person like that deserved to go. Waking her up at this time was unacceptable. Especially since the last few days had been just about as stressful as they could be. Lily's dreams had been plagued with memories of the blood and broken glass at the restaurant. Her days were filled with her friend's heartache and the confusing mess happening to the people around her in the Outfit.

No one trusted anyone.

She understood that much at least.

Groaning, Lily turned back in the bed and promptly dozed off again.

Not thirty seconds later, her phone began to screech with another call.

Damn it.

She should have just silenced the stupid thing.

Knowing the caller might be Evelina, Lily forced herself to wake up again. More frustrated and tired than ever, Lily reached over and grabbed the phone, dragging it to her ear before answering the call.

"Hello?" Lily asked, her voice gravelly with sleep.

"You sound like a real winner in the morning."

The dark molasses tenor of Damian washed over Lily's senses. His voice still had the strangest effects on her insides and she didn't know why. Lily chose not to question it.

"God, Damian, do you know what time it is?"

"You know, that only sounds good when you're saying it to me in bed, Lily."

Lily's cheeks heated and she tried to bury her face deeper into the pillow. "Shut up. I am in bed, okay."

"Not mine."

"Stop. It's too early for this."

"Never too early for that." Damian hummed deeply. "I'm trying to perk you up, Lily."

She grinned into her sheet, pulling it higher over her head. This man was such a serious mind-fuck for her. He didn't have to be sweet and funny or anything like that, but he was. Especially with her. They might have slept together, but that didn't mean anything when Lily considered the fact she was still being made to marry Damian whether she wanted to or not.

It was hard to hate someone when you liked them.

"What are you doing?" she asked.

"I told you, trying to—"

"No, Damian. What are you doing with me?"

"Calling you, sweetheart."

"Why?" Lily asked quietly.

"Because I have a surprise. Get up and come downstairs to the front."

Lily sat up in bed. "A surprise?"

"Yes. Get up, I said."

The call hung up. Grumbling under her breath, Lily found the strength to get out of bed. She pulled on something suitable for wearing outside her bedroom, slid on a pair of ballet flats, and made her way downstairs.

Strangely, Theo was sitting at the dinner table with Dino when Lily passed the kitchen by. For not being very friendly, her brothers seemed to be spending a hell of a lot more time together now.

"Morning, princess," Dino called.

Lily gave her brother a dirty look and flipped him the bird.

"A little early for your attitude, isn't it?" Theo called.

"Somebody woke me up."

Both her brothers laughed. Lily ignored them and continued her trek to the front door. Without looking out through the curtains first, she pulled it open and damn near fell over the threshold at the sight in front of her.

Damian stood with his arms crossed and leaning against one of the most gorgeous cars Lily had ever seen. It sported strong, bold lines making the sporty look of it all the more sleek and sexy. The yellow paint with black highlights was sure to draw attention.

The cobalt blue Porsche sitting beside the yellow sports car was one Lily recognized. It was Damian's car. The yellow one, she didn't have a clue.

Lily gaped. "Holy shit."

"Good morning," Damian murmured, never moving a muscle.

"Whose car is that?"

Damian smiled a sexy sight. "Yours."

No way.

Lily's eyes widened. "You're lying."

"I am not. Stop gawking, Lily, it looks terrible on you."

Her mouth snapped shut audibly.

"That's …" Lily eyed the silver trident emblem on the grill of the car in total disbelief. Sure, Damian had a high-end car and even Lily's brothers drove expensive vehicles. She, on the other hand, had never once owned her own car despite having a license. "Is that a Maserati?"

Damian glanced down at the car, nodding. "It is. A GranTurismo, if you want to be specific."

Holy shit.

"You bought me a Maserati?" Lily asked, her voice faint and unsure.

"I did," Damian said simply.

"Why?"

"Do I need a reason?" he asked.

"Is this like … Damian, that's a six-figure car."

"*Sì.*"

"You bought me a car," Lily said, still in shock.

Damian's grin grew. "Happy birthday, Lily."

Her heart stopped for a split second. Somehow, with all the mess that had been going on over the last couple of days after the shooting at the restaurant and everything else, Lily had forgotten her own damn birthday.

Clearly someone else hadn't.

Damian.

"How did you know?" Lily asked.

"You're intended to be my wife. Of course I would want to know when your birthday was," Damian replied. "And it's been a rough couple of days with you being there for Eve, I know. I wanted to see you smile and this seemed like a good time to hand over your birthday present."

All over again, her heart kick-started with confusion and a strange mixture of bliss. Why would Damian do this? Why did he care about her or act like he did?

I'm not asking for you to fall in love with me.

When he did something like this, she found that hard to believe.

Quiet chuckles rang out behind Lily from her brothers. Obviously they had sneaked up on her when she was otherwise distracted with the dangerously attractive man and the equally beautiful car in the driveway.

Lily glanced over her shoulder at Dino. "Did you know?"

"Yes," Dino replied. "I picked the color. Theo and Damian argued over the model for a good week before D won."

"It's very yellow," Lily said, unsure of what else to say.

"The windows are dark enough that even when people stare, they won't know it's you," Theo said.

Goddammit.

They knew her too well.

"So even when you're in the spotlight," Damian said, drawing Lily's attention back again, "… you won't really be in it, sweetheart."

"You bought me a car," Lily repeated.

Christ. She really was turning into a parrot.

Damian winked. "Take me for a drive, Lily."

"God," Evelina said, her breath hitching on a sob. "I don't want to go in there."

Lily's frown felt like it had become a permanent fixture on her face. Nine days had passed since Mia Conti's death. The officials held back on releasing the body until they didn't have a choice. The means of death was obvious but the motive was unclear.

Lily didn't want to watch her friend have another breakdown but it was probably inevitable. Burying her mother would be like another painful confirmation. It wasn't easy to say goodbye. Lily spent as much time as she could with Evelina over the last week, and she knew it helped her friend, but it was heartbreaking.

Mia Conti's death—pointless and filled with uncertainty—only served to remind Lily of her own mother's death. It felt exactly the same. Everyone knew why Lily's father had been killed. Turning on the Outfit and being caught was a signed death warrant. But Lily's mother? Her murder was simply a by-product of her husband's killing.

Nothing more.

Lily grabbed Evelina's hand and squeezed tight, giving her friend a silent reminder she was there and she was so loved. It was one of the things Lily wished someone had done for her when she was just a little girl burying her mother.

"Thanks," Evelina said. "I know this is hard for you, too."

"Oh?"

"Your parents."

Lily cleared her throat, glancing around the quiet room. They were alone, but Lily still felt like she had to be careful when she discussed her parents in the presence of others. "It's been a long time since I've had to bury someone."

"It's not fair."

"It never is," Lily murmured.

Which was the exact reason she despised this life and the ways of the mafia and Outfit. A murder was just another job. A person was just another body. This was just another day. Business as usual, except for the people hurting. Sure, *la famiglia* would put on a good show for the family with their black suits, remorseful words, and supportive hugs, but it meant nothing. It was all lies.

This shit happens.

Move on.

Evelina wiped under her eyes with one hand. "Dad is so ... confusing."

"Confused or confusing?" Lily asked, her brow furrowing.

"He's weird," Evelina said quietly. "He keeps locking himself in his office. He won't take calls. Even Adriano can't get him to pay attention to anything. And he's mad—really, really mad, Lily."

"His wife was killed," Lily replied simply.

Just because Evelina wasn't angry, or rather, hadn't gotten to that place in her grief yet, didn't mean Riley Conti would hit that level at the same speed as his daughter.

Lily shrugged, adding, "I guess I understand the anger."

"At Terrance, though?" Evelina asked. "At the Outfit? I don't know, it just doesn't make sense."

It did to Lily. She hated the Outfit for a long time after it took her parents. She wasn't sure how the Outfit had been responsible for Mia's death, if it even was, but it probably led back to something involving the mafia in one way or another.

Damian leaned in the doorway that separated the private room from the church's main hall. He offered Lily a small smile. "It's almost time to start, sweetheart. They're just waiting on some last minute people."

Lily nodded. "A few more minutes, okay?"

"Sure."

Evelina sniffled when Damian disappeared again. "He's been around a lot lately."

"Yeah, I guess he has," Lily murmured more to herself than her friend.

Lily didn't mind Damian's constant presence, honestly. It gave her a chance to get to know the man beyond awkward dinners with people neither of them could stand and what he could do to her in his bed. Not that they had fucked again since that first time.

"I heard him on the phone the other day talking to somebody about a Poletti hit or whatever," Lily said. "Retaliation was the word he used, I think. Is that what happened?"

Evelina grimaced. "Yeah."

"What did I miss?"

"I know as much as you, Lily."

Lovely.

Ignorance was bliss.

Evelina fell into another crying fit, ruining her makeup further.

"Sorry, I shouldn't have said anything," Lily told Evelina, wiping the mess from her friend's face again.

"Nothing I don't already know." Evelina glanced in the direction Damian had gone. "He watches you a lot, Lily."

"Does he?"

Lily didn't notice. She'd been so busy the last week trying to keep Evelina entertained and working on details for the wedding that her focus was spread thin enough as it was. She figured she might as well enjoy her wedding day—it would be the only one she got in her lifetime—and decided to have what she wanted instead of letting someone else pick for her.

Evelina and Abriella helped a great deal. Even with this whole ... mess. Lily appreciated them more than she could adequately explain.

"A lot," Evelina repeated quieter. "I know you're not agreeable to marrying him and all that."

"I'm okay with him," Lily admitted. "But I don't like the rest or not knowing why."

Evelina nodded. "Makes sense."

"I got lucky."

"Because he likes you?"

"Because my brother cared enough to pick someone I wouldn't be able to hate," Lily said, finally starting to figure it out.

"Dino always was sneaky like that."

Lily laughed but sobered quickly. "Enough of this, huh? Let's talk about something different."

Evelina shook her head. "No, this is good. I don't want to keep crying."

Lily snagged her friend's hand with her own and held tight. It was the best thing she could offer Eve. "I'm here."

"I know—"

"*You!*"

The angry, vicious shout came from inside the hall. Lily flinched at the vitriol and violence in the one word. She released Evelina's hand and peeked out of the entryway to see men and women flooding out from the church's main doors.

Terrance Trentini stood with Lily's uncle and other men she didn't recognize. His hands were high in the air and his head bowed low. The Outfit boss was dressed fit for the funeral in all black along with his grandchildren. Abriella, Alessa, and Joel said nothing, but it was clear they were uncomfortable when they took a step back from the yelling. Riley Conti stood ten feet away, his face red and his hands balled into tight fists. His entire body shook with tremors. The grief he must have felt wafted off him heavily.

"*You*," Riley hissed again.

Evelina stood beside Lily in the doorway, a crease marring her brow. "See, he's so angry."

Lily didn't say a word.

Adriano took a step toward his father with a hand outstretched. Riley jerked away from his son, pointing a finger at his boss with hatred coating his next words.

"You bastard! I don't want you here. *We* don't want you here. I never—"

"Riley, come on," Tommas said.

"Shut up," Riley barked, turning back on Terrance. "I asked you for one thing, Terrance. *One!*"

"I don't know if it was the Poletti boy's family or not," the boss said quietly. "And this is not the time or place for this discussion, Riley."

"One thing, Terrance, and you couldn't do it."

"I will not start a war when the facts are unclear!"

Riley scoffed, dark and broken. "Was it worth it?"

"Dad," Adriano said, grabbing his father's arm. "Stop."

"Don't, Adriano," Riley mumbled, pulling away.

Lily couldn't help but notice how the people seemed divided. The DeLucas stood on the sidelines closer to the boss. The Conti family gathered behind a hurting Riley. Most of the Rossi family was scattered between the two.

Her air lodged in her throat as she recognized what was happening. What little bond there actually was between these people were being ripped apart because of one murder. How many other murders had they experienced? How many other people had lost their lives and they barely blinked about it?

What was so different about this one?

"Was it worth it?" Riley asked again. "Just to teach that useless piece of shit you call a grandson a lesson? Was it worth my wife's life, Terrance?"

A disgusting grin curved Joel Trentini's mouth as he regarded Riley. "Oh, don't worry. I learned my lesson well."

Terrance scowled. "Joel, enough."

Lily stilled, coldness washing over her.

"Retribution," Evelina said lowly.

It made a hell of a lot more sense, now.

Riley waved at the church doors leading out to the front steps. "Get out. Leave. You're not welcome here; not to grieve with my family or give your false remorse and apologies. They mean nothing—*nothing.* Leave!"

"Riley, just listen to me and think about this," Terrance started to say, sadness clouding his features.

"Leave!"

The funeral lasted longer than Lily thought possible. Through the entire service, she stayed beside Evelina to give her friend what comfort and support she could. Damian sat at Lily's other side in the pew, quiet as usual. Once the final blessings had been said and the casket was free to move to make its way to the cemetery, Evelina and Lily separated for the first time all day.

Lily made sure to keep an eye on her grieving friend. Damian leaned against the brick wall of the church, still and stoic. Without realizing it throughout the day, Lily was only now coming to understand that while she had been Evelina's cornerstone, Damian had been hers.

"Sad day," Damian said.

"It's always sad when someone dies for nothing, Damian."

"It's never for nothing. It always means something to someone."

He had a point. Even still, Lily had a hard time correlating Mia Conti's unfortunate end to something worthy or honorable.

"That was quite a show earlier," Lily said, nodding subtly at Riley Conti as he passed with his son and daughter at his side.

"They've been best friends for years," Damian said.

Lily watched the crowd of mourners separate for the pallbearers as they walked the casket to the hearse. "Who?"

"The boss and Riley. Hell, as far as I understand, Riley was the first person Terrance moved higher in the Outfit after he took his seat."

"Huh."

"It's strange," Damian said. "Seeing them fight like that, I mean."

"He's angry," Lily replied. "Maybe he'll calm down."

"But maybe he won't."

"People are picking sides," she whispered, still gazing over the crowd. "I noticed that."

"It's inevitable."

"You didn't."

"No," Damian murmured. "It's not good to pick sides when you don't know which one will win, Lily."

"Win?" She tossed him a look, hoping it voiced her confusion without needing to ask.

"Little things like these have a way of becoming much bigger problems."

"What does it mean, though?" Lily asked.

Damian's arm found her waist before he pulled her closer to his side. Lily didn't mind the closeness. It reminded her that for the moment, she did have someone who cared. "Means I need to keep you close, sweetheart."

"Close?"

"Very close."

Lily shivered. "Maybe I should like the sound of that, but for some reason, I don't think you mean for me to."

Damian shrugged. "Bad things happen when angry people grieve."

"Sometimes."

"But nothing will happen to you."

Evelina passed Lily another pack of colors to flip through.

"How many different shades of peach can there be?" Lily asked, exasperated.

"A lot," Evelina said, laughing quietly.

Lily smiled. It was the first time in a week since Evelina's mother had been buried that the girl actually laughed or anything of that nature.

"I'll find the right shade," Lily said, tossing two awful swatches into the pile. "Not those, though."

"What did you do this week?" Evelina asked. "When you weren't here, I mean."

Lily grinned. "I wanted to be here, Eve."

"Thanks."

She missed so much time with her friend when she spent those years touring Europe that Lily was trying to make up for what they'd lost. Never once did their friendship feel out of place or like it had grown stale. Some didn't. Some friendships—the very best kind—picked up where they last left off without ever missing a beat.

That was the kind of friend Evelina was.

"Where's Damian?" Evelina asked, leaning back on the couch and glancing over her magazine.

Lily frowned. "I don't know."

"Really?"

"Nope. He's been MIA for the last week."

Which was completely odd. Especially if Lily considered what Damian had told her at Mia's funeral. He planned on keeping her close, yet

Lily rarely saw him all week. He showed up for dinner at her brother's place yesterday, but that was it.

"I've been doing a lot, too," Lily said in explanation. "Maybe I'm just passing him by."

"Maybe," Evelina echoed.

Between Evelina's place and Abriella's, Lily had spent more time out of her home the last week than she had inside it. It didn't make things any easier that Evelina didn't seem to want to be anywhere near the Trentini family for whatever reason. Evelina and Abriella had always been good friends, too, but the divide separating the men in their families had pushed the girls to separate corners, too.

"She's in my wedding, too," Lily said softly. "You do know that, right?"

"Hmm, who?" Evelina asked, looking over the top of the magazine.

"Abriella."

Evelina's face darkened. "What is your point?"

Lily pointed at her friend's angry expression. "That's my point right there. What is going on?"

"It's not Ella that I'm pissed off about, Lily."

"What is?"

"Her family. Her grandfather might as well have held the gun. Pointed it, pulled the trigger; whatever you want to call it. He's responsible."

"She's not them, though," Lily said.

Evelina lifted her shoulders like it didn't make a damned difference. "I know, but I can't get involved or take sides right now. Not with my father being like he is. Better I stay to my side of Chicago and she stays on hers. Maybe it'll work itself out."

"Sounds like you've already taken a side."

"I haven't."

Evelina's actions spoke differently.

Lily chose not to push her friend on that front. "Is your father going to come to the wedding?"

"Yes, I'm in it. He doesn't miss a chance to show me off when I'm dressed up. Unlike you, I'm still on the market, Lily." Evelina's voice didn't hold a hint of sadness about the fact her hand was still for sale in the marriage market, technically. "So yeah, I imagine he'll be there."

"Terrance will be there, too. It's a big thing, remember? Two families inside the Outfit joining or whatever. As much as this whole wedding thing irks me, I would like to have a nice day. One that isn't full of people screaming at one another."

Evelina didn't blink a lash. "I'm sure it will all be settled by then."

"How—"

Evelina's father walked into the living room with a cell phone pressed to his ear. Adriano followed right behind.

"But, Dad—"

"Enough, Adriano."

Evelina tensed and quickly averted her gaze from her brother and father.

"Yeah, is everything good?" Riley asked, his attention back on his phone call. "Perfect, give me thirty."

Riley ended the call and slipped his phone back into his pocket. Like Evelina and Lily weren't even in the room, he turned on his frustrated son and waved his hands wide.

"The answer is no, Adriano," Riley said. "Stay out of it and keep an eye on your sister for me like you've been doing."

"Aren't you worried about what the boss is going to do?" Adriano asked his father.

"I don't care. He should have done it right the first time or settled it for me like I asked."

Lily's brow furrowed as she watched the confusing exchange between father and son.

"They deny it, Dad," Adriano said, his voice desperate.

Riley sighed harshly, his teeth gritting. "Why are you doing this, son?"

"What?"

"This," Riley barked, flicking his wrist in Adriano's direction in the most dismissive way Lily had ever seen. "Fighting with me and refusing my wishes. I raised you better than this. You know what is important—blood, the family, *us*. She was your mother. When someone spills your blood, you answer that by spilling theirs."

"The Lazzari family denies retaliating for the hit on James Poletti," Adriano said firmly. "Other people are talking, too. This might have come from the—"

"No one in the Outfit was looking to kill your mother."

Adriano's gaze narrowed. "You keep saying that shit like someone was pointing the gun at her directly. Laurent took a bullet, too. Terrance was sitting at that table along with members of the Rossi and DeLuca families. Mom was an acc—"

"If you call her death anything less than a disgrace needing retribution, I will cut your fucking tongue out."

Lily gasped quietly, disbelief filling her to the brim.

Adriano sneered. "And this? Disobeying and disrespecting Terrance like this? How will that go over, Dad?"

"It's the only thing that makes sense," Riley replied. "It came from somewhere, and the Lazarri family is the only one Terrance has had issues with. He can clean up the mess when I'm done. The hit is going through."

More blood. More blood was going to spill. More useless, unneeded deaths. More funerals, sadness, and grief.

Lily could already taste it and feel it.

"What the fuck are you going to do, huh?" Adriano demanded.

"Excuse me?" Riley asked.

"What are you going to do, paint Chicago red before you finally feel better? It's not going to bring her back or fix what happened, Dad. She's still going to be dead!"

"Your motives are showing," Riley said.

"What?"

"This is about her again, isn't it? You're worried about her. I am so sick of this bullshit, Adriano. It's not going to happen, not after everything."

"It has nothing to do with her."

"I think it does. Fighting with me isn't going to get you any closer to Alessa Trentini."

Oh. Well, then.

Lily followed Evelina's lead and decided to ignore the two men as their fight spilled into the joining hallway.

"Alessa?" Lily asked quietly.

Abriella's younger sister tended to stick to herself and was a quiet thing. Lily hadn't gotten the chance to talk much to Alessa since returning home.

Evelina didn't look away from her magazine. "Apparently."

"Didn't see that one coming."

"Star-crossed," Evelina said under her breath with a hint of bitterness. "Fucking romantic, huh?"

Lily fingered the swatches of fabric before asking, "Is he going after the Lazarri family?"

"Seems like it," Evelina replied, calm and unbothered.

The Lazzari family was a small criminal family with Italian roots and little connection to the Outfit. Lily didn't know a great deal about them except for some of the things she'd heard in passing between Dino and Theo over the last week as her brothers discussed the divide separating the Outfit between the Conti and Trentini families.

Theo didn't believe the Lazarri family had a hand in the hit.

Dino didn't give an opinion at all.

"Somebody else might bury their mother," Lily said, wanting her friend to understand what her father's actions meant.

Evelina flipped a page in her magazine. "So be it."

"Eve!"

"Don't be so surprised," Evelina said coolly. "Tell me in all your years that you've never once wished someone had paid for the life of your mother and father. I know what your dad did—we all fucking know, Lily. But you still loved them, right? It still hurt."

"It did," Lily replied.

"Look me in my eyes and tell me it's okay with you that nobody ever answered for doing that to you and your brothers."

Lily couldn't.

Lily turned her new Maserati off to the side of the quiet street, threw the gears into park and cut the engine, frustrated and overwhelmed. She'd cut her evening short with Evelina after the show between Riley and Adriano. Lily didn't know what to think about her friend's response or how Evelina acted like retaliation for her mother's killing could be in any way justified.

Lily understood pain. She got Evelina was still in the midst of grieving and maybe her anger was finally catching up with her. At the same time, Lily didn't get it at all. Maybe the lingering pain from losing her own mother and father way back when prevented Lily from accepting the mafia way of taking a life for a life, but no matter how hard she tried … she couldn't do it.

The Outfit had taken people away from Lily once—her view had long been tainted. She knew that. She also knew the people she did care about, her brothers, Evelina, and even Damian, were all involved in a life that hurt her once. They fully engrained their own worlds and rules to fit the mafia.

Lily couldn't help but wonder if she had ever been able to get the retribution deserved for her parents' death, would she be like them, too? Accepting. Tolerant. Unaffected. Would she? If her parents' death had been answered with more blood, would the ache in her heart be mended?

She had always believed that spilling blood did nothing but stain the ground and the hands of the person making the calls.

Her father's death had always been considered justified. Her mother's, a by-product.

A fucking afterthought.

Dismissed.

Someone took away Lily's mother without even thinking or caring about it. They buried her and pretended like it didn't happen. Like that woman wasn't important to three little people who she helped create and who needed her.

Nobody ever answered for that. Nobody ever would.

Why was Mia Conti so goddamn different from Lily's mother?

And why did it bother Lily so much?

Lily blew out a heavy breath, jerked her car door open, and got out. The cool breeze of the late July air swept around her bare legs. The dress she wore fell just above her knees and the skirt blew wide as the wind picked up.

She didn't even care that she was wearing heels and it was colder than normal. Locking her car, Lily started a trek down the street. She needed to clear her head or do something. Just anything.

Being in Chicago and getting a front row seat to what seemed like the beginning of another family feud only put Lily right back into her childhood. She didn't feel like a young girl anymore, but her emotions mirrored that time and threated to take her under with the weight.

More confused than ever, Lily pulled her phone out of her purse and dialed a familiar number. Dino picked up on the second ring.

"Lily," he greeted.

"Why are we different?" she asked right away.

Dino cleared his throat and chuckled. "I have no idea what you're asking me, little one."

Despite how that pet name usually bothered her, especially when one of her brothers used it, Lily smiled that time.

"Our parents and what happened to them. Why are we different, Dino? Why didn't someone fight for what happened to Mom or—"

"Dad turned on the Outfit," Dino interjected gently. "You know that."

"But Mom didn't!"

Dino grunted out, "Yeah, I know. This is way out of left field for you, Lily. Where is this coming from, anyway?"

"I was over at Eve's," Lily replied, hoping that explained it without her needing to go into further details.

"You've always been strong-willed and opinionated about our business," Dino said. "We don't talk about these things, Lily, because you don't want to."

"I want to now."

"Why?"

"Because I want to know what was so different about our mother! I get Dad turned rat, okay. But Mom—"

"Wrong place, wrong time," Dino interrupted softly. "She was in the house with him and it wasn't supposed to happen. That was all Ben ever said to me, Lily."

"Doesn't it make you mad, though? Doesn't that just … enrage you that she was killed? Both of them, even, Dino. Why doesn't it piss you off?"

"It does," her brother replied. "It always has, but sometimes it's better to bide your time, little one. Not everything is black and white."

Lily stilled on the sidewalk, taking in her brother's words and what they might mean.

"Where is all this coming from?" Dino asked.

"I told you, I was at Eve's place."

"And all your scars are getting cut open again."

"Maybe. I don't know, it's just … I don't want to see more people hurt because of what happened to Mia, but at the same time, I think I understand how Eve and her father want some kind of retribution. Doesn't that make me an awful hypocrite?"

"I don't think so."

"You're biased."

"No, not really. I think you've got certain people and the Outfit messed up. It's not the same thing. You're pissed off at the people who took our mother away—the Outfit didn't do that, Lily."

"It's the same thing!"

"It's not, in certain ways. I'm the Outfit. Theo is the Outfit. The Rossi family, your friends, and even Damian. We're the Outfit—*la famiglia*. Certain people inside the Outfit made decisions that hurt us because of *la famiglia*. I know it's hard to understand, but those people don't make up the Outfit, Lily. It is way more than just a couple of people. It is all the people. It's a culture, a lifestyle. We don't choose this life because it's an easy one; we choose it because we believe in it."

"Why does it seem like every man is just out for himself, then?" Lily asked.

To her, that was how the Outfit had always felt.

"Because that's the problem with it. Certain people have forgotten what it's supposed to be. Don't blame the Outfit, blame the people."

"Don't blame the gun, blame the man," Lily muttered.

"Exactly."

"It can't be that simple, Dino."

Her brother laughed. "Yeah, it rarely is."

CHAPTER ELEVEN

Damian rested on the hood of the Maserati, his gaze staying trained on the figure through the darkness. Down the sidewalk, Lily hung up her phone call, put her hand over her eyes, and shook her head.

She'd been too far away for him to understand most of the conversation, but he had heard her use Dino's name at least once.

Lily turned back toward her car, took a couple of steps, and nearly stumbled over her own two feet at the sight of Damian sitting where he hadn't been before.

"Shit," Lily gasped, her new phone dropping from her hand to the pavement.

Luckily, it didn't break.

Damian chuckled as Lily picked up her phone and stood straight again, glaring daggers at him the entire time.

"You almost owed me a new phone again," Lily warned.

"You should get used to this, sweetheart."

"Having a stalker?"

Damian raised a single brow at her statement. "Really?"

Lily made a face. "Yeah, never mind. What are you doing?"

"Keeping you close."

The briefest, tiniest smile tugged at the corner of Lily's mouth. "Oh?"

"Just like I said."

"Where have you been, then?"

"Around," Damian replied, knowing how vague he sounded. "You've been busy and I work better when people can't see me."

"Just like a ghost, huh?"

"Just like that." Damian nodded in her direction, saying, "I had a meeting with some of the Rossi family while you visited with Eve and I just caught you in time before you left. I thought you would be staying later. Didn't you have color schemes to finish or some nonsense?"

"How did you know that?"

"Dino," Damian said simply.

"You're keeping tabs on me and following me?" she asked, her voice pitching high.

"Don't be angry, Lily."

Lily's expression darkened. "That's a pretty bold—"

"You want to have a life," Damian interrupted calmly. "You want to do things and go out. I don't blame you, but there's a lot of messy stuff happening right now, so I have to keep a close eye on you while it happens. I'm sorry if the idea of having someone trail you leaves a bad taste in your mouth, but it's either this, or you won't be allowed to leave Dino's place until shit blows over."

Lily's stance softened. "It's just you watching me, right?"

Damian smiled. "Just me."

"You could have told me, Damian."

"I did—at Mia's funeral. I can't help it if you don't read between the lines. Just because you can't see me, doesn't mean I'm not still around, Lily."

Lily picked at her nails and avoided his stare. "What kind of messy stuff?"

"Distrust and uncertainty. From a lot of people. It makes for a bad situation."

"Oh."

"You're not going to end up some casualty in this mess if I can help it," Damian said, sighing. "Leading me back to point, I almost missed you because you left early. What happened?"

"Nothing," Lily replied too quickly for it to be true.

"Nothing, right. That's why you drove around aimlessly for twenty minutes, pulled over on a random street, and then proceeded to make a phone call to your brother while you paced back and forth. Come on, Lily. Do I look like a fucking idiot to you?"

Lily refused to look at him again. "No, but it's not important. Leave it alone."

"Look at me."

"Damian—"

"Lily, look at me right now," he demanded.

Lily blinked up at him, a wetness shining in her brown eyes. Tears saturated her bottom lashes, threatening to fall. Instantly, Damian's gut twisted with anger and an unusual rush of sadness and confusion.

Christ.

He hated it when women cried.

"Happy?" Lily asked as the first streaks of her tears tracked down her cheeks.

"No. Why would I be happy over your tears?"

Lily sniffed and wiped at her eyes, but it didn't stop the second flood of wetness that came right after.

"I am not a crier," she mumbled.

"You said that once before, but I'm starting to wonder." Damian tried to will away the odd sensations balling in his stomach. Like a shot of rage straight to his veins, all he could think about was finding out who had made Lily cry and forcing whatever goddamn apology he could out of them for it. "What happened?"

"Bad week," she said in explanation. "All of this crap reminds me of my parents and what my brothers and I went through as kids. I called Dino because I couldn't understand how one person's death could cause so much uproar around us like Mia's has. I get she was loved and that she didn't deserve to die, but so was my mother. She was loved, too. Her death was nothing more than an accident, too."

"And no one said a thing about her being killed," Damian finished for her.

"Yeah, in a way. And it makes me feel awful to even think about it."

"I get that. Nothing is ever simple, right? What did Dino tell you?"

"Blame the man, not the gun," she said quietly.

"And who is the gun in this situation?" he asked.

"The Outfit."

Ah.

There it was.

Dino had forewarned Damian before he even met Lily that she had her issues with the Outfit. Most of them could be drawn straight back to her parents' murders.

"He has a good point," Damian said.

Lily didn't bother to wipe the tears from her cheeks as she said, "I know, but it still bothers me and I feel like a fraud."

"Why?"

"I told Eve someone else's mother might die because hers did and at the same time, all I could think about was why didn't someone die for mine, too?"

"You know why though, don't you?" Damian asked.

"My father."

"Yeah, him. Dino saved you kids back then. You know that, right?"

Lily shook her head. "No."

"He was old enough to have a leg stuck in the Outfit and he was working under Ben's thumb a great deal of the time. Because he understood the rules and how badly it made you kids look that your father turned on the Outfit, Dino did what he had to so that your parents' shame wasn't reflected on to you or Theo. Dino separated you from Joseph and Valerie DeLuca."

Lily flinched at her mother's and father's names, but Damian didn't relent. "He took you out of that home, put you in with your uncle immediately, and then threw himself full force into the Outfit. He never finished high school. He's never even had kids of his own or been married, Lily. Because he's spent his entire life working to wash away the shame so that people could see you and Theo as his brother and sister, not the children of Joseph and Valerie."

"I'm not ashamed of my parents," Lily said.

"But you are ashamed of what your father did."

Lily cringed, staying silent.

"You can say it. It's just me here, you know," Damian said. "Nobody else needs to know. You're not protecting dead people by saying something that's true."

"He did wrong by the Outfit," she said instead.

"And the people reacted how they were taught to."

"How do you not blame the gun?"

Damian shrugged. "Because it didn't pull the trigger. It just follows the rules."

"I don't think my mother's death was an accident," Lily told him.

"Why not?"

"I think my uncle knew she would have taken her kids and ran."

"It's possible," Damian agreed. "Ben has always tried to control the DeLuca side of things as much as he could. Don't take this the wrong way, but dwelling on it all isn't going to help you, Lily. All that stuff has already happened. It's been over with for years. I'm not saying you should forgive and forget, but maybe you should start leaving it where it belongs."

"Behind," she murmured.

"Yeah. Back where it can't keep hurting you. Because right now, you're the only one letting it hurt you, sweetheart."

"Is that how you do it, Damian?"

"I'm more concerned about the now to be worrying about buried people, Lily."

"Don't you miss your parents?" she asked.

"I barely remember them, but if you want the truth, I miss the idea of people who were supposed to be only mine and them loving me. I miss what I think that should feel like because I never got the chance to experience it."

"Oh."

Just like that, her tears starting falling again. Damian's gut twisted harder at the sight, making him feel all kinds of terrible. Pushing off the hood of the car, he crossed the few feet between them, caught her pretty face in his palms, and tilted her head up so he could stare down at her.

"Please don't cry," he murmured. "I don't do well with tears. I told you that. Stop."

Lily sucked on her bottom lip but she didn't stop. He figured she couldn't help it. "I'm sorry."

"You're going to force me to do it, huh?"

"Do what?"

"Make you stop crying so I can feel better," Damian said, grinning wickedly.

Lily laughed through her tears. "And just how do you plan on—"

Damian's mouth crashed down on hers, swallowing her words and gasp with his teeth and lips. The sweetest squeak of surprise echoed from Lily before she responded to the kiss and fisted his jacket in her hands. Her mouth tasted of cherries and salt as she kissed him back, tugging him closer. He kept her pinned in place, wanting to feel her mouth on his while he got himself reacquainted with the taste of her.

With every scrape of his teeth to her lips and every strike of his tongue, Damian felt like he owned this girl a little more. Like she was only his and that he was all she wanted. Just the way her body fitted into his and she never shied away from his touch and kiss, Damian knew ... Lily DeLuca was two steps away from falling straight for him.

He didn't mind.

Unfortunately, Damian could still see the tears in her eyes fighting to fall and her breathing hitched, telling him she was holding back sobs.

"Don't cry, don't cry," Damian chanted, kissing along the line of Lily's cheek bone. "When you cry, it makes me want to find the person who made you do it and shove my fist so far down their throat that I could rip their heart out and then force-feed them the organ. Seriously, it bothers me. Stop it, Lily."

"I'm trying," she mumbled as his lips ghosted over hers again. "You made me sad again by talking about your parents."

Great. Now he was the reason for her tears.

Damian couldn't handle this shit.

"I punched a kid in the face for you once," he said, hoping that gained her attention enough to stop her crying.

Lily let him wipe away the wetness on her lashes. "When?"

"You had just turned seven. I wasn't hanging around that much anymore and neither was Theo, really. We were doing ... other things with Dino." Damian shrugged, not wanting to go into all that. "Anyway, that left you to make new friends. Some idiot nine-year-old boy happened to be one of them. He made you run home crying over something. Dino was there when you told Ben what happened. He told Theo, your brother told me, and I hit the kid then next time I saw him."

"That's terrible," Lily muttered.

"Learned his fucking lesson, I bet."

Lily laughed, but another tear streaked down her cheek. Damian cussed under his breath at the sight, willing away her sadness.

"How can you laugh and cry at the same time?" Damian asked, overwhelmed by how affected this girl made him. He could not handle the awfulness welling in his gut because of her crying mess.

"Because I'm sad and happy."

"That doesn't make sense."

"It does, too!"

"You sound like a child arguing with me like that," Damian said, running his finger over her trembling bottom lip.

Lily gasped, hurt filling her gaze all over again.

"I was kidding, Lily!"

She didn't look like she believed him for a second.

"I was," he repeated.

"Still awful."

"You're still crying," Damian pointed out.

"You haven't made me stop yet, so you must not want to feel better. Remember?"

Sneaky little ...

Damian kissed Lily again without warning, tugging her into his chest and turning them both so he could back her down the sidewalk. Their lips didn't part once, not even when they stumbled off the sidewalk and Lily's legs hit the hood of her Maserati. Unable to control the crazy desire thickening his blood, Damian ran his hands up Lily's smooth legs and under her skirt. He could practically feel her heartbeat and blood rushing up to the surface of her skin under his touch. Every sound, every goosebump, and every inch of her was starting to imprint in Damian's memory like a melody he couldn't forget.

He didn't really want to.

The way her tongue swept her bottom lip had his gaze narrowing in on her mouth all over again. He wanted to bite her lip until she begged him for more, so he did just that. The sharp, breathy whine Lily released shot straight down to his aching cock.

But Damian wasn't important. He wasn't interested in getting his own rocks off. No, he wanted to get *her* off.

"Oh, my God, what are you doing?" she asked in a breathless whisper.

"Feeling you. What the fuck does it look like?" Damian grabbed her ass in a firm grip and lifted her onto the hood before dragging his hands back down her legs. "Christ, I swear you've got the best legs in Chicago, Lily."

"Liar. I'm short as hell."

"I like your shortness. I do not lie, I simply omit things for my own benefit."

Lily cocked a brow. "Isn't that the same thing?"

"Ask the right questions to get the correct answers. Nobody ever asks the right questions."

"Huh."

"And why would I lie about your legs, hmm?" he asked, grinning sinfully. "I like them very much, especially when you wrap them around my head and my face is buried into that beautiful pussy of yours."

Lily groaned, biting hard into her bottom lip. "Fucking hell."

"Yeah, that's the goal, sweetheart."

With those words, Damian's hands disappeared under her skirt again. He moved her legs apart with taps of his palms to her inner thighs. Lily glanced around the dark street, a shake rocking her thighs the closer he came to her cotton panties.

"Somebody might see us," she said.

"So?"

"So!"

"What are they going to see, huh? A beautiful woman getting finger fucked on a beautiful car in the darkness. Nothing more. We should give the neighbors a show. I bet they've never seen one like us before."

"Jesus."

"Are you wet for me?" Damian asked.

"Probably," Lily replied. "Someone still might see me."

"I hope they do. And I hope they figure out exactly what I'm doing to you because then they'll know you're mine and only I get to do this." Damian's fingers skimmed the patch of her cotton panties covering the lips of her pussy. She shuddered at the contact. He could already feel her wetness dampening the fabric. "Yes, you're fucking soaked. Pretend all you want like someone seeing us bothers you, but I bet it doesn't. You're so goddamn hot, it's crazy. I can feel it, sweetheart. Tell me what you want, Lily."

Lily blew out a shaky breath and wet her lips under her tongue. "I want your fingers in my pussy making me come."

"Goddamn," Damian hummed out. "Those are dirty fucking words coming from a beautiful mouth. Spread your legs wider, Lily."

She did as he asked before yanking on his jacket and bringing him closer. Her legs hooked around his hips as he leaned down for another searing kiss.

"So soft," Damian murmured against her lips as he stroked his finger along the side of her panties. The bareness of her sex drove him insane. He loved that she was waxed clean; there was absolutely nothing between them when he touched her and she felt all of him because of it. "And so fucking wet."

"Hot," Lily moaned.

"Yes, that too."

Damian slid his one hand under her panties and used his other to grab the ends of her hair. He bunched her hair up to the back of her neck, holding her tight in place, and he swept his fingers over the sensitive lips of her pussy. Soaked was an understatement. With every swipe of his fingers, her fluids slicked them both up. Her juices smeared to his hand as he cupped her pussy and dove in with a single finger.

Lily arched into the touch instantly, the sweetest moan tumbling from her lips at the same time. Without warning, he added a second finger and began a fast rhythm that was sure to get her desire raging out of control and fast. He wanted to see her shattering around him as she came calling his name.

"So hot," he told her. "Like a fucking fire holding me tight. Show your face, Lily. If anyone is watching me do this to you right now, I want them to see exactly what you look like because of it."

Lily's head fell back, Damian weaved his hand deeper into her hair, keeping the fast strokes up between her thighs. It was all his fingers and her sex sucking him in as he fucked her harder on the hood of the car. He reveled in the sounds of her pussy taking him in and the noises of her juices as he fucked her harder with his fingers. She didn't seem to mind the brutal strikes of his digits taking her deep but instead, pushed right back into his palm for more.

Lily shifted her hips, meeting each thrust of his hand with a quiet, airless cry that heated him up from the inside out. Her arousal coated his fingers and he felt her inner walls beginning to flex and flutter around his digits.

"Tell me how close you are," Damian demanded.

Lily's eyes, hooded and dazed, met his. "So close."

The spot he'd found inside her pussy the first time they fucked, the one that seemed to drive her wild, had her gushing around his digits. Damian spread his fingers wide, needing her to feel full of him and only him.

"How badly do you want to come, Lily?"

Her legs shook as she whined. "So bad. More, please."

Damian flashed his teeth in a smirk. "Whatever you want, sweetheart."

Using his thumb to play at her clit while his fingers kept up the tempo inside her pussy. It wasn't long before her head tilted back and her lips parted with one loud shout that was sure to wake up someone on the street if they weren't already.

As her inner muscles contracted around his fingers and the warmth of her come dribbled down to the hood of the Maserati, Damian leaned in and kissed Lily softly. He explored her hot little candy mouth with his tongue and teeth while she rode out the waves of her orgasm. Nothing was sexier than the sight of her coming undone because of what he did to her.

"So good," she breathed as he caught her chin between his forefinger and thumb.

"You're beautiful when you come, Lily."

She batted his hand out from between her legs. "Sensitive."

Damian chuckled. "I bet."

He waved his wet fingers for her to see.

"What—"

He sucked them clean before she could say another word.

"You're wicked," Lily said, using her elbows to hold her up on the hood.

"Very. You're too good to waste, though."

Damian dotted kisses across Lily's forehead. She shivered, humming a pleased sound under her breath. The slightest sheen of perspiration dotted her skin and her eyes were wild and dark with lust. He loved the sight of her on that hood with her legs spread around him, her panties soaked by her own juices, and looking at him like she was ready for another round.

"That seemed to work," Lily said, her voice a little dry.

"Hmm, what?" Damian went about fixing her skirt and panties before placing his hands on either side of her hips. "What worked, Lily?"

She grinned a sexy, slow smile. "You made me stop crying."

He did.

"And now I feel better," Damian mused with a chuckle.

"You're awful."

"As I told you before, you will grow to like it."

Lily eyed him curiously. "Maybe I already do. Can I tell you something?"

"Shoot," Damian said.

"I think I missed you this week."

"Oh?"

"Yeah," Lily said heavily. "And besides following me around, I'd like to know where else you were."

Damian couldn't have missed the hidden meaning in her words if he tried. "Jealousy looks terrible on you, especially considering the fact I'm here doing this with you and not somewhere else doing God knows who."

"Since you just gave me an orgasm on the hood of a Maserati after being MIA for almost a week, maybe you owe me an honest answer."

"Ask a better question," Damian said instead.

Lily's gaze narrowed. "Any women?"

"Absolutely not."

"Who was the last woman you fucked around with?"

"A couple of months ago with someone I met at Tommas' club. I took her to the back office, screwed her on my cousin's desk, and never got her name. I'm not the relationship type, sorry."

"Liar."

"I don't lie, Lily. Stop making me repeat myself."

"You are lying. You're doing okay right now."

Damian cleared his throat, stunned. She was right. "Maybe it's different with you."

"Why is that?"

God, she could be frustrating and stubborn as fuck when she wanted to be. Damian almost hated how he liked that part of her. Except he couldn't hate it at all.

"Better question, Lily."

"You're impossible."

Damian laughed low. "I know."

"Don't fuck with my head, okay?"

"That's not in my plans, sweetheart."

"Sometimes I wonder," she said.

"You shouldn't. Don't. I care. You're important to me. Nothing else matters in the end but that."

"What do you owe my brother?" Lily asked.

Damian froze. "I beg your pardon?"

"I remember what you told me. You're doing the marriage thing because you had to but, at the same time, some of your family doesn't approve. I have nothing to give you, as my inheritance isn't enough to make you a massively wealthy man, not that you'll be able to touch a dime of it. You've already said you didn't buy me from my brother, so he's not giving you anything, either. Which leads me to believe you owe him something. What is it?"

Shit.

"You are far too observant," Damian said.

"So you do owe him something?"

"I do."

"What is it, Damian?"

"My life."

Lily stared at him for longer than he liked before she said, "A life for a life."

"Yes."

"And you're giving yours to me."

"Yes," Damian said again, his throat growing tighter.

"What else did my brother demand?"

"That I give you everything you need."

Which was far more than she could possibly know.

Lily didn't bat a lash when she replied, "You're succeeding."

Damian rolled down his window as Lily stepped out of the Maserati and closed the driver's door.

"Lock that fucking thing," he said.

Lily rolled her eyes but hit the locking button on the auto-start like he told her to. "Nobody would be stupid enough to steal a vehicle from a DeLuca's driveway, Damian."

"You never know. Come here."

Lily walked over to his car and leaned in the window. Damian hooked a finger around one of her wavy strands of hair and pulled her close enough to press a kiss to her pretty mouth. She smiled as she pulled away.

"You're not coming in?" Lily asked.

"Work," Damian said in explanation. "You're here, so I know you're okay."

"You know, I could just text you when I'm going to and from somewhere."

Damian liked that idea. "Yeah, especially if you're going to pull another stunt like today."

"Wasn't a stunt, Damian."

"I don't want to take chances; that's all. It makes me nervous."

Lily nodded and pulled out her phone, looking it over. "All right. Tomorrow night I have to go see Abriella for a fitting. Where are you going to be?"

Damian grinned. "Wherever you are."

"Maybe I'd like to see you when you're there."

"I told you, I work better when you don't."

"Hmm, Ghost, right?"

"Right," he said. "How about I pick you up for breakfast and we do something in the afternoon before you have to head over to the Trentini place. Maybe I'll see if the boss wants to chat while you're there and it'll give me something to do instead of just be bored while I wait."

"Sounds good."

"Tomorrow, Lily."

With a two finger wave and a coy wink, Lily left Damian alone to his thoughts. He waited until she had the front door to Dino's home opened and shut again before he turned his car on. Damian didn't even get the chance to put the Porsche in reverse before the front door opened again.

Dino walked down the steps and across the large driveway.

"Evening," Dino greeted.

"Hey."

"Kissing my sister in my driveway is not a good way to keep me liking you, D."

Damian smirked. "She's not a little girl anymore, Dino."

Dino scowled. "I'm aware."

"And I'm keeping up my end of the deal here."

"As long as she's happy."

"She is," Damian said. "I didn't expect it to be this easy."

"Give her time. Her stubbornness never fails to amaze me when it shows."

"No, that's not what I meant."

Dino crossed his arms, facing the driver's window. "Oh?"

"She's easy to care about, Dino. She makes me want to keep her happy and all that crazy nonsense. I know that's what you wanted to begin with, and I planned on doing that to the best of my ability because I owe it to you, but it has nothing to do with you anymore."

"I am not going to pretend like that bothers me," Dino said.

"Right," Damian muttered with a sneer. "Thanks."

"Why should it bother me, D? For me, this is a good thing. For her, it's still a damn good thing. I don't see what you've got to complain about, either."

"It's a dangerous thing, Dino. I've lived the majority of my life with no ties and no one to concern myself over but me. This is … different."

"Just keep doing what you're already doing, D. I'm just setting her up so she has what she needs once I can't give it to her anymore. You were a good choice. You cared about her when you were a kid and I figured that would bleed over again. So I was right, big deal. What is the problem?"

"I thought I would have to fake it."

"And you're not. Congrats, I thought of you, too. You two are a good match, D."

"She told me earlier not to fuck with her head," Damian said quietly.

"Sounds like Lily."

"She doesn't even realize she's already fucking with mine."

Dino laughed. "Well, as long as she's still alive by the end of this whole thing, I don't care what it takes. Even if that means the things she's got going on inside your head keeps you focused."

"Whatever it takes, right?"

"Right," Dino echoed. "Speaking of which, hear anything interesting?"

"By the sounds of Lily's spiel about Eve, Riley Conti is two steps away from going after the Lazarri family."

"Huh." Dino sucked air though his teeth, glancing back at the house. "I don't think anyone needs to push him along in that, really. He's already on the verge of a nervous breakdown as it is. Might as well let that dog lie until it wakes up all on its own. The Rossi family hasn't taken a side yet, however. They're still pretty neutral."

"Terrance is already pissed off at Laurent as it is over Serena."

Dino nodded his agreement. "The divide is widening. It won't take much for it to get wider."

CHAPTER TWELVE

"Holy shit," Theo hissed, grabbing the remote from Dino. He hit the volume button several times to turn it up louder. "Look at that car, Dino."

Dino stayed quiet on the couch, not even turning to respond to his brother as he said, "I see it."

"License plate was removed."

"Doesn't matter. We know who that car belongs to, Theo."

"Serena Rossi," Theo replied. "Looks like her car, doesn't it?"

Yes, Lily held back from saying.

She recognized the black Mercedes, too.

"Sure does," Dino said. "Ben called. He'll be over later."

"Is he having a fit?"

"Major one. So is Terrance. Riley is threatening retaliation for this, too."

"Christ," Theo muttered. "This is bad."

"It could get a hell of a lot worse, yet."

On the screen, the news broadcast replayed what grainy footage of the drive-by shooting that they had. It wasn't much. The black car could be seen taking a left turn before the window rolled down far enough for something to be stuck out the window. Something round, long, and black.

Lily didn't need to wonder what the item was for long because rapid assault fire blew from the window. It lit up the blackness of the car but never showed the person inside hidden by the dark tint of the window.

Once again, the video clip ended and a live shot came back on the screen. The front of the bar had taken a massive spray of bullets. The windows had been shot out and glass sparkled over the black asphalt. No one had been inside as the business was being revamped for opening the following week.

"Officials have hinted at this being related to the infamous Chicago Mob," the female reporter said. "But they have yet to give real confirmation. This bar, in particular, is owned by a high ranking member in the Chicago Mob. The Conti family has had a long running relation to the Outfit and organized crime in Chicago. Riley Corrado Conti was acquitted just months ago on several rounds of racketeering charges. This shooting is only one incident in several that have happened over the last few weeks. All have some relation to the mob or the people involved can be linked back to the Outfit."

"Officials are digging in," Theo noted.

Dino nodded, still unaffected by the entire scene. "This is really going to piss someone off."

"Terrance is already suspicious enough of Laurent and Serena. This isn't going to help Laurent's case."

"See how it rolls from here," Dino murmured. "I get why it wasn't a DeLuca or Trentini place, as far as that goes."

"How'd—" Theo's words cut off when he noticed Lily standing in the entryway to the living room. "Hey, little one."

Dino tilted his head in Lily's direction. "Morning, You're going to have to stick around the house today, Lily."

"Why?" she asked.

Lily knew why.

The broadcast said it all.

"Trouble," Dino said in explanation.

"Lots of it," Theo added.

"Why would someone shoot up a Conti business?" Lily asked, trying to sound ignorant.

"Maybe to prove a point about something," Dino answered.

"Like what?"

"Which side they're on, Lily."

"At least no one was inside," Lily said.

Dino frowned. "No one had to be for the meaning to be clear, little one."

"Oh. What time did you go to bed last night?" she asked.

"Right after Damian dropped you off."

Dino's master bedroom was directly across the hall from Lily's. She had heard him tinkering around in his room for quite a while before she fell asleep. Her brother liked to work out before he showered and went to bed.

"What side are you on, Dino?" Lily asked.

Theo coughed, failing miserably to hide his surprise.

Dino didn't do a damn thing. "That's an interesting question."

"I think it's pretty simple," she replied. "Which side?"

"Mine, of course."

Well, which side was that?

"Oh, Laurent denies it all," Ben said, frustration writing lines across his brow.

Lily continued prepping the salad while her pasta casserole finished baking in the oven. She tried to appear like she wasn't listening to the conversation between her brothers, her uncle, and Damian, but it was impossible.

They knew she was in the goddamn room. They could move to Dino's office if they wanted more privacy.

"Hard to deny it when it was caught on camera," Theo said.

"Yeah," Ben muttered, laughing bitterly. "That's what the boss said, too."

Damian leaned across the countertop and rapped his fingers down to the marble, catching Lily's attention.

"Smile," he mouthed.

Lily couldn't help it. She smiled for him like he asked.

Damian winked before turning back to the conversation at hand. "Maybe he was trying to make a point about something."

"Like what, Rossi?" Ben asked. "He's your fucking uncle. What does the guy want to prove?"

"Just saying, DeLuca. Besides, whether or not he's my uncle doesn't make a difference to his mind, all right? He's drunk half of the damned time. You know it as well as I do. Alcoholism has a way of screwing someone up and Laurent's been half cut for more years than I care to remember."

Ben's gaze narrowed. "Watch it, Rossi. Elders are still elders."

Damian lifted a single shoulder like it didn't make a difference to him either way. "Maybe he thought this would be a way to deflect all the attention on him."

"Good point," Dino said, waving at Damian. "Terrance wasn't pleased with Serena and Laurent did nothing to put his wife in her place after that mess about Lily."

"Serena didn't say anything that wasn't true," Ben replied.

Damian stiffened. "That's a bit of a stretch, Ben."

Ben DeLuca waved a hand uncaringly. "Not by much."

Lily wasn't surprised that her uncle didn't come to her defense. Ben didn't give a crap. He never had.

"Doesn't matter," Theo said firmly. "Serena has no business running her mouth about Lily or Damian. The arrangement wasn't made between Laurent and Dino. It was made between Dino and Damian. She's got no say and she knows better."

"She's always been a vocal woman," Ben said, dismissing Theo.

Theo scowled. "You defend that woman like you've got a claim on her, Uncle."

Lily didn't miss the twitch of Ben's cheek as he said, "You're toeing a thin line, Theo."

"Drop it," Dino demanded quietly. "Back to the Rossi issue."

Ben jerked his thumb in Damian's direction. "You're about to break bread with one right now. Terrance isn't pleased about this shooting mess, regardless of what Laurent is trying to say about his involvement. Cara and Lea arrived home last night."

Damian perked at that. "From Toronto?"

"Yeah, you didn't know?" Ben asked.

"No."

"Well, they are. And they said nobody left the house."

"It was Serena's car," Dino said. His tone left absolutely no room for argument. "He can't deny that."

"He can't."

"What is wrong?" Lily asked, inserting herself into the discussion, too. She probably shouldn't have. "I mean, if Laurent made a point by going after the Conti business, doesn't that show he's being loyal to Terrance?"

For the first time since Ben arrived that morning, he actually graced Lily with his attention. She wished he hadn't. Mostly, she flew under her uncle's radar and she liked it that way. This didn't feel the same at all.

"This isn't for you to concern yourself with, Lily," Ben said.

Her uncle stood from the table and walked out of the kitchen without saying another thing. Dino and Theo followed behind him shortly after. Damian stayed in his spot with his back facing Lily.

"I hate that man," she said more to herself than Damian.

"A lot of people do," her fiancé replied.

"What is the problem? Will you tell me?"

Damian spun around slowly and placed his hands to the countertop. "The problem is that Terrance wants to make peace. He sees the things happening around him. He sees his men taking sides and separating further. Riley has a great deal of loyalty on his side because he's the front boss for the Outfit."

"Meaning?"

"Meaning he's a lot closer to the guys on the streets and the crews than Terrance is. Riley has power, too, even if Terrance doesn't want to admit it."

"I don't understand what that has to do with the shooting, Damian."

Damian ran a hand through his hair, sighing. "No matter how many times Terrance says he didn't order Laurent to follow through on the shooting, Riley is at a place now where he won't believe him. No matter how many times Laurent says he didn't do it, Terrance is too angry to believe him because he has no one else to blame."

"More problems," Lily said.

"A lot more. All this did was put more of a rift between Terrance and Riley. A bigger one than what was already there before. Some crews, even part of your uncle's crew, are kicking up a fuss on Riley's behalf because of this shooting mess. DeLucas are loyal to the Trentini side of things, or they always used to be. Ben is struggling to keep his people in line for Terrance's benefit. Laurent made a huge statement for the Rossi side of things by going after the Conti business."

"What about the Lazarri thing?" Lily asked.

"That's another issue. Riley still wants blood from them; they still deny the restaurant shooting and Mia's death."

"This is a mess."

"It's not good, Lily."

"Doesn't sound like it."

Damian's demeanor changed in a blink. He winked and ticked two fingers under Lily's chin, grinning. "Don't worry about it, sweetheart. There isn't anything you can do. You've got enough going on as it is."

Like the wedding.

Lily frowned. "Eve is my maid of honor, Damian."

"I know."

"She's not picking up my calls. I tried several times earlier."

Damian's fingers ghosted over her cheekbone with a gentle touch. "I'm sorry."

Was he?

"What are we supposed to do about that?" Lily asked.

"I doubt her father is going to let her be involved with you right now, given everything that's happened. You don't know them all that well, but if my cousins are back in town, I'm sure they'd stand in as an extra couple of bridesmaids while Abriella took on Eve's role."

"Cara and Lea?"

Damian chucked. "The twins won't say no to a good party. They're two years younger than me and closer to your age."

Lily didn't want to seem ungrateful or unhappy, but she wanted Evelina as her maid of honor. Evelina was her best friend. Lily's wedding day was right around the corner. Most everything had been set, scheduled and done for the day but for a few last minute things. Dropping Evelina out of the wedding party wasn't a problem on the technical side of things. But it was a huge problem for Lily's emotional state.

"I'm not the Outfit, Damian. I didn't do this to Eve. What is so wrong with me?"

"Right now?" he asked.

"Yes."

"You have the wrong last name."

"That's not fair," Lily said.

"It doesn't have to be."

The Rossi twins were a hurricane of chatter, red hair, and laughter. Lily liked Cara and Lea almost instantly, as Damian promised she would. The two girls were so identical, it was difficult to tell them apart sometimes. If they dressed alike, Lily was positive she wouldn't be able to at all. Lily came to learn the two women spent time with family in Canada while they finished up college in Toronto.

Despite Terrance and Laurent having their issues over the shooting the week before, the Outfit boss opened his house for the twins' homecoming.

"This wedding is a big deal," Lea said. "We couldn't miss it."

"Huge," Cara agreed.

Lea nodded. "I thought Tommas would have settled down by now."

"Definitely not Damian, anyway."

"Why is that?" Lily dared to ask.

She wasn't sure she wanted to know.

Cara shrugged. "Damian is a loner. He likes his space. Getting married means he plans on sharing that with someone else. It just doesn't seem like him."

"Hey, enough of that," Damian muttered from behind Lily.

"Just telling the truth," Lea said, grinning.

"And she asked," Cara said.

With a lift of his brow, Damian silenced his cousins.

As with Lily's return to Chicago, the Rossi twins had been welcomed home the same way. An informal dinner party at the Trentini home with an open invitation to the families as guests. Lily couldn't help but notice there was a great deal fewer people milling about for the twins than there had been at hers.

Considering the mess going on, it wasn't a surprise. No one from the Conti family showed up. Even a few men Lily knew had been at hers for her uncle's sake hadn't come, either. The tension residing between the guests kept the crowd at a dull roar and little laughter was shared.

One week after someone shot up the Conti bar, and nothing was settled. Things were off in the Outfit. Even Dino hadn't shown at the welcoming home party, but Theo had. Theo dismissed his older brother missing it as something to do with work. A last minute call.

Lily didn't know if that was true or not. The dinner had been a last minute thing, so maybe that was why fewer people showed up to celebrate. Lily had a feeling that wasn't the case at all.

Emptying what bit of white wine was left in her glass, Lily told Damian, "I need a refill. You want something?"

Damian handed over his empty glass. "No, but I'd be thankful if you got rid of this for me."

"Will do."

Lily found the closest maid she could and got rid of Damian's glass and her own. She took the chance to snatch a bottle of water from the kitchen before making her way back through the large home to find Damian and his cousins.

The conversation happening between the Rossi cousins drew her attention. She knew better than to eavesdrop, but she couldn't help it. Lily stayed in the shadow of the hallway and didn't go further.

"Do you like her?" Lea asked.

Damian chuckled. "Why is that any of your concern?"

"Because we care about you, smartass," Cara replied with a roll of her blue eyes. "I'd hate to see you settled down with someone you can't stand. That doesn't seem fair to you at all."

"And Mom said—"

"Fuck Serena," Damian interrupted sharply. "I'm about done dealing with her crazy mouth. Someone needs to permanently shut that up."

"Well, I'm not going to disagree there," Cara said, snorting. "But what Lea was trying to say was that we were told it's business, D."

"It is," Damian confirmed.

"So?" Lea pressed.

"So what?"

"Come on, Damian," Lea said. "You two seem close for it being business."

"I like her," Damian said. "She's easy to like."

"At least she doesn't hate you," Cara replied.

Damian sighed. "Yet."

"What is that supposed to mean?" Lea asked.

"Nothing. So hey, I heard you two were home the night the shooting happened," Damian said quietly. "Or that's what Ben said."

Cara crossed her arms. "So?"

"You didn't see anything?" Damian asked.

"Nothing," Lea said.

Damian hummed under his breath. "No one left?"

"No," Cara said. "Not that we know of. We were pretty out of it. Long flights."

"Really long," Lea said, agreeing with her sister. "And hell, D, the only person we know who could get in and out of the house without someone knowing is you."

Damian scoffed. "That's not entirely true."

"Yes, it is," the twins said together.

"Tommas is sneaky, too, but I'm not saying he did it. Someone must have," Damian said. "It was Serena's car. Did you see the video?"

"I saw it." Cara shrugged. "Sure looked like Mom's car."

"We didn't hear a thing," Lea said again.

Damian laughed. "Yeah, Rossi kids never do."

"About this bachelorette party," Damian said.

Lily let him snag her hand with his own. "What about it?"

"Abriella is planning it, right?"

"Yes."

"Fucking great," Damian muttered.

Lily laughed and bumped him with her shoulder. "At an approved club."

"Approved by who?"

The words might as well have been spit from his mouth. Damian shoved his other hand into his pocket but Lily didn't miss the fact it was clenched into a tight little ball. His brow darkened as he eyed her from the side and his mouth was drawn tight.

Jealous.

Damian was so fucking jealous it was ridiculous.

Lily thought it looked pretty damned hot on him.

"I like that," Lily said, pointing a finger at him and making a circle.

"Hmm?"

"You're all huffy over there."

Damian cocked his head to the side. "Huffy?"

"I'm just waiting for your chest to puff up so you can beat it with your fists."

"Seriously?"

"And you say jealousy looks terrible on a person," Lily teased, smiling.

Damian shook his head, failing to hold back his chuckles. "No, I said jealousy looks terrible on you. I said nothing about how it looks on me."

"So you are."

"Hmm?"

"Jealous," Lily clarified. Before he could say a thing, Lily said, "Too late, you admitted it."

Damian's lips split with the sexiest grin. "You're awful, Lily DeLuca."

"What is that thing you always tell me?"

"You'll grow to like it."

Lily nodded. "And so will you."

Damian caught her wrists in his palms before he backed Lily into her Maserati. His body crowded hers in the best way, promising something lovely and wicked was sure to come. Lily didn't shy away from his form as he leaned over her and dragged his lips across hers softly. His teeth bit down on her lower lip, making Lily whine under her breath. She loved the bit of pain mixing in with her desire. It always made it sweeter. Damian always seemed to know, too. Her hips canted forward, driving her pelvis into something long and hard.

"Christ," Damian grunted.

"You do like this," Lily said, pushing against him again. "Deny it, I dare you."

"You really don't want to know the things going on in my head right now."

Lily winked. "Maybe I do."

Damian cursed heavily. "Stop, or I'll be forced to turn you around, bend you over, and fill you so full of my cock you won't know what to do."

"Is that a promise?"

"Wicked. You are so fucking wicked."

Damian bent down and kissed her again, his tongue sweeping across hers with damning force. Somehow, he managed to make her feel owned by his mouth alone. Lily wasn't sure if she liked that or not.

Her body sure as fuck did.

"Who approved the club, Lily?"

Well, it sounded a lot like a demand.

"Terrance," Lily whispered. "Abriella went the right route this time. Reel the asshole back in for once, Damian."

"I'll try."

Damian hummed, stepping in closer. Lily widened her stance enough to feel his lower half press at the junction between her thighs. Warmth spread from her stomach straight down to her sex. Lily shivered when Damian released her wrists just long enough to grab at her waist and hold her tight. His fingers dug in deep, making Lily's breath catch in her chest.

She couldn't help remembering where they were. Guests had begun filtering out from the Trentini home, leaving the late dinner. How many of them had a front row seat to Lily and Damian's little show?

"People might be watching," Lily warned Damian.

"Let them."

"Damian, be serious."

"I am, Lily. I like for people to know what is mine; marking my territory, so to speak. This seems like a good way to do it without pissing you off in the process."

Lily scoffed. "Right, because we both know you're entirely concerned about that."

Damian smirked. "As long as you know you're mine, we're both good."

Another shudder worked its way over her body. Her attraction to Damian only seemed to grow in intensity the more time they spent together. The darkness edging around the corners of his personality drew her in like a moth to the flame. She couldn't help but want to peel back his layers and find all the secrets hidden underneath.

Yeah, just like a moth to the flame.

Someone always ended up being burned from that.

Lily didn't want it to be her but she didn't think Damian was going to give her much of a choice.

Damian nuzzled his nose at the spot behind Lily's ear as his words whispered over her skin like silk. "And you do know you're mine, don't you, sweetheart?"

Lily bit her inner cheek and said, "I know what is yours."

"Good." Damian's fingers danced up her stomach and over her chest. Sparks bloomed on every spot he touched, waking Lily's lust up even more. It was innocent enough, sure, but it felt entirely sinful at the same time. He stepped back, giving her just enough space to breathe. "I'll keep reminding you when I think you need it."

"You don't play a clean game, Rossi."

"Nothing about me is clean, DeLuca. Which you already know. Don't act so surprised."

Lily poked him in the chest. "What are you going to do when my last name is changed, huh?"

"I'll be happy I can add another way to show you're mine. And—"

Damian's words cut off as his gaze caught something else. Lily followed his stare and noticed a dark suburban driving slowly down the road in front of the Trentini home. Terrance's driveway, blocked by an iron gate, had filled with the leaving guests getting into their cars. The gate began to open.

The hair on the back of Lily's neck prickled with the oddest sensation. Damian's hold on her tightened the closer the suburban came to the front of the driveway. Despite the unusually warm Chicago air, Lily suddenly felt cold all over.

"Oh, it's great to see them home," came a loud voice from the doorway of the large home. "I'm sure they'll be lovely in the wedding."

Lily's gaze traveled back to see Terrance giving his goodbyes to the

Rossi twins. Joel, Abriella, and their parents stood on the steps with Terrance. Ben stood in front of his boss, saying his goodbyes, too.

"Get down," Damian said.

Lily barely heard the words. "What?"

"Get down!"

Damian shoved her to the driveway with enough force to rattle her bones. Lily's skin felt the effects of the asphalt as it scraped her knees and elbows. Her cry of pain was drowned out by the shattering scream of others as rapid assault fire filled the air. The fast popping shredded what serenity had been gained from the dinner.

Lily's heart was in her throat, beating wildly out of control. Damian covered her body with his own, whispering calm assurances in her ear.

"*Shhh*, sweetheart, it's okay," Damian murmured.

Lily didn't believe him. She couldn't breathe as the fear swept over her body with damning intent. Sickness welled in her gut as she clenched her fists against the driveway. Glass exploded around them as bullets rained into her Maserati. She heard the calls of people shouting for others.

There were kids in the driveway.

Her friends were in the driveway.

Damian was in the driveway.

"We're okay," Damian told her like he knew she needed to hear it.

Lily trembled, but no matter how hard she tried, she couldn't hide her face. Damian had laid them flat beside the car for safety. She had just enough view from around the wheel well to see someone inside the black suburban toss out three glass bottles with burning rags sticking out of the tops. The bottles crashed over the top of two vehicles much closer to the gate than Lily's was. The moment the bottles broke, fire lit up across the cars, engulfing them in flames.

Damian's hands ran up and down Lily's sides, soothing her without saying another word. She still shook like a leaf in the wind, but it wasn't as bad with him there.

The screech of tires broke Lily from her daze. The black suburban disappeared before Lily could get another good look at it. Damian wasted no time rolling off her and standing. He lifted Lily's stunned, shaking body up from the ground as if she weighed nothing more than a feather.

"Hey, hey," Damian said, his tone calm and sweet in her ear.

Lily couldn't see him through the haze of panic controlling her senses.

"Lily, look at me!"

Blinking away the confusion, Lily stared at Damian's concerned features. Worry wrote lines over his brow as a frown curved his lips downward. His palms held her face tight in his hands, forcing her to keep looking at him.

"What just happened?" Lily asked, knowing but still unsure. She didn't want to admit to herself what she already knew. Not again. Why did this happen again?

Before he could answer, sirens and lights blew past the Trentini home.

"Shit," Damian hissed, glaring to the side.

Several unmarked police cruisers blocked the gate of the house, keeping anyone inside from leaving. Police spilled from the vehicles with guns drawn while several more unmarked cars with their lights flashing brightly continued on down the road in the direction of the black suburban.

Lily's confusion only climbed higher. "Why are they here? How did they—"

"Issues with the mob," Damian said quickly in explanation. "We've been all over the news. Terrance was bound to have somebody watching his goddamn house. What did you see, Lily?"

Unable to answer Damian because her lungs just wouldn't work properly, Lily stared around at the mess instead. People were helping others off the ground. A lot of guests seemed to have hit the pavement like Lily and Damian had. At the front of the house where the Trentini family had been standing with her uncle and the Rossi twins, a far more devastating scene took shape.

People were shouting, shoving … others on the ground, unmoving. Red stained the pristine white door. Cara Rossi sobbed, her fists shoved in her mouth as she cried out. Tommas rushed up the stairs to his sister's side.

Where was the other Rossi twin?

Where was Lea?

"Ben!" someone shouted.

Lily's ears felt like they were ringing from the gunfire and the catacomb of sounds surrounding her now. She couldn't concentrate enough to understand what the people on the stairs said to one another, but there was fear all over their actions, in their shaking hands and the tears streaking down their faces.

Theo clamored up the steps after Tommas. "Ben!"

Terrance fell back from one of the bodies on his front steps. He put his hands out in front of him, his gaze trained in on the morbid red covering his skin.

"Lea!" Laurent screamed.

Serena Rossi's devastated cry followed her husband's from somewhere down with the rest of the people in the driveway.

God.

More blood.

So much more.

"Lily!" Damian snapped.

He tilted her chin up so he could look down into her eyes in that intense way of his that stopped her heart and made her think there was so much more to this man than she could ever possibly know. She was trying so desperately to keep from falling for him, but something about him that she couldn't deny spoke to her. Something that kept making her trip over her own two feet, surprising her at every turn.

She was falling fast and hard.

He wasn't even trying.

Damian swept his thumb over her trembling lips. "What did you see?"

"Nothing," Lily said quickly. "I saw nothing."

For him, Lily would never see anything.

It had nothing to do with the Outfit.

It was Damian.

Damian nodded. "That's right, sweetheart. It's always nothing."

The hospital emergency room was packed to the rim. Every time Lily turned around, more people seemed to flood the waiting chairs. But with no seats left to take, people were left hanging around doors and littering the outside with cigarettes.

Shaking hands, quiet murmurs, and paranoid stares had become common place. Guessing by some of the discussions filtering in around Lily, she knew the families were pissed and planning. This—whatever this attack had been—would not go unanswered.

War, someone hissed.

Going to the mattresses, said another.

Lily felt sick.

Barely anyone talked to Lily and Damian as they stayed close together in a corner while they waited on news. Some had already come. News that wasn't good and cut as deeply as it could get. Damian seemed calm on the outside, but Lily had to wonder if it was nothing more than a lie. The man wore too many masks for her to tell.

Lea Rossi died thirty minutes after being admitted into an OR for surgery. She'd lost far too much blood and by the time the paramedics reached the scene, there was very little they could do. The cops, with their barricades and questions, refused to let anyone leave the confines of the Trentini estate. The Rossi family received the news about their daughter while police hounded them with questions.

That was how they found out Lea died.

Lily suppressed a shudder, remembering the sound of Cara's cries. It was not an easy thing to hear, but it was even worse to learn the news with people and cops surrounding you. There was no privacy for the family, no seclusion for their hearts to break.

No, their pain simply shattered over wet asphalt while guests and police looked on.

The black suburban hadn't been found. Cops lost the trail as far as Lily understood.

"I'm sorry," Lily told Damian for what felt like the hundredth time.

Damian squeezed her knee tightly. "Don't be."

"But—"

His blue eyes burned into hers with not a sign of wetness behind the irises.

"Don't be," Damian repeated. "I chose this."

CHAPTER THIRTEEN

Damian walked through the quiet ICU with a smooth stride and his head down. Snatching the white lab coat off the back of a nurse's chair while the guy was distracted by a pretty face had been easy enough. It appeared like Damian's attention was thoroughly engrossed by the information on the clipboard he'd stolen from a station outside of the ICU, but actually, he was surveying the people around him.

Like always, barely anyone noticed him as he strolled through the hospital's unit with his white lab coat, dark slacks, and the stethoscope slung carelessly around his neck as any good doctor would do. Between work, patients, and visitors, the nurses on staff were kept busy and constantly moving from one thing to the next. They didn't have time to question the unknown doctor on the floor who could be there simply by request of another doctor or patient's family.

Ben, being a high ranking member in the Outfit, had been appointed a guard by Terrance's request, but Damian had watched that man, too. He had a habit of running down to the cafeteria to grab a bite to eat at lunch and then he was relieved by another guard around supper. He was rarely gone more than ten, fifteen minutes at the most.

But it was enough time.

The drawn blinds on room 6B gave a bit of privacy as Damian stepped inside and closed the door. He locked the door even though he didn't believe someone would interrupt his time. Damian didn't bother to flick the lights on in the room as he glanced around at the beeping machines showing life and making their usual noise. The steady hiss of oxygen and the pump of the ventilator echoed in the space.

Ben DeLuca laid beneath stark white sheets, tucked safely in their confines. The man's eyes were shut and he stayed prone on the bed as Damian crossed the space to get a better look at him. A tube inserted through Ben's throat was attached to the ventilator, keeping him breathing and alive.

For now.

Comatose.

Well, as long as the doctors planned to keep him that way, anyway. The three bullets that the man took shattered a vertebra, tore a bad hole through Ben's right lung, and the third lodged just above his temple. He would likely never walk again, be paralyzed from the shoulders up, and life wouldn't be what it once had been for the DeLuca king.

But he was alive.

The coma had been nothing more than a medical decision designed to give Ben's older body a chance to recover more without pain, emotional distress, and distractions. The ventilator had been needed to support Ben's damaged lungs. According to Dino and the paperwork Ben's wife Carmela received in order to continue on with the medically induced coma, Ben would have a better chance of long term recovery—as best that could be expected—if they went this route.

That couldn't happen at all.

Lily DeLuca needed to be safe in all aspects.

Ben was a problem when it came to that. Hell, the man was a problem because he simply decided he didn't like Damian. Even from a hospital bed, the man could cause problems. The power of a frail, manipulative man should never be underestimated.

Especially once everything was found out. Lily would always be safe. That didn't make Damian any less pissed.

Every single time he thought about the eight bullet holes in the back of Lily's Maserati, his rage boiled, threatening to take him under with the poisoned heat. Too close. That had been far too close.

Setting the useless clipboard aside, Damian unbuttoned the dress shirt he wore underneath the stolen lab coat. Ben's chest continued to rise and fall in a rhythmic fashion alongside the ventilator's timing.

The monitors keeping track of Ben's heartbeat and breathing from the three leads attached to his chest became a game of sorts to Damian. He watched the lines strike up with every heartbeat and the green line monitoring breathing function fly up in time with the ventilator. Every minute or so, the screens would blink out and reset themselves. It gave a quick few second interval that Ben's vitals weren't being monitored.

The ventilator itself was on an entirely different monitor. There were no leads attached for that particular device, but Damian knew it would send out a warning sound to the front station if it was somehow turned off.

Damian didn't plan on turning it off.

Not a flicker of hesitation or concern could be found in Damian's emotions as he continued watching the monitors and Ben's lifeless figure. His own heartrate was calm and his breathing steady. Never had killing someone felt so entirely natural to Damian. He'd always thought a lot about his victims before a job was done, but this one didn't feel the same at all.

Lily had a lot to do with that, of course.

When the monitors blinked out again, resetting their tables, Damian quickly unplugged the leads coming from Ben's chest to the monitor. Before the machines could recognize that they no longer had a set of wires to track, Damian attached another set of leads into the machines.

Earlier, after he'd grabbed the lab coat with the nametag attached, he'd used it to get inside a supply room. There, he'd found vital leads in designated bins. Quickly, so he couldn't be caught, he followed the instructions on the covering of the underside of the sticky leads and attached all three leads to his own chest and abdomen.

As the monitor finally reset itself, Damian watched as his own vitals lit up the screen. There was little to no change between his heartrate and what Ben's had been. Keeping an eye on the ventilator breathing for Ben, Damian inhaled and exhaled in time with the machine so that the green line monitoring breathing function would remain the same, too. As long as the monitors continued reading that everything was normal, the ventilator would remain stable and without warning.

Damian waited for the monitor to blink out again. When it did, he slipped the oxygen monitor clamped over Ben's finger onto his own. Now, the blue line keeping track of the oxygen saturation inside the body wouldn't read anything different, either.

"You'll get it a hell of a lot easier than most of my hits have, Ben," Damian said, knowing the man couldn't hear him anyway.

Damian reached over and unclipped the ventilator tube from the attachment at Ben's mouth. Air hissed from the tube as the machine pushed a steady stream of oxygen through. Immediately, Ben's chest decompressed from the lack of air.

Damian continued breathing in time with the now useless machine. The monitors never changed. They never gave off the warnings they should have to the front desk as a patient was dying in his bed.

A shadow crossed the blind covered windows in front of Ben's room but kept on going straight past. Damian waited a good three minutes and then he waited another two. All the while, his breathing stayed steady and his choices never faltered.

When he was sure Ben DeLuca's heart had stopped beating or his brain function would be seriously impacted by the loss of oxygen, Damian waited for the machines to reset once more. He unplugged his leads from the machine and replaced them with Ben's again. He pulled the oxygen clamp from his index finger and slid it back over Ben's. Damian pressed hard around the rubbery material so any evidence of his fingerprint inside would be gone or smudged with Ben's and he replaced the breathing tube to the apparatus on Ben's mouth. The man's chest began to rise and fall again with the help of the machine, but Damian knew it was already too late.

The machines finally started beeping with their warnings. Flat lines showed across every vital sign.

No life recorded.

No heartbeat.

There was always a slight delay, but not much, before the machines at the front station would show the warnings as well. Damian had watched them over the last couple of days as he and Lily came and went, visiting the few people who had been caught in the crossfire of the Trentini home shooting.

How easily they overlooked a killer. Damian didn't even care anymore. Being able to blend in meant he was just another face in the crowd. His job was so much easier because of others stupid mistakes.

Still unconcerned and calm, Damian buttoned his shirt back up, grabbed the clipboard and left the room. He didn't close the door as he stepped outside and turned to walk back down the hallway in the same way he came. Keeping his gaze down on the unknown patient's paperwork, Damian slipped outside the doors of the ICU, glancing back in just enough time to see nurses rush into Ben DeLuca's hospital room.

Damian had carefully chosen his time to hit Ben DeLuca. With the time at five minutes after twelve in the afternoon, the hospital was just beginning its lunch rush. Staff worked to serve the patients outside of the unit while other nurses, doctors, and hospital employees made their way down to ground level where the cafeteria was located. Family members of patients in the large hospital swarmed the place with takeout as they came and went.

Elevators filled with souls and Damian was lost in the sea of people. Taking the lab coat off, he folded it up and tucked it under his arm. He dumped the clipboard into an unsuspecting nurse's bag as he stood behind her in the elevator. When nobody was looking, he pulled the light brown, short haired wig off, bunched it up, and tossed it into a garbage can as he walked out of the elevator with five other people surrounding him.

Just another face.

Another patient's family member.

Damian walked out of the hospital and didn't look back.

"Handsome," Lily appraised, her hands fluttering over the lapels of Damian's tux.

"Oh?"

"Very."

Lily's demure smile sent a shot of lust straight down to his cock. She acted like she didn't even know.

Damian stayed still while Lily checked the buttons on his tux. He knew she didn't need to. This was the third time he'd gone through a fitting with her. The girl was particular, especially where the wedding was concerned. It seemed like planning for the wedding and getting all the last-minute details together had become a sort of stress reliever for Lily. Damian was more than willing to feed into that for her. When she'd come over to his apartment earlier, he did everything she asked just to give her something else to focus on other than the people in the hospital and the Outfit's mess.

"Dino got a call today," Lily said quietly.

"Did he?" Damian asked.

"Yes."

"About what?"

Lily looked up at him through her thick lashes. "Are you telling me you don't know?"

"Well, I asked didn't I?"

She continued fussing with his tux, saying nothing more.

"Lily," Damian said.

"*Hmm*."

"Tell me what the phone call was about."

"Ben."

Ah.

"I heard," Damian said.

Lily tapped her fingers on his chest, catching his gaze. "It's practically unexplainable. The records show his machines were functioning properly and then suddenly ..."

"Flat line."

"Aunt Carmela is in a panic."

"How long had they been married?" Damian asked, helping her with the knot on his tie.

"Thirty-seven years," Lily answered.

"A long time."

"She's more concerned about the final Will and Testament than his death. She was on the phone with the lawyers according to Theo."

Damian sighed. "Death brings greed."

"Something like that." Lily grew silent as she ran her hands over his tux once more. "They're opening an investigation into Ben's death. They're calling it suspicious."

He wasn't worried. Nothing would be found.

"On the hospital's part?" he asked.

"Apparently."

"Medical malpractice, maybe."

Lily nodded. "Maybe. But maybe you should get rid of that lab coat in your garbage can, Damian."

Damian turned to stone. He'd tossed the lab coat earlier, planning to burn it with some other shit that needed to disappear. Lily showing up at his place unexpectedly when she was supposed to be at Dino's all day had put a kink in those plans. She'd walked into his apartment with one of those frilly coffee drinks she liked so much and then tossed it into the same garbage can he used to dispose of the coat temporarily.

He hadn't even realized his mistake.

Jesus Christ.

It wasn't like Damian to make those kinds of errors.

When Lily came into the picture, Damian's mind went to a completely different place. She was fucking him up left and right but he didn't know if it was a good thing or a bad thing. Nothing about her expression said she was disgusted or angry about finding the lab coat. She wasn't trying her damnedest to get as far away from him as she could, either.

This was not the Lily that Damian thought he knew. He couldn't deny that he liked this unfazed attitude she sported. If their lives were going to be permanently intertwined through marriage, it likely wouldn't be the first time she found something that connected him to a hit. And even if she didn't find something, the girl knew what he was.

"Lily—"

"I saw nothing," Lily murmured, slipping his powder blue tie under the matching vest. "For you, I see nothing."

Well, then …

"Don't you want to know why?" Damian asked.

"As you told me once, a death always means something to someone. His means little to me, so no, I don't care about why. I'm more curious about how."

Damian caught her wandering hands, needing her to be still for a moment. "Ghost."

Lily didn't drop his stare as she said, "I figured."

"Why?" Damian asked.

"Why what?"

"Why don't you care that you found something like that?"

Lily shrugged. "Because I care about you."

Oh.

When her hand skimmed the crotch of his tux pants for the fifth time, Damian smirked. She'd done it more than enough to have his cock hard. The ridge of his erection strained against the smooth fabric. No doubt, she could feel what her light grazes had done to him.

"What game are you playing, Lily?"

She looked up at him with those brown eyes of hers. Nothing about the smile she gave him said innocence. The girl knew exactly what she was doing. "Hmm?"

"You come over here today for a fitting and we both know the damn suit fits me perfectly. What are you really here for?"

Lily's fingers slid along the waist of his pants. She dipped below the band of his boxer-briefs, her fingers threading into the dark hair leading down to his cock. Just the feeling of her hand close to his dick had Damian growing harder by the second.

"You're busy lately," Lily said.

"Sorry."

"I'm busy, too."

"You are," he agreed.

"So I needed an excuse to come see you. This seemed like a good one and it worked to get you settled for an hour."

Damian glanced at the clock. "Two, actually."

"Can we make it a day?" Lily asked sweetly.

A thick, heady groan caught in Damian's throat as Lily's hand slipped further into his pants and circled his aching shaft. Her palm was soft and hot against the sensitive skin of his dick. She stroked him from the base to the tip and kept her eyes locked on his all the while. Her teeth cut into her bottom lip in the sexiest way as her hand tightened just enough to have the air rushing out of his lungs.

"Holy shit," Damian hissed.

How long had it been since he fucked or even felt this beautiful girl under him?

Too long.

She was right; they had been busy with life and nonsense.

"Fuck, keep doing that," Damian demanded when Lily's hand loosened around his dick.

"How about something different?" Lily asked with a wink.

Before Damian could ask what she meant, Lily was on her knees. His ability to speak was fucking lost as she unbuttoned, unzipped, and pushed his pants down around his hips. His boxer-briefs quickly took the same path. Damian grappled for the closest thing he could find for support as the crest of his cock rubbed against Lily's silky, pink lips. That just happened to be her hair.

Lily didn't seem to mind as he fisted the blonde strands between his fingers. She just smiled in the most sinful way, flashing her white teeth up at him as her gaze glimmered with lust.

Fuck.

"Can we make it a day?" she asked, wrapping her hand around the base of his cock.

Something demure and wicked coated her voice. The low, gravelly tone of her words struck him straight in the chest and shot down to his steel-hard length in her hand. He shivered as she stroked him softly but used the tip of her manicured nail to drag along the pulsing vein on the underside of his shaft.

Christ.

"Damian ..."

He blinked out of the daze. "Yeah, we can make it a day, sweetheart."

"Good. I like to play while I suck."

Damian's throat felt dry. "Play?"

"Getting you off gets me off. So when you're fucking my mouth, I'll be getting myself off, too. Sound good?"

"Sounds perfect," Damian said, barely holding back his groan.

With those words, her free hand disappeared under the skirt of her dress. Damian's heart raced as silken, warm lips encompassed his length. Her mouth was a hot, wet paradise. A lot like her fucking pussy. Lily sucked him off slow at first, working her hand at the base of his shaft to the same rhythm as her mouth. Her cheeks hollowed the harder she pulled on his dick and her grip on him tightened, making his stomach clench with anticipation.

There was something about seeing her on her knees like that, taking his dick in her mouth as she watched him above her. The sensation of her tongue pressing to the vein on the underside of his length as her teeth scraped along the swollen head was nearly enough to push Damian over the edge.

Good God. Lily could suck dick.

Damian's grip in her hair tightened as the telltale signs of Lily's masturbating began to mimic the noise of her sucking on his dick. The quiet, wet sounds of her fingers fucking her own pussy drove him insane.

Never once did she look away from him.

Lily let go of his cock and pulled her skirt higher. It gave him a view of her panties pushed aside and her fingers diving into her sex over and over. Juices soaked her fingers. Her thighs shook.

"Fuck, that's hot," Damian managed to mumble. "Let go for a second."

Lily grinned the best she could around his cock before releasing it with a pop. "Why?"

He didn't give her a reply. He simply held the base of his cock and directed it back toward her mouth. Lily opened up and his dick slid past her plump lips and over her tongue as she took his shaft all the way to the base without any trouble.

"Close your mouth," Damian demanded.

Lily swallowed around his cock and he could feel her throat clench as she shut her mouth. Hard, but not quite as fast as when she had been

173

sucking him off, Damian fucked her mouth while he fisted her hair. Her throat relaxed and her gaze darkened as the sounds of her fingers fucking her pussy started up again.

Saliva slicked up his cock and her lips, making a tiny trail at the corner of Lily's mouth as it leaked out. He could feel his heart beating hard in his chest the closer he came to coming. His hands trembled but were hidden in her hair.

"Fucking beautiful," Damian grunted.

Lily blinked as her mouth tightened around his dick in the best way.

Damian couldn't breathe. "Fuck, fuck, fuck."

He came harder than he expected to, but Lily took every drop of his come he gave. His back tensed as heat gripped his spine in a smothering grip. Lily released his dick just as her own orgasm raced visibly over her body. Damian took in the sight of her mouth open, damp with her spit and his come, while her eyes clamped shut and her body rocked into her own hand.

Yeah, so fucking beautiful.

Lily licked her bottom lip as she ran her wet fingers over the head of Damian's dick He was still hard. Just thinking about this woman got him that way.

"A day?" she asked softly.

"All day," Damian said.

"We good?" Damian asked.

"Yeah, I just checked," Dino said on the other end of the phone call. "Lily's out for the night. Christ, she barely made it to her bedroom. What did you two do today?"

Damian smirked. No way in hell was he answering that question. Dino did not want to know what Damian had done that tired Lily out so goddamn much over the course of a day and evening. Dino likely wouldn't want to know considering it involved a bed, no clothes, and a whole lot of sweet sounds from Lily.

"Let's just get to work," Damian said instead.

"All right. I'll open the gate for you. I'll meet you in the back. I've got it covered, so just leave shit alone until I get in there. Sound good?"

"Perfect, man."

Damian hung up the phone and dropped it into the passenger seat. The electronically controlled gate opened not five seconds later. He cut the lights on the Porsche as he drove up Dino's large driveway, not wanting to risk the chance the headlights might somehow wake Lily up. The night was going to be a long one, but if Damian could help it, he didn't want it to be a fucking messy one. That meant getting Dino's job done quickly, quietly, and without anyone knowing.

Including Lily.

Damian parked his car in the driveway where he always did and shut off the engine. Once he was sure the house was going to stay dark, Damian left his car and jogged the length of the DeLuca home. In the backyard, Dino had a large storage building that wasn't attached to the garage or house. A single, small light exposed a garage door entrance and small metal side door. Damian chose the side door.

Inside the building that was slightly smaller than a two-door garage, Damian waited for Dino. He didn't bother to turn on any lights because he didn't know where in the hell the switch for them was.

The side door opened, haloing Dino in the glow of light from outside. Dino hit the lights, illuminating the space in color. Damian's gaze was drawn to the large, long shape covered by a dark tarp.

"Ready to get this done?" Dino asked.

"Absolutely," Damian replied.

"All the tools we need to chop it down are in this garage. We'll beat the hell out of anything even remotely recognizable with hammers until it's a twisted mess. Once it's nothing but bits and parts, I'll call a friend to come get the pieces and take it to a junkyard."

Damian nodded. "As long as they can keep their mouth shut."

Dino chuckled. "It won't even look anything like what it used to by the time we're done. How are you with mechanics?"

"All right. I can check my oil and change my own tire."

"Can you run a wrench?"

Damian snorted. "What the fuck do I look like to you, some city grown kid?"

"You are city grown," Dino said.

True.

That didn't mean Damian was a fucking fool.

"I can run a wrench," Damian muttered.

"Power tools?" Dino asked.

Damian cocked a brow. "Yes."

"Perfect."

Dino grabbed the edge of the dark tarp and pulled hard. Beneath the tarp sat a familiar black suburban. At the sight of the vehicle, Damian's anger over Dino's carelessness at the Trentini home shooting rushed back.

"Still can't believe you almost—"

"Oh, shut up about that," Dino barked, flipping Damian with the middle finger before his companion could get out another word. "I fucking told you it was all good."

"You shot her car up!"

Dino rolled his eyes. "For fuck's sake, D, her car couldn't be the only one in that driveway without bullet holes. Don't you think that would look just a little bit suspicious?"

"We were standing right beside it," Damian growled. "Theo was in the driveway, too!"

"Theo has a cherry red Stingray with racing stripes. Lily's car is bright yellow for a goddamn reason. I took the right shots knowing where they were. You knew I was going to be there, and you handled it like you were supposed to. What is the problem, Damian?"

Damian knew exactly what the problem was even though he didn't want to admit his mistake out loud to Dino. He'd been distracted by Lily at the Trentini home and nearly missed seeing Dino's arrival. Because of that, Lily had almost been hurt. The guilt Damian felt over that was manifesting as anger toward Dino.

"That is not the point, Dino."

"Seriously, what the hell is wrong with you?" Dino asked.

"Nothing. Let's just get this done."

"This is about Lily, isn't it?"

Obviously, Damian thought.

"It's like you didn't even think about her, Dino," Damian said. "Did you think it was going to get this big? Did you think it was going to be this bad? Did you realize how fast this would spiral out of control?"

Dino shook his head. "You're right, it blew up a lot bigger than I thought it would but there's nothing wrong with that, either. It's done. We move on."

Damian's frustration level rose higher. "Ben's dead. You got what you wanted, Dino."

"Yeah, but did you get what you wanted?" Dino asked.

How could he truthfully answer that question? In the simple span of a couple of short months, the things Damian thought he wanted had changed. He was still fully convinced that he was happy in his role doing what he was doing in the Outfit. He wasn't looking to move higher or have more control. But then Lily flickered into his mind and he couldn't help but to consider her, too.

The wedding had never once been a ruse. From the moment Dino approached Damian about his plans, it had been made perfectly clear the marriage would need to happen for Lily's sake. Dino wanted his sister safe, he wanted her to be cared for, and he believed that to make sure her protection and happiness was always guaranteed, she would need to be settled into a safe marriage of good standing.

Because Lily was affiliated to the Outfit, regardless if she wanted to be or not, there would always be a risk that someone else could take control if Dino couldn't. That was where Damian stepped in.

But that girl ... that woman hadn't been anything like what he thought she would be. Instead of simply treating Lily and the marriage as the duty it should have been—the debt Damian was required to pay—he'd ended up letting her in. She got under his skin in the best way, made herself a little home there, and now he was fucking stuck like that.

Damian knew loyalty better than most. Dino earned Damian's a long time ago, but now he was wondering if it was worth the price.

"It's more than Ben," Dino said firmly. "It was always more than Ben."

"For you or for me?" Damian asked.

Dino smiled a cold sight. "Both."

Damian wasn't surprised. He'd never once thought that Dino forgave the people around him for doing what they had back when he and his siblings were younger. Like the smart man he was, Dino waited patiently before striking back.

"I thought you were the one who told Lily not to blame the gun," Damian said quietly.

"Right now, the people are the gun. I'm correcting that shit before it gets worse."

Was he?

Damian didn't know what to believe anymore.

"Let's just get this done," Dino said with a nod at the black suburban.

"Yeah, let's do that."

Damian took the ratchet gun Dino offered and squeezed the trigger to test the tool. It zinged with a loud sound, ready to be put to work.

"I'll get to work on removing the doors, hood, bumpers and back," Dino said. "You get to work on the tires and interior."

Damian didn't care. "Whatever."

Two hours later, the suburban had nearly three quarters of its major parts removed and set aside. It was starting to look like nothing more than a shell of a vehicle. Once it was down to the frame and chassis, Damian and Dino could take a torch and saw to the steel and cut it apart, too. Then, it really would be nothing but scrap metal to be taken away.

Nothing to find.

Vanished.

Damian lifted the mask from his face. He'd put it on earlier to keep from ingesting too much dust and grime as they worked. "How'd you lose the cops that day?"

Dino didn't look down as he ripped off the material covering the suburban's roof. "Hit a small back road quickly and kept going until I was clear. They must have took a different route. I never saw them once."

"Lucky," Damian said.

"Something like that."

"Do you think Theo knows?"

Dino chuckled. "Theo suspects I've had a hand in certain things. Or rather, he believes I've had a hand in pushing certain individuals along. I've never confirmed or denied anything."

Just like how Damian never lied. He omitted a great deal of things. He talked around a lot of shit. His game was good, sure. Lying didn't factor into that at all.

Dino glanced over his shoulder at Damian. "Is there something else on your mind, or what?"

"Yes."

"Spit it out, D."

Damian blew out a harsh breath. "So you shot up the restaurant, which just happened to work in your favor with Mia's death and now Riley's threats of retaliation. You've got the Rossi family fighting with the Contis and the Trentinis."

Dino barked out a laugh. "You did the Rossi mess, Damian."

True enough.

"You wanted a wider divide," Damian said.

"And you could have done that in a million other ways," Dino argued. "Yet you chose to fuck with your aunt and uncle. Why was that?"

Damian refused to provide an answer.

Apparently, Dino wasn't looking for one. "Don't bother. We both know. You're looking to mess their shit up, too. And it worked, so shut your mouth about it. You're no better than me, Damian, you're just sneakier about it. Watch that or it might bite you on the ass someday."

Yeah, Damian doubted that.

"The DeLuca side of things still haven't made a hard and fast choice for either side," Damian said. "Ben's gone, the divide between the four families is so big, you couldn't throw a rock and hit the other side."

"What are you dancing around?" Dino asked.

"What is left? Who's left?"

"The boss."

Damian should have known that.

When Dino first discussed his plans with Damian, there had been no mention of dividing the families. Not like they had ended up, anyway. The issues with the Poletti hit simply tipped the scales in Dino's favor.

It gave a justifiable, reasonable way to keep total suspicion off the restaurant shooting as being an inside job. Dino chose to run with it. Damian had no other choice but follow behind. Like with everything else, the issue only grew. The paranoia grew. Riley Conti's anger helped to cover

Dino and Damian's tracks further.

No one really knew that they were fighting for nothing.

Well, not nothing. They just weren't fighting for the right reasons.

"Are we going after him for me or for you?" Damian finally asked, repeating his earlier words.

"Both."

Well, that answered everything, didn't it?

The anger Damian had been holding back about the bullet holes in Lily's car finally spilled over. He couldn't control it any longer.

"Eight!" Damian shouted.

Dino didn't even flinch from Damian's show of rage. "Eight what?"

"Eight bullet holes across the bumper of her Maserati. Two more went through the back windshield!"

"It's a car, Damian. We'll get it fixed."

"That is not the fucking point," Damian hissed.

"You're dancing a thin line," Dino warned.

Damian was damn well ready to jump the hell over it.

"Too close, Dino. That was too close for comfort."

"Like I said—"

"Too close."

Dino sighed. "Her vehicle wasn't the only one with bullet holes."

"She could have been inside."

Didn't Dino realize that?

"She wasn't."

"She could have been!" Damian yelled, his anger boiling over.

"You made sure she wasn't."

CHAPTER FOURTEEN

Lily padded into the dark, empty kitchen. Pulling a glass out of the cupboard, she tipped the cup under the sink faucet and turned on the water. She'd woken up out of a dead sleep for no other reason than her throat was dry and she needed a drink.

Sipping from the water, she stared out the kitchen window into the driveway. A familiar blue Porsche caught her eye instantly. She nearly dropped the damn glass. Damian's car was parked beside hers and guessing by the dew drops gathering on the blue paint, it had been there quite a while.

He hadn't mentioned needing to come over. In fact, Lily was positive Damian said he had work to do and might not even see her the next day. Their wedding was just two weeks away; Lily didn't mind that he had business to handle because she could always use a day to make sure everything was going smoothly with the two wedding event coordinators that Dino hired. Besides that, Lily had taken up two summer online classes for credits she needed in order to be ahead of the game for school in the fall.

She had a lot of stuff going on.

Damian did, too.

Why hadn't he told her he was coming over?

The digital microwave clock blinked 4AM. More confused than ever, Lily turned the garage light on and looked out the window connecting the garage to the kitchen. Dino's white Bentley wasn't parked beside Lily's Maserati. Damian promised to have her car repaired before the wedding but Lily had been using Dino's car to run errands or to do whatever else she needed in the day. Her brother was too busy trying to keep a firm handle on the DeLuca crew with Theo to be worrying about his car.

But now Dino's car was gone, too.

Listening for any sounds in the house, Lily couldn't hear a thing. Nothing that said her brother and Damian were inside, anyway. Lily dumped the remaining water from her glass down the drain, keeping an eye on Damian's car at the same time.

She figured it didn't matter. Maybe Dino and Damian had business and met up or something. Padding back through the dark house, Lily came to a stop at the foot of the stairwell. The faintest sound, something Lily was sure she had never heard before, hummed from the back of the house. The noise got louder, like metal grinding on metal.

What in the hell was that?

Annoyed, Lily made her way to the back of the house quickly. She slipped on her ballet flats and pushed open the back door leading to the deck. Darkness covered the back property except toward Dino's small storage shed at the far end. White light spilled from the open garage door as sparks flew. Smoke and dust billowed out around the halo of light, illuminating a figure bending down with some kind of tool as the person worked on what looked like a … vehicle? Or rather, the frame of some kind of vehicle.

Maybe she should have turned around, went back inside the house, and pretended like she hadn't seen a thing, but something inside Lily's gut wouldn't let her. Before she even understood her own actions, Lily had walked down the steps of the deck and was half way across the back yard.

The closer she came to that grinding sound and the man in the light, the worse she felt. The tightest sensation wrapped around her heart, filling it to the brim with dread and making every beat hurt.

When Lily was just a few steps away from the garage door, her heart might as well have fell from her chest and shattered across the lawn. The vehicle … She knew that vehicle. She knew the shape of it because the image of it had permanently imprinted itself inside her memories ever since that shooting at the Trentini home. It didn't matter that all that was left of the vehicle was nothing more than a steel frame and twisted black metal.

No, Lily *knew.*

The torch lit up again, blowing into the chassis. The man dropped the tool and picked up what looked like a grinder of some sort. Sparks flew everywhere, lighting up the mask the person wore to protect his face. The awful grinding sound started up again, making Lily cringe from the volume of the noise. Lily's ears ached and the terrible stench the grinder created as it cut through the hot steel burned her nose.

Lily turned on her heel, needing to get away from that vehicle and what it all meant. She didn't make it very far. The grinder shut off just as she took her first few steps. She heard a muffled curse before the familiar voice became a hell of a lot clearer.

"Lily?"

No.

Why?

Everything inside screamed those two simple words. Nothing was right. Everything was so terribly wrong and foul.

Lily spun on her heel in the dewy grass. "Why?"

Damian dropped the welding mask to the cement floor of the building. "Lily—"

"Why is that here?" she interrupted, her voice barely breaking a whisper.

"It's nothing, Lily."

Lily scoffed, dark and hateful. "Right. It's *nothing*. Tell me that's not the vehicle used in the Trentini shooting. Tell me that!"

Damian didn't look away as he said, "I can't."

"Because it is."

"Yes," he confirmed quietly.

Lily's heart broke all over again. "*Why?*"

"Dino—"

No, Lily didn't want to hear that, either. She turned toward the house and bolted as fast as she could away from Damian. The sound of the tool he'd been holding echoed with a bang as he dropped it to the cement floor.

"Lily!"

What had her brother done? That vehicle could only mean one thing. Dino had a hand in the shooting. He'd nearly killed her in the process. And Damian ... he was helping to dispose of the evidence. Damian knew, too.

Oh, God.

Memories and things Lily had overlooked flew into her mind one after the other. Whispered conversations and offhanded remarks made by Dino or even Damian at times.

"This shit happens."

"Right now we have to focus on keeping what is important safe, which I thought someone already understood that."

"She was safe, man."

"Someday, she might actually understand."

"Which side are you on?"

"My side, of course."

"Obviously someone is out to prove a point with someone else in the Outfit ..."

"... sometimes it's better to bide your time, little one. Not everything is black and white."

There was so much. Too much. Lily, blind and dumb to her brother and his schemes, had passed over everything without so much as a question.

Then, there was Damian. That probably hurt her the very most. She'd spent a great deal of the last day in Damian's bed. Her body could still feel the aftereffects of their lovemaking hours after it had ended. Damian touched her like he cared, like he wanted her. He'd made her believe that.

How much of it was nothing but lies?

Had that been a part of whatever plans Dino had, too?

Bile rose in the back of her throat the closer she came to the house. Fresh, hot tears streaked down her cheeks. Nothing had ever felt quite as hurtful before. Betrayal stung on her tongue, making her sicker than ever.

"Lily, just wait," Damian said.

She'd almost made it to the steps but he caught her first. Damian's hands, ones she let touch and learn her body, grabbed onto her wrists and spun her around fast to face him. The moment he released her, she swung at him with all her might. Her palm connected with his cheek, the crack reverberating across the nearly silent backyard. Damian tensed and snapped back from her like he was worried she might smack him again.

"You fucking asshole!" Lily shouted, letting the tears fall freely. "You lied to me!"

Damian licked the spot of blood from his bottom lip and rubbed at his jaw. "Fuck, you've got a mighty swing."

Lily held back her scream of frustration. "You're lucky it was just the one."

"Don't hit me again."

"I beg your pardon? Where in the hell do you get off telling me anything after what I just saw you doing?"

Damian took a step forward, closer to Lily. She backed up one, needing the space. "Just like I said. Don't hit me again. I've never hit you. I would never hit you. Don't hit me."

Lily's sobs caught in her throat, choking her. "Where is my brother?"

"Gone. He got a call from Tommas an hour ago. Riley finally retaliated. The Rossi crew took a mighty hit. Terrance wanted the men to gather and discuss what they were going to do from here on out."

She didn't give a damn.

"You lied to me."

Damian shook his head. "I have never lied."

"Oh, really?" Lily pointed at the shell of a vehicle Damian had been working on. "What do you call that? All of the stuff that's been happening, you've been doing that. You knew and didn't tell me. My friend's mother and your own cousin! You're a sneaky, lying—"

Damian stepped forward, clamped a hand over Lily's mouth, and grabbed her tight. "Hush. I did not do all of it. In fact, I did very fucking little. The only thing I did do was keep you safe while it was happening. Goddamn, Lily, stop it and listen to me."

She struggled in his hold, mumbling curses and anything else she could think to spew at him. She didn't want him touching her or near her. There was no excuse or reason worthy for what was happening around them. Nothing would ever justify useless blood spilling or the heartache of others.

"Listen to me," Damian demanded.

"Fuck you," Lily spat, finally getting her face away from his hand.

"Lily, please listen to me!"

Lily bit his palm. Damian shouted his pain, jerking back away from

Lily. She took the chance to put more distance between them. From the top of her head all the way down to her toes, she trembled in her rage.

"I was there," Lily hissed.

Damian nodded. "I know."

"I was there, Damian! For the shooting, I watched those people … Was that part of the plan, too?"

"No one would look to Dino if you or Theo were at the locations when the scenes went down."

Locations?

Locations!

"More than one?" Lily asked, feeling like the air was being squeezed from her chest.

Damian's cool demeanor didn't change as a million and one emotions washed through Lily. His statement clearly implied more than one. The only other incident Lily had been involved with was the restaurant shooting when Mia died.

The vague conversation and passing looks shared between Damian and Dino when Lily arrived home after the shooting rammed into her mind with an almost painful quality. It taunted her.

How could you not know?

How did you not see?

"He didn't," Lily whispered.

"Yes," Damian said quietly.

"My God! Eve's mother—"

"Was a mistake," Damian interjected quickly. "Dino aimed high, meaning to hit above the heads at the table just to get some shit stirring and questions being asked. He wanted a fuss kicked up and some suspicion inside the Outfit, nothing more. Mia must have been standing when he did the drive-by. Laurent, too. It makes sense considering Serena's spiel. Maybe the argument continued after we left the table."

Was that supposed to help Lily?

It didn't!

"Riley focused in on the Poletti boy's death and wouldn't let that go," Damian explained. "He took the shooting as retaliation on Terrance. It grew from there. Dino went with it. It was never supposed to get this big."

"You texted him that day," Lily said, remembering that fact.

Damian's jaw tensed. "Yes."

"Why?"

"Exactly for the reason I already told you when you asked that day. To let him know we were leaving and I would be bringing you home."

"So I could be there, but not actually *be* there, right?" Lily asked, hatred swelling up in her heart.

"Yes," Damian said softly.

"I was your pawn. Dino's, too. That's all this ever was. And that night. You knew how heartbroken and hurt I was for Eve and over what happened, and I let you fuck me. You used the place I was in to get me into bed, you asshole."

"Absolutely not," Damian growled.

"Liar," she said, waving a hand at him. "You're just like Dino. You're aiming for one place and you're going to use everybody else's backs to step on while you get there. Mine will not be one you break in the process, Damian Rossi."

"Stop!" Damian shouted.

The word slammed Lily straight in the chest, threatening to send her emotions spilling over again. She couldn't handle this.

"I did not know it was going to be this bad but yes, I knew Dino had plans," Damian continued, not giving her the chance to breathe or think. "Certain people—he wanted them gone. I did that, yes. I helped, yes. But shit happened. Instead of only looking at the men inside the Outfit when the restaurant mess happened like Dino wanted, Riley focused outside. Nobody planned for that. Nobody thought of that. It just kept getting bigger.

"I owed your brother my life and he asked for that payment in the form of a marriage to you. He wanted your safety and your happiness to be my payment. That meant I needed to do anything—everything—I could to get you to that place."

"I am not happy!" Lily cried. "I am heartbroken. I am ... *disgusted*."

Damian recoiled, pain flickering in his blue eyes. "Don't say that."

"It's true. After everything, all the bullshit you've fed to me, I hate you."

"It is not true. You can't hate the things you love, Lily."

Lily's felt her entire body flinch inward, reacting to his words and the truth hidden inside them. It only made everything so much worse that she had somehow fallen in love with this dangerous, dark man. Because she hadn't known anything about him at all. She'd taken the bits and pieces he gave for what they were, she trusted him in his actions and words ... she thought he cared.

He clearly hadn't cared about her. Not at all.

But her heart still swelled and pounded, wanting Damian. Lily hated that she couldn't control that reaction because he didn't deserve it from her. None of it.

"Too much," Lily managed to force out. "This is too much."

"I'm sorry."

"No, you're not. All you did was lie to me. You made me think you gave a damn; you made me believe you wanted me. The only thing you wanted was to use me."

"That's not true," Damian said, anger heating his tone. "I agreed—"

"To marry me because of my brother! You never would have looked twice at me otherwise," Lily said, practically screaming at him. "God, Damian, just admit it. For once, tell me the truth!"

"I have never lied to you. I omitted facts because you didn't ask."

"I never asked the right questions; that's what you're dancing around," Lily said, scoffing. "All that means is you're nothing more than a fucking liar, Damian. Is the marriage arrangement even real or was that another one of Dino's distractions?"

The look on Damian's face said it all.

The marriage was real.

Lily couldn't do this anymore. She couldn't stand there looking at the man who had done nothing but lie to her over and over; a man who had used her for his own gain and who she was still expected to marry.

"I hate you," Lily said, needing to hurt Damian like he hurt her. "I hate you so much."

"Lily—"

Lily spun on her heel before Damian could get another word in edgewise. She heard him move toward her as she bolted for the back steps again. Why he couldn't just leave her alone, she didn't know.

Damian caught her just a few steps later. His hand snagged her flimsy sleep shirt and pulled, making her slip on the wet grass. Lily stumbled at the surprise move, falling to the dew covered grass. Damian tried to catch her but ended up on the ground, too.

Angry, hurting, and more confused than ever, Lily rolled to her back and kicked at him. She struck out at him with her fists, shouting every hateful thing she could think to say and spit. All of the pain crushing her heart with a dreadful weight came out in a vomit of words and tears.

"I hate you," she repeated, tasting the saltiness of tears on her lips. "You used the things about me that hurt me, the things you knew would get to me—my parents, the Outfit—you used all of it to get closer to me. All the shit you said to me was nothing more than bullshit. I should have known better than to think you gave a damn. Men like you don't know how to care about anything but yourself. You are a bastard! You made me think you wanted me. You're a monster. I hate you!"

Stop," Damian said, keeping her pinned under his body on the ground. "Please just stop, Lily."

Lily struggled in Damian's hold as his hands cupped her jaw firmly and didn't let go. She refused to listen to whatever he had to say, so she kept fighting him the more he held her down. Her fingernails scored into his cheek, drawing blood. Damian flinched in response, wincing. He never once tried to strike her back. Instead, he continued holding onto her face before he forced her head back, making her stare at him. Her eyes filled with tears all over again, streaking down her cheeks for him to see.

"Let me go!" Lily cried.

"Not until you listen to me," Damian muttered.

With his body on top of hers, barricading her to the wet and cold grass, Lily couldn't get away. Her flats had fallen off and her shorts and shirt were soaked from rolling around on the ground. She was pretty sure her hair was a goddamn mess, too. She wished she could care.

Lily felt Damian's thumbs sweep over her cheekbones as if to wipe away the tears. He couldn't possibly take them away because the flood kept on coming. Every breath she took was accompanied by a sob that ached deep inside her chest.

"Do you like this, huh?" Lily asked, taunting him. "Do you like my tears, Damian? They're all for you this time!"

Damian's teeth bared. "You know I don't."

"I don't know anything about you."

"You know everything that's important," he replied quietly. "Anything I've said and all the things you know, those are important to me."

"Lies," Lily mumbled.

"Facts."

"Asshole."

"Maybe," Damian agreed. "Maybe I am. I told you once that my motives were wrapped up entirely in you and that was the truth. The things that mattered to you, the people who might hurt you or the shit holding you back—I wanted to fix that for you. I never lied to you."

"Yes, you did."

"I did not! There were things you didn't need to know. I don't control Dino, Lily. So I did the next best thing which was keeping you safe while he did whatever the hell he wanted."

"You helped," she spat.

"Sometimes," Damian admitted. "Because I had shit to keep safe, too. I had reasons for wanting this, too."

Lily stilled under his weight. "Like what?"

"Me. I wanted to keep me."

That didn't make sense.

"Let me go," Lily repeated. "I want to go inside. Anywhere away from you."

Soon, preferably.

Damian refused. "Not until you hear me, Lily. You're goddamn well going to hear me whether you want to or not. Things were happening around me that I wasn't getting a say in. Despite what you may think, I didn't do any of this to get myself higher in the Outfit. I did it so someone else could and I was able to stay being just Damian Rossi. Not someone else, just *me.*"

Lily glared. "I—"

"Dino wanted you to be safe long after he didn't have the control to keep you that way. He knew that with certain people gone, a mess might happen. One that would put families in the spotlight and fighting against one another. He didn't want you to be somehow used as a bartering chip between anyone. Not today, tomorrow, or five years from now."

"I don't care."

"Stop it. You know you do. You want to know and I'm telling you. Listen."

Lily sniffled. "I just want to go inside. Please."

Damian acted like she didn't say a word. "In order to make sure you wouldn't be put in that kind of position, he needed you married and already taken. I fucked up a long time ago. My mistakes kept me indebted to Dino but it also made me loyal to him. I understood what he wanted to do and why he was doing it. The Outfit is so fucked up sometimes. Greedy, excessive, and full of bullshit and liars."

"You're a liar," Lily said, hoping that would piss him off enough to release her.

It didn't, not entirely.

Damian's hand let go of her cheek just long enough to smack the ground hard. Lily froze and her gaze widened. "I am not!"

"You're lying to the people around you," she retorted.

"They've never *asked.*"

"Tell me the truth for once," Lily said, her voice a whisper. "Make me believe something you say. Because nothing rings true anymore. *Nothing.*"

"I didn't want to marry you. I didn't want to be married at all."

Lily choked out a sob mixed with a bitter laugh. "Now, that I believe."

"Then I met you," Damian added quieter. "And you were not what I was expecting. We were more alike than I thought. I'd already known you from way back when. You had shit going on—you were *real.* I didn't want you to hate me or to feel like you were stuck with a man who wouldn't care about you. And I did *care,* Lily."

"Why would you?" she asked, refusing to look at him again. "I'm nothing to you in the end. Just another girl, a ring on your finger you'll eventually forget. Nothing, Damian."

"Not nothing. Everything," he murmured.

A shiver worked its way over Lily's body but it had nothing to do with the cold, wet ground. His words washed over her skin and senses with a soothing, truthful quality that only hurt her further.

"You're so good at this game," Lily said, hating him for it.

"No game. Not with you. I would have faked every little goddamn thing I had to with you to make Dino happy, but I didn't have to. With you, I didn't have to fake anything."

Lily wiggled, trying to get away from the feeling of Damian's warm hands sliding down her body. When he touched her, she couldn't think. Damian probably knew that.

"Stop," Lily demanded. "Stop playing these games with me. Leave me alone. I'll follow Dino's rules and keep my fucking mouth shut about what I know. I'll marry you because I don't have a choice, but you can leave me the hell alone while I do it. Find another whore to keep you satisfied, but stay away from me."

"No. You've got it all wrong, Lily. Every bit of it."

Lily laughed darkly. Her tears had finally stopped. "I think I'm right and you're too much of a coward to admit it."

Damian's fingers pressed to the exposed skin of Lily's stomach where her shirt had ridden up. The pressure of his fingertips bit into her flesh with the lightest touch, promising and sweet. She despised the fact there was no denying the hard ridge of his erection digging into her pelvis. It turned her on, despite how angry and hurt she was.

Lily adored this man. She'd went into her affections blindly for him, trusting what he gave to be what it was. She hadn't realized that someone like Damian could have the kind of effect on her that he did until he was front row and center, demanding her attention. Without ever really trying, he'd had her falling head over heels.

She thought he would be standing there to catch her.

Lily was stupid.

Stupid over him. Stupid for him.

Stupid.

God, it was sickening.

"Stop touching me," Lily said.

"No."

"You're an asshole."

Damian shrugged. "You're beautiful."

Lily glowered. "Stop it!"

"You are. I had no reason to let you in, Lily. Not to me or who I was. I didn't need to invite you into my life or bed before the marriage. I didn't have to give a shit about you or even try. I didn't have to like you if I didn't want to but you made it so fucking easy. Don't you get that? I could have treated this arrangement as just that—business. If that's all I thought of it and you, it would have been a hell of a lot simpler just to let you fight it out with Dino and be waiting at the end of the aisle when he forced you down it to meet me. I didn't have to do any of *this!*"

Lily shuddered at what his words implied. "You're lying again. All you did was make me trust you so that no one would suspect what you and

Dino did."

"I didn't have to. That didn't matter to me. I didn't have to hide anything. Dino, yes, but not me."

"You're—"

"Be quiet," Damian said, his blue eyes blazing into Lily's with a fierceness that stopped her breath. "Listen to what I have told you. Think about it and for once, hear me. God, I need you to *hear* me, Lily. Please."

"It doesn't matter. You already said it, Damian. Regardless if Dino forces me down the aisle or not, you'll still be there waiting. I don't have to hear or understand anything for it to make a difference."

"But I want you to."

Lily whined low, feeling his fingers skip around the hem of her shorts. "I don't."

"Why?" he asked.

"You know why."

Damian smiled and the sight only pissed Lily off more. Having her hand free gave her the ability to hit him again, but he caught her wrist before she could. He slammed her hand to the ground beside her head. Lily stilled, shocked. Her body, on the other hand, was hotter than ever.

"Stop hitting me," Damian said, cocking a brow. "You're better than using your hands to show anger. Words work just as well."

"I'm so angry with you."

"I know. I'm sorry."

Lily cried, her tears falling freely again. "I'm angry with me, too."

Damian traced Lily's trembling lip with the pad of his finger before he wiped away her tears. "I hate it when you cry."

"I hate it when you say things like that."

"No, you don't," he argued. "You like it because someone cares."

"Except it's *you*," she said shakily.

"And you're angry because you know I care," Damian replied, never breaking eye contact with Lily. "I care enough to protect you. I care enough to let you in."

"Enough to lie to me, too?"

"Lily, stop making me repeat myself."

"Lying would have been easier!" she shouted.

Lily knew he hadn't lied, not really. In the end, she was the one who chose not to question those around her. She let Damian slip through her carefully constructed walls keeping everyone associated with the Outfit out. She cared about *him*.

"I love you," she breathed, aching inside. "You could have done all of this without making me fall in love with you, Damian."

"I never tried to make that happen," Damian said gently.

But it was so easy to.

"You hurt me," Lily whimpered. "Things you love shouldn't hurt you."

"I'm sorry." Damian swept his thumb over her mouth again with the softest touch as he said, "But you should know that there's so much about you I love, Lily. I love the way you smile because you don't do it nearly enough. I love how you're quiet and you don't need noise when you're beside me to keep you entertained. I love how you let me make you happy even though you don't like a lot of things about me."

"God, stop."

"Not a chance. Hear me."

Lily blinked, willing away the stinging in her eyes. "I wish I fucking couldn't."

But she could.

Damian's erection dug a little harder into Lily's pelvis, reminding her that she had an effect on him, too. One he had never tried to hide. One he always fed into whenever he could. When he bent down to capture her lips in a kiss, she let him. It still hurt but if felt good, too.

Pulling away, Damian dotted soft kisses along her cheekbone. "I love the way you taste and how you always beg me for more. I love burying my tongue into your sweet pussy and how you shake when you come. I love my name in your mouth and wrapping my hands in your hair. I love fucking you because even when it's dirty, it's still beautiful, too."

"So many people are hurting because of this. I can't be okay with that, Damian. I don't know how to look the other way."

"It's never been about just you, but my one priority was you while it happened," Damian explained. "You don't have to look the other way, but when you're ready to, I'm still going to be standing here when you look back at me. I'm sorry you hate me right now, but I love you and I wish you would hear that."

Lily blew out a breath, biting on her lower lip. "Why did you do this?"

"I didn't."

Dino.

"Why did he do it?" she asked.

"I thought I knew," Damian said. "I thought I understood."

"But?"

"I don't think I know much about him at all."

CHAPTER FIFTEEN

Damian's insides twisted into a million and one little knots as Lily lay beneath him, still crying. She cried silently without the sobbing from before. It didn't hurt Damian any less. Her tears still sliced through every inch of his skin, cutting through the muscle and driving into his bones. She couldn't possibly understand how her pain affected him.

"I didn't mean to hurt you," he told her.

"You must have known it would," Lily replied.

Damian's hands were dirty from the ground. Blades of grass and pieces of dirt stuck to his fingertips as he wiped at Lily's face over and over to rid the tears that were ripping him apart. He only made her dirty, too.

"Christ, I'm sorry," Damian mumbled.

Lily laughed but even the sound was sad. "Don't bother. I'm a mess, anyway."

"My mess."

"I don't know how to feel about that," she whispered.

"The same way you always did. This changes nothing."

"I think it changes everything."

Damian frowned though he wished he could hide it. Unfortunately, he was slowly learning that hiding things from Lily never worked out to his favor. "How?"

Lily sighed, using her own dirty hand to rake through her blonde hair. "Because you love me."

Satisfaction filled Damian like he'd never felt before. If she was admitting her belief in his love, the battle was half won on his side.

"I do," Damian said.

"And that just leaves me to wonder about everything when it comes to you." Lily turned her head to stare off to the side. "Is there such a thing as good men who do bad things?"

"I've never claimed to be good."

"I thought you were. You told me differently. Maybe I should have listened."

"I'm still yours," Damian said, leaning down to press a kiss to Lily's dirty cheek.

Lily's eyes fluttered closed. "My friend's mother died."

"I know."

"Your cousin, too."

"Lea isn't my biggest regret," Damian said, tilting Lily's head back so he could see her eyes.

"What is?" she asked in a whisper.

"You already know."

"Maybe, but I'd like to hear you say it."

"Hurting you, sweetheart. Although Lea being caught in the crossfire shouldn't have happened, either," Damian said, the confession slipping past his lips before he could stop it. "I wish it hadn't but I made my choices and now I have to live with them."

"Stop talking."

Damian chuckled. "Why?"

"Because when you talk, I believe everything you say."

"I'll never lie, not if you ask the right questions, Lily."

"I shouldn't have to ask, Damian."

"I don't want to tell you things that put you in danger or might hurt you in some way," he said. "If, or when, you ask, I will always tell you the truth because if you have the sense to ask, you have the strength to handle it. But I will not go out of my way to purposely tell you things just so you have every little last detail about whatever. I won't ever do that, not if knowing them could somehow hurt or harm you. Please understand that."

"I just ..."

"What?" Damian asked, cupping her jaw in his palm. "Tell me what you need, Lily."

"I can't understand."

"Not yet."

"Ever," Lily said.

"Eventually."

Lily sighed. "I hate this life—the mafia life. This is why. People fight and die for nothing; for a belief and rules ... and *nothing*."

"I know."

He'd always known that.

"And I hate the things you've done," she murmured.

"You're allowed to."

"I can't accept it."

"You don't have to," Damian replied quietly.

"But I love you."

Damian nodded. "Yeah."

"It is going to take a while for me to be okay. I need you to understand that."

"I get it."

Lily wet her lips. "So no matter what you say, I have to believe you're a good man who does bad things because otherwise, you're just a man who hurts the things you love for no other reason than you can."

"I love you," he said.

"I know."

"That's the hardest part for you, isn't it?"

"Yes," Lily replied. "It really is."

Damian leaned down just far enough that he could sweep his lips over Lily's. He hated her tears; despised that he'd been the one to cause her any pain. The best way he could think to apologize, if his words weren't doing the job, was to show her. Instead of kissing her hard and deep, demanding she pay attention to his distraction and let it do the job for him, he took his time loving her mouth with his until she slowly began to kiss him back.

"You are, Lily," he said, stroking her cheek as he brushed his lips over hers again.

"Hmm, what?" she asked, breathless.

"Everything to me."

Another sliver of a tear fell from the corner of her eye. Damian wiped it away with the pad of his thumb just as quickly.

"I wish that didn't hurt you to hear," he said.

Lily shook her head. "It doesn't."

"It's true."

"Damian?"

"Yeah?" he asked.

"Stop talking and kiss me again."

Damian cocked a brow. "Don't you want to—"

"I want you to shut up and kiss me again. And not like I'm some fucking China doll ready to break into pieces at any moment. Just kiss me. Please."

How could he deny her when she asked so nicely?

Damian fisted Lily's flimsy sleep shirt and pulled her up from the ground. The thin fabric covering her chest ripped at the force, tearing from the neck line straight down to where he held it tight. Lily gasped a second before Damian's lips crashed down on hers with a bruising force. Her tongue fought with his, her teeth scraping to his mouth as her breaths turned ragged and harsh.

Lily grabbed his shirt in her tiny hands and moaned, spreading her legs wider. Damian couldn't help himself; he grinded his growing erection into her core, knowing there was nothing but his jeans and soft cotton shorts separating his dick from her pussy. A pressure built in Damian's chest the longer he kissed his girl. Nothing would ever be as honest or true as how he felt when Lily kissed him.

"Fuck," Damian ground out when Lily's teeth bit into his jaw. She kissed the spot with the softest touch of her lips before her tongue struck out against his skin to taste. Heat and blood flooded his cock. "Lily—"

"Shut up," she hissed, biting him again.

Sweet Christ.

Damian hadn't even blinked again and he felt her hands working at the zipper and button on his jeans.

"Lily, wait," Damian demanded.

"No, fuck me," she said forcefully, her fist hitting his chest. "Shut up and fuck me."

"*God.*"

Lily laughed, the sound airless but thick. "You always know how to get me saying that in the end."

Shit.

Damian cussed loudly as Lily's hand circled his dick under his jeans. She stroked him once, twice, and then released him just as fast. Clearly, she wasn't going to give him a chance to argue with her further. Lily knew what she wanted.

Him.

Damian let her shove his jeans and boxer-briefs down around his hips. When she pulled his shirt up, exposing his back and chest to the cold, early morning air, he let her do that, too. His shirt hit the grass as he began grinding his bare, throbbing dick into her cotton shorts.

Lily groaned lowly, falling back to the grass and digging her hands into the ground as Damian began yanking down her shorts. He kicked his jeans down further at the same time he pulled her shorts off her legs. Lily was nothing but bare skin, sex, and pussy under her shorts. Her juices were already glistening over her pink folds, showing just how hot she really was for him.

Damian fucking loved it.

He cupped her sex in his palm and ran two fingers through her slit.

"Just like I fucking thought," Damian muttered.

Lily sighed as his fingers pressed into her pussy. "Hmm?"

"Hot, wet, and wanting me, sweetheart."

Damian smeared Lily's arousal over her folds and up to her clit. He circled the little nub, feeling her shake from the attention. He kept teasing her with his touches until she rocked her hips into his hand and begged for more.

"Please, please, please," Lily whimpered. "Fuck me."

Damian smirked, chuckles building in his chest. "I don't know how to tell you no, Lily."

Wrapping his fist in her ripped shirt again, Damian pulled her up from the ground until she was nose to nose with him and her eyes were locked with his. Lily's pupils dilated wide, her breath catching hard in her chest.

"I love you," he said softly.

Lily kissed his mouth gently. "I love you."

Keeping his hold on Lily with one hand, Damian used his other to guide his cock to her sex. He rolled the head of his member through the fleshly lips of her pussy, letting her juices cover the tip of his dick. He let his cock go, letting it rest along the seam of her sex so he could grind his hardness into her soft, wet warmth.

Lily grabbed Damian's wrist, bringing his fingers to her lips. His digits were still wet with her come. She sucked his fingers into her mouth without a word. Damian couldn't hold back the growl forming at the sight of her lips encompassing his digits while her teeth scraped along his skin. He reveled in the feeling of her tongue sweeping at his fingers, cleaning them of her fluids.

"You taste like sin," Damian told her, knowing it was true.

Sin. Sugar. Heaven.

Bliss.

She always tasted like bliss, too.

Lily released his fingers from the confines of her hot little mouth but not before kissing the tips of the digits. Damian rubbed his fingers along her pink lips as he rocked his body into hers one more time. As his cock came down to the entrance of her pussy, he pushed in with a slowness he knew would let her feel every fucking inch of his dick filling her.

"Oh, God," Lily gasped.

He wanted her full, aching, and needing.

Only for him.

Lily's head fell back, exposing the creamy expanse of her neck and collarbones as Damian's cock seated fully inside her clenching walls. He took that moment just to feel her bare, soaking him, and taking all of him.

"Don't you feel that?" Damian asked. "How you fit me, *bella*? How I fill you?"

Lily's tongue peeked out to sweep over her lips. "Yes."

"More?"

"More," she echoed.

Damian pulled out from her sex just as slowly as he'd entered her. When he could feel the head of his dick at the entrance of her pussy, it took all his willpower not to slam right back inside her and fuck her until she was screaming his name and begging for every bit that he could give her.

"I adore you," Damian murmured.

"*Mmm.*"

"I love fucking you."

Lily moaned. "Jesus."

"You're my perfect fit, Lily."

A shudder wracked over her body, vibrating them both. Damian's own shiver worked its way over his spine as he held Lily in place, keeping her from rocking further into his dick. Fuck, he wanted her so badly.

"So beautiful," he told her.

"Yours."

He touched her lips again, feeling her tongue strike out against the pad of his fingers.

"Yours," she said with a tenderness he hadn't expected.

Damian thrust inside her again before retreating much slower than he entered her. Lily whined under him, her fingernails digging deep into his chest and ass. "Look at me, sweetheart."

Lily's lashes fluttered as she sighed in her bliss. The tight, hot walls of her pussy clamped around him as he pushed in faster, deeper.

"Lily, look at me," Damian ordered. "Right now."

Lily met his stare, her lips falling open with a quiet cry. "Damian ..."

"Nothing else matters."

Lily rocked into his cock on the cold grass, holding him tighter. His hand, still fisted into her ruined shirt, shook from the emotions rolling through his body and threatening to take him under. Her hand let go of his ass to weave into his hair. The slight bite of pain ricocheted through his body along with the bliss singing in his blood as she yanked on the strands and arched off the ground.

"There ... right fucking *there*," Lily said, her voice barely above a breath. "Oh, my *God*, Damian."

"Say it," Damian said.

Lily wet her lips under her tongue, murmuring, "Nothing else matters."

"Just this."

Another thrust drove his words home. Her sweet fluids gushed around his cock as he withdrew and slammed right back in, moving them both across the wet grass. Damian yanked on her shirt, ripping it more as he pulled her closer to him. Close enough that he could bite her bottom lip and taste the heat of her blood on his tongue. Lily met every plunge of his hips with her own rocking, tugging harder on his hair the more he kissed and nipped at her mouth and jaw.

Lily's cries turned louder, like the sweetest music to his ears. "So close."

"Just us," Damian said through his clenched teeth.

Lily blew out a shaky breath. "Just us."

He could feel every inch of her walls flexing around his shaft as he fucked her. Damian's hand dug into the soft ground, needing something stable. Lily's legs tightened around his hips, her heels digging into his lower back and pushing him into her with every thrust.

"Fuck," Lily said, whispering the word. "Damian."

She came undone around him shaking, mumbling his name, with a tear streaking down the side of her cheek as her nails scratched a set of lines across his chest. Damian wasn't far behind. He finally let go of the hold he had on her shirt and grabbed tightly to her hips. Holding her still to his body so his cock was as deep as he could fucking manage to get it, Damian released into her sex in thick, ropey streams.

"Shit, shit, shit," Damian chanted, falling forward.

Lily wrapped her arms around his torso and didn't let go. With his face buried into Lily's neck and the feeling of their sex still lingering around his senses, Damian was content. Far more than he had ever been. Peace— that was what this beautiful, strong woman was to him. She brought a sense of completion into his heart, filled his body with fire, and he loved it. He needed it.

"Openness," Lily said softly.

Damian kissed her neck, the waves of pleasure still keeping his cock semi-hard inside of her sex. Nothing had ever felt quite so sublime clenching around his dick. "Hmm?"

"You need to be open with me. Everyday. No matter what. Whenever I ask. No omitting."

"I can do that."

"I don't forgive you," she said.

"This isn't about that."

Lily nodded. "Yeah, I know that, too."

Damian leaned up enough to capture Lily's lips with his own. He kissed her hard and let his tongue war with hers as she sighed into the kiss. Weaving his fingers into her hair, Damian kissed a path over her jaw, down her dirty neck, and over her collarbones.

"Tell me you love me," he said against her skin.

"I love you."

"Need me."

"So much," Lily breathed, writhing under his wandering hands and desire.

"Marry me."

Lily stilled.

Damian didn't relent. "Marry me, Lily. Marry me because you love me; because you don't have to like everything I do or even understand the reasons why I do it. Marry me because you want to; because you want to walk down the aisle and see me waiting there to meet you. Marry me because you need that like I need it, too. Marry me."

"I—"

Damian met her gaze, quieting her instantly. "It's a yes or no question."

"I don't have a choice," Lily said.

"I'm giving you one."

"You can't do that. Dino—"

"Stop," Damian interjected firmly. "I am giving you one, Lily DeLuca. I am giving you what he didn't. You can say no and I will refuse to follow through with Dino's arrangement, regardless of what might happen. That doesn't matter. It will never matter. What does matter at this moment is a yes or a no. That's all."

Tears slipped from the corners of Lily's eyes. For once, Damian didn't try to wipe away the proof of her emotions that usually hurt him so badly.

"Yes or no," he said again.

Lily blinked. "You'll always love me."

It wasn't even a question.

"Yes."

"Forever," she said.

"Yes."

"You shouldn't propose during sex, Damian."

His laughter rocked them both. "It's after, technically."

"No, you're hard again. Every part of me can feel it."

Damian was. "Point taken. But you're deflecting."

"No, I'm not," Lily said, never breaking his gaze. "Be there to meet me at the end."

"Always."

"Then yes."

A grin split Damian's lips. "Yes?"

"Yes," Lily echoed. "But I'm still so angry with you."

"That's okay," he said.

A familiar rumbling woke Damian from the daze he was in. Lily barely reacted at all to the sound, or she didn't hear it like he had. He scrambled off the wet grass, pulling a confused Lily up with him. He fixed his pants and pulled his wet T-shirt over his head. Damian helped Lily back into the shorts he'd pulled off earlier. Quickly, he grabbed her flats she'd kicked off and held them out for her to slip her feet back into. Her shirt was ruined, but at least it wasn't falling off her.

Damian had a hard time keeping his baser instincts under control as he looked Lily over. He'd bitten and kissed her lips a rosy red. Her hair was a mess from his hands and their frenzied fucking. She looked goddamn gorgeous. Like he'd been all over her.

"Is that …?"

"Dino's car," Damian said.

"Crap," Lily muttered.

"Don't worry about it. Just go inside, go back to sleep, and don't act surprised when you see me sitting at the kitchen table in the morning."

Lily frowned. "But—"

Damian interrupted whatever she was going to say by pulling her in close for a kiss. "What did you see, Lily?"

She didn't even think about it.

"Nothing. I saw nothing."

Damian stared at the colorful screen of his laptop, wondering if he should make the call.

"What are you doing?" Tommas asked, tipping back his beer to finish what was left.

"Thinking," Damian replied.

"It's a little late to be having second thoughts."

Damian flipped his cousin the middle finger. "Not about the wedding."

"Good, because you're due at the altar in …" Tommas trailed off, checking his watch. "Fifteen hours."

"Thanks for the reminder."

"You should sleep, Damian."

Damian had too much shit to consider before he could sleep.

"What are you still doing here?" Damian asked. "The party ended hours ago."

Well, if you could consider a few friends hanging around drinking and doing nothing else a party. Tommas refused to let Damian get married without some kind of final goodbye to his single life. Damian consented to his cousin and a couple of Tommas' friends coming over to his apartment for a few beers and a game of poker.

Damian won the poker match. He always did.

"Giving you company," Tommas finally answered.

Damian passed Tommas a look. "I don't believe that for a second."

"Yeah, well, fucking deal with it. I'm not giving you anything else."

Tommas didn't have to. Damian already knew. Abriella Trentini was on a shorter leash than ever before. With the families fighting like they were, it was probably damn near impossible for Tommas to get any time around the girl.

"You're sulking about Abriella again, aren't you?" Damian asked.

Tommas scowled. "I thought you didn't want to know."

"I don't, but I figure it would be rude if I didn't ask."

"That, and you like to know everything."

"Partly," Damian agreed.

"I just … it fucking sucks," Tommas decided on saying.

Damian could understand that. He wouldn't like it very much if the thing he loved was kept from him, either. Even if Tommas' and Abriella's situation was a precarious one simply because of their ages and other minor details. Like her grandfather.

"My place feels empty," Tommas added.

"If you grow a uterus and your dick turns inside out, don't call me to whine about it," Damian said, chuckling.

Tommas opened his mouth to speak, but shut it just as fast. "Asshole."

"I try."

"I should get going," Tommas said, sighing. "Try to sleep."

Well, Abriella would be at the wedding tomorrow standing with Lily. As long as Tommas kept things clean, he could probably get away with at least talking to his lover.

"Are you good?" Tommas asked Damian.

Damian nodded toward the apartment door. "I'm fine, Tommas. Really."

"You sure?"

"Absolutely."

Damian had never been surer of anything in his life like he was of Lily. He adored that woman—loved her entirely.

"Yeah, get out of here," Damian said.

Tommas smiled and pushed up from the chair. "I'll be here to pick you up bright and early. Confession before pleasure, as the saying goes."

Damian scoffed. "I never confess anything."

He had nothing worth confessing. Nothing he wanted forgiveness for, anyway.

"Whatever. It's tradition for the Rossi family. Suck it up. Knowing you, you're going to need a couple of extra hours for penance."

"Hey—" Damian stopped himself before adding, "Probably. Get the hell out of here already."

Tommas' hands flew up. "Going, going."

The moment his apartment door closed, Damian picked up his cell phone and dialed a familiar number. Lily's cheerful voice picked up on the second ring. Damian cringed at the noise level in the background.

Approved club, he reminded himself. There were also a group of body guards Terrance had appointed for the girls for Lily's last hurrah. That did not help the swell of jealousy building inside Damian's chest.

"Hello?" Lily asked.

"Sweetheart."

Damian could practically feel her smile as Lily said, "You're not supposed to call me tonight."

"I think what you're looking for is that I'm not supposed to see you," Damian replied.

"Same thing." The slight giddy tone she sported told Damian his girl had been drinking those ugly green things again. "Oh, he's cute, Ella."

Damian felt the growl-like sound claw outward from his throat. "*Lily.*"

"Hmm?"

"How many drinks have you had?"

Lily laughed. "Definitely not seven."

"You're awful."

"You love it," she shot back.

Damian smirked. "I do."

"Good," Lily hummed.

The final couple of weeks leading up to their wedding had been hard. Not just because of the mess going on around them but because Damian knew how he hurt Lily by keeping what he had from her. They didn't talk about it a lot but he figured they didn't have to for her pain to be clear to him.

She didn't understand. She didn't act like she did.

But Lily loved him.

That was what mattered most to Damian.

"Why are you calling?" Lily asked.

"I just wanted to make sure you weren't making a run for it."

"Liar." Damian flinched. Lily caught what she said quickly enough and muttered, "Kidding. You're still going to be waiting at the other end for me?"

"Always."

"Then I'll meet you there."

"All right. Love you," Damian said.

"Love you," Lily whispered.

Damian ended the call and dropped his phone on the couch cushion. For another twenty minutes, he stared at the screen of his laptop again, letting the opened window for the conference call option taunt him further.

He didn't need to ask for permission to do the final job Dino asked for. Well, the job wasn't only for Dino. Killing Terrance Trentini would work to Damian's favor in a lot of ways. It would take him out of the spotlight as the potential for a future boss and nobody would ever believe that Damian could kill Terrance. Not being as close as they seemed to be.

They weren't really close at all.

Nonetheless, killing a boss could come with consequences. Not just from inside the Outfit, but from families in other states aligned with them. Syndicates had protocols and rules for that sort of thing. They expected some kind of say at the end of it all.

Before he could overthink it further, Damian reached forward and hit the call button on a contact he'd purposely changed the name of in case anyone ever got a look at his list. The trip he'd taken to New York for the Commission and meeting of the bosses had been beneficial in more ways than one.

Just because Terrance didn't like certain families didn't mean Damian couldn't have connections with them. Keeping friends close but enemies closer had a whole different meaning in the mafia.

Damian checked the clock on the bottom, right-hand corner of the screen and noted the late time. He probably shouldn't be calling a New York Don without first going through some form of connections between other men in the family, but Damian didn't have that option at his disposal. Not considering everything.

Just when Damian was about to hang up the call, Dante Marcello picked up on his end. Dante ruled over the dominating family in New York as their leader. Being the Marcello Don also meant Dante had a great deal of control and influence with the other major families of the Commission. He was also what many men considered to be the Boss of bosses. Damian didn't want problems from other families arising because of Terrance's death. Having Dante on his side, one of the most ruthless crime bosses in North America, would certainly help Damian's cause.

"*Ciao,*" Dante greeted as the screen flickered with the Marcello Don's picture. "Marcello speaking. If you talk any louder than a mouse, the next time I see you will not end pleasantly."

Damian laughed under his breath. "Oh?"

The live shot of an office Damian didn't recognize filled the background as Dante sat down in a large, leather chair. Even more surprising was the toddler boy Dante held, snuggled into his chest. The young boy's face was hidden into Dante's neck. In footie pajamas and with just a peek of a thumb sticking out, Damian guessed the boy was sucking on the digit.

Damian grinned at the sight of Dante holding the child like the two were in the midst of snuggling. It was such a contradictory sight compared to the man Damian knew Dante to be. While Damian had been aware Dante had a young, adopted son, he didn't realize the man was such a hands-on Dad.

Apparently even cold men could be daddies.

"Damian Rossi," Dante said, grinning. "This is a surprise."

"Sorry for the late call," Damian said, keeping his voice down for the child's sake.

Dante shrugged. "If it were any other night, you wouldn't have caught me. Michel is having problems with his molars coming in. He keeps us up a great deal of the time. What can I do for you?"

Damian had struck an unlikely friendship with Dante during that meeting of the bosses. Dante was sharp, quick, and brutal when he wanted something. Damian appreciated that. They'd exchanged contact numbers just in case something came up in the future. Damian supposed something had, now.

"It's an interesting situation," Damian said vaguely.

Dante chuckled. "They always are. No beating around the bush, what do you want?"

"Hits on high members should always go through the Commission, shouldn't they?"

"They should," Dante said slowly, raising a brow high. "Usually it's passed through the grapevine and not a direct call with an actual face behind the hit, Damian."

"I'm not the usual, I guess."

"I guess not." Dante sighed, patting the bottom of his son as he asked, "Who's it for?"

"Terrance."

Dante's expression didn't change on the screen at all. "Why?"

Damian shrugged. "Nothing is ever simple and getting into it all would be pointless on your end."

"It would," Dante agreed. "I'm curious though, so indulge me."

"I don't want to be you," Damian said.

Dante smiled. "That was not the answer I expected to hear."

"There's more but that's the most important part."

"I heard whispers about trouble in Chicago, but I wasn't sure," Dante said. "They say it's bad enough for a war."

"Something like that." Damian raked a hand through his hair and asked, "I know the request is supposed to go through all the bosses, but I figured one was enough as long as it was the right one."

"Why am I the right one, Damian?"

"*Capo di tutti capi,*" Damian murmured.

The Boss of bosses.

"I've never claimed that title," Dante said quietly.

"You don't have to."

Not for it to be true.

Dante sucked in a deep breath like he was considering it all. "Regardless of what I say, the hit will go through, won't it?"

"Probably," Damian said honestly. "But I know you've got a few chips in the pool down here and a new boss might do you some good, too."

"Who would take it?" Dante asked.

"Hard to say."

"A new boss would do well. Lucian would love to finally get that apology he's owed."

Damian shook his head. "Is that all?"

"Believe me, in Cosa Nostra, an apology means more than anyone could possibly understand. It isn't too late for the Outfit and the Marcellos to reconcile their issues if the right boss were to take the seat. A boss with the right motives and morals."

"Who's the right boss for you?" Damian asked, throwing the man's question right back at him.

"That's not for me to decide, just make sure he's married when he comes to his first meeting. Make the hit, Damian. What else do you need from me?"

"Keep my name out of it. On all sides."

"Will do," Dante said. "You should have put the feelers out to the other bosses just to be safe."

Damian wasn't worried. "You can say I did."

Dante laughed. "Yeah, that works, too. One more thing."

"Yeah?"

"I heard you're getting married."

Damian cleared his throat, unsurprised. "Tomorrow, actually. Didn't you get an invitation?"

"We did, but declined. I appreciated the thought but you know how it goes."

"No apology, no Marcellos."

"Exactly. Is your marriage for love?" Dante asked.

"Was yours?"

"No, but my wife has a way about her. Are you marrying for love?"

"It wasn't for love," Damian said.

"But?"

"My girl has a way about her."

Dante laughed darkly. "The good women always do. Congratulations."

CHAPTER SIXTEEN

"Eyes wide, let me see them," the makeup artist ordered.

Lily did as she was told, letting the woman fan her lashes further. She wasn't sure how much longer her eyelashes could possibly be.

"Pinky again," another woman said.

Lily tilted her hand to put her pinky out. The nail artist manicuring Lily's fingernails started her work over as a top coat of clear polish smoothed over each nail. Another woman worked on her hair, setting each of the wavy strands into perfectly managed curls that would be set up into a messy chignon.

Oddly, Lily didn't mind all the people working around her or the attention. It wasn't often she preferred the spotlight, but since it was her wedding day, she didn't have much of a choice. She figured she might as well enjoy the pampering and time.

Her wedding morning started out early. Maybe a little too early considering her bachelorette party hadn't ended until nearly two in the morning. Theo woke Lily up with breakfast and a phone call from Damian, which was nice. Theo took Lily to the spa and as far as she knew, was still waiting out in the lobby for her and Abriella to finish.

Dino, on the other hand, hadn't shown himself that morning.

Lily wasn't too worried about it.

"That smells amazing," Abriella said as some coconut oil was rubbed into her hands.

"It does," Lily agreed.

Abriella smiled, tilting her head to the side so she could look Lily over. "Are you nervous?"

Not at all.

"No," Lily answered honestly.

"Excited?"

"Very."

For a day that was usually high-stress and full of nonsense for other brides, Lily's wedding day was turning out to be a quiet affair with little issues. No one bothered her for useless things or demands. Even Theo, who didn't know how to be a quiet man, had given Lily space and silence that morning.

She was so relaxed, it was crazy.

Lily loved it.

Every day should be like this.

Abriella grinned wide. "I'm happy for you. Damian is a good guy."

Lily nodded. "He is."

It just took a lot for Lily to correlate the good man she knew resided inside Damian and the parts of him that did bad things.

"A few more hours," Abriella said.

Only a few?

Lily checked the clock on the wall. Abriella was right.

"What is next?" Lily asked.

Abriella shrugged. "The church. Confession to start out new. What else?"

Great.

Lily sat in the private room, counting on the beads on her rosary. The black globes felt smooth under her fingertips as she recited the words of prayers she couldn't ever forget. Over and over. One more time ...

Penance was never really over.

Touching the rosary gave her a sense of comfort she hadn't expected. The rosary had been a gift from someone—Lily didn't know who—and delivered to her when she arrived at the church from Theo. He'd said nothing when he handed over the sleek, blue velvet box. Only that someone had wanted her to have them. She started her last confession before becoming a married woman with peace settling in her heart.

Something else she hadn't expected to feel on her wedding day.

Clicking each bead on the rosary as she went through the final words, asking to be forgiven and cleansed for her past transgressions, a knock on the private room's door broke her concentration. Lily assumed it was just the priest coming to see if she had finished.

"Come in," Lily called, setting the rosary aside.

The door opened a crack and Theo poked his head in. Her brother flashed her with a smile that was known to dazzle women and set men off-guard. Theo had a way about him. Out of Lily's two brothers, Theo was the more charming, likeable of the two whereas Dino had a roughness around his edges that kept people at bay.

Lily figured nobody really knew Theo well enough to know his demeanor was nothing more than a trick to draw people in. He could be just as ruthless as Dino, but he had a cleaner way about doing it.

"I'm not interrupting, am I?" Theo asked.

Lily waved at the seat across from her. In their church, confession wasn't done in a booth, but instead a private room decorated with beautiful tapestry and rugs. Two chairs, sitting directly across from the other so the priest and the parishioner could look at one another, served as the confessional. The room was then used as a private area for penance if that's what someone wanted.

"No, I'm done. Or as close as I'm ever going to get for today."

Theo laughed. "Tomorrow, new sins arise."

Lily grinned. "Always. Come in."

Theo stepped inside the room and closed the door behind him. Lily waited as her brother moved the seat across from her so that it was positioned beside hers instead. Sitting in the ornate wood chair meant for a priest, Theo kicked his legs out and crossed his shined leather shoes at the ankles. Her brother looked sharp in his black suit with a blue tie and vest to match the color scheme of the day.

Glancing at her from the side, Theo reminded Lily of when she was young and so was he. "How're you really doing?"

Lily shrugged. "I'm doing okay."

"Really?"

"Yeah, Theo. I'm good."

Theo sucked in a deep breath and chewed on his inner cheek. "I wondered. I mean, you keep saying that to everyone but with you, it's hard to tell. You always were good at hiding shit when you needed to."

Lily scoffed playfully. "Church, Theo. Watch your dam—watch your mouth."

Theo barked out a laugh, pointing at her. "You almost said damn."

"Shut up."

Throwing his hands high, Theo conceded. "Fine. I did wonder. I know you didn't choose this, Lily, and it's probably the last thing you want to do."

He couldn't have been more wrong.

"Actually, I did choose it. In my own way and in my own time," Lily said, reaching out to pat her brother's arm gently.

"Good. I was thinking maybe I would have to steal you out of here and run you down to the Mexican border or something."

Lily snorted under her breath. "Right. How far do you think we'd make it?"

"Oh, we'd make it. Don't you worry your pretty little head off about that. I'd make sure of it."

"You would never do it for real," Lily said, teasing her brother.

Theo caught her gaze and held it. The briefest flash of something unknown passed his eyes before it disappeared. "I would have, Lily. I don't want to see you unhappy or pushed aside. You're too good for that, little one. You always were. You should have a man who adores and cares for you because you're everything to him."

Lily's breath came out in a shuddering exhale, emotions rising. "I have one, Theo."

"Yeah, I guess Dino didn't do too badly after all, huh?"

"Something like that," Lily replied.

Theo caught her hand with his own and held it tight, grounding Lily with that one action. Her brothers had never been emotional men, as far as that went. She remembered that as they grew up, the boys had been taught to shut that side of themselves off and give nothing away. Sometimes that bled over to family and Lily. Sometimes it was just cold as hell.

She understood but that didn't make it easier on her when she was just a little girl with no mom and dad and brothers who treated her like she was just another one of the boys. Then again, Lily had always appreciated her brothers involving her in the things they did as they grew up. Especially because the three DeLuca siblings were so far apart in age, yet Theo and Dino always kept Lily close in their own way.

Lily sighed, realizing something she hadn't before. Keeping her close when she was younger had been Theo and Dino's way of showing her their love. She'd always thought of herself and her brothers as orphans without parents, but that wasn't entirely true. They had each other and her brothers had been the best guardians for her.

"I love you, Theo," Lily said, wanting her brother to know.

Theo smiled but only said, "Yeah, I know."

He didn't have to say it back for her to know the truth. Theo loved her, otherwise, he wouldn't be there sitting with her when he really didn't need to be. He hadn't needed to take time out of the day to make sure she was okay. It did give Lily a look into her older brother's feelings about everything, however. Theo usually kept his emotions and opinions locked up tight. She certainly didn't expect him to change that part.

"I have another surprise for you," Theo said.

Lily arched a brow high. "Oh?"

"Yes, but you have to make it quick. It was hard enough getting her here, not to mention someone still has to get her back."

Lily's confusion jumped higher. Theo stood from the chair and fixed his slacks before walking across the room to open the door again. With a quick word to someone out in the hallway connecting the private back rooms of the church, Theo turned and opened the door a little wider.

Evelina Conti stood waiting with her head down and her hands clasped tightly together at her middle. She kept wringing her hands together as she glanced up at Lily with a small smile that quickly faded.

They hadn't spoken since the night Lily left her friend's house. She hadn't even seen Evelina once because Riley wouldn't allow his daughter to communicate with anyone outside of the Conti family and close friends. Evelina had been ripped from her spot in Lily's wedding and replaced, even though Lily hadn't wanted her to be.

Lily's heart grew, happiness swelling inside.

Evelina had come.

She probably wouldn't be able to stay if Theo's words were any indication. She wouldn't be able to stand with Lily like they had originally planned. She would miss the party and sending Lily off. But she had come.

Nothing else mattered but that.

"Eve?" Lily asked, stunned.

"Hey," her friend said.

Theo cleared his throat, gaining Lily's attention. "I'm going to step outside for a minute and see if I can find somebody to take Evelina back home that won't send Riley into a fit. Try not to take too long, okay? I know it's been a while and everything."

Lily nodded quickly "It's okay, Theo. Thank you."

"You're welcome."

Theo stepped outside the room, letting Evelina pass by. Once the door was closed, Lily wasn't sure if she should stand and greet her old friend or stay where she was. Evelina remained close to the door, avoiding Lily's stare as she picked at her fingernails. A blanket of awkwardness covered the small room.

"Thanks for coming," Lily said, breaking the silence.

Evelina flashed another small smile. "I really wanted to. I tried."

"Your father?"

"Yes," Evelina said, sighing. "I'm sorry, Lily."

Lily hadn't been expecting that. Between both of them, Lily should be the one apologizing to Evelina. After all, even if Evelina didn't know, Lily's brother had been the cause of Mia's death. How would Evelina feel about Lily if she knew the truth?

"Whatever it is, don't worry about it," Lily said.

"I should have called or something."

"It's not important."

Evelina shifted on her feet, looking terribly uncomfortable. "You look beautiful."

Lily laughed. "I'm not even in my dress yet."

"So?"

"Thanks." Lily shrugged, waving at the chair beside her. "Sit, Eve."

Evelina shook her head. "I can't. Theo was right, I can't stay for long. Chances are, Daddy will find out from someone that I came, anyway. I don't want to be the next person on his shit-list."

If Evelina wouldn't come to her, than Lily would go to her friend.

Standing from her chair, Lily crossed the space with open arms. Evelina welcomed the embrace with her own tight hug that felt amazing and awful at the same time. Guilt pounded at Lily's insides. Knowing the secrets she did was a horrible feeling.

"I love you," Evelina said.

"I love you, too."

Evelina leaned back, wiping at Lily's cheek with her thumb. "Christ, don't cry. Your makeup is perfect."

"I don't care."

"Yeah, you never really did."

Lily smiled through her guilt and sadness. "This is going to be over eventually, right?"

"The feud?" Evelina asked.

"Yeah."

"Eventually."

"I'll be waiting when it is," Lily said. "I'll be waiting to pick this up where we left off."

Evelina nodded once. "Me, too."

Because the best kind of friendships never really ended. They could be put on pause for a short while or divided by space and time. But real friends—the truest ones—always waited and never missed a beat.

"I have to go," Evelina said.

Lily squeezed Evelina's hand. "Be safe."

Lily lifted her arms to let Abriella and Cara slide the wedding dress over her head. Quickly and quietly, the girls tugged the dress down in place and began doing up the hundred or so tiny little pearl buttons along Lily's spine.

The off-white lace dress reminded Lily that she was only an hour away from walking down the aisle. An aisle she hadn't wanted to walk down at first, but now she couldn't wait. The excitement was beginning to seep in a little more with very passing minute.

Cara Rossi took a step back as Abriella smoothed out the rushing waves of lace. While most of the day had passed with happiness, smiles, and a few joyful tears, Cara was having a rough time. She hid it well, but Lily knew.

"Cara?" Lily asked.

Abriella stood straight, crossing her arms. "Looks good. Just like we thought."

Lily paid Abriella no mind. She was more concerned about her new friend and the permanent frown Cara couldn't seem to get rid of. Lea Rossi's funeral had been a quick, quiet affair. Lily accompanied Damian to the service and grave when Lea was buried. The Rossi family was still suffering from a mixture of shock and pain from the killing.

Cara probably had it the worst. She hadn't just lost a friend and sister, she'd lost her twin. The thing some people considered to be the other half of her soul. How could someone ever settle something like that in their heart?

Lily didn't begrudge Cara for her distraction or sadness.

Lily said the girl's name louder the second time. "Cara?"

Cara's head snapped up like someone had burned her. "Yeah?"

"Are you okay?" Lily asked.

"I'm—"

"Please don't say fine," Lily interjected gently.

Abriella rolled her eyes. "You're the bride, Lily. We're not supposed to upset you today."

"Exactly," Cara said, waving at Abriella. "I'm fine, really."

She wasn't.

Lily didn't care what the girl had to say.

"It upsets me when you fake something for my benefit," Lily pointed out.

Cara laughed a sad sound. "I don't know how to do anything else right now."

"Be honest," Lily said. "Tell me something about Lea and you. Or even just you. Whatever. Give me anything."

Cara didn't look like she knew what to say to that.

"Are you going back to Canada after the wedding?" Abriella asked.

"Yes," Cara said. "I have school."

Lily frowned. "You don't want to stay a little while longer? I know your family is glad to have you back."

Well, Damian and Tommas seemed to really like having Cara home.

Cara sucked in a deep breath. "I need to go back. I can't stay here. This place doesn't feel like Lea at all. The only memories we have here are bad ones from when we were younger. I don't know how Tommas does it. Or even Damian, really. I can't stand being near my parents. I wished they would have cremated her so I could take a piece of her back with me. This isn't home. She deserves to go back home."

Lily watched Abriella blink away the wetness gathering in her eyes.

"I'm sorry," Lily murmured.

"I'm still waiting to wake up and find out this is a dream," Cara said quietly. "But it's not, I'm never going to wake back up to find her here, and that makes it worse."

Lily's guilt only climbed higher.

Abriella opened up the door a crack and popped her head in. "Ten minutes."

Lily nodded. "Thanks."

"By the way, somebody is here to see you."

"Huh?"

Abriella waved at Lily. "Come here, but stay behind the door."

Confused, Lily did as Abriella asked.

"All right, but make it quick. If Dino or Theo catches you, I am not excusing your dumb ass," Abriella said to someone on the other side of the door.

The dark chuckles that echoed in response to Abriella's warning filled Lily with happiness and desire. She grinned as she peeked out the doorway, making sure the wood kept her dress hidden from Damian's view.

As he looked toward the door, she hid behind it again.

"You're not supposed to be on this side of the church" Lily said.

Damian made a dismissive sound. "No, I'm not supposed to see you."

"You're treading a thin line, Damian."

"I can't see you, sweetheart. I am firmly on the right side of the rules."

"For once," Lily teased.

Damian didn't even try to deny it. "Your point?"

"Nothing." Lily turned and looked out the door again, getting just a glimpse of his black tux from the breast down to his waist. Abriella's hand shoved Lily back in the door before she could see more. "Hey!"

"No looking," Abriella barked.

"You're terrible," Lily said, scowling.

"It's only fair," Abriella replied.

Lily was positive the girl was having fun with this.

"I have something to give you," Damian said quietly.

Lily perked at that. "Oh?"

"Yes. I could have handed it off to someone else to deliver it, but I wanted to. I sneaked away from Tommas and Theo while I had the chance. It won't be long before they realize it doesn't take me ten minutes to piss."

Lily laughed, turning her back to the door. "What did you bring me?"

"Give me your hand."

Sticking her hand through the crack of the door, Lily waited. Damian placed something small, round and cool into the middle of her palm. His fingers grazed along all of hers as he pulled his hand back.

"I realized a few nights ago that I forgot something important about this whole thing," Damian said. "I felt like a jackass and had to rectify it. But it never came in until yesterday and you weren't allowed to see me. I really wanted you to wear it when you met me at the end today."

Lily's heart raced, jumping into her throat. She clenched her fingers around the tiny gift as she drew her hand back inside the room. Opening her hand again, a white gold, princess cut two carat diamond ring rested against her skin. It was simplistic in design, but Lily loved that style. She wasn't one for flashy things and Damian wasn't either.

It would make sense for him to pick something like this.

"I know you picked the wedding rings," Damian said.

"It'll match."

"I figured. Do you like it?" Damian asked.

"You know I do," Lily replied.

"Well, I wanted to hear you say it."

"I'll wear it," Lily told him.

"I'll meet you at the end."

Not five seconds after Lily couldn't hear Damian's footsteps retreating down the hallway, Abriella cooed, "*Awe.*"

"Shut up, Ella."

"That man loves you, Lily."

Lily smiled. "Yeah. He does."

Lily linked her arm with Dino's as they waited behind the small progression of the wedding party. Only Abriella, Cara, and a young girl from Damian's extended family acted as the party for Lily. Tommas would stand as Damian's best man while Theo filled in for an usher. For such a large guest list, they chose a small party.

Dino patted Lily's hand softly. It was the first time all morning she had seen her brother and he barely spoke a word to her.

"Are you happy?" Lily asked Dino.

Dino raised a brow at the question. "Shouldn't I be asking you that?"

"I think you already know, Dino."

"Well, I hoped. I'm glad it worked out."

Lily decided not to mention a thing about what she knew regarding the shootings, his involvement, or anything even relating to the subject to Dino. Doing so could put Damian in danger from Dino or worse, someone else. Lily wouldn't do that. Not to Damian.

The doors opened to the church and Cara Rossi gave Lily a small smile before starting her walk down the aisle.

Almost time …

"I'm proud of you, Lily," Dino said quietly.

Lily hadn't been expecting that. "Why?"

"Sometimes I look at you and all I see is this little girl who you used to be. I often forget you're not a child anymore and you've seen nearly as much as I have in life. I always thought Theo and I would forever be watching after you and minding you in some way, but you proved us wrong. You don't need us at all, do you?"

"Why would you ask that, Dino?"

Dino shrugged. "It feels that way today. Instead of handing you off, I'm actually just giving you away. Dad should have been able to do this for you. I don't think I'm a worthy enough man to stand in his place and do it for him. I need to know you're going to be okay, Lily."

"You know I'll visit you," Lily said.

No matter what, when they talked about Dino's upcoming trial or his sentencing possibility, they never discussed it outright. Usually the topic was danced around or vaguely hinted at. Even being as mad and hurt by her brother's choices as she was, Lily didn't want to say goodbye to Dino for twenty years.

She didn't want to say goodbye at all.

Lily watched as the doors opened for Abriella to make her way down the white silk aisle, too.

"You won't visit," Dino said, sounding like he was sure of it. "Because I don't want you to. It's not the kind of place for someone like you."

"Fine, then I'll call."

Dino sighed, chuckling low. "You're too stubborn for your own good."

"I can't imagine where I learned that from, Dino."

"The best, of course."

"And I got my sweetness from Theo," Lily said.

Dino nodded. "That must be it. God knows you never got any of that nonsense from me."

Lily squeezed her brother's arm as the mother of the tiny flower girl urged her daughter through the opened doors. When they closed, shutting out the quiet murmurings of the church and the eyes of the guests trying to get a peek at Lily and Dino, her heart began to calm.

"Did you like my gift?" Dino asked.

Lily's brow furrowed. "What gift?"

"The rosary, little one."

Oh.

"That was from you?" she asked.

Dino nodded. "Yes. It's very special to me. I waited a long time to finally be able to give it to you like I was supposed to."

Lily's hand clenched around the stem of her bouquet, feeling the rosary beads roll under her fingers. "Why is that?"

"You probably don't recognize them. Church wasn't a big thing for Mom, I guess. She only really brought them out on special occasions and whenever she went in for confession."

Lily's heart stopped and she grabbed her bouquet tighter. "It's Mom's?"

"Yes. She used to hang them off the bedpost on Dad's side of the bed because she always said he needed more reminders of faith than she did. She loved him like crazy. I don't think she ever really liked what he was or the things he did, but she loved him. And we came along for the ride, you know."

Lily felt like she couldn't breathe. "Thank you."

"Better for you to have them, Lily. Theo and I, we're going to the same place no matter how much we pray. You're not quite the same."

Lily didn't think so. She wouldn't argue it with Dino.

"You're not giving me away today," Lily said, tugging on Dino's arm firmly to bring him closer to her side. "You're just—"

"Setting you free," Dino said as the doors opened a final time to let Lily and Dino step forward into view. "Because that's what you do with the things you raise and love, Lily. You set them free and you pray they're strong enough that they don't need to come back to you, but you still hope that they do."

Dino turned as the sound of three hundred or more people standing from the pews echoed through the church. Lily let her brother kiss her cheek before he fixed her veil.

"You're going to be just fine," Dino said.

"Will I?"

"DeLucas don't know how to fail, Lily. We never have."

Lily willed away her tears as Dino took his spot beside her again. He fixed her hand tucked into his elbow and then moved them forward. Through the sheerness of her veil trimmed with a delicate lace, Lily ignored the faces of people she didn't know and even those she did recognize. Instead, she focused on the man waiting for her at the front, standing at the bottom of the altar with his hands clasped behind his back.

Damian's smile grew the closer she came. For a man that usually kept his emotions hidden from view, the happiness and joy on his face was written as clear as day. The wedding march reverberated through the church from the organ, hitting every note perfectly.

Lily barely heard it at all.

"Who gives this woman today in marriage?" she heard the priest ask as they came to a stop at the bottom of the altar.

Theo stepped down from his spot on the altar with Tommas to stand beside Dino.

"We do," her brothers said together.

Words exchanged between the priest and the men before Damian took Dino's place. Dino kissed Lily's hand softly before he passed it to Damian. Theo took his place back on the altar without a word. Lily smiled as Damian gave her hand a slight squeeze.

In that one action, she was grounded to his side again.

Right where she was meant to be.

Lily glanced up at the waiting priest.

"Do you come into this union willingly, child?" the man asked her.

That was the million dollar question, wasn't it?

"Yes," Lily said. "I absolutely do."

CHAPTER SEVENTEEN

Damian twirled a smiling, laughing Lily out from his embrace before bringing her in close again. Her back tucked into his chest as he kissed the soft skin of her neck. She smelled like roses and sex.

And she was happy.

He couldn't wait for this night to be over so he could take her back to the five-star presidential suite he'd booked for them. Their honeymoon wouldn't be so much of a vacation, not a real one. But they did have a week of nothing but them and quiet love in a beautiful suite with champagne on ice and chocolate covered fruit just waiting to be eaten.

"You look terribly sexy tonight," Lily said, pressing her backside into his groin.

If she kept that up, Damian made no excuses for them leaving early.

"Shouldn't I be the one telling you that?"

"You already have. Several times. There are a lot of people here," Lily said, turning in Damian's arms.

"There are," he agreed. "At least three-hundred."

"I know maybe twenty."

Damian shrugged, keeping their slow dance moving across the floor as the guests watched on. "I know maybe one-hundred."

Lily's laughter was like a balm to his dark soul. He'd long since decided that Lily was the light to his darkness. Maybe it was true that every person had a better half. Lily was surely his if he considered everything.

Damian caught Lily's cheek in his palm and swept his fingers over her cheekbone. Her painted red lips and dark eyes demanded attention and praise. Lily didn't need the makeup and gorgeous dress to make her perfect, but he loved seeing her all done up just the same.

"Goddamn, you're beautiful tonight, sweetheart."

Lily's smile was anything but innocent. "Oh?"

"So much."

"I spent all morning getting pampered."

Damian smirked. "Did you?"

"Yes. I had my nails, makeup, and hair done. But before that, I went to the massage place and this very good-looking—"

He drove Lily's smaller frame into his body hard, quieting whatever she was going to say instantly. Lily glanced up at him with wide eyes glittering. She damn well knew what she was doing teasing him like that.

"Playing with fire, Lily Rossi."

Lily's tongue peeked out to wet her lips. Damian held back from biting the spot just to teach her a lesson about teasing him. "Just getting you ready for the after party, Damian."

"Isn't this the after party?"

"Nope. The private after party."

Ah.

Fuck.

Damian tried to ignore the way her suggestive words and demure tone had his cock twitching to life under his tux pants, but he couldn't. Hell, if she wanted to play those games, he was up for that.

"You know what my biggest problem was today, Lily?"

Lily frowned. "What was wrong today?"

"I could barely pay attention to the priest at all."

"Why?"

"Because I was too busy thinking about the last time I wore these pants. You know, when you were on your knees with my cock in your mouth and you practically sucked me—"

Lily squeaked the cutest sound before she covered his mouth with her hand. Even with the blush on her cheeks, he could plainly see them redden further. Damian roared with laughter, shaking them both. His loudness drew the attention of several guests close by, but they only seemed to chuckle at his amusement. They probably didn't have the slightest clue what Damian was laughing about.

Lily glowered at him playfully before poking his chest. "Oh, my God, you are awful."

"Hey, I did penance today. I've been sin free for several hours. I have to make up for lost time."

"Damian!"

"What?"

Lily snickered. "Awful, I said."

"You married me."

"I did," Lily murmured. "Thank you for being there at the end."

Damian matched her smile with his own. "Thanks for walking down to meet me."

"I really can't believe how many people showed up," Lily said.

Interweaving their fingers together, Damian glanced around the ballroom. It was bursting at the seams with guests. He'd been ignoring the people for the better part of the day. Sure, Damian did the respectful thing when he needed to by saying hello to the guests, thanking them for coming at the large dinner reception, and all that other nonsense, but he wasn't going out of his way to spend time with people he didn't know.

Frankly, they hadn't come because they knew him, either. No, most of the people came because the Outfit's boss was there and Terrance had made a big deal out of the wedding. Plus, Dino and Theo both had their own motives for inviting whoever they could to the wedding. But none of that mattered to Damian.

Nothing was more important to Damian than keeping his wife smiling and joyful on their wedding day.

Wife.

He was *married.*

"What is that all about?" Lily asked, pointing at Damian's face.

"Hmm?"

"You went all glassy-eyed there for a second."

"Did I?" he asked.

"Yes."

Damian stopped their dance, drew Lily in close, and kissed her. She tasted just the same as she always did on his tongue—life, love, and sweetness on her lips. He took his time loving her mouth with his own, brushing his lips along the seam of hers over and over, and flicking his tongue out to taste her silky skin.

"You're my wife."

Lily's smile was brilliant and bright. "I am."

Before Damian could get Lily dancing again, the lightest tap on his shoulder interrupted them. Turning to see who had cut in on him and his new bride, Damian came face to face with Terrance Trentini.

"You two look lovely," Terrance said.

Lily offered the man a smile that was nothing like the one she graced Damian with five seconds before. Damian had to give her the credit where it was due though, because she never once gave Terrance the slightest inclination that she disliked the man.

"Thank you," Lily replied.

"May I cut in?" Terrance asked.

Damian shrugged. To refuse would be rude even if he hadn't wanted to part with Lily just yet. "Sure."

"Thank you," Terrance said, taking Lily's hand when she held it out. "I'll be leaving soon as I'm not as young as I once was. Abriella, Alessa, and Joel are staying, but I just can't keep up with you younger ones anymore."

"Well, I'll end your night off right with a dance," Lily said.

"Yes, let's do that."

Damian winked at Lily. "Chances are now that someone's cut in on me, the people won't stop, Lily."

"We've done all the important things."

They had. From cake cutting to tossing the garter and bouquet. Everything had gone off smoothly. Mostly, the couple had just been enjoying the last bit of their reception together. In fact, they'd barely spent any time apart. But the night still had hours and hours to go before it could be officially over and the couple could say goodbye.

"I'll be back," Damian told Lily.

He would be … eventually. Damian had things to do. His wedding didn't stop business from being finished. Terrance, without even knowing it, had given Damian an opening. Damian planned on taking it. If he was lucky and quick, he'd get the job done and be back before anyone really noticed his absence for long.

"Will you?" Lily asked.

"Soon," he promised. "Let your brothers dance with you after the boss has his turn."

"Yes," Terrance said. "You must dance with your brothers, Lily."

Damian smirked. "But don't get too tired smiling and dazzling the crowd, sweetheart."

The soft sound of squeaky footsteps padding down the hallway outside of the office broke Damian from his daze. Italian leather always gave off a certain sound when it hit hardwood floors. No matter how quiet you tried to be, the shoes gave a man away every single time.

Not a second later, the office door opened, followed by the sounds of familiar grumbling. The decorative lights above turned on, illuminating the space in a warm yellow tone. Damian didn't turn the large office chair around as Terrance Trentini closed his door.

"You may spin around," Terrance said quietly.

Damian was surprised the man knew someone was in his office. He'd parked his car a couple of blocks away from the home, sneaked in the back under the old willow that was unprotected by security cameras, and got inside the house with little to no problems.

Terrance trusted Damian too much. Maybe that was the problem. In fact, he trusted him enough to give him the keypad passcode to shut the security system off and get inside without anyone knowing.

"I said turn around," Terrance ordered, firmer the second time.

Damian spun the office chair slowly, facing his boss. A brief flicker of shock passed over Terrance's features before the Outfit boss turned stone cold again.

"I should have known," Terrance muttered.

"Probably," Damian replied quietly.

Terrance waved at the chair. "I always push my chair in before leaving my office. Anyone who is smart knows better than to come inside here without my permission. I didn't think it would be you in that chair, Damian."

"Yes, well …"

"I wondered, though," Terrance said softly.

Damian fiddled with the tip of the barrel on his gun. "Wondered what?"

"Ben's unfortunate death seemed a little too suspicious for me. He was nearly cleared after being put into the coma. The way he died … something felt off. Was it?"

"Completely," Damian admitted.

"Why?"

"I owed someone something."

Terrance stared at Damian, but never once did he give the gun and silencer any attention. An understanding dawned on the older man's features as he said, "Dino DeLuca."

"Dino doesn't have much to do with *this*," Damian said.

"He might say that, but I can assure you it is far from the truth," Terrance replied, still unbothered. "That man plays his part well. He makes everyone believe his loyalties are entirely wrapped up with the Outfit, but he lies as well as he breathes. He gets that from his father. Dino never forgave me for killing his parents."

"Maybe so. I wouldn't blame him if that were the truth. He was left to raise two younger siblings and he never even got the chance to have his own life because of it. Nonetheless, I am not here because he sent me or asked for it. And you gave me the perfect opportunity to get this finished when you admitted your grandchildren would remain at the wedding reception and you came home alone. Their parents always stay to keep an eye on them despite the fact they're grown adults. Predictable. Which makes this a hell of a lot easier."

Terrance's jaw ticked. "Damian—"

"Why me?" Damian asked, interrupting Terrance before the man could say anything.

"I beg your pardon?"

Standing from the chair, Damian tapped his gun to the top of the desk. "What is it about me that you liked enough to begin inserting me into your position?"

Terrance sucked in a sharp breath. "My position?"

"Neither one of us are parrots here. Pay attention and listen. Wasn't that what you always used to tell me?"

"When you were a boy I said that. You needed some kind of structure. Moving from place to place like you Rossi kids did wasn't good for any of you. You can't expect children to grow up into well-behaved adults when they have no routine and structure."

"I wasn't your child to raise," Damian said.

"I didn't raise you, I simply helped whenever you were around. Just the same as I did for Tommas and his sisters."

True enough.

Damian chewed over his thoughts, wishing the hurricane inside his head would calm. "I thought you liked me because of the man I was, not because of what I could do for the Outfit."

"I don't know what you're talking about."

"The Commission, the calls from the men, the private consultations about business and the information you've shoveled on me over the years. Are you saying that was all innocent in nature? That you had no other motives for bringing me into your closer circles?"

Terrance raised a single brow. "Of course, I had other motives."

"And I don't want it!" Damian barked.

The boss barely flinched at Damian's show of rage.

"I don't want it," Damian repeated quieter. "I like the place where I am currently at. I have no desire to move higher in the Outfit or be someone else's puppet, Terrance. I never have. I don't want to be the one controlling these greedy, spoiled bastards you call family."

"Is that what you think I was doing?" Terrance asked.

"It's kind of obvious, isn't it? Why else would you put me closer to your side if you didn't mean for me to eventually match you, hmm?"

Terrance eyed Damian with a little more curiosity than before. "You're wrong."

Damian scoffed, disgusted. "I don't think I am."

"You believe I meant for you to be my understudy."

"Yes," Damian said.

"No intelligent man would give away his secret weapon, Damian. Not if he planned on using it without someone else trying to get a hold of it for his own purposes. Clearly I failed in trying to keep mine private if someone else has poisoned your thoughts against me."

Damian wasn't even listening. He didn't care what Terrance had to say and the man's time was quickly running out. Damian's time was ticking down, too. He needed to get back to the reception and soon if he didn't want anyone to notice his absence. The drive was a good twenty minutes from the Trentini place. There was no time for games.

"No one poisoned my thoughts," Damian said. "But you were terribly smart about infecting them with what *you* wanted for me. You were doing it slowly over time so I didn't catch on. You never said a thing about me having control or even suggested that I did, but other people knew it. Other people could see."

"People like Dino," Terrance said, nodding.

"More than him. I have calls all the time from your men that want things."

"Because I've never hidden your closeness to me, Damian. I've always kept quiet about our understanding of your job in the Outfit but hiding our friendship was pointless. It makes sense for men to turn to you if they think it will get them closer to me."

Damian shrugged. "Have your excuses. I don't care."

"They're not excuses. They're facts."

"They're lies," Damian retorted. "Tell me, who do you think would make a good boss, Terrance?"

"I—"

"A name would suffice."

Terrance's gaze narrowed. "There are very few men left in high standing that would be appropriate for this position. I think we both know that."

"Riley is still alive."

Damian knew without a doubt that statement would hit Terrance right where it fucking hurt. Friendships like the one shared between Terrance and Riley didn't end easily, but rather, tore apart all the seams of everything surrounding them. All of the things that they had shared and built together over the years during their comradery would be ripped to shreds. Like families, loyalties, and anything else that was left barely surviving in the mess.

"How long will he stay alive?" Terrance asked. "I think that's the better question."

"Longer than you." Damian smiled, knowing it looked cruel. "And if Riley is also out of the pool, who is left?"

"Nobody worthy, as far as I'm concerned."

"There are men waiting to come out of the woodwork. It's too bad you've been too focused on me to see them." Damian chuckled. "I'm sure it'll be an interesting fight to the finish."

Terrance frowned. "You truly believe that, don't you?"

"That you were grooming me for your spot? Yes."

"I never did that," Terrance said. "It was never my intention to, either."

"Lying will get you nowhere."

Neither would telling the truth, but Damian didn't think he had to mention that. The gun in his hand with a long silencer attached spoke more than he ever could about how their encounter would end.

Terrance slipped off his suit jacket and tossed it over the arm of a leather couch. He said nothing as he kicked off his shoes as well. Damian let the man have his final moments in peace.

"How much has Dino had his hands in?" Terrance asked, taking a seat on the couch. He undid the buttons on the sleeves of his dress shirt and rolled each up his arms. "With this whole mess, I mean. How much of it was him?"

"Practically all," Damian said honestly.

"But?"

"I helped here and there."

Terrance smiled. "Ah, the DeLuca girl."

Damian smirked. "Rossi, now."

"Yes, well, she'll always be a DeLuca at heart. A ring doesn't change a person's blood, my boy."

Damian tried not to react to Terrance's innocent phrasing, but he barely managed to hold his growl back. Things like that had become all too common over the years. Before, it felt like Terrance's way of caring. Now, he saw it as nothing more than Terrance making Damian think he gave a damn.

Maybe he did.

It didn't matter.

"I did think you two were a good match," Terrance said. "I still do. Why kill Ben?"

"You really have to ask that?"

"I think so."

Damian lifted one shoulder, bored with the entire conversation. "He didn't like me being as close to you as I was and he didn't like where you planned for me to go. His vocal disapproval about the marriage arrangement to anyone and everyone who would listen was proof. Besides that, he could have proved dangerous for Lily at some point. I fixed those issues."

Terrance stilled on the couch and glanced up at Damian through dark eyes. "Ben liked you very much."

"No, he couldn't find a way to manipulate me," Damian said, laughing darkly. "Like I said, he couldn't even keep his mouth shut about the marriage—"

"Because Dino didn't give him a say in it," Terrance interjected calmly. "Not once did Dino allow Ben to have any involvement or say in the deal between the DeLuca and Rossi families. Considering Ben was the head of the family, he should have been able to put in his opinion."

Damian shook his head. "That's not important."

"It is but you're not hearing me, Damian. It wasn't you he disapproved of, it was the way Dino went about the entire thing. He was fine with the marriage but he would have liked to be able to be involved. Had you took the time to talk to Ben about the situation, you would have known that. My guess is you took Dino's word for what it was and ran with it. You always were loyal to DeLuca in that way."

Something painful and heavy squeezed around Damian's heart, nearly pushing it up into his throat. A sick feeling balled in his stomach. Terrance was right about everything he said. Most of Ben's disagreement and vocal displeasure had been about Dino's side of things and not Damian's. Ben had barely been included in any of the wedding planning or even for Lily's side of things where family was concerned. It was almost as if Dino wanted the man to seem unimportant to the DeLuca family.

"It doesn't matter," Damian said.

"It does," Terrance replied. "Because chances are, Dino used what he thought would get under your skin the most in order to have you do the work he wouldn't."

Damian barked out a laugh. "Like what? Look at all the things he's done, Terrance. Look at the people he's killed and the problems he's started. What could I possibly do that he couldn't have if he wanted to?"

"Killing me," Terrance said.

The words came out softer than Damian had ever heard his boss speak before.

"You're wrong," Damian said, sure of it.

"I don't think so. Dino always believed I did him and his siblings wrong when they were children. I know I did when I had their parents killed, but Joseph DeLuca didn't give me a choice. I tried to make up for it over the years with Dino and Theo, but clearly my remorse never bled through to the man enough. Or maybe it did and his conscience just won't let him do what yours is capable of."

Damian ground his teeth so hard his molars ached. "And what is that?"

"Killing someone who cares for you."

Fuck.

Damian cocked back the hammer on his gun. "Like I said, it isn't important."

"His lies are," Terrance murmured, staring down the barrel of the gun. "You don't have to, by the way."

Kill him?

Yes, Damian absolutely did. Despite the fact Terrance's statements made a hell of a lot of sense and Damian felt like a wrecking ball had just slammed into his body, the boss still needed to go. Terrance knew too much. Damian would never get away with all he'd done to the Outfit if he let the man live.

"We both know I do," Damian said, never lowering the gun.

"No, my boy." Terrance smiled as Damian's finger wrapped around the trigger. "I meant to say you don't have to apologize. I understand."

"Do you?"

"Yes," Terrance said. "Take this as your final lesson, Damian."

"What is that?"

"Trust no man."

Damian pulled the trigger and didn't look away.

Damian slammed the bathroom door open, zoning in on the figure he'd been searching for in the crowd of people since he arrived back at his wedding reception. No one noticed him gone and no one noticed him return. Damian was smart in that way.

Dino, however, had a few things to answer for.

The man barely got his pants zipped up before Damian fisted Dino's tux jacket from behind. He yanked him away from the urinal and slammed him into the closest wall which just happened to be the side of a stall. The stall shuddered from the impact as Dino cursed his surprise.

Dino's eyes flew wide at the sight of Damian. No doubt, Damian's rage was clear to see if the way his muscles clenched and trembled with the sensations passing through him. It was like someone had kicked him straight in the fucking gut; like he'd been used and manipulated when all Damian wanted to do was stay the fuck away from that kind of shit.

"Whoa!" Dino said, his hands flying wide.

Damian's fist cracked into the stall right beside Dino's head. "Shut your mouth."

"Hey!" someone shouted from inside the stall.

"Get the fuck out," Damian growled.

A man dressed in a sharp suit quickly scurried from the stall without even flushing the toilet and disappeared from the bathroom. Once the door closed, all of Damian's attention turned on Dino again.

"All you had to do was tell me the fucking truth, Dino," Damian said through gritted teeth.

Every breath he took ached. He'd trusted Dino. The man put him in a positon by using lies and bullshit where Damian had to make choices he wouldn't have otherwise.

"What are you going on about?" Dino asked, still not fighting back.

Damian slammed Dino into the stall again. "Ben, Terrance ... ring any fucking bells for you?"

Dino's brow lifted. "Hey—"

"No, be quiet. Unless you're going to give me something worth listening to, I don't want to hear another goddamn thing coming out of your mouth, asshole. I did the final job tonight—I followed that through like I said I would. But it had nothing to do with you, right? That was supposed to be all for me. You're such a liar, Dino. Christ, it's no wonder your eyes are brown. You're so full of shit it's starting to show."

Dino laughed hoarsely. "Me? Take a good look in the mirror."

"You could have told me the truth," Damian repeated, willing his anger to calm. He didn't want to go back out on the floor to find Lily feeling like he was. She would know; his girl always knew. "You could have told me that this was for your parents and what happened way back when. You didn't have to lie to me and manipulate my weaknesses for your benefit. I was loyal to you. I would have done what you needed regardless of the rest, but I didn't have to be one of your pawns. Lily didn't have to be one of your pawns."

"Neither of you are," Dino said, shrugging.

"Right. Even when you're caught red-handed, you still can't tell the truth."

"She wasn't a pawn and neither were you. Everything I said about Lily and what I wanted for her was the truth. And so what, Damian? Who cares if I worked a little bit of revenge into the plan, too? What does it really matter now?"

It mattered a lot.

A war was beginning.

"How long do you think this is going to last, Dino?" Damian asked. "How many more people are going to die because your parents did?"

"A lot," Dino said, grinning. "But I know my brother and sister won't be one of them. Remember what I told you when I first asked you to my place that day? Theo is smart as long as he keeps his heart out of the game. He'll have all the control on the DeLuca side of things now. Keep an eye on him and see how far he goes. As for Lily?"

Damian's jaw ticked. "She's got me."

"Exactly. She's got you. We both know you'll never let a thing happen to her. I got everything I wanted out of this. Your feelings don't matter to me."

Damian swallowed the bitter taste in his mouth. "And what about you, Dino?"

"What about me?"

"Where are you planning on going?" Damian asked.

"Wherever in the hell I want to." Dino brushed Damian's hands off him and pushed away from the stall. "Smile, Damian. It's your goddamn wedding day."

CHAPTER EIGHTEEN

Lily sighed in relief as Damian pulled off her heels. After being in the damn things for a good twelve hours straight, she was happy to see them go. She couldn't hide the little moan that escaped as Damian's strong, deft fingers worked the arches of her feet.

"Feel good?" he asked.

"So good."

Damian hummed and kissed her calf. "Happy to help, sweetheart."

"They're beautiful shoes."

"Well, beautiful on you," Damian said, chuckling. "Sexy, actually."

Lily smiled, watching her new husband as his massage went from her feet to her calves. "Oh?"

"Very. Beautiful legs, Lily."

She pursed her lips. "I'm shorter than you by inches even in heels."

"Don't care," Damian said, humming sexily. "Even if you are shorter than me."

"And you love my legs."

Damian flashed a sinful smirk. "Best in Chicago."

Lily shivered as Damian's hands drove higher under her wedding dress, kneading and pressing into her soft flesh. He worked every single last kink and soreness out of her tired legs without ever looking away from her.

"You're awfully quiet tonight," Lily said softly.

Damian's gaze flicked away. "Am I?"

His inability to look at her again said it all.

"What is up, Damian?"

"Nothing, sweetheart."

"Damian—"

"Lily," Damian interjected, his tone offering no room for arguing. "I said it's nothing."

Lily didn't believe him for a second. She had the distinct feeling that because it was their wedding night, Damian wanted to spend the evening without all the muss and fuss going on outside of the hotel walls. He probably wanted it to be just them and no one else. Lily didn't mind dropping whatever it was.

"You'll tell me tomorrow, right?" she asked.

Damian nodded, hiking the skirt of her dress up around her hips as he dropped to his knees. He yanked her panties down around her knees, his grin growing salaciously. "Yeah, sweetheart. I'll tell you anything you want to know tomorrow."

"Okay."

Damian pulled her panties down further, his eyebrow cocking. "Black lace?"

"There's a whole lot more where that came from."

"I can't fucking wait."

Lily couldn't respond. His head was already buried between her thighs. The little talent Damian had with his tongue always drove Lily insane every time his mouth came anywhere near her pussy. This time was no exception. With blindly fast strikes of his tongue, he'd parted the fleshy lips of her pussy and was already tasting the fluids gathering at her entrance. Lily could feel her sex trying to clench around his tongue with every plunge. She tried to close her legs around his head, wanting more friction on her clit, but Damian's hands kept her thighs pried apart.

"Shit, that feels good," Lily moaned.

Damian's dark laughter rolled over her senses like golden honey. The vibrations from his amusement tickled her sensitive sex as he nibbled and lapped at her folds. She spread her legs wider, needing to see what he was doing. Using her hands for support on the edge of the bed, Lily propped her upper body high so she could watch Damian eat her out. His mouth was smeared with her arousal and she could smell the scent of her sex already wafting in the air. Damian's steel-blue eyes surveyed her from down below, a wicked smile curving the corners of his mouth upwards as he licked a line from her slit straight to her clit.

That had to be the hottest thing she'd ever seen.

"Fuck me," Lily muttered.

"The prettiest sounds," Damian murmured, keeping her gaze locked on his. "You always make the prettiest sounds for me."

"I—"

Before she could get a word in edgewise, Damian's hand came up, pushed her to the bed, and his head disappeared between her thighs again. Lily cried out, her surprise and bliss echoing through the room as his tongue attacked her clit. She struggled under his hand and the pleasure suddenly coursing through her nervous system. The pace of his tongue against her bud was relentless and brutal.

She was going to come and fast.

"Shit, shit, shit," Lily chanted. "Damian!"

Damian's approval came out in a long groan. That was all it took. Lily came undone crying his name, fisting the bedsheets, and feeling like she couldn't breathe. Her orgasm started somewhere in her middle and then shot out in all directions, numbing her fingers and toes.

While she tried to calm, gasping for air in the bed, Damian kissed her inner thighs.

"Up," he ordered.

Lily blinked, unsure if she'd heard him correctly. "What?"

"Up, sweetheart. I want this dress off of you. Despite how beautiful you look in it, it will only hold me back."

"But I'm so comfortable."

Damian laughed. "Oh, well. I'm not done yet."

Lily melted into the soft chaise as Damian's fingertips danced up her lace covered spine. On her stomach with her head resting in his lap, she was comfortable and content. She was also turned on like nothing else as her new husband pampered her with pieces of chocolate covered fruit and sips of champagne. The sheer lingerie she wore hid nothing from his view and his hands started their wandering trek all over again.

"This is downright sinful," Damian said, slipping his fingers between her thighs. Lily sighed as he caressed her sex with sweet, light touches.

"More," Lily demanded, her lust spiking all over again.

"Soon, sweetheart. I want you begging for it."

Lily was ready to do that now.

"Damian—"

"Bite," Damian demanded, holding out a piece of fruit for Lily to take while he kept up the teasing touches with his other hand. Lily glowered up at him even though the angle was awkward and she couldn't hold the position for long before dropping her head back down in his lap. Damian wasn't having it. "Play by my rules, Lily, or I won't give you what you want."

"You don't know what I want."

Damian laughed, the sound coming off deep and throaty. "Maybe not, but I know what I want and I can bet you're going to like it a whole hell of a lot if you just open that pretty mouth of yours, eat this fruit, and let me keep playing with your sweet pussy."

How could she deny him when he talked like that?

Good God, it did the best things to her insides.

Lily sucked the chocolate covered tip of the strawberry between her lips before nibbling down on the juicy fruit. As she chewed on the sweet fruit, two of Damian's fingers sunk into her core without warning. Lily's cry of surprise dissolved into a deep moan as he curled his digits hard into her

G-spot.

Lily swallowed the fruit so she could speak. "Christ!"

"So wet," Damian said, continuing the rhythm with his fingers that had Lily gushing.

"Holy fuck."

"Feel, sweetheart. You're hot all around me. It's fucking beautiful. You love my fingers fucking you."

"I love anything you do," Lily whimpered, wanting more of his fingers.

"You certainly will before the night is over," Damian said. "Bite, Lily."

Taking another bite from the fruit, Lily let the sensations of his fingers wash over her while the juices of the strawberry covered her tongue. She jerked in surprise when Damian used the bit of fruit left on the stem to paint along her naked shoulder. The coolness soaked into her nerves, making her shudder. Without saying a thing, he continued painting her skin with the fruit, finger fucking her pussy, and whispering the dirtiest things up above her.

Damian discarded what was left of the strawberry. Lily thought he was going to get another one, but was surprised when she felt the loss of his fingers inside her pussy. Before she could question his motives, his slick fingers drew a path up to her ass.

Lily froze, unsure.

"Breathe," Damian murmured as just the pads of his fingers massaged her puckered hole.

The sensations of his fingers touching her in a place she hadn't ever let someone go anywhere near before was new and foreign to Lily. She couldn't deny the excitement shooting through her bloodstream but there was trepidation following right behind.

"You know I'd never hurt you," Damian said, his fingers slipping through the clenching ring of muscles. Lily groaned into the palm of her hand, feeling her body stretch around his intrusion. A slight bite of pain mixed with the strangely new desire as it rushed her body. "I only want you to feel good and this will feel so, so good, Lily."

"Will it?" Lily asked.

Damian winked. "You just have to trust me."

Lily spread her legs wider, giving him better access to her ass. Slowly, he pumped his fingers in and out of her tight hole, opening his fingers on the withdraw and making her feel incredibly full.

"Do you remember what I told you?" he asked.

Lily could barely speak. "Told me what?"

"About your body."

"It's yours."

"It is," Damian said, his other hand ghosting down her spine and over the waves of her hair. "And I want every part of it, Lily. I want to be the only man who gets to touch and feel you. I want you to know I'm the only man who gets to fuck and love you."

"You are."

Damian removed his fingers from her body, making Lily whine. She hadn't realized how good that felt until he wasn't there anymore. "Good. Right now, I want to fuck your beautiful ass. Sit up."

Lily did as she was told, confused when Damian stood from the couch. Without a word, he crossed the room and disappeared into the bathroom. A tenderness in her backside from being filled in a way she hadn't experienced before only made her crave more. Lily listened as a tap turned on, making her anticipation grow more.

What he was he doing, washing his hands?

Damian appeared back at the bathroom doorway with two things in his hand. He waved a condom and bottle of lube, surprising Lily further.

"You planned this," she accused.

"I told you once that I wanted to have you any way I could. I wasn't lying."

Lily swallowed audibly. "Oh?"

"No. Spread your legs. Show me how wet you are and play with yourself. I want you to feel how turned on and hot you are right now."

"That's what you want?" Lily smiled coyly, leaning back on the chaise and opening her thighs for him to see. "Are you sure?"

"Very much." Damian's grin turned sensual as Lily stroked her pussy with light touches. Wetness glided her fingers over her labia and up to her clit. She was fucking soaked. "Beautiful, sweetheart."

Lily watched in silence as Damian began to finally pull of his own clothes. He'd stayed in his tux even after undressing Lily. He'd only loosened his tie and unbuttoned his vest when he convinced her to let him spoil her with chocolate covered fruit on the chaise. As far as Lily was concerned, there was nothing sexier than watching Damian undress. He did so in such an unhurried, quiet fashion, like nobody could see him. He must have known what he looked like. A cut figure, ridges of muscles, and smooth, olive-toned skin.

"I didn't tell you to stop," Damian said without looking up as he discarded his pants and boxers. "Keep playing for me, Lily. I want you wet all over."

Lily laughed shakily. "I didn't realize I had, either."

"Continue."

Pressing a finger into her pussy, Lily could feel how tight and ready she was. Her soft flesh was sensitive and drenched. A second finger did nothing to soothe the ache. Damian continued to watch her, saying nothing, as he stroked his own erection.

"Damian, please," Lily begged.

A smirk formed on the corner of Damian's lips as he slid the latex down his length. "Ah, there's what I was waiting for. Nothing sounds better than my name in your mouth while you beg, Lily."

Damian came to stand by the chaise, reaching down to circle Lily's clit with his thumb while she used her fingers to thrust inside her sex. "Christ."

"Damn, look at you," Damian said.

Lily hadn't realized how close she was to her orgasm before it was blowing through. She felt like a mess of cries, sweaty skin, and bliss. Damian kissed her through it, never once pulling away. Before Lily could comprehend what was happening, Damian had picked her up and then sat back down on the chaise with her on top of him. Lily's back pressed into his chest as his arm wrapped around her waist. He kept her hovering above him and when she felt stable enough to hold her own weight, he let her go.

Lily shivered when something cool and slippery dribbled down the crack of her ass. Damian's lips pressed to her shoulder blade where he'd painted with the strawberry earlier and she could feel him stroking his cock underneath her.

"I can't even fucking jerk off anymore," Damian said.

Lily bit her lip. "Why is that?"

"Because nothing gets the fucking job done but you and then I'm left with blue balls if I try myself."

"*God.*"

Damian hummed, his tongue striking out against her skin. "Trust me, yeah?"

Lily nodded. "Always."

"Good. Relax."

Saying it and doing it were two completely different things. Lily tried to calm the nervousness and raging desire coursing through her system, but she couldn't. The head of his cock pressed into her ass and Lily tensed instantly, scared of what might come.

"Lily," Damian murmured. "Stop worrying. Just feel."

Slowly, as he sucked on her skin where the strawberry had made sticky pathways, Damian worked his thick cock into her ass. Lily sucked in a ragged breath as a brief pain from the sensation of being stretched shot up her spine. Damian's hand raced right after, soothing away the immediate chill of fear and relaxing her again. It wasn't long before the pain was replaced by a deep need pounding at her insides as his cock sunk all the way into her ass and she was seated on top of him.

"Fuck," Damian hissed.

Lily whined. "I just ... can't."

Not think, move, or breathe. She was filled entirely. So, so open for him. She felt damp with perspiration and her nerves felt overworked. Nothing had ever felt quite so new and blindingly good before.

"Talk to me," Damian said softly.

"It's ..."

"Hmm?"

"So good," she whispered.

Damian's chuckles rocked them both, making his cock twitch inside Lily's ass. She clenched down around him, suddenly wanting him to move again.

"Yeah, it's supposed to be good, sweetheart," Damian said, his grin forming against her skin. "You're on top for a reason. Take the lead. This is all about you. No matter what, it'll feel crazy good for me, too."

Lily froze. "I—"

"No worries. Move."

She did, carefully and timidly. It took her a while before her body was accustomed to the foreign sensations. But when she did ... oh God, when she did it felt fucking glorious. Like every pleasure point in her body was connected to exposed nerves. Every stroke of his cock deep inside her ass took her higher.

Damian licked, kissed and sucked on her shoulders. "*Mmm*, strawberries and sex, Lily."

Lily laughed breathlessly. "Oh, my God."

"I don't care what anybody says, that's fucking heaven right there."

Damian caught her hand with his and moved them both between her legs. She shuddered as one of his fingers slipped inside her clenching sex before dragging up to her clit. He rolled his fingers in quick, harsh circles, driving her insane. The cries falling from Lily's throat rose in volume until her thighs were shaking and sweat beaded down her back.

Without him even telling her to, Lily thrust two fingers inside her pussy. She fucked herself in time with his cock in her ass and his finger at her clit. All the sensations pushed her straight to the edge.

And when she fell ...

When she fell, he caught her.

Always.

"Tell me what was bothering you last night," Lily said.

Damian held out the bite of fluffed scrambled eggs for Lily to take.

She refused the food, knowing it was just his way of distracting her. "Lily—"

"If you tell me it was nothing again, I'm going to be pissed."

His frown said it all. Damian didn't want her angry.

"Do we have to do this on our honeymoon?"

Lily snorted. "A week hidden away in a hotel isn't really a honeymoon, Damian."

"Yeah, well, it'll have to do for now. The first second I can, we'll skip over to Europe and you can show me all the places you visited and stayed."

"Really?"

Damian nodded. "Absolutely. It was something you loved and it made you happy. I want to see it, too."

"Okay." Lily played with the edge of the sheet covering her. Breakfast and quiet love in Egyptian cotton sheets was one of the best ways to spend a morning as far as she was concerned. "Stop deflecting my earlier question."

Sighing, Damian put the silver tray of food aside. "It's that important to you?"

"Very."

"It's probably going to hurt."

Lily chewed on her inner cheek, not liking what those words could mean. "Oh?"

"Very," he said, throwing her words back at her.

"You left the reception last night," Lily said, deciding blurting the knowledge out was better than dancing around it.

Damian lifted a single brow, eyeing her quietly. "You noticed that, did you?"

"Nobody else seemed to."

"They were very focused on you, gossiping about the nonsense going on in the Outfit, and the party," Damian said. "I used that to my advantage and finished something."

Lily's heart raced. "Will you tell me?"

"I'll tell you that I did a bad thing," he said, shrugging.

And sometimes, good men did bad things.

Lily blew out a slow breath, willing her thoughts to calm. "Why?"

"I thought I knew," Damian said.

Lily didn't need him to finish. "But you didn't know a thing."

"No. And that was my fault."

Well, then.

Lily reached out and intertwined their fingers together. Damian's shoulders relaxed at the touch instantly. "I love you."

Damian smiled. "I know. That's the only thing that matters to me about any of this."

"Is it?"

"Yeah," he said.

She believed him.

"Don't you think it's a little annoying that we have to spend our first day after our honeymoon in church?" Lily asked.

Damian offered her a smile and slipped her hand inside his. "You just didn't want to leave the hotel."

Lily pouted. "Well, you spoiled me all week. What else do you expect, Damian? You created a monster."

"Ah, I see how this works."

"Hush," Dino said behind the couple.

Lily skillfully flipped her older brother the middle finger without even breaking eye contact with the priest at the front. Damian chuckled, lifted Lily's hand to kiss it, and then dropped their still connected hands into his lap.

"Bad girl," he murmured.

"I'm better when I'm bad," Lily said, grinning.

"You are."

"Jesus," Dino grumbled under his breath.

Lily didn't give a damn what her brother had to say. She'd had a fantastic week with it being just her, Damian, a hotel room, and love. Best way she'd spent a week in a long time. The high was still buzzing around her senses. Dino wasn't going to kill that.

Damian tugged Lily to stand when the priest asked. Her husband swept his finger over her wedding band as the congregation was blessed one final time and then dismissed for the day. Sighing, Lily rested into Damian's side as he slid on a pair of dark aviator sunglasses.

"Are you coming over for dinner?" Dino asked as they followed behind the congregation to leave the church.

"Do you want to?" Lily asked Damian.

"Sure, sweetheart."

"Good," Dino said, smirking. "Lily can cook."

"Ass," Lily muttered.

Dino waved a finger in the air as they walked out the front doors into the sunlight. The Chicago wind whipped around the three. "Never denied it, Lily. I'll see you two later."

"Later," Damian replied.

Lily moved to walk down the large steps, but Damian pulled her back to his side. "What—"

Damian shut her question up with a quick, searing kiss. Her surprised gasp allowed him to deepen the kiss. She gave into the dominating strikes of his tongue and the rhythm of his lips as he owned her with the kiss. Lily hummed in satisfaction, fisting his suit jacket and grinning as giggling people passed the couple by.

"That was bad," Lily told him. "We're technically still at church."

"Nothing they haven't already done or seen."

"True."

Damian kissed the tip of her nose. "I know you wanted to stay at the hotel a little longer."

Lily shrugged. It didn't really matter. "Anywhere with you is perfect."

"How about we spend the next week looking for somewhere to call home?"

"Oh?"

"Something for you to call yours and not an apartment," Damian said.

Lily's heart swelled. "A house?"

"Any kind of house you want, Lily."

"Not Melrose Park."

Damian laughed. "Too much Outfit for you, huh?"

"No, too many memories."

"What did I tell you, huh?" Damian asked, giving her a look that pinned Lily in place.

"To leave it behind."

"So do that."

"I'm trying," she said quietly.

And she was. But sometimes it still hurt and she thought it would for a long time. Scars like those didn't heal instantly. It took a while and the constant reminders, like pokes to the wounds, would always leave an ache behind.

"Not Melrose Park," Lily repeated quietly.

Damian nodded, reaching up to caress the apple of her cheek with two fingers. "All right. Time to start making our own memories, Lily."

"Yeah, I think that sounds—"

An explosion like Lily had never heard before pierced the air. Whatever she was going to say was lost as the sight of fire and flying metal caught her eye. Her ears rang from the volume as a blast of heat and pressure covered the church steps. Damian covered her instantly, pushing her back toward the opened doors of the church as screams began to echo.

Lily felt sick. Her heart leaped into her throat.

What was that?

"Move," Damian barked.

Lily couldn't. She stumbled as her husband pushed her again. Damian caught her before she could hit the ground. Over his shoulder, she caught the sight of a familiar car burning in one giant ball of flames.

"*No,*" Lily breathed.

"Lily, move," Damian demanded again.

People shoved past them, trying to get back into the safety of the church. Her heart fell to the cement steps and shattered into pieces as she watched her brother's car be engulfed in another wave of flames.

"No!"

"Lily, please move."

"Dino," Lily cried.

"I'm sorry." Damian wrapped Lily in a bear hug and forced her to move. "I love you."

"*Dino!*"

"It looks like there was a very sophisticated timer set on the bomb," the detective informed.

Lily wasn't paying attention to the man. All she kept thinking as she stared at him was that her brother wouldn't want this cop in his home. Dino would have hated having any official inside his private space going through his things. Unfortunately, they hadn't been given much of a choice in the matter.

It had taken three weeks for the investigation to come back with anything regarding the bomb. Lily didn't give a damn what the police had to say. Things like this wasn't something that could be settled in a courtroom. The officials, no matter how hard they worked or how many leads they had, would never truly know who set the bomb in Dino's car. That was just how it worked in the mafia.

No, it wouldn't be settled in a courtroom.

The streets, but not a courtroom.

Damian sighed, his hand squeezing Lily's shoulder gently. "And how do you know that?"

"There was a significant portion of the electronics that survived the blast. After it was put together and worked over, we discovered it was connected to the Bentley's radio system."

Lily's brow puckered. "So, when he turned it on, it blew?"

"When he turned it to a particular station, it set the timer to begin ticking down. That was why he had already reversed out of the parking space when the bomb went off."

Oh.

That only left Lily with a sicker feeling than before.

"Would you have any idea who would know the kinds of radio stations your brother listened to?" the man asked.

Damian's hand squeezed Lily's shoulder again. She didn't need his silent reminders.

"No, and I think it's time for you to leave," Lily said, standing from her chair.

The detective stood as well, frowning. "But—"

"I have nothing to offer and we've complied as much as we could, even though you didn't give us any choice," Lily interrupted firmly.

By no means would she allow the cops to keep digging through Dino's house.

"Miss, your brother was heavily involved with the Chicago Mob and—"

"Firstly, it's *Mrs.*," Lily snapped. "Secondly, I don't care what my brother was involved in. I buried him. He is dead. I have nothing else to say on the matter."

"Any information you may have could be incredibly invaluable to not only our investigation, but other ones, too."

Lily scoffed, disbelief filling her to the brim. "Turn rat, you mean."

"Lily," Damian said quietly.

"No, that's what he's saying. Or rather, what he won't because he's a coward."

The detective shrugged. "I'm just suggesting that you could be a great help."

Fuck this.

"Get out," Lily said, pointing at the kitchen entryway.

"Doesn't it bother you at all that someone killed your brother?" the man asked.

Lily felt a stab of pain pierce through her heart. "You have no idea how I feel. You don't have the first clue what it feels like to—"

"You're protecting the very same people who killed him."

"All right, that's enough," Damian said, anger heating his tone.

Lily didn't need Damian to come to her defense. "Get out!"

Storming past the detective, Lily made her way to the front of the house. She opened up the front door wide, pointing at the outside. She waited, her agitation rising, as the man took his time putting on his shoes and suit jacket.

Standing on the front steps, the detective turned back to Lily. "If you change your mind—"

Lily slammed the door in his face.

Damian stayed leaning against the wall, his features downcast as he regarded her with a stare that made her sadness swell. Because he knew— her heart was breaking and she couldn't breathe. A meltdown was just around the corner if she couldn't reel it back in and fast.

"Oh, my God," Lily whispered, pressing her palm to her chest.

"Lily, it's going to be okay."

She nodded, but nothing felt true.

"Lily, breathe," Damian murmured.

How could she?

Before she blinked, Damian was standing in front of her. He cupped her cheeks in his palms and tilted her head up so she could see the worry and love swimming in his gaze. Over and over, he kissed her lips with soft pecks until her tears had stopped falling and her lungs worked again.

"It's just beginning, isn't it?" Lily asked.

The fighting between the families had only grown worse since Damian and Lily's wedding. Terrance Trentini's murder seemed to tip the Trentini family over the edge. Lily remembered when Damian got that phone call on their honeymoon perfectly. She was sure he was the cause of the Outfit boss's death.

Lily chose not to ask. She knew he would tell her the truth if she did and Lily wasn't sure if she was ready to hear it.

Nonetheless, things were bad between the four families and getting much worse.

"It's going to be okay," Damian said again.

"Who did that to Dino?" Lily asked.

"I don't know."

"Please don't try to save my feelings."

Damian sighed, using his thumb to trace her lips. "I'm not, sweetheart. No one knows."

"But ... someone must know something, Damian."

"It's war. Nobody has to know anything."

War.

Lily shivered. Somehow, her brother's plans to upset the Outfit had turned on him. "Dino did this for me."

"You, Theo ... himself. I don't even know if he realized what he was really doing."

"How do I settle that in here?" Lily asked pointing at her chest where her heart was racing out of control.

"Lily—"

"He started a war for us."

Damian pulled her close and kissed her hard. Lily let him. "We'll be okay."

"Promise?"

"Always, Lily. You and me, we're the kind of people who survive. That's just what we do."

God, she hoped so.

"My heart hurts," Lily said softly, willing away her tears.

Damian kissed her tenderly. "I'll take it away."

Yeah, he always did.

ABOUT THE AUTHOR

Bethany-Kris is a Canadian author, lover of much, and mother to three very young sons, one cat, and two dogs. A small town in Eastern Canada where she was born and raised is where she has always called home. With her boys under her feet, a snuggling cat, barking dogs, and a spouse calling over his shoulder, she is nearly always writing something ... when she can find the time.

Find Bethany-Kris at:
Her website www.bethanykris.com,
or on Facebook at www.facebook.com/bethanykriswrites,
on her blog at www.bethanykris.blogspot.ca,
or on Twitter - @BethanyKris.

Sign up to Bethany-Kris's New Release Newsletter here:
http://eepurl.com/bf9lzD

CPSIA information can be obtained
at www.ICGtesting.com
Printed in the USA
LVHW081552140220
646995LV00011B/684